2014   10/...

THE REVOLUTIONS

TOR BOOKS BY FELIX GILMAN

The Half-Made World
The Rise of Ransom City
The Revolutions

THE
REVOLUTIONS

Felix Gilman

A TOM DOHERTY ASSOCIATES BOOK
NEW YORK

THE REVOLUTIONS

Copyright © 2014 by Felix Gilman

A Tor Book
Published by Tom Doherty Associates, LLC
175 Fifth Avenue
New York, NY 10010

www.tor-forge.com

Tor® is a registered trademark of Tom Doherty Associates, LLC.

The Library of Congress Cataloging-in-Publication Data
is available upon request.

ISBN 978-0-7653-3717-7 (hardcover)
ISBN 978-1-4668-3136-0 (e-book)

Tor books may be purchased for educational, business, or promotional use. For information on bulk purchases, please contact Macmillan Corporate and Premium Sales Department at 1-800-221-7945, extension 5442, or write specialmarkets@macmillan.com.

First Edition: April 2014

Printed in the United States of America

0 9 8 7 6 5 4 3 2 1

For Zoe

ACKNOWLEDGMENTS

Thanks to both of this book's editors—Eric Raab and Liz Gorinsky—and to everyone at Tor for the outstanding art and design of this thing. Particular thanks to Wilhem Staehle, who produced a dozen wonderful alternative cover art designs; I wish we could have used all of them. And as always, thanks to my agent, Howard Morhaim.

Thanks to Sarah for her comments and constant support, and thank you to William for his patience.

Inspirations for this book are too many to list, but the reader may notice in particular bits of *A Princess of Mars* (especially in chapter 18), *Gullivar of Mars* (chapter 8), *Out of the Silent Planet*, Olaf Stapledon's *Star Maker* (chapter 21), William Timlin's *The Ship That Sailed to Mars*, Margaret Cavendish's *The Blazing World*, and David Lindsay's *A Voyage to Arcturus* (chapter 13). Robert Markley's *Dying Planet: Mars in Science and the Imagination* and Robert Crossley's *Imagining Mars: A Literary History* were both invaluable. Key inspiration came from Alex Owen's brilliant *The Place of Enchantment: British Occultism and the Culture of the Modern*. An early scene in this book is based on a real event described in her book—an 1898 meeting of Frederick Leigh Gardner (stockbroker) and Annie Horniman (theatrical impresario) for occult purposes.

The nineteenth century has run its course and finished its record. A new era has dawned, not by chronological prescription alone, but to the vital sense of humanity. Novel thoughts are rife; fresh impulses stir the nations; the soughing of the wind of progress strikes every ear. . . .

The physics of the heavenly bodies, indeed, finds its best opportunities in unlooked-for disclosures; for it deals with transcendental conditions, and what is strange to terrestrial experience may serve admirably to expound what is normal in the skies. In celestial science especially, facts that appear subversive are often the most illuminative, and the prospect of its advance widens and brightens with each divagation enforced or permitted from the strait paths of rigid theory.

—Agnes Clerke,
*A Popular History of Astronomy
During the Nineteenth Century*, 1902

Unfortunate Mars! What evil fairy presided at his birth?

—Camille Flammarion,
Astronomy for Amateurs, 1904

THE
FIRST
DEGREE

{ *The Great Storm of 1893* }

It was the evening of what would later be called the Great Storm of '93, and Arthur Archibald Shaw sat at his usual desk in the Reading Room of the British Museum, yawning and toying with his pen. Soft rain pattered on the dome. Lamps overhead shone through a haze of golden dust. Arthur yawned. There was a snorer at the desk opposite, head back and mouth open. Two women nearby whispered to each other in French. Carts creaked down the aisle, the faint tremors of their passing threatening to topple the tower of books on Arthur's desk, which concerned explosives, and poisons, and exotic methods of murder.

He was writing a detective story. This was something of an experiment. Not knowing quite how to start, he'd begun at the end, which went:

That night the dome of St. Paul's Cathedral broke through London's black clouds as if it were the white head of Leviathan rising from the ocean. The spire and the cross shone in a cold and quite un-Christian moonlight, and diabolical laughter echoed through the night. The detective and his quarry stood atop the dome, beneath the spire, each man ragged from the exertion of their chase.

"Stop there, Vane," the detective called; but Professor Vane only laughed again, and began to climb the spire. And so Dr Syme pursued.

Which was not all bad, in Arthur's opinion. The important thing was to move quickly. It was only that month that Dr Conan Doyle had sent his famous detective off into the great beyond—chucking him unceremoniously from a waterfall in Switzerland—and the news that there would be no more stories of the Baker Street genius had thrown London's publishing world into something of a panic. In fact, there were nearly riots, and some disturbed individuals had threatened to torch the offices of the *Strand Magazine*. The hero's death left a gap in the firmament. The fellow who was first to fill it might make a fortune. It was probably already too late.

For the past two and a half years Arthur had been employed by *The Monthly Mammoth* to write on the subject of the Very Latest Scientific Advances. He wasn't any kind of scientist himself, but nobody seemed to mind. He wrote about dinosaurs, and steam engines, and rubber, and the laying of transatlantic telegraph cables; or how telephones worked; or the new American elevators at the Savoy; or whether there was air on the moon; or where precisely in South America to observe the perturbations of Venus; or whether the crooked lines astronomers saw on the fourth planet might be canals, or railroads, or other signs of civilization—and so on. Not a bad job, in its way—there were certainly worse—but the *Mammoth* paid little, and late, and there was no prospect of advancement there. Therefore he'd invented Dr Cephias Syme: detective, astronomer, mountain-climber, world-traveller, occasional swordsman, *et cetera*.

Vane dangled by one hand from the golden cross, laughing, his white hair blowing in the wind. With the other hand he produced a pistol from his coat and pointed it at Syme.

"What brought you here, Syme?"

The Professor appeared to expect an answer. Since Dr Syme saw no place to take shelter, he began to explain the whole story—the process by which, according to his usual method, he had tackled each part of Vane's wild scheme—how he had ascended that mountain of horrors—from the poisoning at the Café de L'Europe, to the cipher in the newspaper advertisements that led to the uncovering of the anarchists in Deptford, which in turn led to the something or other by some means, and so on, and thus to the discovery of the bomb beneath Her Highness's coach, and thus inevitably here, to the Cathedral.

Arthur sketched absent-mindedly on his blotting paper: a dome, a cross, inky scudding clouds.

The notion of the struggle on the dome had come to him in a dream, just two nights ago; it had impressed itself upon him with the intensity of a lightning flash. Unfortunately, all else remained dark. How did his detective get there? How precisely had they ascended the dome (was it possible?). And above all: what happened next?

Nothing, perhaps. In his dream, Dr Syme fell, toppling from the dome into black fog, nothing but hard London streets below. Not the best way to start a detective's adventures. Something would have to be done about that. Perhaps he could have poor Syme solve his subsequent cases from the afterlife, through the aid of a medium.

> Dr Syme lunged, knocking the pistol from the Professor's grip, but his enemy swung away, laughing, and drew from his coat a new weapon: a watch.
>
> "We have time," the Professor said. "Dr Syme, I confess I have arranged events so that we might have time and solitude to speak. I have always felt that you, as a man of science, might see the urgent need for reform—for certain sacrifices to be made—"

Arthur's neighbour began to pack his day's writings into his briefcase. This fellow—name unknown—was stand-offish, thin, spectacled. Judging from the pile of books on his desk, on which words like *clairvoyance* and *Osiris* were among the most intelligible, his interests tended to the occult. He closed his briefcase, stood, swayed, then sat back with a thump and lowered his head to his desk. Arthur sympathised. The dread hour and its inexorable approach! Soon the warders would come around, waking up the sleepers, emptying out the room, driving Arthur, and Arthur's neighbour, and the French women, and all the scholars and idlers alike out to face the night, and the rain, and the wind that rattled the glass overhead.

> Midnight! The Professor waited, as if listening for some news to erupt from the befogged city below.
>
> "Well," Syme said. "I dare say I know your habits after all this time. I know how you like to do things in twos. I knew there would be a second

bomb. At the nave, was it, or the altar? I expect Inspector Wright's boys found it quick enough—"

A terrible change came across the Professor's face. All trace of civilization vanished, and savagery took its place—or, rather, not savagery, but that pure malignancy that only the refined intellect is capable of.

Howling, the Professor let go of the cross and flung himself onto Dr Syme.

Pens scratching away. Rain drumming on the glass, loudly now. A row of women industriously translating Russian into English, or English into Sanskrit, Italian into French. Arthur's neighbour appeared to have fallen asleep.

Arm in arm, locked together in deathly struggle, the two men fell—rolling down the side of the dome—toward

Toward what, indeed!

"By God," said Inspector Wright, hearing the terrible crash. He came running out into the street, to see, side by side, dead, upon the ground—

Arthur put down his pen, and scratched thoughtfully at his beard.

His neighbour moaned slightly, as if something were causing him pain. Concerned, Arthur poked his shoulder.

The man jumped to his feet, staring about in wild-eyed confusion; then he snatched up his briefcase and left in such a hurry that scholars all along the rows of the Reading Room looked up and tut-tutted at him.

Rain sluiced noisily down the glass. Lamps swayed in mid-air. Thunder reverberated under the dome as the Reading Room emptied out.

Arthur'd thought he might try to bring out his friend Heath for dinner, or possibly Waugh, but neither was likely to venture out in that weather. Bad timing and bloody awful luck.

He collected his hat, coat, and umbrella. These items were just barely up to the Reading Room's standards of respectability, and he doubted that they were equal to the challenge of the weather outside. Certainly the manuscript of *Dr Syme's First Case* was not—he'd left it folded into the pages of a treatise on poisons.

Outside a small band of scholars, idlers, and policemen sheltered beneath the colonnade. Beyond the colossal white columns, the courtyard was dark and the rain swirled almost sideways. In amongst it were stones, mud, leaves, tiles, newspapers, and flower-pots. Some unfortunate fellow's sandwich-board toppled end-over-end across the yard, caught flight, and vanished in the thrashing air. Arthur's hat went after it. It was like nothing he'd ever seen. A tropical monsoon, or whirlwind, or some such thing.

He was suddenly quite unaccountably afraid. It was what one might call an animal instinct, or an intuition. Later—much later—the members of the Company of the Spheres would tell him that he was *sensitive*, and he'd think back to the night of the Great Storm and wonder if he'd sensed, even then, what was behind it. Perhaps. On the other hand, anyone can be spooked by lightning.

He was out past the gates, into the street, and leaning forward into the wind, homewards down Great Russell Street, before he'd quite noticed that he'd left the safety of the colonnade. When he turned back to get his bearings, the rain was so thick he could hardly see a thing. The Museum was a faint haze of light under a black dome; its columns were distant white giants, lumbering off into the sea. The familiar scene was rendered utterly alien; for all he could tell, he might not have been in London any more, but whisked away to the Moon.

His umbrella tore free of his grip and took flight. He watched it follow his hat away over the rooftops, flapping like some awful black pterodactyl between craggy, suddenly lightning-lit chimneys, then off who-knows-where across London.

Chapter Two

In a quiet Mayfair drawing-room, a man and a woman sat stiffly upright, eyes closed and hands outstretched across a white table-cloth. The curtains were drawn. A single candle on a rococo mantelpiece illuminated a circle of midnight-blue wallpaper, a row of photographs, and a rather hideous painting of the Titan Saturn devouring his children. There was a faint scent of incense.

The woman was middle-aged. She wore high-collared black and silver, and an expression of fierce resolution. The man was young and handsome, fair and blue-eyed, and faintly smiling. He was the subject of most of the photographs on the mantelpiece, posing stiffly, dressed for tennis or mountaineering or camel-riding.

On the table there was a large white card with a red sphere painted on it; they rested their fingers on its corners.

They sat all evening in silence, hardly even breathing, until at the same moment they each opened their eyes in alarm, jerking back their hands so violently that they sent the card spinning off the table into the dark.

The man swore, got to his feet, and went in search of it.

The woman clutched her necklace. "Mercury—what happened?"

He went by the name Mercury when they met. She went by Jupiter.

"A rude interruption."

"*Rudeness!* I call it an assault. They struck us."

"I suppose they did. Yes. Where did it go, do you suppose?"

"We were further than ever before. I saw the gate open before me—the ring turning—did you see it too?"

"Perhaps."

"Then a terrible discord. And shaking, as if the spheres themselves halted in their motions—how?" She took a deep breath, collected herself, and stood.

He crouched. "Aha. It slid under the wardrobe—and that hasn't moved since my father's day. Bloody nuisance."

"They *struck* at us, though we were far out."

"They did, didn't they? Troubling. I thought we had more time."

She glared at him. "Your father's friends, Atwood?"

Martin Atwood was his real name, and this was his house. He stood. "Well, don't blame *me*."

"No? Then who should I blame?"

"I expect we'll find out soon enough. I wonder how they did it? I wonder what they did? Something dreadful, no doubt. Wouldn't that be just like them?"

He lit a lamp, and snuffed the candle.

"If only we knew who they were," he said.

There was the sound of rain at the window, first a whisper, then a clattering, thrashing din.

"Aha," he said. "See? Something dreadful."

Over the noise of the storm there was the shrill insistent ring of the telephone across the hall. Atwood poured himself a drink before answering.

The storm smashed a fortune in window glass. It uprooted century-old trees. It sank boats and toppled cranes. It washed up things from the bottom of the river, rusted and rotten stuff, yesterday's rubbish and artifacts older than the Romans. It vandalised the docks at St. Katharine's. It flooded streets and houses and cellars and the Underground. It deposited chimneys on unfamiliar roofs, laundry in other peoples' gardens, dead dogs where they weren't wanted. It cracked the dome of the Reading Room and let in the rain. It coated the fine marble facades of Whitehall with river muck. Lightning struck Nelson's Column, scattering the few dozen unfortunate souls who slept at its foot like so many wet leaves. The lights along the Embankment whipped free and floated downriver. The London Electric Supply Corporation's central station at Deptford flooded and went dark. Barometers everywhere were caught unawares. Omnibuses slewed like storm-tossed ships, trams detailed, horses broke their legs. Men died venturing out after stalls, carts, pigeons, and other items of vanishing property.

Arthur Archibald Shaw staggered and slid from shelter to shelter. An abandoned bus in the middle of Southampton Row gave him protection from the wind. God only knew what had become of the horses. An advertisement on the side for something called KOKO FOR HAIR took on a fearful pagan quality. What dreadful god of the storm was *Koko?* He stumbled on, clutching at lampposts, and turned the street corner (by now quite lost) just as lightning flashed and snapped a tree in two. He stopped in a doorway and watched leaves and roof tiles whip past. Someone's house. A light in the window. He could expect no Christian charity on a night like this. A horse ran down the street before him, wide-eyed and panicking.

He shivered, wrapped his arms around himself, stamped his feet. He was young, and he was big—running to fat, his friend Waugh liked to say. Well, thank God for every pound and ounce. Skinny little Waugh would have been airborne half a mile ago.

The storm appeared to have engulfed all of London. Lightning overhead flashed signals, directing coal-black hurrying clouds to their business in all quarters of the city.

His fear was mostly gone; what had taken its place was excitement, accompanied by a nagging anxiety over the cost of replacing his hat and umbrella. He wondered if he might defray the expense by selling an account of the storm to the *Mammoth*—he was already thinking of it as *The Storm of '93*—or, better yet, the New York periodicals: *Our correspondent in London. Monsoon in Bloomsbury. Typhoon on the Thames.* An *Odyssey*, across the city, or at least across the mile between the Museum and home. They'd like the panicked horse—it would make a good picture.

He peered back south in the direction the horse had fled. Behind the rooftops and out over the river there was something like a black pillar of cloud. It resembled a gigantic screw bolting London to the heavens, turning tighter and tighter, bringing the sky down. Behind it there was an unpleasant reddish light.

The Isle of Dogs and the West India Docks suffered the worst of it. For years afterwards, those who'd seen the Storm, and those who hadn't, but remembered it as if they had, spoke of crashing waves; the lights of troubled boats swinging crazily in the dark, and then, dreadfully, going out; and bells ringing, and thunder, and timbers creaking, and chains snapping, and cranes falling, and men screaming as the waves swept them off the docks and downriver, perhaps all the way to the sea.

What wasn't much remarked on was that the Storm also flooded Norman Gracewell's Engine—for the simple reason that few people who didn't have business with the Engine knew it was there. Mr Dimmick kept away sneaks and snoops—he was better than a guard-dog, Gracewell liked to say. But there was nothing Dimmick could do to keep out the flood waters. The Engine was mostly underground, which had seemed, when the Company built the thing, like a good way to ensure secrecy, but now ensured that the flood quickly filled all the Engine's rooms. Most of the workers fled before the flooding got too severe, abandoning their desks and their ledgers; but Gracewell himself remained until the last minute, pacing back and forth in his office, shouting into a telephone, demanding an explanation, demanding more time and more money, demanding an accounting for this outrage, long after the flood had severed the wires and the line had gone dead.

Arthur lived in a small flat on the end of Rugby Street. Under ordinary circumstances it was a short walk from the Museum, but that night it took an hour, and by the time he approached home he'd had more than enough weather to last him a lifetime.

Through the rain he saw Mr Borel's stationery shop on the corner. He knew the shop well—he often bought ink and tobacco and newspapers there. In fact, he owed Borel a moderate sum of money. The place was in a sorry state: the sign was askew, the windows had shattered in two or three places, and the door swung open. There was usually a bright blue-and-yellow sign over a basement office that read J.E. BRADMAN, STENOGRAPHY, TYPEWRITING & TRANSLATIONS, but that was gone, too, ripped off its hinges and blown God knows where. Poor old Borel and poor old Mr Bradman whoever he was.

Someone inside—a girl—screamed.

Arthur abandoned caution and ran headlong across the street, sliding and stumbling in the wind, and in through the door. Lightning flashed behind him. When his vision cleared he saw Mr Borel's daughter, Sophia, standing behind the counter, screaming. Her father stood in a puddle, holding a broom. An eel flopped at his feet. Sophia stared at it in horror, as if were a vampire that had broken into her bedroom. It was, no denying it, hideous.

A young woman Arthur had never seen before held a candle, inspecting the eel with a mixture of curiosity and distaste. Her hair was tangled and her dress dishevelled, as if she'd dressed in a hurry. She looked up at Arthur in surprise.

"Hello," she said. "Are you all right?"

"Yes. As well as can be expected. There was—I heard screaming."

"It was a very heroic entrance. I'm sorry—it was! Sophia cried out—well, you can hardly blame her—it's a frightful-looking monster, poor thing."

Strikingly green eyes, he noticed; emerald-like by candlelight. A quick, pleasing face.

He straightened his coat, wiped twigs and leaves from his hair.

"So I see," he said.

"Are you hurt?"

There was blood on the hand that had wiped his hair, but not a great deal. His head stung a little, now that he noticed it.

"Not at all," he said. "Could be worse, anyway."

She looked out the open door behind him and shuddered.

Arthur shrugged off his overcoat. In its current state it would hardly be gallant to offer it to her. She'd be better off without it.

"Mr Shaw," Borel said. The eel snapped at his broom.

Borel's shop was a long way from the river or any fish-market that Arthur knew of, and the eel's presence was a small mystery. He'd heard of hurricanes blowing things all over the place in the sort of places that had hurricanes, but one didn't expect it in London. No doubt it was even more puzzling to the eel.

"Hello, Mr Borel. Is everything all right?"

It quite plainly wasn't. The door had blown open, shelves had fallen, and Borel's stock was soaked. Tins of tobacco and creams and medicines lay scattered on the floor. The wind and the rain had made sad heaps out of German newspapers, French photographs of dancing girls, and the magazines of various obscure trades. Arthur realised that he was standing on a ruined copy of the *Metropolitan Dairyman*.

"By God. It's extraordinary out there. Extraordinary. You'd think you were in the tropics. I lost my umbrella. There was a horse."

He closed the door. The wind opened it again. He sat on the floor with his back against it.

The eel thrashed. It appeared to be getting weaker. Borel poked it again.

The green-eyed woman said, "Your coat."

"My coat?"

"To pick up the eel. I'm afraid it might bite otherwise."

He tossed his coat to Mr Borel, who groaned and wrestled the creature out through one of the shattered window-panes.

"Good," Arthur said. "Well. Glad I could be of service. Perhaps I should go and see what's come in through my own windows."

"Oh—I wouldn't. It's dreadful out there. Besides, you're the only thing holding the door closed."

"Well. Yes. That's best. In my current state, I feel just about competent to be a door-stop."

Wind howled and thumped at the door.

"The fellow downstairs," Arthur said. "The typewriting business—that sign's gone too."

She looked up in surprise.

"Oh God. Where?"

"Halfway to the moon, for all I know."

"I'm sorry. A silly question. God, what an awful night!"

"You know the owner, Miss . . . ?"

"I do. I *am* the owner, Mr Shaw. Or, I *was*, I suppose."

Arthur was very surprised.

He introduced himself as Arthur Archibald Shaw, noted journalist for *The Monthly Mammoth*, and author of detective stories—*aspiring*, he acknowledged. *J. E. Bradman*—whom he'd vaguely imagined as gnarled, grey-bearded, and whiskery—turned out to be *Josephine Elizabeth*. She had the office downstairs, and lived in a tiny flat upstairs. She'd come down to help when she heard Sophia screaming.

"Perhaps," Mr Borel said, "we could move a shelf to stop the door. And of course you may be guests here until this storm departs."

They bustled about, making what repairs they could by candlelight. Sophia fell asleep somehow. Arthur and Miss Bradman talked as they worked, between interruptions from thunder and branches crashing against the window, with Borel as an odd sort of chaperone.

They talked about detective stories while they picked up and dusted off Borel's jars of ointment. She seemed to have some very distinct ideas about how a detective story ought to go, though Arthur wasn't sure he followed everything she said. Blow to the head, perhaps. He wondered if she were a literary type herself—this being Bloomsbury, after all. After some cajoling, she confessed that she was a poet. "But not for a while. One can't find the time."

"Time," he agreed. "Time and money!"

She glanced sadly at the window. "That sign was practically new! And awfully expensive."

"Typing, it used to say, if I recall. I suppose that means—I don't know—document Wills? That sort of thing?"

"From time to time."

He helped Borel heave a shelf upright. "And you do translation, of course. French? Italian? Russian? I came here from the Reading Room, if it's still standing—one hears every sort of language around there . . ."

"Greek; Latin."

"Scholarly monographs, that sort of thing?"

"In a manner of speaking," she said, and busied herself arranging the magazines.

"A manner of speaking?"

She turned back to him. "You promise you won't think it odd?"

"Tonight, Miss Bradman, nothing could seem odd."

"In the safe downstairs I currently have a half-typed treatise on the Electric Radiance by a Lincoln's Inn barrister; a monograph on Egyptian burial rites by a clerk for the Metropolitan Railway Company, who wants the whole thing translated into Latin so as to be kept obscure from rival magicians; and an account of a telepathic visit to Tibet by a—well, I shouldn't say more. She's been in the newspapers. An actress."

"Good Lord."

"You do think it odd. I knew you would. I'm telling you this in confidence, Mr Shaw."

"Of course."

"The thing about—about that sort of person, Mr Shaw, is that he or she will quite often pay very well for a certain . . . trust. Confidence. A kindred

spirit. Anonymity. And Greek and Latin, of course. I have a certain reputation."

She went to calm Sophia, who'd woken in a panic at the sound of thunder. Arthur watched her with a certain amazement.

"How does one get into that line of work?"

"Accident, I suppose."

"Accident?"

"Most things in life are, aren't they? May I ask how you came to be
writing about science for the *Mammoth*?"

"My uncle, to be frank. Old George—"

Outside there was a terrible crash, possibly a tree falling. Sophia
shrieked. Mr Borel told her to go and make coffee. At the prospect of hot
coffee, Arthur lost his train of thought.

"The accident," Miss Bradman said, a little later, as they stood around
the stove.

"Yes? Please, do tell me."

She took a deep breath. "It was after I came to London, though not
long after. My father, having left me a little money for an education—he was
the rector in a little village you've never heard of, but forward-thinking,
and he believed in education. Anyway, after Cambridge there was a little
left over for a typewriter, though hardly a room to put it in; and for enroll-
ment in the Breckenridge School for Typewriting and Stenography. From
whose dingy and dismal premises I stepped out one bright spring afternoon to see a silver-haired lady of dignified appearance staring into the
window and weeping. Naturally I asked if I could help her."

"Naturally."

"As it turned out, her name was Mrs Esther Sedgley, and her husband
was just lately deceased. From time to time she suffered what you might
call memories, or you might call visions—I don't know—she herself was
never sure what to call them. The sight of her reflection in a window might
bring them on, or a flight of pigeons, or all sorts of things. It reminded
me of—well, now I'm wandering off from my story, aren't I? You must tell
me if I do it again, Mr Shaw. By this time we'd already moved to Mrs Sedgley's parlour, and then she invited me to dinner, which I was certainly in no
position to refuse. We quickly became friends."

Miss Bradman sipped her coffee.

"Her husband had been a barrister—quite a good one, I think, though of course I wouldn't know—but also the Master of a . . . well, a sort of society, a club for discussion of spiritual matters, and the esoteric sciences, and so on. And so after the poor fellow died, my friend had found herself presented with a bewildering array of mediums offering to call him up by spirit-trumpet, or table-rapping, or what-have-you . . . So that summer she engaged in travel all across London, and she was lonely. Besides, she needed a secretary, and a witness, because she considered it her business to sniff out fraud and imposture and nonsense. And so Mrs Sedgley and I went to Bromley to see Mrs Hutton's spirit-trumpet."

"Good Lord," Arthur said.

"And we saw Mrs Gully turn water into rose-water in Spitalfields, and Mr H. C. Hall lift a spoon by animal magnetism in St. John's Wood. And together we attended the re-launch of the *Occult Review* where Miss MacPhail—the actress—said that we were all Exemplars of the Super-Man. Though of course I'm sure she says that to everyone. I saw Brigadier MacKenzie fail to levitate, and I saw Mr Wallace's spirits play the piano. A lot of those sort of people come to the meetings of Mrs Sedgley's society, for which Mrs Sedgley employs me to take the minutes. And in the course of all that I suppose I earned a certain reputation. The Brigadier had a monograph he wanted typed, and Miss MacPhail wanted to learn Greek—and so on, and so on. And so—since you ask, Mr Shaw—it's because of that chance meeting that I fell into that sort of company; and it's because of *that* that I came to be here—renting the office downstairs, that is, and the room upstairs. Aren't chance meetings terribly important, don't you think?"

"Did the spirits really play the piano?" Sophia said.

"A good trick if they did," Arthur said. "A good trick either way."

"I don't know. I will say this: that for every fraud I have met, I have met a dozen sincere and intelligent seekers after truth. After all, isn't it nearly the twentieth century? And is it more outlandish, Mr Shaw, that there should be revolutionary advances in the science of telepathy, or clairvoyance, than that there should be electric lighting, or telephones?"

"I won't deny that," Arthur said.

Miss Bradman stared down at the hem of her skirt, which was soaking wet. "I've said altogether too much, haven't I? You let me talk too much,

Mr Shaw; you should have said something. I don't know quite what's got into me. It must be the storm."

After a while Mr Borel found some relatively dry playing cards and the four of them played whist by candlelight. They were by that time all quite merry, in the way of people who've survived the worst of things and have nothing to do for the time being but wait. Every time lightning flashed they cheered—even Mr Borel. God knows what the hour was. Already Arthur felt as if he'd known Miss Bradman all his life.

By chance their hands touched across the table, and there was a sensation that Arthur would later swear was a sort of electric shock. The candle flickered. Something lurched inside Arthur, too, at the thought of how big London was, and how many people were in it; and at the thought of how fast the world moved, whirling through the dark, and how improbable and uncanny it was that any two people should ever, under any circumstances, meet—and that they should then find themselves talking to each other, and playing cards around a table, as if it were all perfectly normal.

Miss Bradman flushed red and drew back her hand. She went to the window and peered out into the dark.

Chapter Three

The sky was beautiful the next morning, full of an unusual flickering rose-pink light, and odd tall towers of cloud that slowly, over the course of the morning, crumbled to cloud-dust—but few people had the time to notice it. There was damage to inspect, losses to calculate, repairs to make; hands to shake and congratulations and condolences to extend to one's neighbours and friends; rumours of miraculous escapes; and tragic deaths to pass on.

The most newsworthy rumour, which had spread all over London before it was time for breakfast, concerned the death of Augustus Mordaunt, Duke of Sussex. The origin of the rumour was variously thought to be a nurse, a servant in the ducal household, or a policeman. The circumstances of the old man's death were somewhat mysterious—he certainly hadn't been out and about on the streets at night in the storm.

Arthur slept late that morning. He heard the news at lunchtime, when he called at Borel's shop to offer to help with repairs, and in the hope of running into Miss Bradman again.

"Sad news, Mr Shaw," Borel said. "Sad news indeed."

Borel adjusted his spectacles. He looked anxious. Arthur had heard that the Duke had been the landlord for half of London; his death would be as disruptive in its way as the storm.

"The old fellow was in London for Christmas," Borel added.

"The storm did it," Sophia whispered. "The noise and the lightning. He was always afraid of bad weather—that's what people say."

"Good God," Arthur said.

If he hadn't already lost his hat, he would have taken it off.

The fact was that he'd always thought of the Duke, in so far as he'd thought about him at all, as something of a figure of fun. The Duke had been a staple of the newspapers since long before Arthur was born. He

was a second cousin—or some such complicated and mysterious relation—to the throne, and it was said that after the Prince died he was one
of the very few people whose company Her Majesty could tolerate. In his old
age he had become a reformer, an advocate for the education of women,
and exercise, and modernization of the prisons, and other more contro-
versial causes. His health was said to be bad; there were stories of rare and
dreadful ailments and eccentric remedies, strange foreign doctors, and
obsessions with mesmerism and meditation and hieroglyphics and telepathy and reincarnation and spirit-writing and astrology. He'd lavished a
fortune on the construction of a tremendous telescope near Hastings, but
did it fifteen years ago, when astronomy was not nearly so fashionable as it
had recently become. *The Monthly Mammoth* had published a memorable
cartoon—it was pinned up in the *Mammoth*'s offices—in which he wore a
turban, and levitated slightly, while he proposed the transport of convicts
to the Moon.

"Her Majesty's beside herself," Sophia whispered. "She's locked herself in the church beside his body, and won't let the doctors near. They
say he used to talk to the old Prince for her—rest his soul—they say—"

Mr Borel frowned. "Do not tell stories, child."

Sophia lowered her head, scowling.

Borel took off his spectacles. Arthur recognised that gesture; it indicated that Borel was about to raise the unpleasant subject of the money
that Arthur owed him. He excused himself.

Overnight, in one of those sudden reversals that the public mood
sometimes experiences in the presence of death, the Duke became
a hero of the nation, faultless and universally loved. No one recalled ever
saying or hearing a bad word about him. The death was an occasion for
national mourning; a brief ecstasy of sudden and rather theatrical grief.
Her Majesty—by all accounts confined to her chambers, too heavy-hearted
even to get out of bed—set the tone. London's battered streets unfurled
black banners. Flowers appeared on fences, tied with black ribbons.
Wreaths hung from lamp-posts. Little shrines appeared in windows. Bells
rang sorrowfully through the fog. the *Times* suggested that it was, perhaps, not too much to say that, in a way, an Augustan Age had passed. At
Arthur's church, prayers were said for the late Duke's soul and for a griev-
ing nation. Sunday crowds on the Embankment wore black, and even the

sellers of roast chestnuts and iced lemonade and apple fritters somehow contrived to do their jobs in a mournful way. All along the cold grey
river there were broken jetties and cranes and half-sunk boats, all left
where they'd fallen, as if the whole city were in too dreadful a state even
to think of doing anything about them.

The courtship of Arthur Shaw and Josephine Bradman began con-
ventionally enough—if one didn't count the storm—with an exchange
of New Year's gifts. Arthur bought Josephine a pair of gloves that he
couldn't afford; she sent him a card that was so forward that as soon as she
dropped it in the post she blushed to think of him reading it, and immediately decided to refuse to recall what it had said; indeed, it hardly seemed
that it was her hand that had written it. He appeared at her office the next
afternoon wearing his least-bad suit. She glanced at him only long
enough to decide that he looked very handsome in it; then, as she
stared down fixedly at her typewriter in something of an uncharacteris-
tic panic, he started to speak. He was—she could tell—inwardly praying
for another storm, so that he could strike a properly heroic figure; while
outwardly suggesting—as if the idea had just occurred to him as he happened to be walking past—that from time to time he had a little typing
he needed done, this or that, and he was thinking of writing a book, as a
matter of fact, possibly about Darwin, or a sort of detective thing; but in
any case it wasn't just a question of typing, but rather, since, as she could
surely see, words weren't his strong suit, the eye of a poet might . . . Almost without thinking she stood, and suggested that they go for a walk to
discuss the matter.

The park was full of toppled trees and strewn debris. They didn't
mind. As they navigated the treacherous paths her panic evaporated, replaced by a sort of elation. When evening came she pretended not to notice the cold. They talked about everything except business. They talked
about nothing. He came again the next day and they took a different
route around the lake, and again the day after.

Passions that could not be acted upon or even uttered aloud expressed
themselves instead through signs and codes. She illustrated for him the
various meanings that could be found in the folding of gloves, the tip of a
hat-brim, flowers. The tapping of gloves on the left hand like *so* meant:
Come walk with me. She'd read it in newspapers and manuals of etiquette.

The placing of the folded glove against the left cheek for an instant meant: *I consider you handsome.* To run one's finger around one's hat-brim *this* way meant *yes*, and the other way *no*. To take off the hat and hold it like *so* was a sign that was not to be invoked even in jest, except after the most careful consideration. When she ran out of signs she could remember she started making them up, and soon they both dissolved into laughter.

That night she wrote a letter to a friend in Cambridge, asking if perhaps she was going a little mad.

There was no one to tell them to stop, no one to disapprove; no one in all of London, or anywhere else for that matter. Miss Bradman's father was deceased, and her mother had rarely left her bed for the past three years, laid low by nightmares and waking visions of hell-fire; she predicted doom and catastrophe so reliably and monotonously that Josephine had long since stopped asking her opinion on most things, and she did not ask her opinion on Arthur.

They walked together in Regent's Park, or along the Embankment, arm in arm, for hours. He cajoled her to read him one of her poems. It was mostly about Plato, and about the soul, and about visions of variously brightly coloured heavens; walking through the white forests of the moon, disputing philosophy with the Cyclops in his cave in a red desert. Arthur had always considered philosophers prior to Newton to be more or less bunk, and Heaven as he imagined it was not very different from the Reading Room of the British Museum, or a holiday in Brighton, or a well-equipped transatlantic liner. The words were good, though. It made him wish he hadn't been such an idler at school. Miss Bradman was actually rather relieved that he didn't know what to say; she didn't trust men with opinions about poetry.

They exchanged letters—mostly about nothing at all, expressed in the most florid and fervent terms that convention and the English language allowed. He addressed her, tentatively, as Josephine. She didn't object. Her friend from Cambridge wrote back to say that it did *perhaps* sound as if she were acting a *little* hastily, and Josephine wrote angrily to tell her that it was none of her business after all. They each woke, night after night, thinking of the other, and—as if by some telepathy—knowing that the other was thinking of them.

"Animal magnetism," Arthur explained to his friend Waugh.

"Magnetism, now, is it?"

"Man is a part of nature, from a scientific point of view, and subject to the animal passions—"

"Passions! Now, that's more like it."

(Waugh spent his father's money fortnightly on a particular prostitute, and called it love).

"I swear to God, Waugh. It's quite uncanny."

They had dinner with Arthur's rich uncle George, the writer, who pronounced Josephine to be a *good egg*. Arthur's friend Waugh, who thought of himself as poetic—solely, so far as anyone could tell, on the grounds of a fifty per cent admixture of Celtic blood—declared that she was a muse. (She rather resented this.)

She told her sister about Arthur, in a letter. Her sister told their mother, who sent a letter, in a scarcely legible hand, warning her of terrible consequences if she didn't repent and leave London at once. Hell-fire and damnation and et cetera; but she was always saying that sort of thing.

"I wouldn't worry about hell-fire," said her friend Mrs Sedgley, who had modern views, and believed in the Spirit World, but not in Hell.

They sat in Mrs Sedgley's parlour, in the big empty house in Kensington she had once occupied with her late husband. Rain pattered on the windows, and Mrs Sedgley's cat Gautama rubbed curiously against Josephine's leg.

"Though a touch of caution might, perhaps, if you don't mind my saying—"

"I have always preserved my independence, Esther."

"Of course."

"Esther," Josephine said. "Do you believe that two people can . . . well, that they can share certain thoughts, or dreams, or . . ." She fell silent, and to cover her sudden embarrassment she reached down to scratch Gautama's ears.

"Am I to understand," Mrs Sedgley said, carefully pouring more tea, "that you and the young man—Arthur—have experienced such a . . . phenomenon?"

"I don't mean it in a vulgar sense—that is, a literal sense."

"Certainly not."

"What-colour-am-I-thinking-of, what-card-am-I-holding, and so forth. But rather . . ."

"In a spiritual sense."

"Yes. Well—yes."

She was in the habit—Mrs Sedgley had introduced her to it—of keeping a journal of her dreams, at least in so far as they had poetic or spiritual significance. Since the night of the storm, she and Arthur had both been visited by dreams of stars, rushing water, roses, and distant mountains—though not always on the same nights—and Josephine had woken on several mornings with ideas for detective stories.

"I don't know." She sighed. "I shouldn't like you to think I'm being foolish."

"Oh, my dear—never!"

They listened to the rain for a moment.

"Certainly"—Mrs Sedgley sipped her tea—"there *may* be such a thing." She sounded a little sceptical. "Between two sensitive souls, who knows what might be possible? I remember when Thomas and I were young. . . . What does the young man think?"

"Telepathy, he says, or thought-transference."

"Hmm. He's . . . educated in these matters?"

"Not at all. Not until a few weeks ago. But he's taken an interest now. As soon as they reopened the Reading Room he began studying the journals—the *Proceedings of the Society for Psychical Research* and so on. It's rather flattering."

In a matter of weeks he'd become conversant in the *lingo* of psychical research, and could happily discuss—scratching his head, puzzled, as if hoping that some rearrangement of the terms might spell out the answer to a question he could not quite define—such arcane subjects as *telepathy*, and *telekinesis*, and *hyperpromethia* (which referred to a supernatural power of foresight), and *psychorrhagy* (which referred to the breaking free of the soul from the confines of the body).

"A scholar," Mrs Sedgley said.

"He writes detective stories."

"Oh? Does he have a good income?"

She had to admit that he did not, and that it was a source of some concern. The prospect of a literary sort of marriage rather appealed to her; poverty did not; yet the two seemed inextricable from each other.

Mrs Sedgley frowned.

"Is he . . ." Mrs Sedgley sought with difficulty for the right word. She liked to consider herself forward-thinking and somewhat bohemian, and was reluctant to utter such a conventional thought. "Is he a *solid* sort of person?"

"Oh, my dear—yes. I can't quite explain it, but I feel he is the most *solid* person I've ever met; as if nothing else since I came to London has been quite real."

"I see." Gautama jumped up into Mrs Sedgley's lap. "Yes, hello, boy; hello."

"Does it seem hasty? Not to me. It seems that the storm was six months of ordinary life in one night. I think that I love him, Esther."

"Yes, Gautama, yes; there's a handsome boy. Josephine, I think I should like to meet this young man."

L ondon in general was in something of an excitable mood. The flood of fashionable mourning for the late Duke carried an undercurrent of morbid—frankly paranoid—speculation. Though rivers of ink had been spilled on the subject of the Duke's death, the cause remained somewhat unclear. He left no heirs or family. Influenza, the doctors said, but this was widely considered an unsatisfactory explanation. A well-known East End medium declared that the spirits had revealed to her that he'd been murdered—she couldn't say how. She wasn't the first or the last. Fortune-tellers (who were ten a penny in London) unanimously held the Duke's death to be a bad omen. The stars were very bad in general for the coming year.

The police denied foul play. The Duke had been elderly, after all, and frail. Yet rumours persisted. Bombs, a shooting, a poisoning. The body was not displayed. Political motives for the crime—if it *was* a crime—were hinted at in Parliament, whispered in pubs. The news got out that the police were seeking persons in connection with an investigation; of what, they wouldn't say. The newspapers recalled the deceased's various lifelong occult interests, his fraternization with spiritualists and fortune-tellers and practitioners of Eastern religions and—well, you never knew with those sort of people, did you? No doubt the great man had been taken advantage of. A man of his breeding had no defences against the low cunning of common frauds. Was there perhaps blackmail involved, or something worse, something the criminal law didn't precisely have a word for? High time to shine a light on that netherworld (said the Bishop of Manchester, in a letter to the *Times*).

The Prime Minister spoke in Parliament, calling for calm. The *Times* criticised the failure of officials to make arrests, and hinted at conspiracy so vaguely and with such discretion that no one was quite sure what they were saying. Some American and Parisian newspapers, less circumspect, called it *murder*, though they couldn't get their story straight as to method or suspects or motive.

A New York newspaper reported that Dr Arthur Conan Doyle had been invited by the police to lend his expertise to their investigation of whatever it was they were investigating, or weren't investigating. Arthur read it in Mr Borel's shop one afternoon when he went to call on Josephine.

"Can you believe that?" His own detective story had fallen by the wayside, rather. Between the Storm and Josephine, he'd spared few thoughts for Dr Syme in recent weeks. Still, he couldn't deny feeling a certain small pang of jealousy.

Borel glanced at the headline. "I can believe anything, Mr Shaw."

"Well now! Dr Doyle! If that isn't desperation, I hardly know what is."

Borel said nothing.

Arthur returned the paper to the window. "What do you think, Mr Borel?"

Borel removed his spectacles and studied them, sighing, as if examining their lenses for imperfections. "Mr Shaw, I have suffered considerable expenses in the storm."

"I dare say."

"I have borrowed money to make repairs. I did not like to do that. The sum of money that you owe me is now considerable. I do not like to have to remind you."

"I know, Mr Borel. I know. But the fact of the matter is I find myself hard up at the moment. The *Mammoth* owes me money—and the rent must be paid before all else."

"We must all pay rent to someone, Mr Shaw. I am sorry."

Borel put his spectacles back on and blinked at Arthur as if he were surprised to see him still in the shop. Arthur took this to mean that their conversation about money was over. Borel was a decent enough fellow. He didn't like to rub it in.

Arthur gestured at the newspaper. "What do you think, Mr Borel? Foul play, yes or no?"

"How could I know, Mr Shaw?"

"No smoke without fire. One hopes they'll catch the villain responsible soon; put things back in order."

"One hopes. I think there will be trouble."

There'd already been trouble. In Whitechapel, Jewish windows that had survived the storm were broken by stones. A German bookshop near the Museum was burned, and a Russian businessman was found dead in Notting Hill. The *Daily Telegraph* hinted that Afghan agents were at work in London, and the *Omnibus* suspected Indian malcontents. The police raided Limehouse. A lot of Indians and Frenchmen and Irish and sailors and gypsies and fortune-tellers and radicals of various sorts were rounded up and arrested for various petty crimes, but no murderers were discovered by those methods. Astrologers said that the stars promised discord, and that the coming year was a bad one for engagements, business ventures, and childbirth. Mr Borel had forbidden his wife and daughter to go outside.

Josephine and Arthur were oblivious to most of this. London's bad mood didn't infect them. They were suddenly out of step with their times: blissfully, almost sinfully so. They spent the winter walking, and writing long letters, and exchanging cards, flowers, gifts, poems, love-notes. *Dearest love. My own darling heart, my only, my fondest, my soul.* They compared notes on their dreams, and attended lectures. They made plans to move to the seaside, to Brighton perhaps, where Josephine would write poetry in a room looking out on the sea, and Arthur would take the train into London twice weekly to meet with newspaper editors . . . They kissed in Regent's Park by the lake, in the spot where the rotunda had been, under the disapproving glare of police officers.

Arthur proposed towards the end of February, at the edge of a half-frozen pond in the park, the words turning crystalline in the cold air as he spoke them. A mere formality by that point; an inevitability. The main impediment to their engagement was that it took Arthur two weeks to get his foster-father to send him his late mother's ring down from Edinburgh—the old sod dragged his feet, counselling against marrying a clever woman.

In fact, the winter would have been entirely blissful, and quite dream-like, if not for one fly in the ointment; the usual: money.

Several of Josephine's clients, being highly strung types, had fled London after the storm. Meanwhile, the *Mammoth* had gone silent. A lightning-struck warehouse and flooded printing press had put it out of commission. It hadn't paid Arthur in a month; then two months; then three.

I should acquaint you," Arthur said, "with the system of my debts."
Josephine frowned. "You have a system?"

"One may regret the necessity but be proud of the engineering. First the *Mammoth*—a notoriously forgetful beast—pays me late. A tradition of long standing, but my landlord and the grocer, not being literary folk, don't see the charm of it; so to pay *them* I borrow from Borel, or from Waugh—who has a good inheritance, and, besides, will one day be a doctor. To pay Waugh and Borel I borrow from Uncle George—who is something of a big man in publishing and makes a very good living off comic stories about chaps messing about in boats, and is forgiving of debts, but only up to a point. And so *in extremis* I borrow from my foster-father in Edinburgh to pay George. The old man is *not* forgiving. It is for God to forgive, he says, as if that were the most baffling and ineffable of all His attributes. And then because of the money I send to Edinburgh, the rent is late. And so on."

"A well-oiled mechanism."

"Except that the storm has played hob with it. Sand in the gears. Old Borel has windows to mend, and George has a roof to mend, and Waugh—*same boat*, Waugh says, *same bloody boat, old chap*. And I wonder if the *Mammoth* hasn't absconded entirely."

He didn't mention that he had received that morning a letter from his foster-father, expressing disappointment at Arthur's impecuniousness and fecklessness, and scolding him for his refusal to apply himself to any manly profession. The old man himself had lost a £500 investment in the *Annapolis*, wrecked in harbour at St. Katharine's, and expected no pity for this, but nor did he plan to throw good money after bad. He said that it was madness for Arthur to think of marriage, his prospects being so utterly, disgracefully bleak.

"Well, then," Josephine said, taking his arm. "We shall simply have to find a new system."

At the end of March, Arthur went to pay one last visit to the *Mammoth*'s offices. He found the door locked and the windows shuttered. Nobody answered his knocking. Nobody had answered his letters for weeks. He pried open the letter-box and shouted into the void.

It was drizzling, and he still had no umbrella. He stumbled for refuge into the closest pub, the Moon & Star. Inside it was empty and dark, low-ceilinged. There was a terrible reek of stale tobacco. The man at the bar nodded to him in vague recognition. Arthur couldn't remember his name—big fellow, bald, Tom or John or something of the sort. No doubt Arthur was the last of the *Mammoth* folk who would ever enter the man's establishment. The storm had been a bad business all round, and it kept getting worse.

They shared a gloomy drink. There was an old newspaper on the bar, and Arthur pored in silence over the employment advertisements—God, could he contemplate teaching? Would Josephine be a teacher's wife, out in the country? The thought of a roomful of schoolboys made him order another drink.

"Impossible," he said.

"Hmm?"

"Oh—nothing."

"As you like, sir."

He pushed the newspaper away. The landlord picked it up.

A story about the late Duke's funeral caught the landlord's attention. A photograph showed the stately procession: the long thin coffin on the great black gun-carriage, the cavalry in their snow-white plumes, and Her Majesty's black and windowless coach.

"Empty, of course." The landlord pointed with a stubby finger at the coffin.

"Empty?"

"You haven't heard? Being a journalist, sir, I would have thought you'd have heard. Everyone says—there was a few fellows in here saying it just the other day; said they heard it from His Lordship's own servant—there never was a body, sir. He burned, poor sod."

"Burned?"

"Oh, it happens, sir! It happens more than you'd think. *Spontaneous combustion*, they call it. Sometimes a fellow's just minding his own business and *whoosh*, or he takes a lady's hand or puts on his hat too fast, and up in flames he goes. It's been proved by science. Could happen to any of us, just like that, one day—who knows. Like lightning, if you get my meaning, sir."

"Whoosh. Well. Certainly a theory."

"They say"—the landlord warmed to his theme—"it happens more often these days. Sunspots, or the influence of the stars—"

Bells interrupted. It was five o'clock, and Arthur had an appointment. "God," he said. "Sorry. Stars, eh? Must run." He drained his drink and hurried out into the rain.

THE
SECOND
DEGREE

{ *The Modern Age* }

Chapter Four

Josephine stepped out of her office into the rain. She opened her umbrella, checked her watch, and sighed. Mr Borel nodded to her through the shop window and she waved to him. She stretched; she'd been typing all day and had a half-dozen little aches to show for it. Then she hurried to catch the bus across town, to an address on Blythe Street, in Kensington, a large and handsome house with lilies in the window. By the time she arrived, the rain had stopped but the sky was darkening. Arthur was there, waiting in the street for her, red-faced and a little short of breath, as if he'd run all the way. She took his arm and he took her umbrella. He smelled of beer and bad news. She gave him a look.

"Nothing," he said.

"Nothing?"

He sighed. "Dead as a dinosaur."

"Oh. What awful luck."

"Left in the lurch, rather. Perhaps your wizard friends can help."

"Please don't call them that; they take themselves awfully seriously." She rang the doorbell.

A servant opened the door. Behind him stood Mrs Sedgley, in a white mutton-sleeved dress and a necklace of gold and pearls. There was the sound of a young woman singing something vaguely Celtic somewhere inside.

Mrs Sedgley peered myopically out into the night before putting her glasses on. "Oh, good! There you are, Josephine."

"Good evening, Matron. This is—"

"Arthur Shaw," he said, bowing.

He was rather looking forward to making Mrs Sedgley's acquaintance. He'd never given much thought to this sort of thing before he met Josephine. A whole new world. Just what he needed.

"Hmm. Yes. The writer. I see. Well, come in, come in, Mr Shaw; the meeting is almost ready to begin."

They entered the premises of the Ordo V.V. 341. Arthur paused to say good evening to a very handsome grey cat asleep on a side-table in the hall. Mrs Sedgley said that his name was Gautama, or George, if Arthur preferred.

The Ordo V.V. 341, though it pretended to a certain immemorial tradition, had in fact been founded not very many years ago by the late Mr Sedgley and a few friends, all of whom had previously been members of Mr Mathers and Mr Westcott's Temple of Isis-Urania. The V.V. 341 had broken away from its parent order after a row, which—depending on whom one listened to—was either about Mr Sedgley's scandalous discovery that the Hidden Secret Chiefs of the Temple were merely a fraud, or about an unpaid £200 loan. In any case, it involved doctrinal schism, threats of litigation, and several months of open magical warfare, during which Mr Mathers and Mr Sedgley wrote half a dozen letters each to the *Occult Review* and the *Proceedings of the Theosophical Society* describing the terrible forces they'd been forced to invoke, the unspeakable curses they'd performed. It ended with both magicians declaring themselves the victor. The Temple went on to become one of London's most fashionable spiritual fraternities, with an illustrious membership and successful satellite temples in Paris, Edinburgh, and Bradford; while Mr Sedgley went on to considerable success as a barrister before dying of a heart attack, leaving the care of the V.V. 341 to his widow.

This was the Order's first meeting since the storm. They met in a room at the back of Mrs Sedgley's house: large and comfortable, lined with bookshelves, and thick with the scents of coffee and liqueurs and cigarettes, perfume and incense and paraffin lamps. Ornamental columns in the corners were decorated with fat plaster *putti*, and the paintings on the wall displayed beautiful and gauzily-dressed nymphs. An imposing oak table dominated the centre of the room; Mrs Sedgley explained to Arthur that her late husband had acquired it at auction, and that it was of prehistoric druidic origin.

"Druids," he agreed. "By God."

He circled the room, shaking hands. Mr Innes (the Hegemon) seemed to have taken a liking to him. They discovered a shared fondness for Sherlock Holmes, and decided to treat it as if it were a remarkable and significant coincidence.

Josephine sat down near the window and took out her shorthand pad.

MEMBERS PRESENT:
Mrs Esther Sedgley (Matron V.V. 341º)
Mr James Innes, Esq. (Hegemon V.V. 300º)
Mr Mortimer Frayn (Officer)
Mr John Hare, Esq. (Officer)
Mrs Lottie Hare (Officer)
Miss Florence Shale (Probationer)
Miss Roberta Blaylock (Student)
Mr T. R. Compton, Esq. (Student)
Mr Henry Park, Esq. (Treasurer)
Dr A. D. Varley (Adeptus Major)
Mrs A. D. Varley (Adeptus Minor)
Mr Martin Atwood (Guest)
Mr Ranjit Chatterji (Guest)
Miss Eliza Hedges (Guest)
Mr Llywelyn ap Hywel (Guest)
Mr Arthur Archibald Shaw (Guest)
Miss Josephine Bradman (Officer; Minutes)

Josephine excelled at shorthand, thanks to the Breckenridge School of Typewriting and Stenography. If she chose she could let her mind wander while her hand worked, as if she were in a trance.

THE MATRON called the meeting to order at half past eight.
MRS HARE blessed the proceedings, and commanded that all ill-wishers reveal themselves or be bound eternally to silence.

MR FRAYN remarked upon the absence of many close friends from the proceedings, in particular MR and MRS GODALMING, who were recovering from injuries sustained in the Storm.

MISS SHALE opined that the Storm had been of supernatural origin, and MR HARE and MR PARK agreed.

THE MATRON reminded all present that mere superstition is the bane of true psychical research.

MR HARE noted rumours concerning the death of the late Duke of Sussex, and suggested that in these troubling times all spiritualists might be in danger of being falsely considered radicals or revolutionaries, and sought proposals as to how best to allay the suspicion of the unenlightened.

THE MATRON observed that an Age in which spiritual science had been a matter of interest at the highest pinnacle of the British State had come to an end, and called upon all present to pray that the true science would not fade away in the coming years, but would rise to new and greater heights.

MR SHAW (GUEST) rose to observe that the press, and those who make their fortune by their pen, have a weighty duty in these times, this perilous and confusing modern age in which a scrupulous love of truth is the highest calling, to neither strangle a revolution in thought in its crib, nor spread falsehoods through laziness or corruption. He also thanked all those present for their kindness in inviting a mere ink-stained wretch such as himself to their august gathering.

THE HIEROPHANT called for prayers for the Duke's soul, and for the speedy capture of the guilty party, should there be one; and the members prayed accordingly.

MR PARK observed that three persons (who would remain nameless) had failed to pay their dues for the month of February.

DR VARLEY presented his astrological observations. It was his opinion that in the wake of the Storm there had been a great disruption among the Spheres, such that the Austral signs had taken on an unseasonable declining aspect, and the House of Mercury now encroached upon the House of Venus, while the House of Saturn was in ascendancy. MR PARK challenged DR VARLEY's conclusions. Consensus was not obtained, and THE MATRON proposed that the discussion be adjourned.

MISS SHALE announced that she felt an Outside Intelligence taking
hold of her. She sang, and danced. MR HARE played the piano.
MR CHATTERJI presented his photographs of Indian temples.

Mr Chatterji and Mr Atwood were both new to the meetings of the Ordo
V.V. 341. Chatterji was tall and rather imposing; a lawyer, of exalted caste
and aristocratic bearing; just recently arrived in London from India, or
so Josephine had heard, and already a much-desired guest. Arthur ap-
plauded each one of his photographs, which were all intended to elucidate
some point regarding Indian spiritualism, the architecture of temples,
and the stars. Arthur had an interest in amateur photography, albeit a
mostly theoretical one. Chatterji answered Arthur's questions about
lenses, collodio-chloride, and other such arcana with aplomb, and corrected various misconceptions about India with great patience.

Martin Atwood was handsome and well-dressed; perhaps twenty-five
or at most thirty, small and slight and rather boyish. He wore a black
frock coat of an athletic cut, and a loose black tie. His hair was fair, and
he had a neat pointed beard. He smiled at everyone, politely but vacantly.
Without ever quite stooping to rudeness, he gave the impression that he
had found himself in Kensington by mistake on his way to somewhere
infinitely more fashionable and important, but intended to make the best
of his evening now that he was here. He dozed through Miss Shale's
dance. He leaned forward to peer at Chatterji's photographs. He met Josephine's eye once, and winked at her; she wasn't sure what he meant to
convey.

MR INNES blessed the conclusion of the proceedings, and closed the
circle against evil.

When the blessings were done, Mr Innes lit the lamps, waking several
dozers. Chatterji gathered up his photographs in a leather briefcase; then
he left without making conversation. Preserving the aura of mystery, Josephine supposed. Servants brought out wine and coffee. Miss Shale,
who had fainted, was examined by Doctor Varley. Josephine tucked her
notes away, collected her fee from Treasurer Park, and went in search of
Arthur. She found him on the other side of the room, sharing a drink
with Mr Hare and Mr Innes and comparing stories about the storm.

Mrs Sedgley waved to her. "Josephine, my dear! A moment of your time?"

"Of course, Matron."

Mr Atwood stood at Mrs Sedgley's side, smiling. "Miss Bradman," he said. "I'm really the one who should be begging your pardon; I'm the one who's taking your time. I wanted to make your acquaintance."

Mrs Sedgley raised her eyebrows and attempted to wordlessly communicate that Atwood was a man of importance, and that Josephine should indulge whatever odd whim he had in mind.

"Miss Bradman; may I ask what you were writing?"

"Of course, Mr Atwood. Nothing of great interest: it's my duty to keep the minutes of the Order's proceedings."

"Ah. Very wise. Let nothing of the great work be lost."

"Quite," Mrs Sedgley said.

"The preservation of learning," Atwood said.

"Yes," Josephine said, feeling that she was expected to say something.

"A vital task. When one thinks how much learning has been lost to the world by the inadequate taking of minutes! Who is that, I said, who was taking such assiduous notes, and the Matron told me your name and a bell rang in my head—Bradman, Bradman, Josephine Bradman . . . I'm certain, I said, that I remember that name . . . such an awful lot of clutter in the attic, such an awful lot of empty space, too, but also all sorts of interesting people—have you read Bruno on the art of memory? No? I expect the Matron is familiar with the technique. I'm not half as good at it as I would like to be. Think, Atwood, think, I said; then light dawned. A bright star in the great infinite darkness of my own foolish head. The poetess!"

Josephine couldn't conceal her surprise. She wasn't used to being recognised for her poetry, which had been sparingly published, and so far as she knew, quickly forgotten.

"Hah!" Atwood clapped. "I thought as much."

"I'm very flattered, Mr Atwood."

"I'm relieved. My head is still of some use."

Arthur appeared, drink in hand.

"Fascinating," Arthur said. "Fascinating. The whole thing. I'm sorry there wasn't a séance, though. I think I may have put my card in, so to speak, for membership. It's hard to say. Mr Hare has an awfully indirect way of speaking. Mystical, I suppose."

He turned to Atwood and introduced himself.

"Atwood," Atwood said. "We were discussing Miss Bradman's poetry."

"Splendid stuff. Are you a poet, Mr Atwood?"

"Good Lord, no."

"Josephine," Mrs Sedgley said, "is a treasure; simply a treasure. Poetry is *so* very important; indeed, I believe that poets are our truest guides to the spiritual realm; poets are waking dreamers, awakened spirits—"

"Quite," Atwood said.

"Are you a member of this club, Mr Atwood?"

"A guest, Mr Shaw."

"Same boat, Mr Atwood. Same boat."

"I should never have expected to meet the poetess Josephine Bradman here. But London is a very small place, sometimes, isn't it? I expect Josephine's quite tired of people talking to her about her poetry."

"It happens infrequently," Josephine said.

There was something oddly unnerving about Mr Atwood. He smiled too much.

Astonishingly, he began to recite. "Oh moon! Halt not thy ceaseless roll—oh sun, astride thy golden wheel—oh wake, oh wake thou sleeping soul—oh something something something stars . . . Oh, Mr Hare, are you leaving? Well, good-bye, good-bye, my best wishes to your wife. Miss Bradman, do I have those lines right? Please say I do."

"Close enough, Mr Atwood."

" 'Dream Verse,' I think you called it."

"Oh, probably. One never knows what to call things."

"Well done." Arthur clapped Atwood on the shoulder. "Well done indeed."

Atwood looked down at his shoulder with curiosity, as if a butterfly had suddenly landed on it.

Mr Park and the Varleys had stopped to listen.

"Atwood," Arthur said. "What do you do, if you're not a poet?"

"Nothing in particular. I understand you're a journalist, Mr Shaw?"

"That's right. I write for the *Mammoth*."

"I've heard that the *Mammoth* is no more."

"That's true, too. News travels quickly."

"London is a *very* small place." He turned back to Josephine. "Miss Bradman, was it?"

"Was it what, Mr Atwood?"

"Composed in a dream?"

"No. I wrote that poem over the course of a long, cold winter's worth of evenings in Cambridge."

"Miss Bradman, would you possibly—would you mind reading the poem for me?"

"Oh, no—I couldn't. I don't think—"

"Oh," Mrs Sedgley said, "I'm sure there's no harm in it—and she *does* have a very fine reading voice."

"Hear, hear," Doctor Varley said.

She couldn't reasonably or graciously refuse. Nor could she quite say why she felt like refusing—like running away, in fact. There was something excessive and unseemly in Atwood's curiosity.

"Now, steady on," Arthur said. "Bit late in the evening for poetry, isn't it? I know I'm a little tired—head full of India and Saturn and Mercury and all that. Perhaps another time."

Atwood glanced at Arthur, appearing to fully take in his presence for the first time. Then he produced a pen and a card from his pocket, and swiftly wrote something down.

"An address, Shaw. I gather that you're out of work?"

"Between engagements, Atwood."

"Well. I leave it in your hands. They may be able to use you."

Atwood turned to Josephine then, as if Arthur was simply of no further relevance.

"Miss Bradman—if I may?"

Atwood held out an arm, almost touching her hand. Then he swiftly and gracefully interposed himself between Arthur and Josephine—so that when Arthur said, "Hold on a moment, Atwood," he found himself suddenly face to face with Dr Varley; while Josephine, without quite meaning to, or even recalling taking a step, found herself by the wall, at the back of the room, under a large ugly gilt-edged mirror, with Atwood standing quite close. Someone seemed to have dimmed the lights.

"Miss Bradman," he said, very seriously. "Please."

The words of the poem rose unbidden to her lips. *Awake, awake,* and *et cetera et cetera. Whirling wheels* of this and that. The subject of the poem was the doctrine of reincarnation: the journey of the soul up through the various heavens towards God, and down again into the body; through the House of Venus, with its bright hot gardens, through the silent Caverns of the Moon. It had been written under the influence of a great deal of Greek philosophy, and some long conversations with a friend—born to parents in the civil service—about the doctrines of the Hindus. It was all rather overheated. The fact was that she was rather embarrassed by it now; it had been published in a small Cambridge magazine and it had never crossed her mind that it might surface again. She looked for Arthur—he'd somehow entirely lost sight of her, and was peering around with his wineglass still in his hand, but in entirely the wrong direction, over towards the *chaise longue* in the corner, where Miss Florence Shale was now much recovered, and was earnestly holding Miss Roberta Blaylock's hands and instructing her in something or other. Mrs Sedgley was bustling over, waggling her eyebrows to communicate who-knows-what vitally important message.

She wasn't more than five lines into the poem before Atwood's smile vanished. He glanced over her shoulder in sudden alarm.

"A-ha. I apologise, Miss Bradman—I do apologise. I've been rude."

"No," Mrs Sedgley insisted, "not at all!"

"I have. I'm sorry. Miss Bradman." He flashed a forced smile. His eyes didn't meet hers.

Josephine glanced over her shoulder to see what could have upset Mr Atwood so. Nothing but the mirror, in which she saw the reflection of her own face; and Mr Atwood—who was now rather theatrically checking his watch and announcing that it was time to leave; and behind him Arthur, approaching at last, looking cross; and behind Arthur the arched entrance of Mrs Sedgley's hall, Mr Hare in the distance, taking his umbrella from the stand by the open door, and Mrs Sedgley's cat Gautama jumping down from his sleeping-place on the table and dashing off.

"Well," Atwood said. "I do hope we meet again, Miss, ah, Bradman. I'm afraid I have to run."

He left. He very nearly *did* run, glancing back over his shoulder as if pursued; brushing past Arthur without a word and nearly knocking Dr Varley's wine-glass out of his hand.

"What an odd fellow," Arthur said. "Josephine—are you all right?"

"Of course." But it was a great comfort to take his offered arm.

"*Josephine,*" Mrs Sedgley said, contriving to suggest that the whole awkward scene had somehow been Arthur's fault, and that she did not entirely approve. Then she set off in pursuit of Atwood, just in time to have him close the door in her face.

Arthur toyed with the card Atwood had given him. It was blank, except for the address Atwood had written on it. Somewhere in Deptford.

"Well. Something always turns up, doesn't it?"

"I think," Josephine said, "that you should throw that away."

"Do you think so?" He looked disappointed. She did think so, though she couldn't say exactly why.

"I'm afraid the poor man may be a neurotic," she said. "It's regrettably common in these circles. No sense in indulging him; it would probably be an utter waste of your time."

"I don't know," Arthur said. "One never knows. Don't you always say that? One never knows, these days."

O n the way home they talked about money, and the closing of the *Mammoth*, and the future. It wasn't until she got back to Rugby Street, and had said good night to Arthur, who was still turning the card over in his hand—in fact, it wasn't until she was half-way up the dark stairs to bed that something odd moved in her memory. She stopped on the stairs with her hand on the bannister, and she thought back to the conversation with Atwood—the odd moment when his mood had changed. In her memory, she saw Mrs Sedgley's ugly gilt-edged mirror again. Was it a trick of her imagination, or had there been, now that she thought about it, a fifth person reflected in the mirror—out in the street, peering in through the open door, his face gaslit and half-obscured by rain? A pale stranger with dark eyes. Then Gautama had distracted her, and in the next instant, he was gone.

The product of an overactive imagination, no doubt. That was what came of too much reading.

Chapter Five

In the morning Arthur set off for Deptford. The tram deposited him outside the central station of the London Electric Supply Corporation—which at the time (so Arthur had written for the *Mammoth*) was the world's largest power station, an unsurpassed triumph of engineering, one of the jewels in London's crown. It had flooded on the night of the storm, and the engines were out; it sat silent, like a great fog-shrouded Egyptian tomb. Beyond there were cattle-markets, stinking slaughterhouses, and yards full of milling herds of livestock, each poor beast branded with the icons of its owner and the inspectors of Her Majesty's Government, each one marked for its ultimate destination; and beyond that were fish-markets and tea-markets, small bank branches, and the offices of maritime clerks. He bought ham sandwiches and coffee from a stall and read the newspapers in a shop window. The latest outrages in Kabul, good news regarding Her Majesty's health, a murder in Mayfair, the progress (negligible) of Dr Conan Doyle's investigation into the Duke's death . . .

Beyond all that lay Bullen Street.

Bullen Street was a narrow space between some warehouses and the river. A single building occupied most of the street, long and low and flat; a face of dull red brick, an unmarked door, boarded windows. The little buildings on either side of it looked abandoned, vandalised. Behind it, crowded and dilapidated terraces stretched away into the distance.

Somehow the building gave an impression of intense activity, intense *heaviness*, as if it would be a terrible time-wasting rudeness to interrupt it for anything but the most urgent business. It took a considerable effort of will even to cross the street.

Arthur rang the bell. An electric buzzer sounded distantly somewhere inside.

The sensation that he was wasting the building's time had faded; now it returned, redoubled. Before Arthur knew what he was doing he'd turned as if to leave—but then he stopped, shivered, told himself not to be such a great bloody fool, and rang the bell again.

The street reeked of the river, and of rats. Out in the distance there was the noise of gulls and the horns of passing boats.

The door opened. Arthur stood to attention.

A short and ugly man stood in the doorway. Behind him was a desk, and a heap of boots and hats and umbrellas. Beyond that was a long hallway with a multitude of doors leading off from it.

The man rapped his stick on the steps at Arthur's feet. "Eh?"

"Is this Mr Gracewell's establishment? I'm inquiring after work."

"Are you now? How's that, then? Who told you? Who sent you? Saw an advertisement in the paper, did you?"

"An advertisement? No. A Mr Atwood sent me."

"Who?"

Arthur had the sense that he was being made fun of. "Look—can I come in or not? It's bloody cold out here."

"Shoes."

"I beg your pardon?"

"Shoes. Coat. Hat. Hup! Hup! Go on. Big slow fellow that you are. Over there. Then come along quick. Time's wasting. You've had good luck—Mr Gracewell's *in attendance* today. They call me Dimmick."

"Arthur Shaw. Why do you need my shoes?"

"Slow now, slow! Gimme your hand, it might get bit—that's just a joke, Mr Shaw. Shoes, coat, hat, hup, hup, hup."

D immick led the way down the hall, moving with a slight bounce that made Arthur think of an acrobat, or an ape. His shirt was frayed and stained.

"I don't understand—"

"The shoes?" Dimmick shrugged. "Don't know. Don't ask neither. One o' Mr Gracewell's rules. He has his little ways. Feet cold?"

"No." There were holes in his socks, and he felt a fool. "It reminds me of India. The temples there, they take off their shoes before they enter, as a mark of respect, I suppose."

Dimmick looked briefly interested. "India? Soldiered, did you?"

"No. I've never seen India. I read about it."

Dimmick lost interest.

The hallway was windowless. To Arthur's astonishment it was lit by electrical light-bulbs. He was impressed. Certainly one wouldn't have expected the luxury of electrical light somewhere like this odd and shabby-looking place. He thought that it was very modern, and admirably industrious.

On the other hand, the light-bulbs were mostly dim or failing. Arthur supposed it was a wonder they were lit at all, after the damage the storm had done to London. In the dim, erratic light it was hard to see how far ahead the hallway extended. It might already be quite hard to find the way back if he had to do it alone.

The doors were numbered. Most of them were painted green, but the paint was peeling. Behind them there were sounds of coughing, muttering, and turning pages.

Between the doors, at irregular intervals, were what looked like dumbwaiter hatches. They were marked with letters: A, B, C, *et cetera*.

In the hallway ahead, a door marked 14 opened and half a dozen young men emerged in a row. All of them were barefoot, bareheaded. Arthur thought they might have been Italian, perhaps, or Spanish. They whispered to one another as they approached, nodding at Arthur and glancing nervously at Dimmick, who rapped his stick on the wall so loudly that they jumped. At almost the same moment one of the nearby light-bulbs hissed and went dark. The six clerks trooped past and went into the door marked 11, a little way back down the hall.

Arthur turned to Dimmick. "What does Mr Gracewell do here?"

"He's the Master."

"I mean, what sort of work does Gracewell & Co. do? There's a lot of men working here—far more than I imagined. There must be about as many men here as work for the Bank of England."

"Maybe! Never been in a bank."

"Well, what are they doing?"

"Numbers," Dimmick said.

"A scientific enterprise of some kind?"

"Numbers."

"Insurance? Accounts? Out here by the docks, I rather thought it might be something, well, maritime."

"Numbers," Dimmick repeated.

Arthur began to wonder if Dimmick was quite right in the head. "All right, Mr Dimmick. Numbers, numbers it is."

A quaint figure, this Mr Dimmick. Short, and square, muscular almost to the point of absurdity. He had bad teeth, uneven ears, and a much-broken nose. A Wedgwood-blue hint of tattoos under his thin linen shirt. Arthur wondered if he might be a naval man. Easy enough to imagine him clambering the rigging. He had what Arthur thought might be the accent of a sailor or a soldier; that is, he was quite clearly of rustic origin, but he was a well-travelled rustic, with something of the East End in his voice. Something of the sea. Scars on his broad knuckles, from which Arthur imagined a detective might read a history of violence; or possibly just factory-work, or haulage, or bad luck, or who knows what.

Dimmick poked open the door marked 14 with his stick. On the other side of the door was something like a schoolroom, reeking of sweat and chalk and feet, of dust and headaches and old india-rubber. There were five rows of desks, in ten close-packed columns, with a narrow channel down the middle. Fifty desks in all; perhaps a third of them occupied. The occupants of the desks were mostly around Arthur's age. There were some men Arthur thought might be Greek, and several Indians. Each man was engaged in identical efforts; each bareheaded, barefooted, with rolled-up sleeves and ink-stained forearms. Each had a ledger in front of him, in which he was industriously making notations. A crackling light-bulb overhead cast chessboard shadows. At the front of the room there were three red bell-ropes, a blackboard with chalked instructions, and a little shelf that held a black telephone, with a hand crank and ringer box.

Dimmick moved so quickly across the room and out the door on the other side that Arthur had no time to read what was on the board. He saw one man raise an arm to wipe his face—was his nose bleeding? Then he hurried after Dimmick and out into a narrow corridor. Beyond that there was another door, another room, much the same as the last, except that this time a short round man stood in front of the board. He was chalking some kind of instructions on it.

He wore a shabby, patched black coat. Bare feet, unkempt yellow nails. He was ugly. His eyes were round and watery, his eyebrows prominent and black and spiky, like little voles or marsh-rats come to drink at a puddle. His hair was plastered across a balding scalp.

He stopped writing, and rubbed his face as if exhausted, getting chalk in his beard.

"Mr Gracewell, I presume? I'm Arthur Sh—"

"Well, Dimmick—where'd you dredge up this one?"

"Didn't, sir Came to us—lost sheep. Rang the bloody bell! Bold as you please."

"Did he? Well."

"A Mr Atwood sent me."

"Atwood! Interfering in my business. Telling me who I can and can't use. Do I interfere with his experiments? I have a good mind to have Dimmick throw you out. But no—God knows we need men. All right—come along."

Gracewell's office was on the second floor. A window revealed a stretch of grey river and smoky sky. The office itself contained a desk, three chairs, two oak filing cabinets, a telephone on a shelf, a typewriter, a heap of ledgers, a smell of tobacco, a number of odd photographs behind glass. Mr Gracewell sat at his desk, behind a row of pipes and a small pile of correspondence.

"Right." Gracewell reached for one of the pipes. "What's Atwood told you?"

"Nothing. I met him at a—a sort of party. He said that you had work."

"Can you count? Can you read?"

"Yes, Mr Gracewell."

"Seven times seven. Nine times six."

"Forty-nine and, ah, fifty-four."

"Well, many can't. You'd be astonished at some of what Dimmick drags in. We're looking for a very particular sort of fellow, and that means we have to take 'em where we can find 'em. Some of them are animals. Enough to make you give up all hope for England's future. Then again, last month Dimmick found us an Oxford man! And he didn't last a week. More precisely, five days. Do you believe in telepathy, young man?"

"Telepathy? I don't know."

"Clairvoyance?"

"Yes and no."

"Fortune-telling?"

"I can believe in any number of things if it would help."

Gracewell didn't smile. "What's your name?"

"Arthur Shaw."

"Educated man, from the sound of you. University?"

"A little."

"A little. Hmm. More precisely?"

"Ah—I began my studies at the University of Edinburgh. Medicine."

Gracewell looked annoyed. "Began?"

"Yes, Mr Gracewell."

Shaking his head, Gracewell began to rummage in the drawers of his desk, possibly for tobacco.

Arthur glanced again at the photographs on the wall. Reflections on the glass obscured their contents, but he thought that they might be an astronomer's sketches of the moon; all blotchy grey seas and mysterious black lines.

"I see you have an interest in astronomy, Mr Gracewell."

"Began." Gracewell closed the drawer. "But not finished."

"Well, no."

"Your father?"

"Excuse me?"

"*Was*, you said. Departed?"

"Yes."

"Madness in the family?"

"Madness?"

"Yes."

"No."

"No there isn't or no you won't answer?"

"The former, Mr Gracewell. At least, not to my knowledge."

"A history of unlucky accidents?"

"I don't see the pertinence of any of this."

"I dare say you don't! Answer, please, or stop wasting my time. How did your father die?"

"In an accident; boating on a lake in Switzerland. I was eight. My mother too, if you must know."

"Hmm." Gracewell showed no sign of sympathy.

"I still don't see the pertinence of it."

"Unusual coincidences?"

"No more than usual."

"Shaw. Arthur Shaw. Do I know that name?"

"I don't know, Mr Gracewell. Did you read the *Mammoth*?"

"What's that? A newspaper? I don't have time to read newspapers."

A bell rang somewhere below. Gracewell lifted one finger, waited, as if for the bell to ring again. It didn't. Gracewell's finger slowly lowered, and he turned his attention back to Arthur. He blinked twice.

"Where were we?"

"The *Mammoth*, Mr Gracewell."

"Oh. Yes."

Gracewell raised his voice. "Dimmick! *Dimmick!*" Gracewell's voice was not pleasant to listen to; it cracked when he shouted.

"Mr Gracewell—"

"*Dimmick! Get in here! It's a bloody journalist.*"

"Mr Gracewell! Sir! I'm not a journalist. The *Mammoth* is gone. I'm here—"

"Are you here to snoop, Mr Shaw? Are you here to pry? Are you here to tell stories? You wouldn't be the first and you won't be the last. But by God you will hold your tongue or Mr Dimmick will know the reason why."

The door opened. Gracewell held up a hand.

Arthur heard Dimmick's footsteps behind him, and the tap of his stick on the floor. He smelt Dimmick's stale odour—tobacco and sweat. Arthur's throat went dry; there was suddenly nothing quaint or comic about Dimmick.

"Mr Gracewell—I wouldn't dream of—there's no call for that sort of—I have debts, Mr Gracewell, and I'm engaged to be married, and I need the money—that's all—I'm not here to tell stories. The *Mammoth* is gone."

"Engaged?" Gracewell appeared confused for a moment. "Oh yes." He slowly lowered his hand.

Dimmick chuckled, then gave Arthur's shoulder a rough but not un-friendly shake. Then his footsteps receded and the door closed behind him. Arthur tried to hide his relief.

"Well then." Gracewell sat. "Far be it from me to thwart young love. Or to thwart Atwood, for that matter. But you won't tell the young lady to whom you are engaged what you do here, and by God you won't write about it." Gracewell shook his head. "Writers. Perhaps a third of the men are poets. It seems disproportionate. But it's all one to me so long as they follow the rules. For six pounds a week, I expect obedience."

"Six pounds a week?"

"Is that not good enough for you, sir?"

"On the contrary, it's . . ." Six pounds a week; more than three hundred in a year. It was far more than he'd expected.

"Well." Gracewell shrugged. "Not every man can do the job. Few last. A question of *will*."

"Mr Gracewell—I—I've never seen anything quite like this."

"Well, there's never been anything quite like my Engine. And there's your answer; or more precisely, there it isn't. Now, to begin with: you will be paid six pounds a week. If you do not run away there will be more—last a month and it will be seven."

"Seven!"

"Rapid ascent. You'll earn it. You'll see."

Mr Gracewell took a card out of a drawer and pushed it across the desk. It read:

COPY THESE WORDS

I, THE UNDERSIGNED, DO SWEAR BEFORE GOD THAT I
COME HERE IN GOOD FAITH, AND WILL DO NO SABOTAGE,
AND WILL NOT REVEAL WHAT I SEE HERE TO ANYONE.

Gracewell pointed at one of the typewriters. "Type it. Sign it."

Arthur did so. Gracewell took the paper without looking and filed it in one of the cabinets.

"A word of advice, Mr Shaw. Pay off whatever debts drove you here as soon as you can. Debt is weakness. I will have you beholden to no one but me."

The ringer box in the corner of the office started to sound. Gracewell picked up the telephone.

"Find Dimmick, wherever he's got to. Tell him we're giving you to Mr Irving. Off you go."

The next morning there was a postcard under the door of Josephine's office. It came from Borel's shop, and depicted a sunny seaside vista. On the back of it she recognised Arthur's handwriting.

Dearest love—I could write all day and not say half of what I could wish to say—nor do I know yet what quite what I mean to say—so first an apology: I did not take your advice. I went to Deptford. But one never knows these days where or when fortune may strike— and struck it has! I have employment, at six pounds a week. Under- line that—it is no joke. And that is all I can say, because I cannot say yet what they mean to have me do (because I do not understand!) and so if any friend asks you what your dear heart does, you shall have to say you do not know, but you know that he does it at six pounds a week—soon to be seven—and you may reckon for yourself what that will mean for the two of us, and how soon.

She didn't see or hear from him for another week, though she wrote and called round. He was out at all hours. His landlord hadn't set eyes on him since Tuesday, when Arthur had knocked on his door and pressed the rent into his hands, late, but with interest. She began to worry about him. She slept badly. On Sunday he arranged for flowers to be delivered to her office; but there was no note of explanation. She saw him by chance on Monday morning, in the street, frightfully early. Not, of course, that she'd woken early in hopes of catching him—she had errands to run, and she couldn't sleep. He was hurrying to catch the omnibus in the rain. He'd found time to buy a new umbrella, she noticed.

He turned when she called out, blinking as if he hardly recognised her.

"A week?" he said. "Has it really been that long?" He counted off days on his fingers, in obvious surprise.

"Arthur—are you all right? You look tired. I got your postcard. Did you get my letters? Are you working for Atwood now? What on earth does he have you doing?"

"Not Atwood. A colleague of his, I suppose. Gracewell. Conspiracy, so to speak; oh, Josephine, I shouldn't say any more."

"Why not—is something wrong?"

"Nothing! It's—it's quite extraordinary. I don't understand it fully my- self. But I swore secrecy. Even from you. It's—well, it's rather like working for an insurance firm, or a bank, or the civil service, I suppose—nothing sinister. Only with an oath of secrecy, as if one were a freemason. But the six pounds a week is real."

She stood as close to him as their umbrellas would allow, and studied him. He looked exhausted and hungry. He had an odd and slightly feverish air about him.

He lunged forward and kissed her, taking her quite off guard. He held her for a very long time. She felt his heart pound. Then he let her go and turned away, checking his watch.

"I'll be late. Gracewell can't abide lateness—he says it's a sort of imprecision. What day is it?"

"Monday."

"Monday!" He started counting on his fingers again, as if calculating something. "Thursday, then—a half-day. I'll find you then. Wait, Josephine—take this!" He pressed two gold coins into her hand—then, after a moment's thought, a half-crown for good measure. "For Mr Borel. That squares us, I think. Would you?"

He started off for the bus. Then he turned back and took her hand. "Steer clear of Atwood," he said. "Now, don't worry. Don't worry; nothing's wrong. It's just—it's just awfully odd."

"What do you mean?"

"The whole thing. I don't understand it yet. Promise me you'll steer clear of him."

"Of course. Wasn't it me who told you to throw his card away? Arthur—are you in danger?"

"No. I don't think so. It's terribly hard to explain. I don't have the time."

He turned and ran.

Chapter Six

The Ordo V.V. 341 met again next month, on a balmy evening at the end of April. Mrs Sedgley's rose-garden bloomed, birds sang, bees drifted lazily from flower to flower, and the house was packed to the rafters. Somehow Mrs Sedgley had persuaded the celebrated American spiritualist Emma Bloom, recently arrived from New York, to pay a visit—her first engagement in London—to the Ordo V.V. 341. Mrs Sedgley was inclined to believe that Mrs Bloom—of whom she was a great admirer—had recognised in her letters the spark of a kindred soul. Josephine suspected that Mrs Bloom's secretary, confused by the flood of invitations from unlikely sounding persons and entities that had greeted her on her arrival at Claridge's, had picked at random. In any case, the visit had attracted publicity. Guests bartered for invitations, and elderly members who'd hardly left their houses in years journeyed in from the suburbs. Three journalists were in attendance, from the *Morning Chronicle,* the *Spectator,* and the *Occult Review.*

Mr Atwood was there again, standing at the back of the room. He wore black tie and tails, and an expression of quiet amusement. Josephine approached him at once, meaning to ask for an explanation of last month's awkward scene, who on earth Gracewell was, and what was going on; but by the time she'd forged her way through the crowd he was gone, and it was too late to pursue him further because the meeting had come to order, and Bloom was about to speak.

Bloom was very tall, strikingly handsome, and had exquisite poise. Her dress was burgundy, her hair a perfect black, her skin lily-white, her eyes sharp emeralds. She had not the slightest trace of false modesty, or any other kind. She spoke slowly and carefully, to be sure that the journalists captured her every word. She told her audience that she had come to London to attend the memorials for the Duke of Sussex, who'd been such a patron of spiritual pursuits. She said that she brought condolences from all of New York and from her contacts in the world beyond. She said that she could not say whether she had or had not been invited by the Metropolitan Police to lend her psychic resources to the investigation; nor could she say for sure yet whether his death had left London under a curse; nor whether the murder of the Duke was or was not, in her view, connected to the storm or to the terrible Whitechapel murders of the last decade.

Mr Innes and Mrs Sedgley begged her to put on a display of her abilities. Bloom put on a great show of reluctance, explaining that she was tired from her long journey, that her spiritual powers were not parlour tricks, and so on; but finally she relented. She asked to be given space alone at a table, and silence, and darkness. Mr Innes dimmed the lamps.

"We shall see," Bloom said, "what the spirit world has to teach us tonight—if anything."

She called for a sheet of paper and a pen to be placed in front of her, and for a blindfold. Mrs Sedgley provided her with a black veil.

"The spirits," she said, "will write through me, if it suits their plans to communicate with us."

She held the pen over the paper like a dowsing-rod, and began to softly hum.

Most of her audience closed their eyes and sat in reverent silence. The journalists watched Mrs Bloom, and Mrs Sedgley watched the journalists. Josephine sat massaging her wrists. From where she sat, a row of heads at the other side of the room was silhouetted against the window. A muffled glow came through the curtains from the streetlights outside.

Innes coughed, and his wife hissed at him. Miss Shale started humming along with Bloom, then stopped, apparently embarrassed.

It seemed to Josephine that a strange light had crept into the room.

Josephine was not credulous. She was not the sort of person who swallowed every story of table-rapping and saw fairies under every flower. In fact, she thought of herself as rather less credulous than the average person. She'd seen her fair share of hidden mirrors, blacked threads, and concealed compartments. At one memorable séance, she'd felt what she thought at first was a mouse brushing against her foot, and had peered under a table to see a small girl crouched there, her bony hands and face bright with luminous paint. She didn't reveal her. Mrs Sedgley, on the other hand, was a fiend for nosing out fraud, and merciless when she found it, banishing the guilty party from the premises of the Order and sparing no efforts to expose them in the letters pages of the *Occult Review* or the *Journal of the Society for Psychical Research*.

So when Josephine perceived that there was a faint red light in the room, her first thought was to wonder how Bloom had tampered with the lamps, and what Mrs Sedgley would say if she found out. She looked around the room to see if she had an accomplice. It could be done with phosphorous oil, or with a mirrored lantern.

The light was both a rather vulgar display—not the sort of thing one would expect from a person of Mrs Bloom's sophistication—and rather splendidly eerie. The odd thing was that no one else appeared to have noticed it. The room was quiet; the journalist from the *Morning Chronicle* stared idly at the ceiling.

Bloom lowered pen to paper, and began to scratch.

Josephine supposed that she might have had an accomplice standing outside the window with a red lamp. But how, then, to explain the *shape* of the light: a faint and trembling sphere?

It wasn't bright. Its faded colour awoke a memory.

When Josephine's father died, he had left a collection of specimens, curios, and oddities. He was an amateur antiquarian, and a man of varied and eccentric interests. There were old farmer's almanacs, and rusty nails that he had marked as *Roman circa AD 400?*, and a verdigris'd sextant, and a small collection of saints' fingernails, *et cetera*. Among the collection were four cases of butterflies, which Josephine had never seen before—and did not see again, because her mother promptly sold them. That was shortly before her mother, who'd always been of a nervous disposition, began to suffer headaches, and night terrors, and then waking visions—hell-fire and warring angels—as if those awful visions had been held in check by her husband's rather mild and scholarly form of religion and released upon his death.

There'd been well over a hundred butterflies in the cases, of many different and beautiful colours. Josephine had studied them for days after her father's death. She remembered one beautiful creature in particular; it had occupied an undistinguished position near the bottom left of its case, with nothing written on the scrap of yellowed paper beneath it except "*AFRICA (?),*" but its wings had been the most extraordinary shade: a deep and dusty damask-rose, edged with azure and indigo; a morbid and passionate and sad and violent colour; the same colour that hovered now over Mrs Sedgley's table, slowly revolving.

Josephine couldn't quite judge its size, because as soon as she started to think too closely about it she felt dizzy, and she had to hold on to the edge of the table. (Miss Shale, watching with one eye open, saw Josephine holding the table and followed suit, so as not to be left out).

From the far side of the room came the sharp sound of glass cracking.

Mrs Bloom started at the sound. She dropped her pen and it rolled off the table. Mr Innes got up in a hurry and moved about the room igniting the lamps, and gaslight banished whatever Josephine had seen or thought she'd seen.

Mrs Bloom sat veiled and very still at the head of the table. The pen had burst and her hand was soaked with ink, but she hadn't flinched in the least; she had controlled herself utterly. Everyone else pushed back their chairs and inspected behind themselves and underneath the table for something broken, until Mrs Sedgley thought to pull back the curtains, revealing that one of the windows had a crack running down it from top to bottom.

"*Well*," Bloom said, in a voice that silenced all whispers. "The spirits have made themselves known to us. But what is their message? Clearly they are agitated. I can see that I may have to prolong my visit to London; this investigation will be a challenging one."

Josephine's hands shook as she packed away her things.

On the way out she noticed that the mirror in the hallway was gone. In fact, now that she thought about it, the mirror in the drawing-room was gone too, replaced by a painting of some sheep. She asked Mrs Sedgley what had happened to them.

"Oh, yes. That was Lord Atwood's idea. He says that mirrors are a way for evil influences to get in."

"*Lord* Atwood?"

"Oh, my, yes."

"Who is he, Esther?"

"Ah—that's a question, isn't it? He has a very interesting reputation—or so I've heard. I've heard it said that he was a close acquaintance of the late Duke—and one can plainly see that he's a man of unusually penetrating and forward-thinking intelligence . . ."

Mrs Sedgley appeared uncharacteristically flustered, as if she couldn't quite recall what she'd heard about Atwood, or where she'd heard it.

"Anyway, we're very lucky that he's taken such an interest in us—very lucky. Mr Sedgley would have been very proud. One in the eye for Mr Mathers's lot—don't you think?"

As Josephine hurried to catch the omnibus, she saw Atwood leaning against a lamp-post. When he took off his hat to her and smiled, she had no choice but to stop and say hello to him. "Well," he said. "Miss Bradman—may I call you Josephine? What did you think?"

"Of what?"

"Bloom. A dull performance, no?"

"Dull?"

"Dull! Between you and me, Bloom doesn't have a sensitive bone in her body. I can tell. She might just as well have stayed in New York."

"I thought she was rather interesting."

"I don't think I'll be visiting the old V.V. again. The whole thing's been rather a bore, and it's time to move on."

"Mr Atwood—*Lord* Atwood—I consider Mrs Sedgley a friend."

"I'm sorry, Josephine. I'm sorry. Sometimes I forget my manners. Which brings me to the matter of my apology. I don't make them all that often—but I was rude when we last met. My eagerness got the better of me. And then I was terribly sorry to have to leave in such a hurry. As a matter of fact, I came to Bloom's little show tonight hoping I might see you again. I meant it when I said that I was impressed by your poems. I should say that the editor of the *Theosophist* is a, well, an acquaintance of mine, at the least . . . not to mention old Stead . . ."

By Stead, she supposed he meant W. T. Stead, editor of *Borderland*, the fashionable new occult quarterly; he was dangling an offer. He held out his card to her.

"Arthur," she said.

"Hmm? Oh yes. The young man. A friend of yours?"

"You sent him off to your—your accomplice in Deptford—"

Atwood shrugged. "He struck me as short of money. Was I wrong? I thought he could be put to use. Has he not been happy in Deptford?"

The fact was that she'd hardly seen Arthur in weeks. She was growing accustomed to his absence again—which pained her. Whatever he was doing for Mr Gracewell out in Deptford, it had begun to obsess him. He was released from it only at night and on occasional and unpredictable half-days. He was haggard, exhausted, snappish. Whatever strange telepathy they'd seemed to share was fading now—or perhaps it had never existed at all. Perhaps she'd imagined it; or perhaps she was imagining her current fears. She blamed Gracewell's work for coming between them. She blamed money. The last time they'd walked out together, they'd quarrelled, fiercely. She'd probed; she'd said his new work worried her. Six pounds a week, he said, that was all he could say. He took offence; God knows what he thought she'd meant to insinuate. She made some little private joke, of the kind that not long ago would have made him laugh, and he took it badly. As if he didn't have enough in his head, he said, without more little codes and puzzles . . .

Atwood was staring at her, waiting for a response.

"But what on earth is he doing there?"

"Work. For which he is no doubt well paid. You'd be wasted there, Josephine—I have a better use for your talents."

She was getting a headache, and starting to lose her temper.

He leaned close. "What colour was it?"

"I beg your pardon?"

"What colour was it?"

She took him to be referring to the apparition in Mrs Sedgley's drawing-room. "Red."

He nodded, as if she'd confirmed something very important. "I would like to extend an invitation to you."

He offered her his card again, and this time she took it. Then he put his hat back on.

"Sir—what happened tonight? Did you see it too?"

"She uses an electric light, Mrs Bloom."

"Oh."

"Well, you didn't think it was real, did you? Red light, and an accomplice outside to throw stones at the window; and imagination does the rest. Yes? Or am I wrong?"

He whistled.

A cab waited idly on the street corner. The driver and the horse both perked up their heads at Atwood's whistle, and the cab came round at a slow trot.

"For Miss Bradman," he told the driver, counting out money. "Take her home—no, I insist—home, or wherever else she wants to go."

He made to help her up into the cab, and she stiffened. He smiled, held out his hands as if to show that they were empty, and turned and walked off.

The driver watched Josephine with frank curiosity. His horse sniffed the air.

The card bore a Mayfair address. Nothing else.

THE
THIRD
DEGREE

{ *Perdurabo* }

Chapter Seven

Notes on a mystery—begun April 3.

Strictly forbidden, of course, this writing. God forbid that the secrets of Mr Gracewell's business should fall into the wrong hands. But if I can manage not to leave my journal on an omnibus in a fit of exhaustion, I expect all will be well.

—April 4

Let us begin with Mr Irving. It is to his service that I have been assigned, in Room 13. Christian name unknown. Somewhat menacing aspect—tall, heavy-shouldered, quite bald. Shuffles, heavy-footed. Taciturn. Always there in the morning when the men arrive, and always there at night when we depart. The look of the new schoolmaster, of whom one isn't quite sure, who might have Done Things when he was a soldier. He is the Master of Rooms 11, 12, and 13. A veteran of the old Engine—of which more later.

His days are spent moving between the rooms of his domain, watching us as we work, as if he were invigilating an examination. From time to time he takes out his chalk and alters the instructions. He distributes the ledgers. He makes whispered reports on the telephone—the only time one sees him speak, presumably to Gracewell himself.

Every room has its own telephone! Extravagant beyond all reason.

When I began a week ago, fourteen of the room's fifty desks were occupied. The other Rooms—there are at least fourteen, not counting all the little store-rooms and cupboards—appear equally half-empty. Or half-full. We are undermanned.

By the middle of the week, our number had climbed to sixteen. Two of the new men brought news to us of Room 8, from which exotic location they had been transferred. "Same bloody thing, Shaw—different boss." One quit; we are down to fifteen. Some of us were insurance clerks, or stockbroker's clerks—young men of some education who labour under debts. Some are very poor; it is a miracle some of them can read or write at all; and yet we have writers of poetry, and painters, and we have would-be aesthetes who it seems to me do very little, but aspire to do it beautifully. We have all sorts; but all of us need money.

And in the various rooms there are men of what must surely be representatives of all the races of Man, or at least all that can be found in London. The Work obliterates all distinctions among men. On my left in Room 13 sits Mr Vaz, who I believe hails from the Portuguese province of Goa; I cannot say with certainty, because even he claims not to know his birthplace. Born at sea, as in Stevenson—a sailor. If half of what he says is true, then he has seen a good percentage of the Earth; and though he is no older than me, he claims to have been ship's steward, cook, navigator, good-luck mascot, fortune-teller, diver, and nurse, at various times and in various far-flung locations. He speaks very good English and he claims to speak half a dozen other languages more or less well. His moustache is long and thin; he is short and thin. Quick to make conversation and a quick hand at the Work, which he says reminds him of his days working at a telegraph office in Mombasa.

To Mr Vaz's left are five scowling and secretive Liverpudlians: Mr Harriot, who was once a solicitor's clerk, and then a painter, and now works here; and Mr Morley, who is working on a novel about the grim life of the factory worker, and will tell you about it if you are not careful. On my right is a sandy-haired fellow called Simon, who says he is a medical student. He is sickly most of the time.

It is hot under electric light and we sweat like men in a foundry.

Rooms 6 and 9 and one or two others are occupied by women, barefoot and bareheaded like us, with whom we are forbidden to fraternise. Also an odd lot. Perhaps even odder.

A long omnibus journey in the dark and cold brings one down by the river at the building's door by eight—at the latest, for we must be in our desks by half past or the whole great machinery might run wild—and there a mob of men and women remove their shoes and hats under the supervision of Mr Dimmick, who struts and shouts like a sergeant-major. A crush in the hallway as we sort ourselves into our various rooms and desks, where the ledgers and instructions await us. More in due course.

—April 10

The ledgers are thin, and bound with black card. Damnably cheap. What Gracewell spends on telephones and electric light he saves on paper and ink. They appear for the most part identical, except for a tiny row of numbers hidden away on the spine. I suppose these numbers mean something to Mr Irving. Somewhere there must be a ledger of ledgers, and perhaps a ledger of ledgers of ledgers.

Sometimes you might find the same ledger on your desk two days running, but rarely three, and most days the thing is new. At occasional intervals and at the end of the day Mr Irving will collect the work and transmit it upstairs by means of the dumbwaiter hatch in the corridor outside.

It was Vaz who brought the numbers on the spines to my attention. He shares my curiosity. He has been here longer than me.

"Once," Vaz told me, "when we were idle, I asked to see everyone's ledgers. The ledger I worked on the day before had ended up with the man at the back of the room—he's gone now. All the others were different. After that I started keeping count. In my head. I have a good memory."

"Excellent! I wish I did. And what have you learned?"

"Nothing, Mr Shaw. I can make no sense of it. Yet."

Idle is what we all call it when the Work stops for any reason; for instance, when Mr Irving shuffles into the room, wipes the board clean, hunches over the telephone for a few minutes, then chalks up new instructions.

—Friday

A half-day! An error in the calculations, transmitted like a disease through all the ledgers, requires a halt to work and Gracewell's personal attention—God help the fellow responsible!

The Work—one can't help but think of it that way, as if it were something religious—the Work continues on Saturdays and Sundays. I suppose that all the men have made their accommodations with their various gods. It seems to me that God in His infinite wisdom would understand that the Sabbath comes every week, but six pounds comes but rarely.

—*April 15*

We are counting something, calculating something, but not money; not insurance, or accounts, or banking—so far as I can tell. Someone is paying Mr Gracewell a very large sum of money to do it, though. Fifteen rooms, each one-third full: more than one hundred men and women. A telephone in each room. Electric light. I am too tired to add all this up, and my head aches terribly. To bed.

—*April 16*

At the front of the room, printed on a placard above the instructions, is the motto *PERDURABO*. Latin is not one of Mr Vaz's many languages, and he was under the impression that it meant something to do with perdition and hell-fire. So was I, at first. But Mr Harriot has a classical education, and informs me that it means *I WILL ENDURE TO THE END*.

What End?

—*April 17*

"I will be frank," Vaz whispered to me. "At first I thought this was a bank or a counting-house. But not for long. Soon I thought perhaps it was something—Mr Shaw, may I say this to you? Something criminal."

"Well," I whispered, counting off facts on my fingers. "We have a motley assemblage of young men—women, too—and we have an unmarked building by the river. Money without apparent legitimate purpose. Secrecy, codes, conspiratorial oaths. Dimmick, a thug if ever I heard of one. It doesn't take a master detective to smell a rat, does it, Mr Vaz?"

"I have said the same things to myself, Mr Shaw. Many times."

"And Atwood, of course; sinister in his own way, I've started to think."

"Atwood?"

I described Atwood, and Vaz agreed with me that he sounds a bad sort.

"You cannot trust a man who smiles too much," he said.

"But what sort of crime? It must involve numbers. Falsifying bank accounts? Inflating a bubble? I don't see how. What would one say to the police? We've uncovered a conspiracy to perform unusual mathematics?"

"Ah," Vaz said; but then Mr Irving clapped to indicate that we should resume the Work.

—Friday

A half-day. Told Josephine: a place at the seaside. Good-bye to London. Clean air, sunshine, the blue sea. Quarrelled—don't know why. Can hardly think of anything these days but the Work.

—April 22

Simon, the medical student, has coughing fits, a burden to those of us who sit next to him, causing us to lose our train of thought. Mr Irving makes no allowance for distractions. He mutters: *discipline yourselves.* Simon follows these fits with a nervous and ingratiating smile, as if he expects sympathy; but there's none to spare. He says he intends to work for Gracewell only long enough to clear up some debts, and that he is not, appearances to the contrary, sickly or dying.

We all have coughing fits, or headaches, or bloody noses. Or shivering, or bouts of lassitude, or moments of creeping unease. Our dreams are troubled.

"Worse things happen at sea," Vaz says. And certainly, the battle for life may be fought more fiercely elsewhere; yet there is something peculiarly uncomfortable about the Work. Something unnatural about the numbers themselves. I do not know how to describe it.

Mr Vaz himself suffers headaches, and fainting fits, from which he once woke up quite convinced that, through a window that had opened in the ceiling, an unfriendly eye was staring at him.

He does not have a family, and says cheerfully that he never intends to be burdened with one. His ambition is to one day own his own little ship, and have a crew to call him sir, and to trade back and forth across the ocean; in pursuit of this ambition he is willing to endure Gracewell's Work with less complaint than most. He had already been there for nearly two months when I arrived, and that makes him something of an old hand. Few last that long.

"Before this place," Vaz once told me, "there was another place. It was lost in the storm. That's what the *real* long-service men—longer even than mine—say, but they won't tell you anything more. They're not supposed to talk about it."

I shall record the story of how he came to be working for Gracewell.

"I told this same story," he said, "to the fellow who used to sit where you sit now."

"Where did he go?"

"I don't know. One morning he didn't come in. The nightmares, I suppose. But please, you asked to hear my story. I'll tell you. I'm a sailor. That has always been my profession. I could climb a rope before I could walk. It'll be my profession again when Mr Gracewell's lunatic enterprise here collapses. Perhaps they'll come for him and put him in a hospital for madmen. Perhaps they'll ship him out to India to govern something. In the meantime I am making more money than I have ever heard tell of in my life."

The room idled. Mr Irving chalked up new instructions. Simon, the medical student, sat with his head in his hands and moaned.

"I was between services. This was shortly after the storm, which I am sure you know was a bad night for ships. The *Viceroy* lost her top mast to lightning! Well, that was not such bad luck for me. I was bound in service for another two years to the *Viceroy*. If the storm had come a few days later I would already have been at sea, far from here; and I suppose I would never have heard of Mr Gracewell."

"It's an ill wind that blows nobody any good," I said.

"I was enjoying my freedom in a lodging-house over a shop in Shadwell, where I shared a room with three or four very good friends. And one morning, as we were playing skittles in the garden, and arguing about money, Mr Dimmick interrupted us. I suppose he climbed the fence; one moment we were alone, the next he was there, leaning on the fence and tapping his stick for our attention."

He shook his head sadly. "No Englishman had set foot in that garden in years. You can't be too careful in London these days, Mr Shaw. *Get out*, I said, *whoever you are. Get out. We did not kill your bloody Duke and we do not know who killed him.* I mean no offense to the Duke, but there has been trouble of that sort lately. He said, *shut up.* Tapping his stick on the cobbles—*shut—up*—like so. Anyway—he said that he was looking for me. He knew my name, Mr Shaw. I said, *What do you want*, and he said that he had heard it said in the pubs that I could tell fortunes."

Vaz shook his head. "I said certainly not, because I thought perhaps he was a policeman. But it's true, I have made a little money here and there telling fortunes. Sailors appreciate a glimpse of the future. I have picked up a trick or two in this port or that, and when I was a boy I could roll my eyes back in my head and speak in strange tongues. I consider it an honest profession, though the law of London disagrees."

I explained that recent events had caused me to have an open mind on the subject of clairvoyance.

"I said that he should leave, because I was not in the business of telling fortunes. He said that he was a sure hand at fortune-telling himself and so he could tell that soon I would be working for him. I said that I wished him good fortune in his endeavours, and he said what did I mean by that, was that a sort of curse? He said that he supposed that, as a heathen, I probably had all kinds of charms and amulets lying around, and I probably thought I could put the evil eye on a man and was probably accustomed to communicating with devils."

Vaz shook his head.

"Now, my friends are not the kind of men who take such insults lightly. I thought it was very bad manners myself. So they said some harsh words of their own to Mr Dimmick, and they approached him roughly. Mr Shaw, Dimmick's stick struck like a snake—I hardly saw it move."

"A nasty-looking implement, that stick."

"My friend did not like it either. Dimmick had knocked him to the floor. *Peace*, I said, *peace, we are all reasonable men here.* I said that I was only a sailor, and that if he wanted to hire a sailor I might work for him, but if he wanted to hire a mystic he should go somewhere else, and quickly. Plenty of frauds in London would take his money! He said that he did not want sailors, and was I deaf, had he not been clear? He wanted clerks. I said that perhaps he was deaf, because hadn't I said I was a sailor. *Shut up*, he said, *and I'll give you two pounds to come with me and let the boss explain.* Well—I was afraid of him, but I have done more dangerous things than follow a madman to Deptford, and for less money."

Others tell much the same story as Mr Vaz—the unexpected visit from Dimmick, that is. One or two were recruited from jail, I regret to say.

Mr Vaz has shared his cure for the headaches.

"When it gets too painful," Vaz advises me, "I close my eyes and think of God; and when that does not work, I think of women."

"I think of Josephine," I say. I have told him about Josephine.

"Aha!" he says.

"Sometimes I think about food."

"Ha! Food!"

"Ham," I say. "Bacon. Oxtail soup, curried fowl, meat puddings, pea soup, roast—"

We have these conversations two or three times a day. Talk of food makes poor Simon moan.

—April 24

Graves was gone today. Coe left us on the nineteenth of the month. Parrington and Singh on the fifteenth—Singh had been suffering from something that resembled consumption. I forget other names.

A letter from Josephine. Could hardly make sense of it.

Awful confession—her letters pile up beside my bed, unread—unopened. Can hardly think about a thing but the Work.

—April 26

Dimmick gave me a long hard look this evening, as if he suspects that I have been keeping notes. But then that's Dimmick's way—the scowl, the menacing *tap-tap-tap*.

Yesterday, Dimmick caught me trying to sneak into a room not my own. I was confused, I said, bloody place is a maze, isn't it? The scowl, the *tap-tap-tap*.

—April 27

Starry night as I walked home. Struck by a quite unreasoning sensation of utter terror, I clutched to a lamp-post as if to a mast in a storm, and was mistaken for a drunk. A light in Josephine's window, but I did not know what to say to her. All this is for her; and yet I cannot tell her. Not a

Had to put this away. Could hardly read the page before me. Troubled all day by visions and now the symbols of the Work dance before my eyes.

—May 10

Quite forgot this thing. Not a great success. The Work leaves little time to reflect; and for a while there I was unwell. Let me try again.

Every morning the ledgers contain numbers, written in the left-hand column of the leftmost page. *Numbers* is something of a simplification. They are dots and dashes, somewhat like Morse code, though so far as I know, it is not. We think of them as representing numbers. It is rather like learning a new language. In amongst the dots and dashes are a few other symbols. Today I encountered α, φ, ψ, and Ω. My classical education was poor, but I know those to be Greek. There are a few other symbols—not many—that my education had not equipped me to recognise at all, such as ♉, or ≈, or ↢. Over the course of the day, the job is to perform certain operations on those dots and dashes *et cetera*, transforming them as they march across the columns from one side of the ledger to another.

Vaz believes that the ledgers circulate among the rooms, so that operations that began in Room 1 might be continued in Room 6 and concluded in Room 12 and revolve back to begin again in Room 2.

The instructions Mr Irving chalks on the board set the rules of the game.

Mr Harriot, who works at the back of the room, advised me to think of it as a game. He says it's trying too hard to understand what it's all for that causes headaches and worry and sickness, and the thing is to play the game the best you can. He is a rugby man.

The operations that we perform are generally not very difficult, but there are a great many to be performed in a day. Mr Irving never makes threats or speeches, and Gracewell never shows himself in Room 13, but no one doubts that errors will not be tolerated, and speed is of the essence. There is a spirit of competition in the room.

The instructions are sometimes very simple:

> DESKS ONE TO TEN: COMBINE THE FIRST AND SECOND
> ROWS

Often we are little more than overpaid scriveners. The instructions tell us to copy one ledger into another, or to do it in triplicate.

Sometimes the instructions are more complicated:

> IGNORE THE SECOND COLUMN IF YOU ARE IN DESKS ONE
> TO TEN. OTHERWISE THE SECOND COLUMN IS THE SUM
> OF EACH NUMBER IN THE ROWS BELOW THE NUMBER IN

*QUESTION IN THE FIRST COLUMN AND CONTINUE IN THE
THIRD COLUMN ETC ETC ETC ETC ETC ETC*

Tedious, and so far as I can tell, pointless, but at least clear. Sometimes
the instructions are merely exhortations:

FASTER.

And sometimes they are utterly obscure:

ONE IS WHITE. TWO IS BLACK.

Or:

ONE IS YES. ZERO IS NO.

And besides, how precisely is one supposed to add ψ to $\approx$, or subtract
$\underline{\Omega}$ from Ω?

"Do what seems right," Vaz says. "If you have done it wrong, I expect
they will let you know."

Every so often Mr Irving summons someone out of the room, for a
conversation from which they return silent and pale. I confess that it worries me. I fear error. Most of what the instructions call for is nonsense, so
far as I can tell, and the remainder is pointless; therefore there is no way
to know if it's being done right, or wrong, or even if there is such a thing
as right or wrong, or if we are being judged on some other ground, or not
at all. Sometimes I worry that the Work doesn't make sense even to Gracewell, and that at the end of the day Irving shovels it all into the fire, laughing at our wasted efforts.

When the instructions call for an impossible or absurd operation, I
take Vaz's advice and simply trust to intuition; I close my eyes and let my
hand work. I think it is these leaps of intuition, not the long hours or the
close airless room, that cause the headaches *et cetera*. It is no doubt significant that quite a number of the men believe themselves to be sensitives,
in one way or another—fortune-tellers, weekend mediums, table-rappers,
fairy-spotters.

One feels that the Work has a shape, somehow. One has a sense of forging into airless heights; of the numbers as spiralling—revolving—a pattern forming of which my work is but a tiny, tiny fragment. A thing being woven together out of dots and dashes, my work a single thin filament; turning and turning, rising up, bearing us with it. As if we are measuring something, or mapping something, or filling some volume of empty space with numbers so that one can plumb its depths. From time to time I have thought of that famous painting of the Tower of Babel, spiralling around and up in an endless procession of arches and ladders and scaffolds.

"Come let us build ourselves a city, and a tower with its top in the heavens."

—May 16

Waugh and Heath called round while I was at work, leaving a note. It occurs to me that I have not touched a drop of drink since I began at Gracewell's. No doubt it does me good. There is a kind of discipline to the Work that does away with other distractions. Rather like one imagines soldiering might be, or being a monk.

Towards the end of the day Simon stood quite suddenly at his desk and announced that he would not do it any more. He would not, he said, he would not, he simply would not, he had decided that he would not, would not, would not, would not. Then he started to scream. His eyes rolled back in his head and he cried out as if he were lost, alone, in some dark starry emptiness, beset by monstrous spectres. I held the poor fellow by his shoulders and tried to talk some sense back into him, but it was no go. Strong, as they say men in a fit often are. In the end he had to be removed from the room by Mr Dimmick, who appeared out of nowhere and forced him into submission, as if he were a rabid dog and not a frail medical student, and then led him out with his arm twisted behind his back, muttering *now then now then come along hup hup my boy hup*. Then a long idleness as the ledgers and instructions were rearranged to account for the new configuration of the room.

Hardly a week gone by since the fire. Already it seems like some awful dream.

God, what a mess.

What on earth have I got myself into?

Martin Atwood's house—number 22, according to the card he'd given Josephine—stood on the south-west corner of Hanover Square. It was palatial, in a discreet, rather austere way.

Five rows of white windows were set into a grey immensity of brick. The door was set back behind four square white pillars, a fence of black railings, a moat of basement windows. The windows and the golden letter-box in the middle of a large black door caught the last violet light of the evening.

At first nobody answered Lord Atwood's door-bell, for so long that Josephine began to wonder if nobody was home, not even the servants. After all, she'd come unannounced, on a whim that had surprised even her, after ignoring Atwood's invitation for several dutiful weeks, just as she'd promised Arthur she would—having, in fact, gone so far as to lose Atwood's card in a desk-drawer, so that when she'd decided that afternoon to pay Atwood a visit, she'd had to spend an hour searching for it, and was now later than she'd meant to be.

She tapped her foot. One or two passers-by looked curiously at her. While she waited, halfway across London, a little flame hatched in a rusted bucket in a cupboard at the back of Mr Gracewell's Engine and began to explore its surroundings, feeding itself on greasy rags and old ledgers and newspapers.

When the door opened it revealed Atwood himself, not a servant. She felt instantly shabby and poor, and she flushed. He smiled at her as if—it was not quite friendly, though not unfriendly either—as if her presence confirmed a hypothesis.

"Josephine! I thought you might come."

"I hope you don't mind. You said—"

"I extended an invitation; you accepted it. And with auspicious timing, too—there must have been something in the air."

He led her into a long hallway, lined with paintings, of mostly Arcadian subjects—women in flowing white silk draped about green willows—she didn't do more than glance at them. She supposed they were all very fine, and very tasteful. She was already intimidated enough. She'd rehearsed what she meant to say on the way over, but now, in the face of Atwood's obvious wealth and station, she nearly forgot why she'd come.

She allowed him to lead her towards a staircase. "I hope I'm not interrupting anything."

"Not at all. I have some friends here. Members of my company. We were almost ready to begin—but they'll be delighted to meet you. It will be better with nine."

"Begin?"

"You'll join us, won't you? A séance, of sorts. The hour is very nearly upon us. No doubt you sensed it."

"Your Lordship—I didn't come here for a séance. I came to talk about Arthur Shaw."

"Arthur Shaw? Oh, yes. I recall."

Yet another of her letters to Arthur had gone unanswered. The final straw. She had been in the dark for altogether too long, and it seemed she would be in the dark for ever, unless she did something to bring light to it. Perhaps Atwood *was* dangerous—but if so, it was Arthur who was in danger, not her. It was Arthur who was becoming so hopelessly caught up in Atwood's and Gracewell's affairs that he might never be able to extricate himself from them—whatever they were. She remained certain that Arthur would have had nothing to do with anything truly criminal, or thoroughly wicked. But it was plainly undesirable, and unhealthy; and she had decided that it was time to swallow her own misgivings about Lord Atwood and pay him a visit to tell him so.

As Atwood led her downstairs—first unfastening a red rope from the top of the staircase, then refastening it—she launched into her case. It was her right to be told what was going on, as Arthur's fiancée and, she hoped, as Atwood's friend; furthermore, whatever was going on in Deptford was quite clearly harmful to Arthur's health, not to mention his sanity; and besides, it was a waste of his talents; and so on, and so on. Atwood was quite plainly not really listening.

"Josephine, Josephine—this is not a night to discuss money."

"Sir! It's not a question of money, it's a question of—of simple decency."

"Is it? How dull."

"I thought you might help."

"I thought you'd come to help *me*. We have very little time, and a great deal to do to prepare."

She was curious despite herself. "For what?"

Atwood smiled, and pointed the way forward down a low-ceilinged, electric-lit corridor.

"I recall Mr Shaw," Atwood said. "I recommended his services to Mr Gracewell, didn't I? It's very important work, Josephine, very important; but I grant you it's unpleasant. I wasn't aware of Mr Shaw's finer qualities, which you have so eloquently adumbrated. I'll speak to Gracewell."

"Who is Gracewell? What on earth is he doing? What—"

"He assists the Company with calculations."

"But what does that mean? Why is all this secrecy necessary?"

"Will you permit me to show you?"

For a moment she was afraid he might open a door to reveal Arthur chained up in a cupboard, shovelling coal or something of the sort.

"You're just in time to witness one of our experiments. Our company—you can see what it's all for, and why it's so tremendously urgent. You're not superstitious, are you, Josephine?"

"Superstitious? I don't think I am."

"Good! It's a source of constant surprise to me how many people can't tell psychical science from ghost stories. So many sensitives waste their gifts, led astray by superstition—and I think that you have a quite remarkable gift, Josephine. I don't say that lightly. Why, if every girl in London who claims to be sensitive really were, it would be a wonder that London doesn't levitate! Fortunately, I have an excellent sense for the real thing. I dare say you feel it too; when two true sensitives meet, there's an undeniable *spark*, isn't there? The uninitiated might mistake it for something baser, something carnal. And what a waste, when such energies could be put to higher purposes."

It was impossible to deny that her heart was pounding.

He paused with his hand on a doorknob.

"I can't say more unless I know you'll join us. Will you?"

"Mr Shaw—"

"We can discuss him later. Will you join us?"

"I confess, Lord Atwood—I'm curious."

"You'll have to stop calling me that. Call me Mercury. It's a game, but rather an important one—we don't use the names of ordinary life here. All are equal. All seekers in the dark, aren't we? Our common goal is *understanding*, and we are all equally distant from it. Besides, you can't have Mr Smith the butcher or Mr Boggs the bank clerk stamping about in the astral stuff, knocking things over. Or Lord What's-his-name of What-have-you, for that matter. So—you need a new name."

"A *nom de magicienne*? Something Latin, I suppose?"

"As a matter of fact, I was thinking *Venus*."

Josephine thought that was very inappropriate, and said so.

Atwood smiled, and opened a door onto an upper gallery of a large library.

A wrought-iron staircase led down to the library's floor, where a little group of men and women stood, making conversation, or carrying out obscure preparations. A large circular table occupied the centre of the room. In the middle of the table there was an arrangement of spherical electrical lamps glowing in a variety of odd hues; the room was otherwise gloomy. A man in a black coat bustled around, wiping the glass of the lamps, adjusting their flames and nudging them in slight orbits around one another, with the care of an artist. Every time he moved a lamp, ripples of dim glinting light ran across the book-bindings on the walls of the room, shimmering like schools of fish.

There was a pattern painted on the parquet floor, in blue and red, green and purple and gold. It had something of the look of a star-map rendered by an astronomer in the grip of either hysteria or genius. Thick curving lines, with arrow-heads pointing in all directions; lines made of characters that Josephine couldn't recognise; a series of concentric circles, the outermost of which reached all the way to the feet of the bookshelves at the edge of the room. The table sat near the centre of these circles, nearly but not quite at the heart of the pattern.

On one wall there was an immense grandfather clock. In a corner there was an untidy collection of musical instruments; in another corner lay a heap of tools—a broom, paintbrushes in a bucket, a ladder, a rifle.

Atwood leaned over the railing. "Now, that's Jupiter down there, in the black dress. She has a temper, and considers herself one of the great brains of England—which she may very well be, for all I know! I don't consider myself more than a stumbler in the dark, after all—and so I make up for my deficiencies by having a circle of talent always around me. And that chap there in the green, the bald one with the philosophical beard, he's a theologian—he goes by Uranus, when he's a guest here. The chap who resembles the Prime Minister goes by Neptune. Do you see the rules of the game? We have a vacancy for a Venus. Now that I think of it, we've never had a poet before! Ah, and the Indian fellow there—"

"Mercury." The woman Atwood had named Jupiter called up from below. Her voice was sharp, ringing, impatient. "Can we begin?"

Atwood glanced at Josephine and rolled his eyes. Then he turned back to the door behind them and performed a quick series of gestures with his hands, rather like the stations of the cross, and muttered something too quiet and quick for Josephine to hear.

He leaned over the balcony again. "It's safe," he said. "As safe as anywhere in London these days, anyway."

The woman he'd called Jupiter pointed at Josephine. "You invited a ninth, without telling me?"

"A happy coincidence. Can we squeeze her in, do you think?"

"I think you've been keeping me in the dark, Mercury, and you know I dislike that. Now, come down, and stop playing the fool."

"Wait," Uranus said. "How do we know she's not one of theirs?"

Atwood sighed, turned to Josephine, and took both of her hands in his. "Are you," he said, "one of *theirs*?"

"I hardly know who *you* are."

"Well, that's good enough for me."

Atwood descended the staircase, and Josephine followed.

The man they'd called Uranus grumbled but returned to his conversation. He was talking to a fat, pale young man in a turban; discussing the news of the campaign in Afghanistan, where the Army was encountering difficulties. Hangings all round. Crack of the whip. So on and so forth. She was both relieved and disappointed that their conversation was so utterly conventional.

It all reminded her in an odd way of her first arrival at Cambridge.

The book-lined room and the stuffy opulence. The sense of ancient ritual and a club to which one was being admitted, on sufferance; the cast of eccentrics, bores, wits, and geniuses; the looming threat of Examination.

"Well," said Jupiter. She was arranging cards on the table, and rearranging the lamps, while the man in the black coat—who gave Josephine a business-like nod—arranged the chairs. The man who went by Uranus and the young man in the turban were now talking about the depreciation of the rupee—or, at least, Uranus was lecturing and the younger man was nodding. The turbaned man did not look Indian; the man Atwood had identified as Indian—solid and dark and white-haired—wore a bright red tie, and no turban.

Atwood took Jupiter's hand, smiling, and kissed it.

"Not now," she snapped. "You—Venus, if you're to join us. Has Mercury troubled himself to *tell* you anything? Or has he been playing his usual games?"

"He was . . . intriguing."

"Hah," Atwood said.

"I'm certain he was. Are you a believer?"

"A believer, ma'am? I don't quite know. A believer in what?"

Jupiter raised an eyebrow. "Hmph. That's a fair answer to an unfair question, my dear. May the gods preserve us from believers, spoon-benders, table-rappers, psychometrists, levitators, mesmerists, tea-leaf readers! Well—all you must do is follow instruction. Please sit. There."

Josephine sat. Something about the woman's voice brooked no question. In Josephine's experience, where an occult fraternity had secret names, like Mercury or Jupiter, there were also hierarchies and titles and inner and outer circles. This was clearly the inner circle of something-or-other . . . except perhaps for the young man in the turban, who had the air of a novice, a supplicant, eager to please. There would usually be a circle within the circle, two or three individuals who were first among equals: they might be very quiet, or they might boom and fizz with energy, but in either case they would be the sort of person who commanded attention. Atwood and Jupiter both fit the description well enough.

Uranus and the young man in the turban sat down on either side of Josephine, and took her hands in theirs. The old man's hand was dry, and the young one's hand was damp.

Atwood sat across the table. He winked, then sat back, his face obscured by a lamp.

Josephine counted nine lamps, each glowing a different shade: golden orange, aquamarine, damask-red, sap green, amaranthine. . . .

The business-like man in the black coat set up a camera on a tripod. Then he lit incense in a little brazier and sat down between Atwood and the Indian man, placing his hands over theirs.

"Your bloody chairs are bloody heavy, Mercury."

"Quiet," Jupiter said. She walked around the table.

The pale young man in the turban leaned in close and whispered. "I know that look. I'm new here too."

"Hello. You must be, ah . . ."

"Saturn."

He had an odd, nervous laugh. She smiled politely.

"It's all a bit odd, isn't it? But Lord At—that is, Mercury's company has the most intriguing reputation. Doesn't it? I don't think we've met. Sorry. I'm rather nervous, frankly. One wants to make a good impression. Do you have any notion of what we're supposed to *do*?"

The scent of the incense filled the room. It was pungent; sweet and oily. Josephine's head began to swim.

"I don't know," Josephine said. "They're very secretive."

Another nervous laugh. The camera clicked.

Jupiter sat. "You, and you." She was looking at the camera, but she seemed to be addressing Josephine and the anxious young man in the turban. "Decide now: stay, or go. There is risk in staying. It will not be great, if you follow instructions, but it is there. I tell you this because there must be *trust*."

Josephine said nothing. She was a little alarmed; but she'd heard that sort of dire warning before. Mrs Sedgley often warned of the great peril that the members of the Ordo V.V. 341 faced, peering too deeply into the spirit world.

"I will stay," said the man in the turban.

"I did not say speak. I said stay or go. I hope you can follow instructions better than *that*! Now, look at the cards in front of you."

In front of Josephine was a white card, with three symbols on it. There was a black hexagram—somewhat off-kilter, in a way that appeared deliberate. Beneath it was a small circle, violet striated with black, and then a sort of cone made up of whirling lines. Mr Turban's card was roughly similar.

The camera clicked again.

"Please," Jupiter said, "Understand that our methods must be *very* precise. Everything must be done in the proper moment and in the proper way. We are engaged in a great experiment."

"Tonight," Atwood said, "we swim the aether."

"That," Jupiter said, "is a characteristically unhelpful way of putting it. We are engaged in a project of scientific investigation—you may consider it essentially astronomical—though we work not with telescopes and spectrographs, but with the will alone—will and perception. Do you understand what Mercury means by *aether*?"

"Our new Venus is a scholar," Atwood said, smiling. "Of course she does."

"Ah," said the man in the turban, "I think I read about this; something about electricity, or, or, I think I read about a scientist chap electrocuting a frog? Or was it a cat?"

"Nonsense," Atwood said, happily.

"In Aristotle," Josephine said, "it would be the fifth element; the stars and the planets are made of it."

"Its properties?"

"I'm afraid I wasn't expecting to be examined. Well, let's see: pure and unchanging. Airy and invisible. Eternal and perfect; not like the gross decaying matter of the earth. And whereas earthly matter rises and falls and moves in straight lines, the aether's nature is to move of its own accord in perfect circles, for ever; so the heavenly spheres go round and around, sun and moon and stars."

"Now, hold on," said the young man in the turban. "Do you—"

"Air and fire," Atwood said. "But we too are made of star-stuff. Our bodies are gross matter; our minds full of the chatter of newspapers and advertisements and train timetables and money and other nonsense; but our souls are made of the stuff of the heavens. And so we call across the void, each to each. If we can but pull back the veil, and take a peek behind it . . ."

"Mercury is a romantic," Jupiter said. "For tonight, all that is required of you is that you follow our instructions. And that if there is fear—and there will be fear—you do not falter. Now pay attention. Listen to the ticking of the clock. There will be a series of chimes; they will be your guide. You must not stray from the path . . ."

Josephine stared at her card. She felt the turbaned neophyte's—Saturn's—palm sweat rather horribly into hers. She struggled to remember Jupiter's instructions. Thank God that she and Saturn were excused from joining in the chant. Everyone else, eyes closed, hands entwined, chanted nonsense syllables. Over and over and over. If not for the perfect interweaving of their voices, she might have thought they were all improvising. Jupiter's sharp clipped voice set the pace rather like a metronome, intertwining with Atwood's drawl. One man at the table had a thick Yorkshire accent. The Indian fellow's accent was equally thick, and a woman whose face was obscured by a round and greenish electrical lamp sounded French. Jupiter's pencil scratched at the paper. Josephine couldn't see what she was drawing. The camera clicked at regular intervals. The incense was sweet, oily, dizzying. She wondered if it was drugged. The thought was a little frightening; not unpleasantly so. She listened intently to the grandfather clock that loomed behind her, just as Jupiter had instructed, awaiting the chimes. It clack-clacked in a somewhat irregular way, as if it was following several different cycles at once, some of which were faster than others. She kept expecting it to chime at any moment. She told herself to be patient, and to keep her breathing steady, her hands still. Saturn's hand really was very unpleasant to the touch. Uranus' hand trembled. She tried to ignore both of them. Jupiter had been quite particular in her instructions: they must concentrate on the chime, on the chant, on the images on the cards before them. Very well; Josephine could do as instructed. But what was it all for? She'd heard of certain talented mediums who could project their astral selves among the stars, or to the moon, or at least who said that they could. Was that all this was? Would the lights come on soon and they would all stand around telling themselves that *of course* we had felt the most extraordinary sensation of *departing from the body*. . . . Or was this one of the more refined sort of fraternities, where it was understood that when one spoke of travel to the stars, it was of course not meant to be taken literally, nothing so vulgar; rather, one meant a spiritual awakening, a discovery of the recesses of one's own soul? Perhaps. Most likely. Atwood was no fool.

How *had* he talked her into this, precisely, and distracted her from the reason she'd come here? The camera clicked. She realised that she'd drifted off for a moment, and sat up straight. There was now a low musical tone in the room, coming from no clearly identifiable corner; it sounded rather like a cello. There might be a cellist hidden somewhere, or perhaps a phonograph. The camera clicked again. The odd thing about the cello was that its tone was always descending, down and down for ever, yet never changing. The camera clicked. Jupiter's pencil scratched. The clock chimed and, as instructed, she shifted her attention to the orange sphere and closed her eyes. There was darkness for a moment, then a ray of violet light rose up from the infinite darkness below her into the infinite light above, and into it slowly descended the shadows of Mercury and Jupiter and Uranus and the others, and she felt herself opening up to lend them her strength, and they revolved together as they descended—or perhaps they rose; she could not tell if those words had any meaning any more. *De profundis*, Atwood whispered, as if in her ear, *ad lucem*, while behind her the clock chimed again and again as if time itself poured brightly into the void like quicksilver.

W hen she opened her eyes it was pitch dark, and there was screaming and shouting in English and French and what was presumably Hindustani. There was broken glass in her lap. Something flopped on the table in front of her, scattering what was left of the lamps. She had a sense of having *fallen* so powerful that she was afraid to move for fear that she would find that her bones were broken. The thing on the table in front of her made a keening, fluttering sound. It was like nothing she'd ever heard before.

"Bastards," someone shouted. "Bloody buggering bastards, they—"

"No," Atwood said. "We did this."

"*Novices.*" That was the Frenchwoman's voice. "Idiot novices."

"No." Atwood's voice. "No, no, no. What is that infernal noise? Who is that? Everyone stand away from the table, and stop shout—"

"Bloody Gracewell," shouted Uranus. "Another bloody error!"

"*What*," said Jupiter. Her voice was tight to the point of snapping. "*What—is—that?*"

Somebody swore. It sounded like they'd stumbled over the camera.

"What did we bring *back*?"

"Impossible!"

"Oh God—oh God, it's *real*."

"I have matches," Mr Turban said. "I have matches!"

The thing on the table lurched. Josephine felt something soft and lace-like brush her face. She screamed and jumped out of her chair.

"Light. Light!"

"All right, all right—wait—oh, bloody hell—there!"

A match flared red.

The chimerical apparition that lay on the table, flopping in broken glass, was . . . She didn't know what it was. It appeared shapeless at first—or perhaps she simply couldn't make any sense of its shape. Parts of it were a bright cobalt blue and parts of it were mottled indigo or pink—Josephine couldn't tell if she was looking at shimmering vari-coloured scales, or tattoos, or bruises, or blood, or clothing. In places it had the shine of scale, or enamel, or silk. Sharp ribs in a narrow chest heaved for air. It had a tangle of limbs, long, flailing, jointed in an irregular way—or perhaps they were broken. It lay in a heap of purple matter—folds of diaphanous silk and lace, a peacock's tail, petals, the leaves of fern, the fronds of a jellyfish—bathed in shadow and flickering matchlight. She couldn't make sense of it. The face—oh God, there was a face!—had what she thought of as rather Chinese-looking eyes, except they were pupil-less, silvery, nacreous, blinking in what might be panic. It was screaming.

Mr Turban started sobbing like a baby. Jupiter slapped him.

Struggling on the table as if pinned there like a butterfly. Were those things on its back wings? Just as she thought she was about to make sense of what she was seeing, the match went out.

Someone took her hand and pulled her away—he lit a match and she saw that it was Atwood, pointing to the stairs and mouthing *up, up*. She was too stunned to argue. When she turned to look back the—the *apparition* had rolled in its agony off the table and onto the floor, where the experimenters all crowded around it, obscuring her view, holding up matches—with the exception of the man in the turban, who'd fainted, and the man in the black coat, who'd gone to fetch the rifle from the corner of the room. Over the noise of the experimenters' astonished jabbering, she could still hear the creature screaming. She thought that she might never stop hearing it.

Atwood pulled her out into the corridor.

"What—"

"I don't know. Impossible. Unprecedented! More than I dared imagine. Is it dangerous? Most certainly. I have to think . . ." He laughed, running his hands through his hair. "Ha!—I was right to add you to our circle . . ."

Was it somehow her doing? She didn't know. She recalled nothing clearly. She remembered colours, darkness, motion; a great turning ring of light, and another, and another. She remembered straining, yearning, a homesick longing for the stars.

"Go home. Say nothing. Do you understand? Nothing."

Atwood put his fingers to her mouth. He'd cut them on the broken glass, and they smeared blood on her lips.

"Nothing," he said, in a tone of command.

He led her to the door.

She said, "I . . ."

"For your own sake, Josephine: say nothing. This is no game. Now go, before Jupiter decides to lock you up in the pantry."

He smiled suddenly. "You were splendid, though. Ha! At last!"

Then he practically shoved her out into the street and shut the door in her face.

Her lips were warm. She wiped blood from them. Outside it was evening, and the rain had stopped. A man across the street was selling newspapers. A couple of cabs rolled briskly by. Two gentlemen strolled past in the other direction, talking business. One glanced at her and *tut-tutted*.

W hen she returned, Mr Borel's daughter Sophia, who was sweeping the steps, gave her a disapproving look. Josephine patted at her hair and found it a dreadful mess. Well, there was nothing she could do about that now. She said good night to Sophia and babbled a few words of explanation, not quite knowing what she said.

She went up to her room, and sat on the bed, shaking. She felt terrible, as if she'd been drinking to excess or had swallowed poison.

She desperately wanted to tell someone. She wanted to never speak of it again.

It had been no sham.

Madness. Stranger than any vision her mother had suffered. But Atwood and the rest had seen it too.

That beautiful, terrible, wounded creature.

She was still awake hours later, pacing up and down, when someone started banging on the door below. She threw open the window to see a large tramp in the street, reeling away from the door, bellowing her name. It took her a moment to realise that it was Arthur. He appeared to have been in a fire.

Chapter Nine

That night Arthur had stayed late in Room 13, explaining to Mr Dimmick at chucking-out time that he thought there were certain errors in the Work he'd done that afternoon, and it was a bloody nuisance but he simply had to fix them. Dimmick thought this was improbable but since Gracewell wasn't there to appeal to, and Dimmick certainly didn't understand the Work, he'd grudgingly permitted it. In fact, Arthur was hoping to snoop on the night-time operations of the Engine. Mr Vaz had remained for the same purpose. Two other workers—Harriot, and a clerk named Malone—had insisted on staying, apparently out of a determination that nobody in the room should show themselves more diligent or ambitious than they. Arthur was waiting for them to go away.

They sat in silence, pretending to work. Now that the room was nearly empty, it had gone cold. The light-bulb hissed. There was hardly a sound from the other rooms; only a skeleton staff remained at night to continue the Engine's operations.

The first sign of the fire was distant shouting, from the direction of the lower-numbered rooms. That gave Arthur a chill, but it hardly surprised him; not after what had happened to Simon.

He said, "Another one gone."

"Poor fellow," Vaz agreed.

"Ah well," Malone said.

The shouting continued and the sound of men running in the corridors joined it. Vaz closed his ledger and looked around, smiling rather nervously. Harriot and Malone bent closer over their desks. Arthur stood. The bell at the front of the room began to ring, yanked by the rope that stretched up into the ceiling and thence to who knows where. At the same time the telephone rang.

If it was meant to convey a message, Arthur didn't know what it was, or where it originated. His understanding was that the bells of each room were connected, but their signals were meant only for the foremen—Mr Irving and his ilk. Meanwhile, the noise of running feet subsided.

The telephone continued to ring. Harriot and Malone lowered their pens and stared at the telephone. Like the bell, the telephone was for Mr Irving's use, and no one but him ever answered it. This was a message the men of Room 13 were not prepared for, and did not know how to answer. It was as if, during a suburban séance, the table had begun to *rap*, *rap*, *rap*, the noise of the spirit-world echoing through the dark room but no medium there to interpret.

Arthur said, "What nonsense!" walked to the front of the room, and answered the phone. He held the glistening black trumpet to his ear and waited for someone to speak but heard only ghostly crackling.

Many of the men in Room 13 had never seen a telephone before they came there, and most had never listened to one, so the thing was widely regarded with a sort of superstitious awe. As if there weren't enough that was strange about Gracewell's enterprise, without inventing superstitions!

Vaz said, "What?"

"There's no one speaking," Arthur said. "Nothing."

"Sit down," Harriot said. "That's Irving's business. You'll make trouble. What if we miss a day's instructions because you're fooling about with the telephone; and then a whole day's work gets—"

Vaz shrugged. "We are paid the same for idleness as for the Work."

Harriot banged his fist on his desk. "Shut up, you! Shut up."

Arthur lowered the telephone back into its cradle.

There was most certainly a smell of smoke in the room.

The light-bulb went out. The room went utterly dark.

"Bugger it," said Malone as he lit a match. He was a sickly looking fellow at the best of times, and the shaking light did not flatter him.

The room was on the edge of panic. Arthur supposed that it fell to him to lead them. God help them all, he thought.

"Smoke," Vaz said. "Fire."

"What did you say?" said Malone. "What did he say, Shaw? What did he say?"

Vaz got up and walked to the door on the right-hand side of the room, and looked down the corridor. He uttered a string of obscenities. Arthur understood very few of them.

The air was singed and acrid. The light-bulbs were out and the corridor was dark, except for a frightening red light from the open doorway of one of the nearby rooms.

"Fire," Vaz said. "Fire!" He slapped Arthur on the shoulder and ran past him into the corridor, where he stood, looking from side to side, then set off to the left.

"Fire?" Malone said.

Arthur shouted, "Yes! Fire!" then ran in after Vaz. Harriot and Malone followed.

They ran past closed doors leaking smoke and light from their cracks. They stumbled past open doors through which they could see the fire at work, crawling up the bell-ropes, playing across the desk-tops, and eating red holes in the walls. Somewhere along the line they acquired three other men, strangers from a distant room. They doubled back when their route was blocked by flames and fallen timbers. They cut across the rooms into another corridor, and then another, where three young and terrified women joined them. They left the doors to the Rooms wide open as they ran, and the fire took advantage, rushing in to fill the open spaces of the Rooms, hurrying joyfully down the paths laid out for it.

"Down," Vaz kept saying, "down!" He meant that they should stoop low, to avoid breathing the smoke, which pooled blackly on the ceiling everywhere they went. Arthur was dizzy, and his eyes stung as if they were being tormented by devils.

Gracewell's building was something of a labyrinth, and they were all quickly lost. The building had only one exit, and the fire had forced them in quite the wrong direction to escape that way. The question, then, was where to find a window. The building had a few, though not many.

Arthur said, "Stop! Stop. We have to get our bearings." At least, he meant to—it came out as a wordless roar, then a splutter.

He stopped by a closed door. He leaned with his hand against the wall and he peered closely at the number on the door, blinking away tears and attempting to read the number. It was more than ten, and less than twenty. That was all he could make out before the door swung open, and Dimmick came charging out.

Dimmick looked wild and in pain. His eyes darted furiously from side to side before settling on Arthur.

Arthur said, "Dimm—"

Dimmick seized Arthur by his collar and shoved him against the wall. His ugly face was war-painted with soot and hideous red scars. His hair was patchy, his eyebrows gone.

"Bastards," he said. "Who did this?"

"Dimmi—"

"Who did this? Eh?"

"Let go, Dimmick—don't be a fool, let go—let go!"

Arthur shoved. Dimmick's eyes flared with rage as he struck Arthur's legs out from under him with his stick.

"Eh? Shaw?" Dimmick crouched over him, his stick at Arthur's throat. "Was it you, then? Sneaking about—was it you? You working for them, are you, Shaw?"

"Dimmick, I—"

"I'll kill you first, you little—"

Vaz's face appeared behind Dimmick's shoulder, as Vaz lifted up his leg and brought his foot down with great force on the back of Dimmick's neck.

Dimmick grunted, fell on top of Arthur, rolled off, swore, bounced back up, and had his stick at Vaz's throat almost at once—almost before Vaz's foot had touched the ground again.

"Eh? You in it with him? Hey? *Hup.*"

Dimmick's head snapped forward into Vaz's nose. A gush of fresh blood covered them both.

"Up, up! I'll gi' you a—"

Arthur stood, swaying.

He'd been good at boxing at school. His old lessons came back to him; he squared up to Dimmick and threw a punch, which Dimmick effortlessly evaded. Dimmick grunted and turned to shove Arthur so hard that his feet left the floor. Arthur fell through the open door and landed on his back, sliding across the dusty floorboards of the dark room until he hit his head on the leg of someone's abandoned desk.

When Arthur woke he was lying on his back in an empty Room. He didn't know how much time had passed. Not more than a minute or two, he supposed; but that might as well be an eternity. He was alone. Smoke hung thickly from the ceiling and it was agony to breathe. The corridor he'd come from was fire-lit. He got to his feet and staggered across the Room to the other door and out into yet another corridor, which was dark. He navigated with a hand on the wall, his eyes closed. He saw Josephine's face in the dark before him. She was still, she said nothing, and he could think of nothing to say to her, except for the obvious things.

When he opened his eyes again there was light. The corridor ahead of him was on fire. Beams had fallen to block it. On the other side of the fallen beams he saw a man approaching.

It was Mr Irving, the Master of Rooms 12, 13, *et cetera*. His suit in tatters, his face streaked with soot, his eyes red. Under his arm he carried a number of ledgers. Despite his sorry condition he stood straight and seemed remarkably calm.

"Hey there!" Arthur called. He waved, then started coughing. "Hey! Irving!"

Mr Irving approached the obstruction. He peered through the flames and smoke and nodded to Arthur as if making a note of his tardiness.

"Irving!" A croak, unintelligible. Feeble.

Mr Irving put the ledgers down on the floor, and held up a hand for Arthur to be silent. He seemed to be thinking.

It looked as if the corridor behind Irving was also blocked by fire. The man was trapped, but he showed no fear. Mr Irving's calm was in its own way as unnerving as Dimmick's fury.

"Irving!" Arthur wasn't sure what he meant to say. *Go back* was futile, *help me* was futile.

Mr Irving reached out to move the fallen beams from his path. Instantly his sleeves caught fire and the skin of his hands reddened and swelled and blackened and cracked. He didn't flinch or retreat. Arthur had never seen such extraordinary self-control. Irving leaned in, shoving at the timbers. His shirt went up. He didn't make a sound. Arthur reached out to help him but the heat drove him back. Irving pressed forward. His hair went up with a sudden flash. He stumbled. The beams were too heavy, jammed so that he couldn't move them. Arthur looked away as he fell to the ground.

Arthur turned and staggered back the way he'd come.

Josephine, my dear, he thought to himself, *I think I am going mad.*

I think I have already gone mad. As a matter of fact, I don't see how I can go much madder.

Set aside the mystery of Irving's superhuman calm. Where had he come from? From his office, perhaps, where some of the men imagined that he slept. Perhaps the fire had woken him. But his office was just outside Room 13. If that was Irving, and if Irving had perished in the vicinity of his office, then Arthur had run in a circle.

There was a dumbwaiter hatch on the wall. Arthur wiped his eyes again, and saw that it was labelled *D*. He tried to remember what the hatch outside Room 13 had been labelled.

Then he let out a great roar of joy, and he threw himself forward and flung up the hatch.

Behind it was a rope, and a chute into which he was just about able to squeeze once he'd abandoned his coat. His shirt tore at the shoulders, and his elbows scraped and bled as he squeezed his way with frantic violence up the chute. He supposed he must have resembled an overgrown chimney-sweep—a chimney-sweep who'd indulged in one of Alice's potions and now found himself swelling, stretching, his head fit to burst! He felt dizzy. He thought he might be stuck. Smoke tickled his feet. He kicked and bellowed.

The hatch at the top of the chute opened onto a dark corridor on the building's second floor.

The second floor of Gracewell's building had no rooms, no workers. So far as Arthur knew it held nothing except storage rooms. Perhaps the bell-ropes led there, too.

The corridor ran all the way to a window, which he broke. It opened onto fresh cold air and an expanse of flat rooftop.

At the end of the rooftop he lowered himself down then dropped to the ground. He stumbled away as far as he could before he came to a fence. He leaned on it, heaving and retching.

Behind him Gracewell's building was ablaze. Hellish flames reflected out over the river. A crowd had gathered in the firelight. He couldn't make out who they were. Workers who'd escaped the fire, he supposed, or neighbours who'd come out to watch the blaze.

He didn't join them. Dimmick might be among them, and he had no desire to see Dimmick again.

He breathed in freezing air and winced. His throat was in agony and he thought he might have a broken rib. His head was still ringing. His legs wobbled.

Vaz and Harriot and Malone had either escaped Dimmick and got out, or not. Nothing he could do about it now.

He wanted to go home. He wanted to see Josephine again.

He walked all the way back to Rugby Street, barefoot and bleeding through the cold night—dead beat and staggering and half-frozen. All the way home he thought of Josephine. He thought of the warm and boozy offices of *The Monthly Mammoth*. He thought of his uncle George, and his friends Waugh and Heath, and he even spared a few fond thoughts for his foster-parents, who were not such bad sorts after all; he would write to them, he thought. He thought of hot coffee, and curried rabbit, and bacon, and sausages, and oxtail, and kidneys, and fried fish, and hot pea soup, and ragout of lamb—and sometimes he thought of Dimmick, or Irving, or whatever had happened to Mr Vaz, and shuddered.

He got to Rugby Street shortly before dawn. In his exhaustion, it didn't strike him as at all odd that instead of his own home, he'd come to Mr Borel's shop, and Josephine's flat above it. Where else would he go? He banged on the door until Borel came out clutching his broom, and Josephine came downstairs to meet him.

She clapped a hand to her mouth in shock.

"Arthur! Where were you? What happened? What happened to your moustache—Arthur, what on earth happened to your *shoes*?"

He swept her up in his arms, lifting her bodily from the floor, and kissed her. She smelled extraordinarily sweet.

His knees started to wobble, and he put her down again. He saw that his hands had left streaks of blood and ash on her face and on her dress. He noticed that she was fully dressed, though it was the small hours of the morning, and briefly wondered why.

"Arthur—"

His legs seemed about to give out entirely.

"There was a fire," he said. "I handled myself tolerably well, I think. I shall tell you about it one day, but now I think I should go to bed."

He stumbled. She tried to catch him as he fell toward the floor, but missed.

*　*　*

He spent the better part of a week in bed. The bruise on his head swelled and he developed a fever. He had burns on his hands and his face and the back of shoulders, where falling cinders had burned through his shirt. His moustache was mostly gone. His friend Waugh, the medical student, came to help move him from Josephine's bed to his own, at the other end of the street, and gave a lot of advice about draining this and elevating that and compresses and not being such a bloody fool as to walk into a burning building in the first place. Then Waugh assured Josephine that if Arthur *had* walked into a burning building, it was no doubt for good reason, and that he had probably acquitted himself heroically. She thought perhaps Waugh was a little drunk. He kept winking at her.

She nursed him for a few days. He could hardly stand. She was no Lady of the Lamp but she managed to feed him soup and dab his burns with hot water and apply all the compresses and ointments that the housekeeping magazines recommended. She tried not to upset him with questions, or to wake him when he moaned in his sleep. He wouldn't say anything more about the fire than that it had been an awful accident, and that the worst part was that he thought his job was gone. She read him the newspapers. It really was remarkable, they agreed, how a clever newspaper writer could make *DUKE'S KILLER STILL NOT FOUND* into a new story every day for a week, or at least into something that seemed like a new story long enough that you were half-way through it before you noticed. She said nothing about Atwood or the events of his séance. At first she didn't want to frighten him; then after a while the secret grew too big to be released. She was afraid of what he might say, or do. She was afraid he wouldn't believe her; she was afraid he would.

Arthur's condition improved. On Wednesday afternoon he asked what day it was (the answer made him groan). By Thursday he was well enough to sit up and take her hand as she sat beside his bed reading him the newspapers. He said that she looked troubled. She said that she wasn't; then she said that of course she was, of course, of course. She fell against him, suddenly tearful, frightened but overjoyed to be alive. He winced—his ribs. She laughed. He was solid, sane, apparently indestructible. He laughed too, and kissed her. She kicked the newspaper away. Then the bristly remains of his moustache were tickling her neck, while she traced the bruises on his ribs with one hand under his nightshirt—the other hand fumbled with the sheets. The bed was too small for the both of them. He was suddenly on top of her. He still smelled faintly of smoke—not unpleasantly. They both breathed heavily, as if from the sheer joy of being alive and breathing. She could hear her heart beating like a metronome, its rhythm alternating with his. She closed her eyes and remembered Atwood's words: our souls, made of star-stuff, burning bright. Arthur tugged urgently at buttons. His fingers on her skin were electric. That spark might, Atwood had said, be mistaken for something carnal. Good, she thought; she was happy to be mistaken, then.

It was silly, she thought afterwards, but his bruises and burns had made it all seem rather—well, *chivalrous*, as if he were a wounded knight or a lost explorer, and that made it all rather less alarming than it might have been, and sweeter. She lay awake listening to him snore, studying the red scars on his back with a mixture of trepidation and excitement, as if they were a map of some unexplored and dangerous territory.

There would be consequences, she supposed. Well, so be it. She felt that nothing in the world could scare her; not after what she'd seen.

It was a fine, warm night, and the moon shone brightly through the window and across the floorboards. She wondered what Atwood and Jupiter were up to.

THE
FOURTH
DEGREE

{ *Analysis* }

Arthur was up on his feet again in no time. Sooner than Waugh had predicted. He should have bet money on it! Well, he had the best nurse in London, and the best medicine, and no time to waste.

After thinking on it for a day or two, he decided that the only decent thing was to tell Josephine everything. A clean sweep of all his secrets. He considered his oath to Mr Gracewell to have been cancelled—if not by fire, then by Dimmick's attempt to murder him. He told her about the numbers, the instructions, the ledgers, Vaz and Simon and Harriot and Malone and Dimmick. He told her about the headaches, and the nightmares, and the other unpleasant side-effects of the Work. He edited the confrontation with Dimmick a little, so as not to worry her unduly—and hadn't it just been a misunderstanding, after all? He left out the Irving Incident entirely, having half-convinced himself that it had been a hallucination brought on by the smoke.

She was appalled to hear that he intended to go in search of Mr Gracewell, to try to get his job back.

"Look, Josephine—a little while longer, that's all. That's all we need."

"I don't like Gracewell; I don't like Atwood. We don't need the money that badly."

"It won't be long; and it will make all the difference in the world."

"Arthur—what if . . . What if they pay so much because what they're doing is . . ." She seemed to be struggling for the right word. ". . . something *wrong* somehow?"

"Then I'll find out what it is, and go to the police. But first I must find out. I'll be careful, I promise."

She stared down at her feet and said nothing. She looked angry.

"But I don't even know where Gracewell's got to, that's the thing. What about Atwood? Atwood must know. But how do I get ahold of Atwood? Does he still come to meetings of the, what were they called, the Order V.V. whatever it was?"

"Oh no—he was far too fashionable to stay there long. Men of his sort get bored very quickly."

"Hah. Yes, that would be altogether too easy, wouldn't it? Where's the challenge in that? What rotten luck. Oh well."

M̲r Gracewell's enterprise lay in ruins. The fire had spread to some nearby buildings, too, and caused God only knows what expense and waste and loss of life.

The building's walls were mostly gone now, so that one could see the whole structure of the thing laid out as if in a diagram. The second storey had fallen in. White gulls perched on black timbers and dogs nosed among the ashes. Otherwise it was abandoned. There wasn't even enough left for vagrants to take shelter in. Arthur entered carefully, alert for the warning sounds of further collapse, and even more alert for the sounds of Dimmick. He heard only gulls taking flight, the wind from the river whistling through the building's bones, and the usual noises of ships.

In two places, he came across wrecked machines. These were large columns of steel and brass and wood that once had intricate parts, levers and cylinders, like typewriters or telegraphs, but were now ruined—melted and broken and fused. They lay like fallen asteroids. He thought they had been on the upper floor, and had dropped through when it collapsed. They were in the heart of the ruins, which was perhaps why no thief had scavenged them. Or perhaps they were just too heavy to move.

No bodies. No bones.

What little paper had survived the fire had been ruined by rain. Arthur found what he thought were the filing cabinets from Gracewell's office, but someone else had already emptied them. Dimmick, perhaps; creeping back at dawn, streaked with soot like a savage, to steal away the evidence under the very noses of the police . . .

Probably the police had already been and gone. No trail, no clues. He poked around until it started to rain, then went home.

He asked at Guy's Hospital and at St. Thomas's after a student by the name of Simon, nervous fellow, recently unwell. No luck.

He went out to Shadwell, in search of Mr Vaz. It was a fool's errand. He was lost at once. He asked after Vaz in half a dozen pubs. *Never heard of him*, the landlords said, or *I know a dozen by that name. Sailors come and go. But if you want to hire some men, there's a load of 'em out in the garden playing skittles . . .* In the bleak concrete garden around the back of the Sovereign, a dozen dark young men halted their game, froze stiff as their skittles, glaring at him. He made them uneasy. It was possible that they thought he was a policeman, or an agent of the shipping companies.

Mr Vaz had very probably saved his life, and for all Arthur knew the man was dead; dead, and London had already quite forgotten him.

He asked at the docks after the *Viceroy*, on which Vaz said he'd once sailed. It had departed London. Nobody could tell him about its crew.

T he Registrar of Companies had no record of a Gracewell & Co., or any other company of similar name.

H e went with Josephine to a Theosophical lecture in Hampstead. A very tall American woman by the name of Mrs Bloom talked for an hour. Perhaps it was interesting, but Arthur didn't listen to a word of it; he was busy scanning the packed hall for Mr Atwood. No luck. Afterwards he struck up conversations with some likely looking people and tried to steer them round to the subject of Atwood, but nobody seemed eager to gossip.

Dear Mr Sidgwick,

My name is Arthur Archibald Shaw. I am a writer, lately employed by The Monthly Mammoth, *and I have lately taken an interest in some of the goings-on among the spiritualist & occultist fraternities of London. I have read in the newspapers that your Society for*

Psychical Research has done sterling work exposing some of the fraud & humbug of that world. I write to you, in hope of your confidence, to inquire if, in the course of your invaluable investigations, the name of a "Mr Gracewell" has come to your attention. I hope you will forgive me if at present I can say no more.

Yours in confidence,
A. A. Shaw

Dear Mr Shaw,

The name "Gracewell" is not one with which Mr Sidgwick is familiar, nor is it found in the records of the S.P.R. If you believe that the S.P.R. should open an investigation into this person's activities, all I can suggest is that you offer a fuller account of them.

Yours sincerely,
Roger M. Morley,
Secretary to Mr Sidgwick,
President of the S.P.R.

P.S. *I regret the demise of* The Monthly Mammoth.

He missed the Work. That was the truth. He hardly understood what it was, yet it had been the biggest and most important thing that had ever entered his life—well, apart from Josephine, of course, he reminded himself. He performed the operations in his sleep; he muttered them to Josephine when she was trying to talk about something else. He couldn't help it. At dinner with his uncle George and George's wife, Agnes, when George tried to talk to him about work (there were a multitude of magazines that would employ him, George promised, a multitude!) he couldn't listen; instead, he traced the symbols of the Work with his soup-spoon. Out at dinner with his friends Waugh and Heath, Arthur fell silent in a corner and let the conversation drift away from him, until Waugh reached out and snapped his fingers in front of Arthur's eyes.

"Hypnotised, Shaw? Mesmerised? The sweet sleep of the poppy?"

"I was thinking, Waugh."

"Thinking, is it? Day-dreaming, more like it. Heath, you bored him into a coma, poor chap."

"I was thinking."

"You were dreaming of Josephine."

"I was thinking about work."

"Good God, why?"

He couldn't explain.

He searched for the name Gracewell in the hundred and one thick blue volumes of the index of the British Museum Reading Room. He found the author of a fifty-year-old medical treatise, the author of a positively ancient book of theology, and a few other blind alleys. He also found several references to a Doctor Norman Gracewell, Lecturer in Mathematics, Kings College.

This Dr Gracewell had published a note in the *Proceedings of the Royal Astronomical Society* in 1873. Some predictions regarding the 1874 Transit of Venus, which had turned out to be wrong, if Arthur remembered correctly. After that the same man had published a series of very complicated-looking papers on life insurance, and, in 1883, a monograph, *General Theory of an Analytical Engine*. It was dedicated to the Duke of Sussex and to the Countess of Lovelace.

> In the past half-century a handful of ingenious engineers have, following the path set out by Mr Charles Babbage, created working models of a simple *difference engine*, for the calculation of logarithmic tables. Mr Babbage's far greater achievement, the general-purpose *analytical engine*, remains merely theoretical. I am not alone in considering this one of the few great failures of British science. I hope that this humble volume may bring us some small measure closer to achieving its creation, in an economical and practicable fashion. I propose three methods by which the operations of the engine might be simplified. First . . .

An *analytical engine*. Was that what Gracewell's Engine was supposed to be?

He read on, but the rest of the volume was incomprehensible. Equations ran across the pages, and diagrams of circular, looping, and utterly obscure processes.

Gracewell's last publication, according to the catalogue of the Reading Room, was a short volume dated 1883. It was entitled *The Final Analysis of the Method of Analysis*. It was dedicated to *Kether*, and *Yesod*, and *Yaldabaoth*. It began:

Last winter I was contacted by an Intelligence from outside the Cosmic Sphere in which we conduct our ordinary lives. The first of several such contacts occurred while I was walking on Blackheath—beside a lamp-post, & in the company of a dog. I have since determined to call the Intelligence in question *Yaldabaoth*—though it gave me no name for Itself, having no need for names in Its Sphere of existence—which is the Sphere (it encloses our own, as I will explain) that lies beneath ours in the Cosmic Ordering. We know it in the sky as the Red Planet. In conversation with this and other Intelligences from the Red Planet I learned the futility & triviality of all our modes of thought & mathematical analysis. Subsequently I was dismissed from my post, depriving the young scholars of Kings of the benefit of my discoveries—& I have learned to keep these discoveries to myself. In this final volume (published at my own expense) I shall confine myself to a demonstration that mathematics as it has hitherto been understood and as it is practiced by the faculty of Kings College is nothing but a snare & a delusion. There are one hundred & twenty-two proofs of this undeniable fact.

Arthur's heart sank at the prospect of reading 122 proofs of anything. Before the Reading Room closed that evening, he read ten proofs, all of which were gibberish. The man had gone mad. Yet someone had believed in him enough to back whatever it was he'd built in Deptford.

On the way out of the Reading Room, Arthur noticed an advertisement pinned up by the door promising a free public lecture, not far away, on the methods and the latest discoveries of Mr Pickering's Arequipa Observatory in the Andes. Arthur had nothing better to do with his evening, and the lecture was interesting enough, as it turned out, though quite technical, and often interrupted by questions from the audience about canals and life on the red planet and so on. When the lecture was done, Arthur remained in his seat for a little while, thinking about his day, so by the time he got up to leave, he nearly missed catching a glimpse of Norman Gracewell filing out from the lecture-hall, opening his umbrella as he stepped out into the dark.

Arthur followed. He hung back, resisting the urge to run, to tap Gracewell on the shoulder. He wasn't quite sure what to say. He thought about perhaps striking up a conversation about astronomy.

Gracewell moved faster than his heavy-footed trudge would suggest. He was heading north-east, towards St. Pancras.

Quite suddenly, Gracewell stopped, searched his pockets, then turned and stepped into a railway ticket-office.

Arthur ran up to the ticket-office, fumbling for the money to pay the clerk. The earth beneath him rumbled as he ran downstairs into the Underground. Across a dim and cavernous platform thick with steam and the stink of coal he glimpsed the windows of the train whipping past, a string of lights disappearing one by one into the dark of the tunnel, taking Mr Gracewell with them. As the last window passed, he thought he saw a fellow he recognised from Room 12—a big, silent, florid-faced German fellow; he didn't remember his name. Reading a newspaper. Quite possibly on Gracewell's trail too, and ahead of Arthur—of course, he wouldn't be the only one, would he?

All through the next morning Arthur waited outside the station. In the afternoon, when Gracewell emerged, Arthur folded up his newspaper and followed him. He watched Gracewell purchase a newspaper of his own, then proceed east into a small brick building near St. Pancras Station.

It appeared to be an office. A plaque beside the door read THE EUROPA COMPANY.

Arthur waited at the corner of the street. He scratched absent-mindedly at his newly clean-shaven face. He bought some peanuts.

Gracewell emerged, putting out his hand to test for rain—there was only a slight dampness in the air. Then he stepped out into the street and walked briskly west. He stopped in at a grocer's shop on the Euston Road, and came out carrying a parcel. He entered a tobacco-shop on the Marylebone Road. When he exited, fiddling with his pipe, two men stepped out of a waiting cab, grabbed him by his arms, put a hand over his mouth, and dragged him towards the cab's open door.

Arthur nearly choked on a peanut.

Then he shouted "Hello!" and charged in.

It was a busy London street, on a sunny mid-afternoon. It simply didn't occur to him to be afraid.

He shouted again, and hit one of Gracewell's assailants in the jaw. It hurt like blazes, but the bugger recoiled.

Arthur shook his hand, thinking that it was rather a pleasure to hit someone, after the last two months of frustration and headaches.

Arthur took a good look at them both. They were pale; almost as white as paper. Arthur thought he'd hit them hard, but not hard enough to account for that sickly pallor. What's more, he could swear that their eyes were inky-black under the shadow of their hat-brims. One of them wiped black blood from his nose with his sleeve.

They spread out, so that Arthur couldn't quite keep his eye on both of them at once.

There was a third one up on the driver's seat of the cab, watching the proceedings.

Arthur stepped back. Gracewell had dropped his pipe when they grabbed him, and Arthur crunched it underfoot. The two pale men now flanked him, one on either side. Now it occurred to him to be afraid. He tried not to show it.

Gracewell leaned against the wall, fumbling in his pockets, as if for a weapon.

Arthur called out for help, and some passers-by came running up.

"You," said the man on top of the cab, pointing at Arthur, "will die far from home."

The other two jumped into the cab, and the driver whipped the horse into motion.

Someone put a hand on Arthur's shoulder and asked him what all that was about.

He said, "I don't know."

Gracewell whistled up a cab. He climbed half-way into it, then turned back to Arthur. "Come on, then, if you're coming."

Chapter Eleven

"Mr Gracewell, I—"

"Shaw, isn't it? You were one of—ah, that's right, one of Mr Irving's, in Room Twelve."

"Thirteen."

"Thirteen, then. Well, I can't remember everything. Now listen—what do you want? Were you following me?"

"Yes. I was hoping to ask you about the Engine."

Gracewell looked somewhat reassured. "Hah," he said. "You want work? It'll be months before we can rebuild. Months. All in disarray."

"It was a sort of difference engine, wasn't it?"

The cab rattled down a street of red-brick houses, at the end of which a great traffic light stood idle and unlit.

"Yes," Gracewell conceded. "More or less. More precisely, no. But yes."

"With men instead of mechanical parts."

"Yes." Gracewell sighed. "More precisely *in addition to.*"

He pulled out a handkerchief and dabbed at a cut on his lip. He gave Arthur a long look, and seemed to reach a decision. "Ahem. Hah. Now, a *difference engine* is a toy, Shaw—a mere adding machine. More precisely, it operates by repeated addition. Crank the handle, and it adds; that's all it does. Thus it can generate tables. Nothing you or I couldn't do, though less prone to distraction and error. Now! An *analytical engine* is a more interesting notion. A hundred variables, a thousand variables—a thinking machine of universal purpose, subject to instruction, capable of *all* of the functions of mathematics and logic. The equal in reasoning to a man. His superior for precision, reliability, and complexity of calculation. Moreover, men are expensive, unreliable, and nosy." He glared at Arthur, then dabbed fresh blood from his lip. "Ow. I think I've a tooth loose."

"Hmm," Arthur agreed, gently rubbing his swollen knuckles.

"Still, though man is inferior in some respects, there's more to life than mathematics, more to the mind than logic. No merely mechanical engine can ever perform all the functions of which a man is capable."

The driver shouted at someone in traffic.

"An engine," Gracewell said, "of which each critical variable is a man, who can therefore perform not only simple operations of addition and multiplication and division, but can also apply to his task the vital forces. The whole much greater than the sum of its parts, capable of resolving psychic operations too vast for one mind."

He paused dramatically.

"Babbage proposed a thinking machine. What I've made is a *perceiving machine.*"

"It's a—some sort of an occult engine, then."

"A Vital Engine, if you must give it a name. This is science, Mr Shaw, the modern science. You look sceptical."

"And the headaches and—"

"Never enough men, that was the problem. Too many faltered. The Work made unusual demands on the spirit. Uncharted territory, calculating the revolutions of the spheres. It called for intuition, perception, what Atwood's lot call *clairvoyance*. So we recruited fortune-tellers, mediums, poets, that sort of person. At first, at least. When we ran out we found insurance clerks worked adequately. Atwood says the Sight can't be taught, but I believe that you can drum anything into a man's head if he's hungry enough."

"It was Mr Atwood who recommended me to you."

"Oh yes. I recall. Oh Hell!"

"Excuse me?"

"Loose. The tooth. No question."

They listened in silence to the noise of traffic for a while. "Why were we all barefoot?"

"Good God, Shaw, is that what you hunted me down to ask?"

"No. But I always wondered."

"Because," Gracewell sighed, "the variables were barefoot on one of the earliest successful tests. Coincidence? Probably. One never knows what might make the difference. It's so delicate, and we're under such time pressure. This is an entirely new science, Shaw."

"But what is it *for*?"

"I'm not at liberty to say. Suffice to say that it is of tremendous importance."

"May I guess? I've had a great deal of time to think, since the fire."

"I hardly see how I can stop you from guessing, Mr Shaw."

"Well, then—first, whatever you were doing, someone was paying for
it, and paying a quite extraordinary amount of money. I don't doubt that
whoever invested those sums expected a profit. Second, it involved numbers. Third, you maintained secrecy. Fourth, you have rivals who will
stop at nothing to steal or stop your work. Fifth, you tell me that the work
had to do with telepathy and clairvoyance—I don't know that I believe
that, but I don't know that I don't, and at the very least I believe you believe it. Sixth, it made nothing physical. It seems to me that your work
must have something to do with money itself—with speculation. What if
you had built, or believed you had built, an engine that could predict and
calculate risks—let's say, the weather; storms off the Cape of Good Hope,
perhaps, or bad harvests in the Azores. Warehouse fires in Bradford.
What'll the Bank of England do next, before the bankers themselves
know. Now, that would make a fine profit, and would have to be kept quite
secret—you could hardly make a profit on predictions if everyone knew of
them. And suppose your backers are a consortium of financiers: those
outside the circle would have reason to fear and oppose them. Am I on
the right track?"

"Hmm," Gracewell said. "I can see why you throve in journalism."

They were stuck in traffic. There was new road being laid down somewhere; the smell of hot tarmacadam was overpowering.

"Blackfriars," Gracewell shouted.

Arthur said, "What's in Blackfriars?"

"Nothing. But by the time we've been there and back those men
should be long gone."

"Who were those men?"

"I don't know. Pale fellows, weren't they? Bad habits, I expect."

A flick of the whip, and the cab was off again. Gracewell pulled a
packet of tobacco from his pocket.

"You dropped your pipe," Arthur said. "I'm afraid I stepped on it."

"Oh, hell. Well, I've answered your questions, as far as I intend to.
What else do you want from me, Mr Shaw?"

"I saved you from those men, Mr Gracewell—I think you owe me more answers."

"I assure you, I was quite capable of defending myself." Gracewell put the tobacco back into his pocket, took out his watch, and started to wind it. "But that's not to say we don't need man-power. We're going to rebuild it, of course. The Engine."

"We? You, and Atwood, and the Europa Company?"

"Hmm? Oh. You saw that, did you? Where else have you been poking around, I wonder? Anyway, we shall rebuild. Again. I suppose you never saw the first Engine. We built it near the West India Docks. Underground, for the most part. For safety, we thought! Bloody thing flooded, of course. In the storm. Next time, who knows what they might do? Bomb us, perhaps, like a lot of bloody whatchamacallems, nihilists. Hmmph. Anyway. So you've been reading about analytical engines, have you?"

"Yes. I read your monograph."

"Oh yes?"

"I read about your, ah, your vision of the Intelligences from M—"

Gracewell clacked the watch shut, and his mouth went tight. "That was a long time ago. I suffered at the time from exhaustion. I experienced a nervous collapse."

"But—"

"My son died in '84. He was a soldier. Africa. My wife, soon after. It upset me, Mr Shaw. I suffered visions."

Gracewell leaned forward and called directions to the driver. It was clear that he would say no more on that subject.

Arthur asked him if he knew who among the men of Room 13 had survived the fire.

"Don't know. Scattered all over London. Months of work wasted."

"Mr Vaz?"

"Who?"

"Dimmick?"

"Unwell. Sulking. Between you and me, I think he went a bit mad there, towards the end."

"He wasn't the only one, was he? I saw him drag men out of the rooms, screaming. *Unusual demands on the spirit,* you said. Why? What happened to them? What became of—"

"Listen, Shaw. They were well paid for the job and I owe no apology. Ours is a great enterprise and some must suffer for it. That's life, isn't it? Some must fall so that others may rise. Now: on that subject. Perhaps I can use you, Shaw. Not in the rooms. A higher calling."

The cab had stopped in traffic. The driver was making small talk about the weather with the driver of a donkey-cart.

"Do you box, Shaw?"

"At school."

"I thought so. Well, your education was not wasted."

He directed the driver to turn back towards St. Pancras.

"I need help, Shaw, and you, you have ambition. Now take this." He dropped the watch and chain into Arthur's hand.

"Mr Gracewell—"

"Payment for your assistance back there. I won't be indebted, you hear? Open it in the event that you run afoul of those thugs again; it will protect you. Now this squares us, do you understand? Open the watch in the event of danger. Not otherwise. Now, you're looking for work."

"For answers, Mr Gracewell."

Gracewell took an envelope out of his pocket. "I think you might work for nothing, if only I promised to pay you in secrets; isn't that right, Mr Shaw?

"Certainly not." He was rather afraid it might be.

"Hah. But, as it happens, money is nothing, and secrets are far more dear. I'll pay you—I don't know, let's say twenty pounds—to take this envelope to St. John's Wood."

He held out the envelope until Arthur took it from him.

Twenty pounds to take an envelope to St. John's Wood, and as if it were nothing! That was a kind of magic, as impressive to Arthur in its way as if Mr Gracewell had summoned up an imp, or turned water into wine.

The cab deposited them both outside St. Pancras. Gracewell entered the station.

Arthur set off walking towards St. John's Wood, through a bright spring afternoon. He went slowly, keeping an eye out. He watched for assailants who might jump from behind lamp-posts or out of alleyways, or pickpockets in the crowds and noise. He kept clear of the road, for fear that some thug in a cab might come rushing past, hand outstretched to snatch the precious envelope from him.

It was an ordinary white envelope, sealed. It was marked with an address on Charles Lane, and the word PRIVATE. Both were written in a firm square hand that resembled the way Gracewell wrote his instructions. Inside was a folded letter. Arthur couldn't read what was written on it, though he stopped and held it up to the light.

The watch was also quite ordinary. It was made of silver, rather tarnished, rather scuffed. On the back were the letters *N.G.* and the name of the manufacturer. Otherwise it was plain and smooth. The chain was also silver, and showed signs of mending. Arthur couldn't see the face without opening it, which Gracewell had ordered him not to do. He considered opening it anyway, to prove to himself that he didn't take Gracewell's absurd order seriously.

The address belonged to a little red-brick house, with a brass letter-box, and flower-pots in the window.

Arthur put the envelope half-way in through the box, then changed his mind. For twenty pounds, one should knock.

A tall grey-haired man answered, took the letter, tore it open, scowled, and said, "Gracewell. Tell him yes. Damn it, tell him yes." Then he closed the door.

Arthur took the bus back to St. Pancras. He walked to the offices of the Europa Company and rang the bell. A young clerk—not Dimmick, thank God!—opened the door, paid Arthur his twenty pounds, and told him that Mr Gracewell said to come back at noon tomorrow.

O ver the following week Arthur carried letters to Aldwych, Bethnal Green, Bromley, Camden Town, Kilburn, Poplar, and Shoreditch (twice). Sometimes he took letters back. Undemanding work. Why Gracewell couldn't simply use the post-office like anyone else, Arthur didn't know. He supposed there was a great deal Gracewell wanted to keep secret from his rivals. Clearly he was conveying offers and counter-offers for the work of reconstructing the Engine—brick and lumber, iron and copper, labour and machines, electricity and licenses and contracts. Once the thing was running again there would no doubt be opportunity for advancement, for a man who'd earned Gracewell's confidence. There would no doubt be answers.

He visited carpenters, masons, and foremen at the docks, and law-yers at Lincoln's Inn. Each saw only a part of the operation; but Arthur began to see glimpses of the whole.

Josephine still didn't like the work. He supposed she was right. He didn't quite believe Gracewell's vague talk about *unusual demands on the spirit*, and *clairvoyance*, and so on, but there was unquestionably something sinister about the whole business. It was quite possible that something terrible had happened to poor Mr Vaz. He considered going to the police; but not yet, not until he knew what it was all about. He'd quit, he promised Josephine; soon, but not yet.

Chapter Twelve

Josephine sat at her desk, staring at a white page, quite unable to bring herself to type a word of Mr Albert Potter's alchemical monograph. It was absurd, pure nonsense. It made her want to scream. It was also two weeks overdue, but she could think of very little else these days except for Gracewell, and Atwood, and whatever danger Arthur was getting himself into; and above all the stars, the heavens, the revolutions of the spheres, and that *manifestation*. Dreadfully pagan and outlandish things to think, shortly after lunch on a Wednesday, sitting in a basement in Bloomsbury in front of a new-model Remington Standard Typewriter with a sticky *R*! She had to tell Arthur. She couldn't keep it all to herself very much longer, or she'd burst. Besides, he had to understand the danger he was in.

He said he was only taking messages, a sort of overpaid postman, an insignificant cog in Gracewell's new Engine. And perhaps that was true, but the nature of that engine was unearthly, sinister, unnatural. But how could she tell him? Blurt out, while they walked in the park, *Did I mention that Lord Atwood and I—who, by the way, says hello—met a moon-man the other night? Bagged him, in fact, like a pheasant* . . . Perhaps she could mention the moon a lot in conversation, or mention the weather on Venus at dinner, and test his reaction. She was afraid he'd think she was mad, the way her mother had gone mad. And suppose he believed her; would he understand how strange and frightening the whole thing had been? Or would he go knocking on Atwood's door, eager to see it for himself?

How *could* she tell him; but how could she not?

Quite a lot of time seemed to have passed while she sat and thought, and she had typed nothing but *Atwood* and then a little later the words *moon-man*.

She sighed, and stretched, then yelped in surprise. There was a man at the window, ash-pale face pressed against the glass. Two inky black eyes peered out from under a black bowler hat.

She'd seen that face before, she realised—or one very much like it—reflected in the mirror at Mrs Sedgley's house a few months ago, spying on Atwood.

She jumped up from her chair, grabbed the key from the hook by her desk, and darted for the door. She was too late; the man at the window had a companion, who opened the door in her face, pushed inside past her, and sat down in her chair, drumming grubby fingers on Mr Potter's manuscript.

The one who'd been waiting at the window ambled up and leaned in the doorway, hands in the pockets of a long grey coat.

Her heart pounded. She squeezed the key in her hand very tightly, finding it gave her a certain comfort.

They said nothing at all.

"There's a shop upstairs," she said, "And people in the street. If I scream, someone will call for the police."

The man in her chair nodded, acknowledging her point.

"Atwood," he said. His voice was very low and flat.

She waited.

"Yes," she said. "I am acquainted with him."

"Atwood," said the man in the chair, "is dangerous."

He poked aimlessly at the typewriter's keys. Then he turned his attention back to Potter's manuscript. Josephine supposed he was waiting for her to say something.

Outside, an omnibus went by.

She wasn't sure what to make of them. They reminded her in an odd way of policemen. They were both rather badly dressed, and there was something strange about their movements and their expressions, as if they were not quite in control of themselves, but were sleep-walking. Their eyes—glistening black—were the only memorable things in their faces, which were otherwise pale, unshaven, indistinct, and tired.

Not so long ago she would have assumed that they were an unusual sort of albino, or wearing odd glasses, or something of the sort. Having seen what she'd seen in Atwood's library, she wasn't even sure they were men. She was quite willing to believe that they were ghosts, or spirits, or who knew what. Perhaps they were the consequences of Atwood's ritual, of poking one's nose in places where it didn't belong, some sort of frightful supernatural nemesis. Or perhaps they had something to do with Arthur's work.

Arthur's employer had dispatched him out of London that morning, to Gravesend, on some mysterious errand. He wasn't expected back until the day after tomorrow, so there was no possibility that anyone might interrupt, unless one of the Borels happened to come downstairs for some reason. She hoped they wouldn't. Menacing though they were, these odd intruders seemed to show no inclination to lay hands on her; but who knew what they might do if they were startled?

The one in the chair looked up from Potter's manuscript, as if he'd just remembered that she was there, and said, "You won't marry him."

"I beg your pardon?"

He smiled as if he'd just tasted something delicious.

"What do you *want*?"

Neither of them answered that. She supposed that was part of their method, part of their way of being menacing.

Suddenly the one behind her—the one in the doorway—grunted in surprise. The one in the chair stood, reaching into his pocket, as if for a weapon.

She turned to see the woman who called herself Jupiter coming down the stairs—boots first, and then the rest of her, all in purple and black: tall, narrow-waisted, high-shouldered dark purple, her black-and-grey hair pinned up. An imposing figure.

The man in the doorway glared at Jupiter but stepped aside to let her enter. She acknowledged him with a contemptuous glance.

"I know what you are," she said. "I know who you belong to. Tell your employer there will be consequences if he continues to menace my colleagues.

There was a long silence, in which it seemed that no one in the room but Josephine was breathing. Then the two men walked out without another word. The bell rang as the door closed, leaving Josephine alone in the room with Jupiter.

She didn't feel a great deal safer.

"Walk with me," Jupiter said.

* * *

It was a sunny day, and street-traders were out in force, forming fragrant barricades of soup-stalls and cake-stalls. Scholars and poets and assorted ne'er-do-wells wandered back and forth between the Museum and their attic rooms, not looking where they were going. A procession of nurses advanced behind black perambulators, huge and implacable as Juggernaut.

"Those men were employees of one of our company's rivals," Jupiter said. "Any great enterprise has its enemies, of course. The jealousy of little men. I expect they meant to unnerve you."

"They did."

"Well—that's to be expected."

"They didn't seem to unnerve *you*."

"Their master might; not them."

"Their master?"

"If I told you, you would think it mere slander."

No trader ever accosted Jupiter. No one got in her way. The perambulators and rude nursemaids circled around her. This seemed to happen without any particular effort on her part.

"What can I call you, ma'am? I can't call you—"

"I believe in anonymity. No one comes to *my* house uninvited, you can be certain of that."

"But—"

"You may call me Moina."

"Thank you. Moina, then. Moina—will those men come again?"

"Perhaps not. I expect they imagine they've made their point. Did they give you dire warnings of what would happen if you ever spoke to us again?"

"I suppose so. They were—circuitous."

Now that she was less afraid, she was starting to be very angry. "What *will* they do if I speak to you? What will they do now that you've sent them away?"

"Perhaps nothing. Their quarrel is with me and with Atwood."

"Perhaps?"

Jupiter shrugged.

"How did you know they were—they were in my office?"

"I didn't. Good fortune. A good omen, don't you think? I came to speak to you. The young man you met at our last meeting—the one who affected the turban—has decided not to return. He wrote Atwood a very long letter, complaining of the shock he'd had, and departed for Switzerland to calm his nerves. That leaves us at eight. Nine is greatly to be preferred. Are *you* our ninth, Miss Bradman?"

"I don't know. I've had rather a shock too."

"You saw what you saw. You know that our work is real, and important."

"I don't know what I saw."

"Of course you do! You have a rare talent. Atwood showed me your poetry."

"Oh. He did?"

"I don't intend to flatter you. What interests us is that your report of the heavens resembles, in certain respects, our own observations. In dreams, or in religious ecstasies, one may stumble into the very states of perception that we are attempting to observe and control through a process of rigorous experimentation. We need such talents."

"Who are you, Moina?"

"I do *not* like to waste my time. Will you be our ninth, or not?"

Josephine found that she rather liked the woman's manner. She was rude, but she was frank. It was preferable, at least, to Atwood's coy secretiveness.

If she said no, what would Jupiter do? She could hardly kidnap her and force her to take part in their rituals. If she said no, she need not fear things from the stars, or menacing black-eyed men at the window, or mirrors.

And Arthur—she shuddered at the thought of the danger Arthur might be in, all unknowing.

"What happened to the—the manifestation?"

"Manifestation?"

"You know what I mean, Moina."

"It's safely locked away."

"Is it hurt? May I see it again?"

Moina walked in silence for a while.

"Once upon a time," she said, "when I was as young as you are now, I had a notion that I might make a career for myself in astronomy. My family, you may imagine, disapproved quite strongly—and yet I applied myself diligently to the study of mathematics, and to the mastery of Kirchhoff's theorem and Kepler's laws and Herschel's hypotheses. I did indeed succeed, through certain work in mathematics, in attracting the patronage of some learned long-bearded astronomers. Perhaps I should have been grateful. But I was not. I was impatient. I am a terribly impatient person, Josephine, as perhaps you can see. I had no time for fiddling about with telescopes, or waiting twenty years for a comet to pass, or growing old. I still do not. I believe that there is a better way to seize the heavens, that a revolution in thought is possible—indeed, inevitable."

"You and Lord Atwood—"

"The very first time you joined us, we achieved something we had never achieved before—never dreamed of. In forty-four experiments, our travel has been merely psychic; a matter of the perceptions. That night we worked something *quite* different. A *conjuration*. I know no better word for it. A *tulpa*, Atwood calls it . . ."

Moina stopped and looked into Josephine's eyes, as if she were searching for something behind them. "Was our circle incomplete, Miss Bradman, until we found you?"

"I simply don't remember, Moina. I don't remember what happened that night before we woke, to see that, that extraordinary thing—"

Moina sighed. "I *cannot* have will-you or won't-you, I *cannot* have nerves and weeping and girlishness. We meet tomorrow night. The hour cannot be postponed. You see that our enemies nip our heels. Will you join us?"

"Why are you here, and not Atwood, Moina?"

"He dithers. He has a soft spot for you, Miss Bradman."

"Then the experiment is dangerous."

"Of course. What worthwhile enterprise isn't?"

Josephine didn't know quite what to say to that.

It was a pleasant afternoon, the streets were crowded, the shops bright and full of inviting and curious things. They paused to admire the window of a glass-maker's shop. Glass soldiers mustered beneath electric-light; a profusion of brightly-coloured bubbles and stems and spheres of glass hung overhead.

A boy ran up and tried to hand Josephine an advertisement for a photographer's studio. Jupiter tweaked his ear and sent him running.

"Does Mr Gracewell do what you ask him, Moina?"

"He's Atwood's creature. But I have influence."

"Then these are my terms. I will join you; God help me. But only for tomorrow night. And afterwards, in return, Mr Gracewell will let Arthur go—with a fair sum for his trouble; I have a figure in mind—and then you and Gracewell and Atwood and all the rest of you will never trouble either of us again."

Chapter Thirteen

The boat to Gravesend bobbed and lurched in busy Thames traffic, belching smoke and soot. On the bench beside Arthur, two old women ate an endless succession of noxious sandwiches from a hamper; while on the other side a youngish father argued with his three sons, who were not looking forward to their holiday by the sea and intended, by God, that everyone should know all the reasons why not. In other words, all the usual irritations of travel. But the fact was that, after a couple of months as a variable in Gracewell's Engine, Arthur found that he had a wonderful immunity to everyday irritations. The city slid by under a bright summer sky, church spires gleaming. The boat emptied and filled again. It passed into the cool shadow of a great industrial steamer, a towering metal behemoth making its way east. Arthur half-dozed, and woke at Gravesend.

He stopped in at St. Andrew's Hotel on the High Street, and arranged for a room for the night. After all that water he was in no mood for fish, which was the hotel's specialty, but they made him a very decent lunch of chops and stewed apples. Then, with his stomach settled and some strength in him, he set off on the next stage of his mission, which was rather a hike out into the country. A policeman at the pier gave him directions.

He wore his suit of good walking clothes. He set a brisk pace; away from the river and out of the wetlands, past little villages and mossy graveyards. Country lanes and hedgerows. A summer's day and butterflies. Up and over a stile, and across a wheat-field. A muddy path through the woods. Stopping at a farmhouse for directions. All those other touches of homeliness and civilization, without which (in Arthur's opinion) no landscape could be said to be truly beautiful. Crows. Sheep. Gnats. Sunburn. Getting lost and stepping in who-knows-what. *Et cetera*.

✳   ✳   ✳

In the late afternoon he came to a house half-way up the side of Rudder Hill, on the outskirts of a village so tiny and so unkempt that it seemed almost accidental. Looking back along the path, he could see for miles through clear skies, all the way to the river and the smoke and the tiny toy houses of London.

The house was made of grey stone, grown over with ivy and moss; the roof was thatched and uneven. Ramshackle wooden sheds sprouted from it. In the garden a rusty red pump stood in the tall grass, garlanded with weeds and violet flowers.

He knocked on the door, to which a sprig of something had been nailed.

The man who opened the door was something of a giant. He was half a head taller than Arthur, who was by no means small; the outstretched arm that held the door was muscular, and also spattered with black mud. He wore wading boots and an apron. He had a square face, under a head of black hair as flat as a cap. His eyes, under heavy brows, were strikingly dark, and oddly inexpressive. He said nothing.

Behind him a voice called out, "Who?"

Arthur peered around the man in the door and into the gloom of the cottage. It was cluttered beyond belief. It resembled a tool-shed.

The big man stepped aside. Behind him stood a witch.

That was Arthur's first thought: *witch*. She was ancient, and tiny, and bent; she wore shabby black, and her hair was white and wild. She was sharp-nosed, sharp-eyed, yellow-toothed. She had the look of something left behind from a bygone century.

Arthur said, "Mrs Archer?"

She wrinkled her nose. "Who's asking?"

"I have a message from Mr Gracewell, for Mrs Archer, on Rudder Hill."

Arthur offered her Gracewell's envelope—a thick packet of papers, which had been folded uncomfortably inside his coat.

Mrs Archer nodded. The big man took the packet, tore it open, and handed the papers inside to her. They were covered in dots and dashes and other symbols of Gracewell's Engine. Arthur didn't know what exactly they meant.

"Hmm-hmm," she said. A bent finger traced the lines. "Hmm-hmm. Where's Dimmick?"

"Dimmick?"

"Dimmick. You know. Your master's usual dogsbody."

Arthur didn't like *dogsbody*.

"Mr Dimmick's unwell. My name's Shaw."

"Ha! Dimmick's not the type to be unwell, like a fainting maiden! Tell me, where's he gone to? What's he about? What's he up to?"

"There was a fire, Mrs Archer—he was injured in it. I'm here in his place, I suppose."

"I know. I know about the fire! Not that your master had the decency to tell us. Not even a letter or a pigeon. A fire that stopped Mr Dimmick— there's a thing! Well, off with you. Go on."

"Now, wait," Arthur said, putting his foot in the door. "They said I was to wait for your answer to whatever that is."

The big fellow scowled, and closed the door regardless. It seemed to Arthur that he would've quite happily broken Arthur's foot clean off if he hadn't moved it.

A moment later the door opened again.

"Sit," Mrs Archer said. "Over there by the fire. Have some tea."

An iron kettle hung over a smouldering fire. Arthur sat on a rickety stool beside it, and the big fellow offered him a cup of tea, which tasted of the river.

The big fellow stared at Arthur, but rebuffed every attempt at conversation. After a while Arthur began to wonder if he was in fact staring, or if his eyes were merely open, while his attention was elsewhere, or nowhere at all. There was something very odd about the man, something that went beyond mere rudeness. Arthur wondered if he was half-blind, or in some way not quite right in the head.

The room smelled of tea, and straw, and dirt, and old age; and beneath that something less wholesome—rat, perhaps, something bitter and pungent. The corners were cluttered with tools, rustic brass nonsense, and dead rabbits. Tied-together twigs hung by string from the ceiling. A rat crawled out from behind a heap of rubbish, and nosed around the edge of the fire. Nobody but Arthur seemed to mind.

Archer sat at a table by the window and read Gracewell's papers, trac-

ing the lines of dashes and dots with her gnarled finger. She made notations of her own in a leather-bound journal.

"He thinks I'm old-fashioned," she said.

"Hmm?" Arthur had been drowsing a little in the heat.

"Your master. Thinks I'm old-fashioned. Won't come out here himself.
Scared, I reckon. How's he going to do all the things he wants to do if he's
scared of a little moonlight?"

"I don't know about that. What is it you do for Mr Gracewell, madam?"

She gave him a long flat look. "We all do our part," she said. Then she
went back to her work.

Arthur felt ready to hit the next person who presented him with a
mystery, or uttered a Delphic word in his presence.

The big fellow was still scowling.

"Your friend and I don't seem to hit it off very well, Mrs Archer."

"That's my son," she said. "My big beautiful boy."

The big fellow continued to scowl.

Evening crept up on them. The window darkened, and insects buzzed
and chirped outside. Archer didn't believe in dinner, it seemed. She looked
like she might live on tea, but Arthur didn't see how the big fellow managed it.

Arthur closed his eyes and summoned in his mind the menu of the
St. Andrew's Hotel.

"Put your feet up, why don't you, while I work!"

He opened his eyes.

He'd been asleep for a moment. Not long.

"Those are Mr Gracewell's calculations," he said.

"Yes."

"From his Engine. Or plans—plans for the next Engine."

"I reckon. Could be."

"What in the world could you know about analytical engines, Mrs
Archer?"

If she was determined to be rude, Arthur didn't see why he shouldn't
respond in kind.

"Nothing," she said. "Not one thing. Not a jot or a tittle. Not a speck.
But I know the stars."

She smiled.

She stood. "Come on, then."

"What? Where?"

"Up." She pointed out the window. "Up Rudder Hill." She pronounced it *rodor*.

She handed Arthur Gracewell's pages of calculations, now rather dirty and crumpled, and her own papers, which were covered in numbers and geometry. She went to a corner of the room and bent over. Rummaging in the clutter, she produced a large and expensive-looking telescope, an equally fine sextant, something very old-fashioned and etched with symbols—an astrolabe, perhaps—and some other implements Arthur couldn't begin to name . . . the sort of things you might imagine Copernicus hunching over, or Magellan navigating by, or Stanley carrying down the Nile.

"Good God! What is all this, Mrs Archer? Do you have a Gatling gun, too?"

"Ha!" She began to shove the implements into sacks, from which long brass legs and odd sharp points stuck out. In amongst the brass and copper there were things made of sticks and twigs and bone. "Come on, then."

"What's up the hill?"

"Your job is to carry," she said, "and keep an eye out."

"What about him?" Arthur said, nodding sideways at the big fellow.

"He keeps the house. That's his job. You come with me."

She took down her cape and walking-stick from a hook by the door. "Quick now."

Outside it was a summer night, clear and starry and windless. Archer walked around to the back of her house, where a gate in a tumbledown fence opened onto a path up into the woods.

She set a good pace, despite the dark and the steepness of the path. Arthur clanked behind, sacks over his shoulder, grumbling as telescopes overbalanced him and tripods caught on branches.

"An eye out for what?" he said.

"Dimmick wouldn't have had to ask that."

"I'm not Dimmick, am I?"

"Could be all kinds. They have all kinds of ways."

He slapped at tormenting insects. Archer appeared immune to them. His stomach rumbled.

"Who does?"

"The other lot. Ah! I remember what happened to Lord Atwood—the old one, little Martin's father. Now, *he* was someone who respected the old ways of doing things." She made a throat-cutting gesture. "Not that *I* know what happened to him. Not that *I'll* spread gossip. But it was bad blood. There were rumours. And now there's Gracewell's Engine, and all the rest of it. Well, how could they stand for that? How could they, after what he did? Be fair. There'll be war, and it'll get worse. And poor old bloody me in the middle. Stayed out of it all these long years—out here, let others fight— let the young fight each other. Survived that way. But I couldn't say no, could I, not in the end? Greed. It's greed that gets us all, young man."

Arthur stumbled and dropped a large ornate bronze implement.

"*Don't* drop that!"

"Sorr—"

"Well. Well! So now Atwood and Gracewell have got me working for them, and the other lot won't forgive that, will they? What'll they do next, I wonder? It was them who did that Storm, you know. Their work. You know why they did it?"

"Did what?"

"The storm?"

"No one can make storms, Mrs Archer."

She looked disgusted.

"If they could, though, I'd say their motive was to flood Mr Gracewell's first Engine."

"No! No! No! They did it, young man, they did it, they called that bloody thing up, damn and blast 'em! Bloody London know-it-alls! They did it for the sake of *buggering about with my bloody stars!*"

She started on up the hill again, shaking her head. The trees thinned out, so that Arthur thought he could see the top of the hill—though hills were tricky things, and there was usually one more peak beyond the one you could see. For a little while he had been able to make out a square structure on the horizon against the starry sky.

He kept a wary eye out for assailants, but it seemed they were alone.

"Mrs Archer—"

"Shh. Thinking. Said too much already, haven't I? Not right, asking all those questions of an old woman. Not right."

That was all she said until they stepped out of the woods and onto the crown of Rudder Hill.

A tower stood on the top of the hill. It was plain and windowless, circular, and made of brick. Arthur guessed it was about sixty feet tall. It had a conical top, out of which stuck an enormous telescope.

It was an extraordinarily impressive structure. At a quick glance, Arthur believed that the telescope was the equal of that of the Royal Observatory. He could not imagine what it was doing out in the woods, in the apparent possession of Mrs Archer. It looked quite new—no more than a few years old. It must have been staggeringly expensive.

The night sky above was so clear that Arthur could recognise no constellations, because it was all one field of a million stars, all of equal brightness. The Milky Way looked like something you could walk on. Arthur guessed it was midnight, or thereabouts.

Archer took one of the implements, a thing like an astrolabe on a tripod, and she set it up beside the tower. She crouched down and stared into a pinhole, and sighted the thing up at the stars. She grunted, and called for her papers. She made notes.

Arthur said nothing. The fact of the matter was that the sight of that telescope had unnerved him.

After a while she unlocked the tower's door and went inside. Stairs spiralled up into the dark. She hiked her skirts and hurried on ahead. The stairs looked steep, and the implements were terribly unwieldy and heavy, so Arthur left half of them behind, planning to make another trip. He was glad of it. With each turn of the stairs he felt heavier and heavier, and shorter of breath. He soon lost sight of Archer, who climbed without apparent effort.

By the time he'd caught up to her, panting and wheezing, she was already at work. The domed room at the top of the tower was dimly lit by stars and by candles, and cluttered with God knows what—chairs and hat-stands by the look of it, as if it were nothing more than an attic. Yet the huge telescope that dominated the room was a fine piece of work, so fine that Archer appeared able, with a turn of a wheel beside the door, to rotate it on its shining tracks with no effort at all.

He set up her implements as she directed, then hurried back downstairs for the rest. On the walk down his footsteps lightened; but as he went back up he felt even heavier than he had the last time, as if he were carrying himself on his back. He planned for a third trip. Archer seemed busy—buzzing about, *hmming* and *haaing* and making observations and corrections and drawing circles and epicycles and taking notes. Her activities bore no more relationship to astronomy as Arthur understood it than the calculations performed by Gracewell's Engine did to everyday accounting.

When he next returned to the foot of the stairs—his legs aching from the effort—he glanced out the door and had a terrible shock. Someone stood at the clearing's edge, beneath the trees; a great tall heavy-shouldered shadow with two faintly visible eyes.

The man from Archer's house. He was watching, arms folded across his chest. A faint breeze rustled the branches overhead, and for a moment shadow swallowed him. He remained silent and still. Not so much as a nod in Arthur's direction. What on earth was he watching for?

Arthur's third trip up was his last. This time he felt heavier still, as if the shock of seeing Archer's whatever-he-was had left his legs weak. He nearly got down on hands and knees. At the top of the tower there was a sensation of great weight, quite unconnected to any obvious physical cause. He all but crawled into the room, dropped the last of Archer's implements with a clang, and fell into a chair. She grunted as if to acknowledge his efforts, but didn't look round. She was squinting into her telescope, muttering to herself.

He put his head between his knees and breathed deeply. Sweat ran from his forehead. The air was so dense that it seemed to murmur. He glanced up once or twice to see Mrs Archer still at work. She seemed to pay no special attention to the telescope. Instead she shuffled about in the gloom, examining her various odd little instruments, her bits of brass and bone and twig; except that sometimes she would pass the telescope and genuflect to it: a stiff curtsey, an awkward little dance like a diminutive and wizened priestess at the foot of a great golden idol. She'd hung something on it, something made of twigs and bone and God-knows-what. She was so busy and the room so full of clutter and shadows that sometimes it seemed there were two or three or a dozen of her, all performing their odd little dances. Windows overhead were unshuttered and star-light poured in. Arthur was scared to look up. God knows what those stars would look like; God knows what one might see through the lens of that telescope. Not, he was quite certain, the same heavens one might see at the Royal Observatory. He felt an urge to sneak up behind her and steal a peek. He felt an equal and opposite urge to run away. Instead, he remained where he was and struggled to breathe.

Archer tapped him on the shoulder. He snorted, jumped up.

"Fell asleep," she said, almost as if to reassure him. "Didn't you? Great silly fool."

"I may have caught forty winks, Mrs Archer. It was a long journey from London."

He stretched. The *weight* was gone from the room. He felt quite normal, though his legs ached from stair-climbing and hill-walking.

"That's that, then." She shoved a messy stack of papers into his hands. "There. Tell him these are my observations, whether he likes 'em or not. Still not there, is he? Still not there."

"Who are you, Mrs Archer? What is Mr Gracewell paying you for?"

"I'm a very old woman who's been looking at the stars for a very long time. And he's paying me to keep on doing it."

"What's Gracewell trying to do? What does it have to do with the stars?"

"I don't exactly know, young man. That's the honest truth. He pays me, him and his lot, and he sends me his estimations, and I tell him what I see in that big telescope he bought me. He keeps his secrets, that one."

"It's a fine tower, Mrs Archer. A fine telescope."

"How could I say no? Just a handful of winters ago I had nothing, nothing but the old house and my beautiful boy and the hill and the stars. Then they came for me—your master and his master. Little Lord Atwood, full of pride and his father's money—well, I should have said no, shouldn't I? Stay out of London's business, keep to myself, the way it's been all these long years. Greed, young man. It gets all of us in the end. And curiosity! Would you come out to Rodor Hill again, Mr Shaw, if you ever learn what they're up to?"

"I might, Mrs Archer."

"Promise? Would you ally yourself with me?"

He said nothing.

"Good. Wise. Now, pick up. Nothing will carry itself."

When they got back to the cottage, nobody offered Arthur so much as a cup of tea. The big fellow—who was waiting in the house, as if he'd never left—took Mrs Archer's tools back, and then he slammed the door in Arthur's face.

Arthur got back to Gravesend in the small hours of the night. The hotel had given away his room to some late-arriving holiday-makers, so he stood in the lobby and made a bloody fuss until someone woke up and found him somewhere to sleep.

He overslept terribly. He'd planned to take the train back to London, but there was some problem with the signals, so after waiting a long time he decided to go by river instead. In the end he didn't get back into London until early on Thursday evening.

By the time he disembarked at London Bridge, he had decided that he would go to the Europa Company's offices, storm past any clerk who tried to stop him into Gracewell's office, throw the papers on his desk, and demand answers in full—or else.

In fact, when he got to the offices of the Europa Company the door was ajar, and nobody answered the bell.

He poked the door open with his foot.

He stepped into the dark hallway, and he called out, "Mr Gracewell?"

He heard sounds of shouting and struggling and saw some dark shapes come down the hallway towards him. There were several men, holding little round Mr Gracewell by his arms and carrying him between them. Gracewell's spectacles and one of his shoes were gone and his legs bicycled helplessly in the air. He saw Arthur and called out for help.

Arthur squared himself in the doorway and said, "Stop there!"

As the men came up to the doorway he threw a punch at one, tried to stand in the way of the others, and grabbed someone by his collar, but it was dark and there were several of them. With no great difficulty they shoved out past him, carrying Gracewell out into the street. Arthur started to give chase, but now the situation had been reversed, and three men stood between him and the door.

They seemed to be the same unpleasant sort of person as last time. They were pale, and even in the dark of the unlit corridor it was clear that there was something very odd about their eyes.

Arthur resigned himself to a beating.

One of them pulled a nasty little knife out of his pocket. That was when Arthur first became really afraid.

He retreated back down the hall, thinking about looking for a weapon somewhere, like a table-leg, or a lamp, or a candlestick.

One of them smiled.

"Arthur Shaw," he said, as if this was an interesting new piece of information.

Arthur was quite suddenly blood-boilingly angry. He charged them, roaring. He feinted, making as if to overbear the one who'd spoken, then turning at the last moment to swing a fist at the one with the knife. His guard was down and Arthur knocked him over. One of the men jumped in Arthur's path, but he might as well have jumped in front of a steam engine. Arthur fell into him with all his weight and the man went down. Arthur heard the bastard's ribs crack as he stepped on him. He threw himself at the door, ran outside, and jumped up onto the back of a passing omnibus.

Chapter Fourteen

He was bleeding. One of the bastards must have cut him as he'd shoved past them, through his coat and into his side. Painful, but not that deep, Arthur thought, or he wouldn't be moving about. Well, no great loss if someone carved the fat a little. But people on the bus were looking at him in horror, and he was afraid someone might start shouting for the police. He jumped off the bus again. God, it hurt!

Arthur didn't quite know where he was. He knew where he was going: back to Rugby Street, to find Josephine. His head pounded an alarm. Those men had known his name. Agents of the enemy—Gracewell's enemy, but his enemy too, now; no doubt they knew where he lived. Same bastards who'd set the fire. Josephine might be in danger. He had to warn her. Hadn't she tried to warn him, hadn't she said it was dangerous to work for Gracewell? She'd been right. He was light-headed. Most of his torso felt numb. He needed her to tell him what to do.

He took off his coat. He folded it under his arm, as if he'd taken it off because of the summer heat, so that it hid his wound. He felt the weight of the watch in the pocket. Gracewell's watch. The one he had said would be *a measure of protection*. A fat lot of bloody good it had done, he thought.

He caught a cab, surprised anyone was willing to take him. He must have looked on the edge of death. He paid the driver well.

He got home. He shouted up the stairs for Josephine. There was no answer.

Mr Borel's shop was closed. Arthur pounded on the door. Borel answered, took one look at him, and said, "You are hurt—what's that there? You're bleeding!"

Behind Borel stood his daughter, Sophia.

"What is this? Mr Shaw, what is this? What has happ—"

"Where's Josephine?"

"Miss Bradman? I don't know. What—"

Arthur pressed money into Borel's hand.

"Go to the sea. Please. Mr Borel, you and your family, go on holiday. Tonight. Now. Take the train. It isn't safe here. I beg you. This is—this is all the money I have with me, but I can send more."

He gave Borel the name of the Hôtel Métropole in Brighton, which he remembered because it was where he and Josephine had thought of honeymooning.

Borel looked appalled. Sophia looked fascinated.

"Please, Mr Borel—it's not safe here. I'm sorry. But where's Josephine? Have they taken her?"

Borel said, "Taken? Who? Not safe? What is this?"

"She went to one of her meetings," Sophia said.

"Quiet," Borel said. "Do not interrupt."

"She went to one of her meetings! It was the one where she puts on the silver necklace—not Mrs Sedgley's meetings, because she doesn't dress up for those; the new one. She doesn't take her shorthand things with her, either, and last time she came back looking a fright—I'd swear she'd run all the way home! And she wouldn't talk about it, and usually she talks all about it whether anyone cares or not—sorry, Mr Shaw. Sorry, sir. She went again tonight. I think she said she was meeting a Mr At-something, Atwell?"

"Atwood?"

She smiled. "That's it!"

Mr Borel had a spare key to Josephine's office. Arthur ran downstairs, unlocked the door, and rifled through the address book that hung from the nail on the wall. It was there, the address, just as he'd feared. *Atwood. 22 Hanover Square.* What was she doing there? What danger was she in? Things were worse than he'd thought. His fingers got blood on the book.

To the sea!" he shouted at Borel, as he staggered out into the street. Somehow he made it to the cab-stand by the Museum, and somehow he prevailed on a driver to take him. In the cab's seat he pressed his coat to his wound and breathed deeply. Bright red blood surfaced through the fabric. The pain was enormous, and he nearly fainted. He practiced the techniques he'd learned to endure the aches and pains and terrors of Gracewell's Work, and he mastered himself. He began to understand how Mr Irving, who was surely very advanced in those dubious exercises of discipline, could walk through fire as if it was nothing.

22 Hanover Square was as big as a castle. Atwood was rich. No surprise. Arthur banged on the door until a servant appeared. A lanky horse-faced fellow, whose immediate reaction to Arthur was to brandish a stick and order him away from the door. Arthur pushed forward and the servant pushed him back. Arthur stumbled, far too weak to fight, and cringed as the servant raised his stick. He clutched at his side and felt the watch in his pocket. He remembered Gracewell's promises about the watch's properties in case of danger. Madness; but it felt *right.* As the servant's stick descended, Arthur opened the watch. There was a *click*, and for an instant it seemed as if everything in the world slowed down, but Arthur did not. The stick halted, then began to fall with stalagmite slowness. The servant's horsey face was frozen in a ghastly expression of anger, and spittle hung from his open mouth. Arthur knocked him down and ran inside.

He called out "Josephine! Josephine?" as he stumbled down Atwood's hall, bleeding on his floor, leaving blood-prints on his doorknobs. He fumbled the watch back into his pocket. He heard sounds of chanting from below. He found his way downstairs. He tried various doors, and he interrupted two more of Atwood's servants playing a card game. They ran for help. It crossed his mind that he was certain to be arrested for assault, burglary, trespass. He didn't care. He didn't understand what was going on, but he was so afraid that he could hardly think. He was sure it was his fault that she had got herself mixed up with Atwood.

He found a locked door, and he broke it open with his shoulder. He fell into a gallery above a library. The room was dark, with a dim but many-coloured light coming from a table in the middle of the room. Nine men and women sat around the table, eyes closed, heads tilted back, holding hands. One of them was Josephine. There was an ecstatic expression on her face, and in that weird rosy light she was as beautiful as Arthur had ever seen her.

He ran to the table and pulled Josephine away from it.

"Josephine—it's not safe. We have to go. I've been a bloody fool."

The other eight of them jerked as if slapped, and their eyelids fluttered—opening and then closing. The two men on either side of where Josephine had been stretched out their hands, as if instinctively, and closed their circle again.

Josephine was limp in Arthur's arms, and her eyes were closed.

"Josephine. *Josephine*. We have to go—what's wrong? Wake up."

The sitters opened their eyes. They let go of one another's hands. They shook their heads, rubbed their temples, and started banging their fists on the table and swearing.

"God *damn* it!"

"Blast!"

"*Fichtre!*"

"What *bloody* happened?"

"Who's that? Who are you? How did you get in here?" Atwood stood and pointed at Arthur. His hair stood up on end and he looked distraught. "How the *hell* did you get in here? What are you doing with Josephine?"

Josephine was still sleeping. Arthur felt her warm breath on his neck.

"What have you done? Atwood, what have you done? What's wrong with her?"

Atwood breathed deeply and mastered himself. He smoothed down his hair. "The fiancé, I presume," he said. "Arthur Shaw, isn't it?"

A severe black-haired woman, still seated at the table, said, "How did he get in, Merc—oh, to hell with proprieties. Atwood?"

"I don't know," Atwood said.

"What's wrong with her?"

"I don't know, Mr Shaw. You interrupted while we were far out. At a tremendous depth. God—she could be—oh God."

"This is a disaster," said the black-haired woman.

"What do you mean, 'far out'? Atwood, what do you mean?"

Atwood had gone pale. He looked horrified. "I mean she's gone," he said. "Her soul—her astral self—stranded! Amongst the—Because *you* bloody *barged in!*"

"Stranded?" Arthur said. "What? Stranded where?"

Atwood glanced at the black-haired woman, who rolled her eyes in exasperation.

Atwood put his head in his hands and said: "Mars."

THE
FIFTH
DEGREE

{ *The Liber ad Astra* }

Chapter Fifteen

Arthur stumbled. Atwood cried out and ran to take Josephine's weight before Arthur could drop her. Arthur was too weak to fight the man off, though he had a desperate urge to box his arrogant bloody ears. A stocky white-bearded Indian gentleman helped Arthur into a chair, wrestled his coat off, looked at his wound and hissed. Atwood swayed and sat down, holding Josephine, her head on his shoulder. He looked horrified. She was smiling faintly.

Arthur said, "Mars."

"No," said the black-haired woman.

"Perhaps," Atwood said. "Perhaps! She's so very strong—she may have kept on going—or fallen back. Our momentum—"

"*Momentum*," Jupiter said, "does not pertain to those realms. As you know."

"I *don't* know. Gracewell—we need Gracewell."

A girl entered the gallery above. She looked down on the scene in horror, and put a hand to her mouth. From her attire Arthur took her to be Atwood's maid. Atwood shouted at her to get out.

"Find needle and thread," boomed the Indian gentleman. "And bandages, or clean linen if you have none. Bring sal volatile, vinegar, and nitre if you have them. Scissors. Boiled water, and a clean basin."

"Don't order my bloody servants around!"

"Would you prefer to have a dead man in your library?"

"I don't care if he lives or dies, quite frankly!"

"Shut up," Jupiter said.

"Mars," Arthur repeated.

Two men from Atwood's party lifted Josephine out of Atwood's lap and laid her on the floor. Arthur couldn't avoid noting the resemblance of her posture to what's-his-name's Ophelia. The thought made him sick.

"Not Mars," Atwood said. "Or not precisely." He waved a hand at the ceiling, as if to indicate the heavens. Looking around, Arthur noticed for the first time that some pack of lunatics had vandalised the floor with a huge shaky-handed maze of paint, a mass of nonsense scribbles.

"Precisely," Arthur said. *"Precisely?"*

"We were exploring certain energy states within the astral light," Atwood said. "The aether, as you may know it—Mars is the sign or symbol of that Sphere of Being. We had slowed our vibrations to the point of—"

"Stop jabbering. Speak English. What have you done to her?"

"We *appear* to have lost her," Jupiter said.

Atwood got up and paced, jabbing an accusatory finger at Jupiter. "You don't know that!"

Arthur thumped the table. "What have you done to her, Atwood?"

Atwood thumped the table too. "I should have you arrested!"

"What have you done to her? Is this poisons? Or hypnotism? Or, or, or—"

"I wouldn't expect you to understand. God damn it!" Atwood turned to one of his party, a man who oddly resembled the Prime Minister. "Call Gracewell. Bring him here this instant—tell him, tell him we need new calculations. We must retrieve her—"

"New calculations?" Jupiter said. "Delay and distraction. Now is not the time."

Arthur and Atwood both shouted *Delay?* Jupiter raised an eyebrow.

The Prime Ministerial-looking fellow hurried out of the room.

"Wait a moment," Arthur said. "Gracewell? The calculations—you mean from his Engine? But Gracewell's gone."

Atwood stopped pacing. "What do you mean, gone?"

"Kidnapped, I suppose; by the same men who cut me."

Jupiter threw up her hands in exasperation and walked away from the table.

The maid came back, with a butler in tow. They had a kettle, a silver basin, and a tray with needle and thread and scissors, *et cetera*, which they laid out on the table. The Indian gentleman called for better light, and started to cut Arthur's shirt open. The man had strong hands, square fingers, and a golden ring with an ornate design that Arthur couldn't quite make sense of.

"Arthur." The woman who spoke had been silent until now. She was dressed in black velvet, fair-haired and pale, perhaps in her forties, and very beautiful. She sounded French. "Arthur: who were these men?"

"I don't—ow! God damn it—I don't know."

Beside the Frenchwoman was a much younger woman, in colourful Indian-style attire, who appeared to be on the verge of fainting. In a corner of the room a long-bearded and beaky old chap in a green velvet coat stood talking to a man of rather square proportions in a black suit, who was holding a rifle. That appeared to be the whole of Atwood's party.

Arthur tried to stand. The Indian gentleman restrained him, politely but firmly.

"Let me go, damn you."

"You may call me Sun, Mr Shaw. Now sit, before you do yourself further injury."

"Bloody *lunatics*," Arthur said. "Mayfair warlocks and table-rappers—this, this, bloody Mad Hatter's tea party. What will you do if I don't sit? Turn me into a frog?"

"If necessary," Sun said.

"This is all nonsense. No one can go to Mars—no one can go to Mars by sitting around a table calling each other stupid names. It's bloody nonsense! You've drugged her. I'm taking her to a doctor."

"Come here," Atwood said.

Jupiter said, "No."

"Yes! Come here, and see if it's *nonsense*, Shaw. Mr Sun—please help him."

He walked away, towards a door in the corner of the room.

Arthur followed, leaning on Sun's shoulder, thinking that—wound or no wound—if he jumped on Atwood from behind he could break his little neck.

Atwood unlocked the door and turned on an electrical light. Behind the door was another, much smaller library. It smelled strongly of dust and of dead flowers. All of the books were locked away behind glass and wrought iron; Arthur supposed that this was the pride of Atwood's collection. There was a fine oak table in the middle of the room, on which lay what Arthur first took to be a little girl, in a dress of blue and purple lace, curled up and sleeping.

On a second glance, it was not remotely similar to a little girl, but nor was it a great deal more similar to anything else in Arthur's experience. It had long thin limbs. Four of them; two arms and two legs. Normal enough, but each leg had two double-jointed knees, so that they could fold up in a way that no human being's limbs could, not even those of a circus contortionist or yogi. The creature was wasp-waisted beyond a corset-maker's wildest fantasies, while its chest was deep and powerful-looking. It might have been tremendously tall if it were standing, but it folded up into a tiny thing, like a flower shrinks when it dries. What had reminded Arthur briefly of a frilly dress was part of its body—wings, perhaps, though they did not look strong or solid enough to fly. It was breathing, though with apparent difficulty. Its face resembled nothing quite like any of the races of the Earth: long and thin, almost noseless, a bright petal of a mouth . . .

Arthur felt the world shift beneath his feet.

"What's . . ." His throat was dry. "What is that, Atwood?"

"We don't know," Jupiter said. "We brought it back by accident on our last exploration. We were investigating the border of the Fourth Sphere. Somehow we pulled it along in our wake."

"We bagged it by accident," Atwood said. "But nevertheless we bagged it. A native."

"It's—it's alive."

"In a manner of speaking," Atwood said. "I believe that its consciousness became intertwined with ours—perhaps it was conducting a similar experiment from the other side, perhaps merely studying the stars—and when we pulled it back with us . . . well, Shaw, I don't want to dazzle you with jargon. I believe it to be a thought-form. The thing, finding itself in what must appear to it to be Heaven, or Hell, managed—in what may have been an unconscious exercise of the will—to clothe itself in a memory of its proper flesh. A memory condensed from the stuff of the aether and from the powers we had invoked that night. It appears to have exhausted the last of its strength."

"Balderdash," called the old man in the green coat. "It's an angel."

Atwood locked the thing away again. For a moment he looked thoroughly pleased with himself, as if a brilliant idea had struck him; then he glanced at Josephine and his face fell.

Sun helped Arthur back to the table. The Frenchwoman watched him with a certain ironic sympathy. Her panicky young colleague appeared to have fled.

He was aware of the debates amongst astronomers over the possibility of life on other worlds, and whether the lines that were visible by telescope on the face of Mars were or were not canals. The *Mammoth*'s readers took a heated interest in Mars; it was fashionable, and entertaining, and it seemed to many people that the question of the progress or decline of Martian civilization was full of urgent significance for the progress or decline of England, and indeed of Earth. Arthur had always been something of an agnostic. He'd always doubted that the "canals" were anything more than shadows, smudges on the lens, figments of the astronomer's imagination—a product of the very human desire to see pattern, order, and purpose in the universe. On the other hand, it had always seemed to him that Mars *ought* to be inhabited; it would be a rather second-rate Creation if God had left most of it empty.

But what kind of God would make that—*thing*? And in whose image?

He looked at Josephine and was suddenly angry again. He was so tired and confused that he hardly knew where to direct his anger.

"She wouldn't!" He thumped the table. "Why would she get involved in—in—in whatever this—something so dangerous, so mad? That *thing*—did she know? Did she know what you were doing?"

Atwood stiffened. He seemed to take offense. "Yes. Of course. Do you think I am a—a kidnapper of some sort? She came of her own free will."

"Why would she do that? Why wouldn't she tell me?"

"She's a woman of exceptional sensitivity, Shaw, exceptional talent—she understood the importance of this experiment. No doubt she could see you wouldn't understand."

"I visited her," Jupiter said.

Atwood turned to her. "What?"

"I visited her, and I urged her to join tonight's experiment."

Arthur said, "You? Why did she—why would she?"

Jupiter looked at him, and at Atwood, and then said, "I offered her two hundred pounds from the Company's general fund. And I instructed her not to tell you, Atwood, because I knew you would make a fuss."

Atwood stared, open-mouthed. "A *fuss*?"

Arthur slumped in his chair. He felt faint.

Jupiter shrugged. "You said it yourself, Atwood—she had talent. Look what happened, the very first time she joined us! We needed *strength*. She needed money. And we *cannot* have further delays."

She looked around the room, and sighed. "Good Lord, we hardly need enemies when we have jealous lovers!"

Arthur tried to stand—possibly to throttle someone, he wasn't sure—but his leg went out from under him.

The Indian gentleman steadied him. "Sit still, Mr Shaw, or you may die before you can answer our questions."

Gritting his teeth, Arthur permitted Mr Sun to see to his wound.

W hile Sun cleaned and stitched, the remaining members of Atwood's party conferred. Arthur learned that the Frenchwoman was called Thérèse Didot. The bearded, beaky old chap was called Uranus, or Donaldson, and had a professorial, pedantic manner. They all quickly reached agreement that Gracewell had to be rescued from wherever he'd been taken.

"No," Arthur said. "To hell with Gracewell—you have to help Josephine."

"Yes," Atwood said. "Of course. But first we need Gracewell. We need Gracewell's Engine to calculate her whereabouts."

"Her *whereabouts*?"

"Don't be dense. I mean, the whereabouts of her consciousness, within the astral realms."

"But his Engine's in ruins."

"He's rebuilding it. All the more reason not to waste time."

"I certainly agree we must recover Gracewell," Jupiter said. "I see very little hope of finding Miss Bradman without him."

"No," Atwood said. "No, no—only he can determine our energy at the time, our trajectory of descent, our . . . Look, Shaw, make yourself useful. Who took Gracewell? Where?"

"Bring her a bloody pillow, at least."

"What?"

"She's lying on the floor, Atwood. Send your maid for a pillow."

"Oh. Oh, yes, yes . . ." He went off to ring the bell for one of his servants.

"Who took Gracewell?" Jupiter said. "Describe them."

Arthur looked around the room. Jabbering madmen, broken glass, nonsense painted on the floor, that, that *thing* in the next room . . .

"I won't leave Josephine's fate in the hands of you, you, you *maniacs*. We have to save her. I'll—I'll—"

The Frenchwoman leaned forward and touched his hand. "Who took Mr Gracewell, Arthur?"

Jupiter toyed thoughtfully with her necklace. "Perhaps you can help us, Mr Shaw."

"If I must. If I must."

"We *do* need a ninth," said the Frenchwoman. "I think perhaps we need a ninth *and* an eighth, because I think that little thing and her Indian dress may not be coming back . . ."

Atwood returned to the table.

Jupiter said, "Mr Shaw wishes to join our company. If not until he attains enlightenment, then at least for the duration of the present hostilities."

"What? I didn't say—oh, bloody hell, all right, if I must. Ow, damn it, that hurts."

Atwood looked at Arthur, and then around the faces at the table. "Oh. Hmm. Well, then. Around and around, changing chairs. Will we employ Mr Lewis next, or the cook? Clearly Lewis is unsuited to be a doorman."

"Gracewell was able to make use of Mr Shaw," Jupiter said. "And so long as the girl is in peril, we can trust him."

"It goes against the grain to poach from the Engine. Not the done thing, somehow. But these are desperate times."

Sun, having finished stitching, lit a cigarette and asked if all were agreed.

"We are," Atwood said. "Welcome to the Company of the Spheres, Mr Shaw. Now, speak. Tell us how you lost Mr Gracewell."

"I wasn't his bloody bodyguard. Nobody told me I was anybody's bloody bodyguard. Besides, he'd sent me off to the country to see a Mrs Archer—"

Miss Didot hissed. Jupiter leapt to her feet. "Archer! What does that awful old woman have to do with this?"

"She was working with Gracewell—something to do with the stars. Good God, is that what it was all for? For—this, this—"

"Who's Archer, then?" said the man in the black suit.

"A woman of notorious reputation, in certain circles," said Jupiter. "Quite notorious. Atwood—did you know? How long has she been involved in all this?"

"Yes. For some time. We needed her. I knew you would be upset! But she knows nothing, and I can control her, if need be."

"Ha!"

"Please, my dear—not now. Let Mr Shaw finish."

Between them, Atwood and Jupiter and Sun and the Frenchwoman explained to Arthur that the purpose of Gracewell's Engine was to carry out astrological and astronomical calculations, to a degree of refinement that would have been unimaginable to the sages of less enlightened eras, who had rarely managed to project their consciousness farther into the astral light than the very nearest-at-hand shadows of Earth, or at best the near side of the Moon. It was one thing, Atwood said, to calculate the revolutions of the heavenly bodies—the Greeks had made a good start on it, without even the calculus on their side!—but to calculate the revolutions of the *heavens* required an entirely different order of thought. The Engine was therefore staffed with what Atwood described, rudely, as low-grade telepathic talent: a lot of fortune-tellers, and other such riff-raff. The goal was to refine Atwood's Company's rituals to the point where it was possible to project a human consciousness entirely out of Earth's sphere of existence and into the higher or lower Cosmic Spheres: up toward the Sphere of Venus, down toward the Sphere of Mars.

It all sounded rather like drug-induced dreams, or religious ecstasies, but the Company quite clearly believed that they were not merely experiencing visions, but travelling *somewhere*—if not in the ordinary spatial dimensions of *up* and *down*, then in corresponding dimensions of spirit, or energy, or soul-stuff, or Astral Light, or the aether. It made Arthur's head hurt.

All they'd achieved so far, Atwood said, were just clumsy experiments. He likened them to the ventures of the very first explorers of ancient times, who set out across unknown oceans in primitive rafts and coracles. But with the aid of Gracewell's calculations, they would build a road to the Cosmos. The thing in the next room was proof that they were on the right track.

Atwood said all of this in the matter-of-fact way that a newspaper might tell you about the building of the Panama Canal.

"You have to understand," Atwood said, "that there have always been magicians in London. Old stick-in-the-muds, a lot of them. Old-fashioned. Many of them—most of them, to be frank—oppose our efforts. Over-cautious. Jealous of the power and learning that might be ours. There's a sort of, well, something of a fraternity of our enemies, you might say."

Atwood and Sun and Jupiter all agreed that the kidnappers—pale and black-eyed—sounded like Podmore's men.

"Podmore?" Arthur said. "You don't mean *the* Podmore—*Lord* Podmore?"

They all looked at him curiously.

"Yes," Atwood said. "Do you know him?"

"No. That is, you could say I used to work for him. I wrote for *The Monthly Mammoth*, and I believe he owned it—but of course he owns the *Evening Standard* and the *Law Times* and half a dozen other magazines and newspapers and . . . Do you really mean Podmore, the newspaper magnate?"

"None other," Atwood said. "In addition to his business enterprises, Lord Podmore is a magician of great skill, and a dangerous man. One of my father's acquaintances, in the old days."

"We knew that his men were sniffing around," Jupiter said. "Threatening, in that unpleasant way that they do. But kidnap Gracewell! He has gone too far. I warned him there would be consequences."

Atwood said, "He'll be well protected."

"Yes," Sun agreed. "An assault by the direct method will fail."

The maid had brought coffee along with the pillows, and Sun sipped at it.

"Gracewell was well protected, too," Atwood said. "So is this house, for that matter—or so I thought. I should fire Lewis for letting you in."

Arthur pulled the watch out of his pocket and put it on the table. "Lewis is the horse-faced fellow at the door? He did his best to stop me. But Gracewell gave me this. I thought he was talking nonsense, but—"

"For the love of God," Atwood said, "why would he give you that?"

Sun picked it up. "I made that toy for Mr Gracewell," he said. "For his protection. The time in it is mine, not yours. I think I shall take it back."

Sun closed his hand, and when he opened it the watch was gone. Arthur experienced a quick succession of mental associations involving watches and the urgency of vanishing time and he looked again at Josephine, lying asleep on the floor, lost to him—perhaps for ever. If what these madmen said was even half-true, then half of her was here, and half of her so far away that it would take a thousand years, a million years, to reach her by any sane or rational means. . . .

Then his wounds caught up with him and he collapsed with his head on the table.

Chapter Sixteen

Either his wound had been shallower than it had looked, or Sun was a master surgeon, because Arthur was soon on his feet again. His thoughts turned to Borel, who, if he'd taken Arthur's advice, was probably half-way to the seaside by now.

Atwood permitted Arthur to use his telephone—which occupied a room of its own, like a sacred object, a little black-and-gold Ark—to consult with the clerks at the Hôtel Métropole in Brighton. Around midnight, clerks of the Metrôpole at last brought Borel to the telephone. By that time the rest of Atwood's Company had gone to their various homes.

Borel's voice sounded very distant as it emerged from the glistening black speaker—as if he were calling not from the seaside but from the bottom of the sea. He was lost, and anxious, and confused. He kept shouting, as if he didn't entirely understand what a telephone was.

"You said that there was danger. My daughter, Mr Shaw. What are you involved in, Mr Shaw? My shop. Is it—*political*?"

"Political? Oh—no! No, not in that way, Mr Borel. Josephine—Josephine is very ill, Mr Borel."

"Miss Bradman?"

"It's a—it's a sort of sleeping sickness, Mr Borel."

Borel was slow to answer. "Is there danger or is there not, Mr Shaw?"

Arthur covered the speaker and asked Atwood if the house on Rugby Street was safe.

Atwood shrugged. "Perhaps. Perhaps not. If I knew what Podmore and his fellows would do next, we wouldn't have lost Gracewell, would we?"

Arthur could feel Borel's silent anger over the line.

Shortly after that the connection was lost, and Arthur couldn't reach the Metrôpole again. He resisted the urge to smash Atwood's telephone to kindling.

"I'll have a bed made for Josephine," Atwood said. He glanced at Arthur with obvious irritation. "You may stay, of course."

The maid and her candle led the way as Arthur and Atwood carried Josephine upstairs to bed, past what seemed to Arthur like an endless series of rooms: one full of half-finished paintings, presumably Atwood's; another that contained nothing but a very fine Turkish carpet on a dusty floor; rooms cluttered with furniture under white funereal shrouds; empty rooms; smartly appointed rooms that looked as though no one had set foot in them in years; rooms full of vaguely Egyptian bric-a-brac; and a room with crossed foils over the mantelpiece, and above them crossed oars . . . though, to Arthur's eye, Atwood looked a head too short to be a rowing man.

They found a bedroom, and Atwood's maid found clothes suitable for Josephine to sleep in. Throughout the whole process Josephine breathed steadily, but never opened her eyes. The maid was nervous and tongue-tied, as well she might be, and said few words. Arthur talked and talked to fill the silence, about how Josephine was only a little unwell, and how she would be right as rain again in no time. After a while he had almost convinced himself of the truth of this.

"A lot of hocus-pocus," he said. "Mars, indeed! It's hypnotism—that's all it is. I dare say she *thinks* she's on Mars, but in the morning it will be a strange dream—wait and see."

The maid wouldn't meet his eyes. "Yes, sir."

"Yes indeed!"

When she left, he locked the door behind her.

He'd told Borel. He supposed next he should write to Josephine's family. But how could he possibly explain what had happened? To them, or to anyone. God, he could just picture it—Waugh would want to offer medical advice, he just knew it. The lies he'd have to tell!

On the other hand, she might be herself again in the morning. Wake with a smile. Just a bit of fun. Find her own way back. Was that possible? He didn't know. He was quite as out of his depth as anyone had ever been. He wanted to shake her awake, and ask her what to do.

Her eyes fluttered open. An empty gaze. She didn't see him. She didn't see the ceiling, with its fussy white plaster mouldings. What *did* she see?

Of course, it was unthinkable that he should sleep in the same bed as her. Too awful and uncanny to even imagine it. It was agony even to touch her. He made himself a bivouac of bedclothes and lay on the floor. He lay on his side for an eternity, his wound aching and itching, thinking of all the terrible things Josephine might be suffering. He thought of all the things that the astronomers had to say about the horrors of space, of the cold and the vacuum and the dreadful solar winds. But if you could travel to the stars in spirit, and lock up a Martian in your library, then everything astronomy had to say might be wrong. He spent another hour thinking of all the other things that modern science had to say that might be wrong, until he felt as if the floor beneath him might vanish in a puff of uncertainty, and the Earth with it.

Two hundred pounds. That was real, and certain. She'd put herself in danger for two hundred pounds; which was to say that she'd put herself in danger because of his impecunity, his fecklessness, his idleness, all the things that his foster-father had always accused him of.

When he finally slept, he dreamed of Mars. Oddly, despite all his waking terrors, the dream was lovely. He dreamed of red plains, cloud-capped mountains, forests of violet flowers, cyclopean aqueducts of white marble carrying sparkling blue water across vast unknown continents. And blue men, tens of thousands of them, aloft on Martian winds.

He woke in a panic. Someone was banging on the door. He leapt to his feet thinking of fire or Podmore's thugs or worse, and snatched up a poker. He opened the door to see Atwood standing there.

"Well? Shaw?"

"Well what?"

"Put that down, unless you intend to strike me with it. Has her condition changed?"

"See for yourself," he said.

She couldn't be woken, not by shaking or shouting or sal volatile or pleading, not by tears or by whispering sweet nothings, not by lighting matches or ringing bells or singing or cymbals or familiar songs on the piano, not by Arthur's kiss, or by the various spells Atwood uttered, or by anything else that occurred to them in the course of the morning. Sometimes she smiled. Sometimes she furrowed her brow. She could be coaxed to swallow water. Atwood had a servant make soup, and Arthur managed to make her eat a little. Sometimes she sighed, or made other small motions—matters of habit. Her mind and her soul were elsewhere.

Atwood's guilt seemed quite genuine. For most of the morning he looked like he might be sick at any moment. Then, around half past ten, he decided that it was somehow all Lord Podmore's fault, and he went off to plan his revenge.

Of course his affections for Josephine were quite plain. He hardly troubled to hide them, which was insulting in itself. Arthur didn't for a moment suppose that Josephine had succumbed to Atwood's dubious charms, but that didn't mean he had to like the bastard.

Atwood returned for dinner. The cook produced a late meal—pork cutlets in tomato sauce. Arthur ate at the table in Atwood's parlour. On the wall facing him was a hideous painting. It depicted the Titan Saturn devouring his children, or at least Atwood said it did. All Arthur knew for sure was that it depicted a twisted old man in the dark eating a child, and that it did nothing for his digestion, and that he did not consider it art. Otherwise, the room was decorated with photographs of Atwood on bicycles, or in fencing garb, or hiking. Atwood sat primly, legs crossed, watching Arthur across the table. He claimed that he wasn't hungry.

"Listen, Atwood." Arthur pointed his fork at him. "I can't call these people *Jupiter* and *Mars* and *Halley's bloody Comet.* Twinkle twinkle little bloody star. What are their names?"

"Our Company has always had nine in its inner circle, and we have always been identified, in our ritual roles, by the names of the planets."

"Immemorial tradition, and all that."

"On the contrary—we're scarcely five years old; and tradition means nothing to me, except when it's of use. We go by ritual names to facilitate the correct mental state for our experiments. And because some of us are secretive. I don't know who Jupiter is—not in the way you mean. She goes by *Moina,* but I believe it to be an alias."

"Hmm."

"And why should I care? She is a woman of extraordinary perception—one of the few in London I would consider my equal. She is—perhaps you will understand this, Shaw—she is the other half of my soul. Between us there is a profound communion, as of the Moon and the Earth. Why should I want to know more? Why should I want to know that she is married to a solicitor, let's suppose, or lives in Chelsea, or if she has children, or *God,* what their names are?"

"If you say so, Atwood."

Arthur chased sauce around his plate, and tried not to let his gaze wander to the horrible painting. "And you must be some sort of grand something-or-other. Lord of something, I expect."

"Yes."

"Thought as much. And Sun is a prince of some sort? Hmm? The bloody lot of you!"

Atwood raised an eyebrow. Arthur continued eating. He was far past the point of ordinary deference.

One of Atwood's flunkeys had left a pot of tea on the side-table. Arthur attacked it with gusto.

"What are our plans, then, Atwood? For getting Mr Gracewell back, that is, if that's the only way to get Josephine back."

Atwood picked up a knife and toyed with it.

"Well?"

"I don't know, Shaw. We will confer. I don't know where Gracewell is. Lord Podmore will be well defended. Sun will counsel patience—he always does."

"I always say the way to attack a problem is by thinking clearly." Arthur ignored Atwood's expression of unmitigated contempt and went on. "Let's hear about these enemies of yours, Atwood. These rivals. Who are they? What are their numbers? Their motives? Their—"

"I don't know precisely who is or isn't opposed to us. I suspect Mathers is one of their fraternity. But Mathers is mostly show—a posturer. Dr Sandys at King's College has made his opposition to our experiments plain. But . . . some of our enemies may be men I meet at my club every morning, and talk to about the newspapers, and exchange cards with, and consider friends, while behind my back they are bent on my destruction. Podmore was a friend of my father's. Until quite recently, I would have said we were on cordial terms. I once offered to bring him into the Company, as a matter of fact."

Atwood sighed, and poured himself tea. "The forces arrayed against me are great. And subtle. Any beggar I pass by as he lies in the road may be my enemy. Any woman who smiles at me or glances my way. Any shopkeeper or cab-driver or policeman. I do not even trust the cats or the pigeons. My enemies are not some criminal conspiracy. They are London; they are all of its old magic."

"Those kidnappers looked like common criminals to my eye."

"So much the worse for your eye, Shaw."

"Podmore owns a lot of newspapers. Man about town. I'm certain we can find out where he lives."

"Of course. I was a guest at his house last November! But to attack him in his place of strength would be disastrous."

Atwood sipped his tea, then frowned at Arthur's sceptical expression. "My enemies are not to be taken lightly."

"I take them very seriously, indeed. I expect the police would too—arsonists and kidnappers and knife-wielding maniacs . . ."

"I refer to their magic. They caused the storm last winter."

"So I've been told."

"Oh, you have, have you? I hope I'm not boring you."

"Mr Gracewell believed that they caused the storm, and so did Mrs Archer. Which reminds me: who is Mrs Archer? Your friends seemed quite put out to hear you've been employing her."

"*Archer*," Atwood sighed. He went to the mantelpiece and found a case of cigarettes. "Archer! You're quite right, Shaw. I kept her involvement a secret from the others. You put me in an embarrassing spot. Jupiter will want an explanation."

"Well—who is she?"

"An awful old woman. You have no idea how old or how awful. Even my father was scared of her. There are—Mr Shaw, there are old ways of doing things. Do you understand what I mean? Old-fashioned superstitions. Bats and rats and eye of newt. The calling up of devils."

"Devils?"

"Black cats. *Et cetera*. Nonsense, of course. The modern practitioner of the art understands that there are no devils; there is only the will. Nothing but. But old nonsense is sometimes more efficacious than the new-fangled kind. Nobody in London knows the stars quite like Mrs Archer. Nobody has watched them for quite so long. And so I enlisted her aid, yes, that's true—it was necessary in the construction of the Engine, Shaw! The others don't always understand necessity."

He lit his cigarette, tossing the match into the fireplace.

"She doesn't know what we're doing. Piecework, that's all. She has certain talents that we can use. We told her nothing. You steer clear of her, do you hear, Shaw?"

Arthur poured himself some thick black tea.

"So Lord Podmore caused the storm," he said. "Mrs Archer said it was . . . how did she put it? She said they did it to bugger about with her stars."

"No, no—well, in a way. The storm that you saw was merely a side-effect. The wind, the rain, and so on. That was the smoke, not the fire. The shadow, not the act. No, Shaw—they moved the spheres. Or, rather, they moved the Earth in relation to the spheres. Ever so slightly—ever so very slightly—just the tiniest degree, almost immeasurable, even if there were tools to measure it."

He held up his thumb and forefinger, almost touching, to illustrate—as if that somehow made anything clearer. "Can you imagine the strength that would take? What it must have cost them? How much they must hate and fear me? And yet, that was enough to render years of calculations, and experiments, and observations, and plans quite obsolete. Jupiter and I were engaged in an experiment at the time, and it was a miracle we weren't stranded, too—we *fought* our bloody way back! And in the physical realm it caused floods and wind—did they mean to flood Gracewell's Engine, or was that luck? I don't know. A good magician is always doing two things at once."

"You know, if it weren't for the storm, I would never have met Josephine."

Atwood said nothing. He stood beneath that horrible gory painting, smoking, while Arthur drank the last of the tea.

"I should see if Josephine's all right," Arthur said.

"No, no. I'll send someone up to ask Abby."

"Abby?"

"The maid," Atwood said. "Who helped you dress Josephine last night, and is presently sitting with her."

"Ah. Yes. A good girl."

"Come with me. I want you to see something."

"No, Atwood." Arthur stood. "I've seen quite enough for one night."

Atwood smoked his cigarette, breathing in until the tip of it was bright red. Then he quickly stubbed it out on the mantelpiece.

The room went dark, as if the cigarette had been the only light in it, though Arthur was sure that just moments ago there had been a lamp on the wall behind him. In the darkness he could make out the shadow of

Atwood's head, the line of the mantelpiece, the white face of hungry Saturn in the painting behind Atwood's head.

Saturn lifted his mad bloodshot eyes up to meet Arthur's, and opened his long bloody maw to speak.

Arthur swore and dropped his teacup.

"Ha!" Atwood said.

The room was lit again—as it had always been—and the painting was still.

"What—"

"A parlour trick! Shaw, you won't last five seconds if someone like Podmore sets his sights on you. If you mean to be of any use, then come with me."

They went together down to Atwood's library. Arthur scratched at his stitches as he followed Atwood. His wound was hot, and itched furiously. A good sign. Whatever else he was, Mr Sun was clearly a first-rate doctor.

Servants had tidied the library a little since last night. The multicoloured lamps that had stood on the table were gone, replaced with a single, sensible white light. The paraphernalia in the corners had been straightened up, and the rifle that Arthur had last seen in the hands of one of Atwood's Company—the fellow in the black suit—now hung on the wall over a writing-desk.

Atwood collected something from a shelf. Two pieces of card and a book. "Sit," he said, and they sat at the table. Atwood tossed one card across to Arthur, and placed another one in front of himself. He opened the book to a middle page and consulted it, his finger tracing slowly down lines of what appeared to be Greek.

The two cards appeared identical. Both were made of thick white card, and were about the length and width of a book. On one side they were blank. On the other there was a painted design consisting of a black dot surrounded by a circle of pale watercolour yellow, which in turn was surrounded by a ring of pale blue, and around the outside of it all was a ring of pale red.

"What—"

"Shh." Atwood turned a page, and continued reading. His lips moved, like an actor committing his lines to memory.

"What is this?"

"A *tattva*," Atwood said, with the air of someone explaining to a hopeless bumpkin which fork to use.

He closed the book with a *thump* that echoed in the empty library. He stood, and lit a little stick of oily incense.

"Opium?" Arthur said.

"You do have a vivid imagination. Are you afraid I plan to *shanghai* you?"

Arthur said nothing.

"Now—you have a little magical talent," Atwood went on, sitting again. "Certainly you don't have the gift that Josephine has. But we shall see what we can do with you."

"Get on with it, will you?"

"I want you to understand where Josephine is."

"Mars, I'm told."

Atwood shook his head. "Listen. The Cosmos is ordered into nine spheres of being. Each has a different energy state, and different laws. The planets are the signs of those spheres within our own sphere."

"But—"

"*Listen*, Shaw! Ordinarily you would have to suffer through many years of initiation to understand this, but we have no time, and I have no patience. The Sphere of the Sun is at the peak of creation, *fons et origo*. The Sphere of Mars lies below ours in the Cosmic Ordering. That is to say, it has a lower energy state—it is colder, and slower. 'The light is not above one-half, and its heat one-third of ours.' Daniel Defoe said that. Not so cold as icy Jupiter, or the unthinkable depths of Saturn, but cold enough. If it has inhabitants, they may be like our friend in the room next door—simple and frail creatures. Do you see? Ripe for exploration."

"Exploration."

"Yes."

"And what do you plan to do there?"

"We shall test our courage and our will against the universe itself."

"This is madness, Atwood."

"We won't go far tonight. An evening stroll down a country lane; that's all. But you must see, and understand."

"I'll see what there is to see, I suppose."

"You say that as if that isn't the very hardest thing in the world to do.

Now, listen. Focus your gaze upon the black dot—there, do you see? On the *tattva*. Empty your mind; think of nothing but my voice. Do not blink. Do not move your gaze. Not yet! When I say. Soon you will see that the red circle will vanish, then the blue, and lastly the yellow . . ."

It worked just as Atwood said it would, though it took some time, because at first whenever one of the circles began to fade to white Arthur found his attention drawn to where it had been, and then there it was again. But with a little discipline, the card was soon white as a snowfield, but for the black dot. Arthur thought it a very striking optical illusion. Meanwhile, Atwood chanted something. It was Greek, Arthur thought, or mostly Greek, and he didn't know what it meant. But sometimes there were words of English in it—for instance, sometimes Atwood said *Up!* and Arthur felt a tug that nearly caused him to stand. Sometimes he said *Down!* and Arthur felt his stomach lurch as it does when one wakes from a dream of falling. At the edge of his vision, the walls of the library seemed to recede. He felt that he was on the verge of fainting.

Arthur stared at the dot. He'd taken it at first for a tiny spot of black paint, but further investigation revealed a very small and intricate design. It must have taken extraordinary patience and a steady hand to paint so small. The dot was a black hexagon. Within that was a black hexagram. Within that was a circle. And within that was another hexagon. Around the edges of his vision there were lights now, as Atwood named the planets and the stars. Within the hexagon another hexagram, and within that, another circle. Up! and Down! Atwood named the numbers and the gods. A hexagon, a hexagram, a circle. He fell. A hexagon, a hexagram. A ray of black light spiralling down into the dark, touching each point of the star as it descended: a black star, weaving a black star. When Atwood's voice said *Wake! Now!* Arthur jumped up from his chair. Up and up, weightlessly. There was no chair. He was nowhere at all. All around him was darkness, lit with stars. He looked down and couldn't see his hands or his feet or anything at all.

"Steady." It was Atwood's voice, from behind Arthur's shoulder, or where his shoulder would have been; but Atwood was nowhere to be seen. Arthur felt terrible vertigo. Unwisely, he looked down.

Above him and around him were stars. Beneath him, at an unthinkable distance, was London—or, more accurately, Atwood's house. Most of the rest of the city was fog, except for Rugby Street, the Museum, parts of the river. Atwood's house was fog too—it was made of fog—a shape in the clouds—faint fog in a mirror. Arthur could see dimly through its roof, as if it were the wax-paper window of a doll's house, and he could see himself and Atwood sitting around a table, faint grey demi-solidities in the mist . . .

He felt himself descending.

"No," Atwood said. "Not until I permit it."

End this trick at once, Arthur tried to say, but he couldn't speak.

"Look up," Atwood said.

The stars, again, all around, and darkness. In the infinite distance, where one might on a clear night ordinarily expect to see the Milky Way, there was a faint rainbow of coloured light. A cold wind rushed past Arthur's head, or where it seemed to him that his head should be—as if he were standing atop Nelson's Column at night.

"The first gyre. Thank me, Shaw. There are thousands in London who would give up all that they have for such a vision."

Arthur tried again to demand that Atwood end his trick—that he let him *down*.

"No," Atwood said.

Arthur was afraid, and very angry.

He looked down again, and tried to *will* himself down. Atwood's voice boomed *No*, and Arthur shook, buffeted by the wind. The misty earth below him reeled as he spun weightlessly and at great speed, tumbling in orbit. By the time he regained control of himself and looked down again, the misty scene far below might have been Africa, for all he could tell, or the Pacific.

"See, Shaw? You have a great deal to learn."

Atwood's self-satisfied voice sounded from just beside Arthur's ear. Arthur stumbled and turned towards Atwood as if he might somehow be able to hit him. Atwood breathed *no* and Arthur was off again, tumbling head over heels, over Antarctica and the Cape of Good Hope and Bombay—he thought he saw great grey cloud-elephants in the zoo—and Land's End and who knows where else. *A girdle 'round the Earth*, he thought, *in forty minutes* . . . but forty minutes was for ever, it seemed. Overhead, the stars were all shooting—white lines of pure crystalline motion. He dug in his heels—or he would have, if he'd had heels—and came to a halt over John O'Groats. Grey rocks and grey sea and ragged islands. Atwood was there behind him laughing *no!* and Arthur was off yet again, the clouds tumbling beneath him, the stars zigzagging above. Like a cat Atwood followed him, and as soon as he next came to rest, Atwood repeated his trick. Arthur was furious. He had a sudden notion of what it might look like to someone below, if they'd looked up, if there *was* a *below*: a great fat oaf of a comet in shirt-sleeves bouncing back and forth across the sky, uttering curses! He laughed, then, and he began to master his anger. He told himself that the clouds, the stars, were only illusion. He'd been hypnotised. The clouds weren't there, and he was still in Atwood's library.

He came to rest. When Atwood spoke behind him, Arthur concentrated with all his strength on the notion that he was *not* moving, he was not falling, he was still. He was twice Atwood's size. Atwood could not bat him about like a cat with a mouse.

He was still.

He felt Atwood's red-hot irritation.

He planted himself more firmly.

Hot winds buffeted him.

Atwood said, "Enough."

At once they were back in Atwood's library. There was no wind. They were both sitting at Atwood's table, and Arthur was panting and holding the white *tattva* card in his hands so tightly that his fingers hurt. His heart beat as if he'd run to and from all those places he'd glimpsed in his vision.

For just a moment Atwood looked flustered, and sweaty.

"Well," he said, smoothing his hair. "Not bad for a beginner. But you have a lot left to learn, Shaw."

Atwood got up from the table. He went to the far side of the room and replaced the cards and the book on the shelf.

Arthur stole a dizzy glance upwards, and saw to his relief that the ceiling was real and solid. No stars were visible. He got to his feet. He touched his face, ran his hands across his scalp. He ached. His skin was raw, as if he'd stood out in a high wind for hours.

It occurred to him that he wasn't really a raw beginner in this sort of thing. Certainly he'd never attempted magic before; but two months in Gracewell's Engine was a solid foundation in the art of self-discipline.

He looked at Atwood, standing by the shelf, head bowed, as if studying the spines of the books. Infuriating, sinister; undeniably somewhat magnetic. A madman, perhaps, but not a fraud or a fool. He knew that he was being stared at, of course. Like an actor, he seemed to take it for granted.

At last Atwood sighed and said, "Josephine is far more remote. Adrift in utter darkness. She will not find her way home unaided."

"I believe you. Good night, Atwood. I'm going to see that she's comfortable."

"That was a game. Our real goal is a thousand times more difficult and more remote. Past the moon and onwards. We cannot reach it without Gracewell."

"Well, Atwood: in the morning we can plan again."

Arthur was half-way up the winding stairs that led to the gallery when he heard a knocking noise. He stopped. It came again.

"Do you hear that, Atwood?"

Atwood had not moved from where he stood. He was watching the door in the corner of the room—the door that led to the little side library where he kept his rare books, and the native of the Spheres.

Something behind that door knocked and scratched and scraped.

Atwood slowly approached the door. Arthur went to stand beside him. If Atwood were brave enough to open the door, Arthur didn't see how he could in good conscience do any less.

The knocking and scratching ceased.

Atwood took the key down from its hook. His eyes were bright with excitement and anticipation, and his hands shook as he unlocked the door. It stuck. "Shaw—help me. There's something . . ." Arthur put his back into it and the door opened. The weight that had blocked it rolled over. It was the creature itself, slumped against the door, curled up on the floor. It was still alive; its mottled indigo hide rose and fell with soft fluttering breaths. There was an overpowering stench of dead flowers and stagnant water.

It leapt to its feet, faster than Arthur's eye could follow, legs extending to their full impressive height. It began to flap its long arms about in rapid herky-jerky motions like a puppet being shaken. Perhaps it was trying to signal something, but Arthur had no idea what, and the flurry of motion lasted only instants before it charged. Arthur tried to block it, but it dodged around him with ease and then it was out into the library.

It leapt effortlessly up onto the table. It appeared frenzied, as if this was the last strength of its dying moments.

"Stop!" Atwood commanded. "This is my house. I bind you, creature of the Spheres, in the name of Earth, Terra Mater! I bind you in the name of the Sun! I bind you in the name of God! I bind you in the name of Mercury! I bind you in the name of . . ."

Arthur got a good look at its silvery eyes. He didn't like what he saw. They seemed to him to be full of malice.

It leapt up off the table and into the air. Its legs were thin but they were long and springy, and it weighed very little, so it reached a good height—rather like a grasshopper. At the height of its jump it fanned out its wings with a noise like sails snapping full of wind. No question any more that they were wings, wide and blue and complex in their structure, but they found no purchase on the dusty air of Atwood's library. The creature fell back onto the table and rolled onto the floor.

Arthur ran for the rifle. The creature didn't try to stop him. Perhaps it didn't know what a rifle was. It leapt again, caught the edge of the gallery with one long-fingered hand, and pulled itself up. It looked around. It didn't seem to recognise the door as a means of escape. Arthur was terrified regardless, thinking of Josephine upstairs, Abby watching over her. God bless Abby, who seemed like a stalwart girl to have put up with all that she had put up with, but if that monster crashed through the door of the bedroom, there wouldn't be much Abby could do to stop it . . .

He shot at it. He missed and hit books instead. Atwood kept up his chant, which seemed to leave the creature quite unimpressed. Arthur worked the rifle's bolt. It was an old Lee-Metford, which was a stroke of rare good luck, because he'd once written about the Lee-Metford, freelance for the *Military Recorder,* and had shot at tin cans with one or two. He wasn't a wholly bad shot. He fired and missed again. The creature wouldn't keep still.

It darted back and forth along the gallery, then climbed over the railing, stumbled, and fell back down to the floor of the library. Arthur was sure it had died. Atwood came and stood over it. Just as he said, "What a waste!" it lurched up and slashed his cheek with its wing. He cried out and fell.

The creature rose to its full height. It fanned out its wings, which began to change colour, rapidly and kaleidoscopically, while from their motions there arose a strange high thrum.

Arthur shot it.

It fell. The stench of dead flowers filled the room, and he gagged.

Atwood stood. Blood ran from his cheek down his collar. Good, Arthur thought; serves him right. He was mumbling unpleasantly, urgently, wetly—*what a waste, poor thing, imagine it, lost in our world!*

Instead, Arthur imagined Josephine, lost in theirs. A horrible thought. *Good shot,* Atwood mumbled, *well done, still, what a waste.*

"It was dying anyway, Atwood. I think it—it started to fall before I shot it. It was . . ."

Could it breathe on Earth? Could it fly? He tried to take into account the atmosphere of Mars, surely thinner than Earth's, its gravity, the physical difficulties a native of Mars might experience here. He was too tired. Besides, was it from Mars? Or Venus? Or the Moon? Or none of those places, but from some other realm separated from London by more than mere distance? He didn't know. He knew nothing, and understood nothing.

"It looked wild," he said.

Atwood had found a little folding hand mirror, and was examining the gash on his cheek. He was mumbling still, swearing and venting his frustrations. Arthur didn't give a damn. The wound in his side had started to hurt again. He supposed he'd probably torn something.

He went to the desk and put the rifle back on its hooks.

"I'm going to bed," he said. "We can plan tomorrow. But I will not have Josephine spend another night in this God-forsaken house; do you hear?"

Chapter Seventeen

The Company maintained their learning in a dozen or more hand-written journals, which Arthur was permitted, under an oath of utter secrecy, to study. Jupiter referred to them as *the notes*, and Atwood called them the *Liber Ad Astra*, or *A.A.* for short, or the Book.

It was a hodge-podge of Masonry, Greek myth, Egyptian fantasy, debased Christianity, third-hand Hinduism, and modern and ancient astronomy, promiscuously and nonsensically mixed. Some of it was in Atwood's handwriting, some of it in Jupiter's. Parts of it were in Latin. *SAPERE AUDE* was written on the frontispiece: *DARE TO KNOW.* Atwood's notes hinted that the parts of the Book that had been entrusted to Arthur were merely the *outer learning*, and that certain other books might contain higher and deeper and more exclusive principles, and the identities of the *Hidden Masters* from whom those principles derived. Arthur took that to be a sort of bluff. Josephine had told him the way this sort of odd little occult fraternity generally operated: the esoteric knowledge that was not shared with initiates and therefore could not be questioned; the rumour of hidden sages in Tibet or Russia or Paris or other places more interesting and romantic than the Edgware Road, or Bromley, or Surbiton, where the ancient knowledge had almost certainly been cobbled together last Tuesday.

The Book was riddled throughout with paradox, and absurdity, and contradiction. Thinking too long or too hard on it caused something like vertigo; it was as bad in its way as Gracewell's Work. But after a week or two of study, Arthur began to enjoy it. He felt guilty about enjoying it, but he did. There was some satisfaction to be had in learning the secret rules that governed the universe. It was like being in a rather important and exclusive sort of club. He even developed a sneaking suspicion that he was rather good at it, despite what Atwood said. He supposed there were worse things to be good at.

I: SUN

First: the Company imagined a sort of Copernican cosmos of invisible concentric spheres, which carried the visible planets in their rotations through the heavens. Of course these spheres were not mechanical things—nothing so crude—but nor were they mere metaphors. They were made of something that was not quite like earthly matter, but not quite nothing either: *aether.* They were best understood as states of energy, or consciousness, or vibration, or perhaps *spirit*, whatever *spirit* meant. Atwood was fond of quoting Corinthians: *Not all flesh is alike . . . There are celestial bodies and there are terrestrial bodies, but the glory of the celestial is one, and the glory of the terrestrial another.* It was in their nature to move in endless, perfect circles.

The Sphere of the Sun stood at the centre and apex of Creation. It turned endlessly, and each atom of it was like a rose of ten thousand angels endlessly revolving—and yet it was unchanging. In the lesser spheres, Atwood believed, time was circular; the centre of things was timeless, or alternatively time moved so rapidly there that it might as well be timeless. If the Sun had an inhabitant it was God: singular, and self-sufficient, like the God of the Jews.

The Company had also discovered (or hallucinated) a complicated system of occult correspondences between the heavenly spheres and the things of the Earth. Among other things, the Sun corresponded to the colours gold and white; to fire, diamonds, musk, and the lion; and to the Ouroboros and Kether, the Crown of the Sephiroth. The manipulation of these signs and correspondences was at the heart of the Company's magic.

The man who occupied the role of Sun refused to give Arthur any other name. One was enough, he liked to say. The Company sometimes called him *Mr* Sun, as if it were the name he'd been born with. He was stocky, white-haired and bearded, with dark intelligent eyes. He dressed in the English manner, in dark suits, but always with a touch of vivid aestheticism: a bright tie, a golden tie-stud, some fine fur. The golden ring on his index finger depicted the Ouroboros. He clearly knew some doctoring. He carried himself like a man with important business interests. He was muscular despite his age: wrists thick and powerful, hands callused and square. Atwood said that Sun was an importer of antiquities—he made it sound shady. At the Company's meetings Sun spoke little, listening thoughtfully while Atwood and Jupiter argued and paced and argued again, and Thérèse Didot made sarcastic interjections. When he spoke, his deep voice startled everyone, and demanded attention.

He counselled patience. In matters of magic, your enemies will destroy themselves, he said, and storms will exhaust themselves on a strong roof, and if you wait long enough by a river the bodies of your enemies will float past you. Shorn of poetry, Arthur understood that to mean that Sun thought the Company should dig in, defend, and wait for its enemies to overreach themselves. Well, Arthur thought, that was all very well for Mr Sun. He didn't have to feed and wash Josephine every night. He didn't have to listen to her every heartbeat and breath, afraid that it might be her last.

II. MERCURY

As the nearest world to the Sun, Mercury was also the fastest-moving; for each second on Earth, a thousand years flashed past on that blazing star. If it boasted civilization, and it likely did, then it could be home only to the golden cities of angels. An Italian astronomer had discovered in recent years that one side of the world was always turned towards the Sun, and was always in light; what better home, Atwood argued, for angels? It was doubtful that any human spirit could survive there. If the heat and the light didn't drive one mad, then surely the wit and beauty and insight of its inhabitants soon would.

Mercury corresponded to Hermes and to Nishubur, to the Archangel Gabriel, to elephant-headed Ganesh, to the eagle, to topaz, to the bow and arrow; to wit and laughter and pure reason. The hours governed by Mercury were favourable to rites of projection, seeking, and clairvoyance. Its symbol was "☿," which Arthur recognised from his time in Gracewell's Engine. It stood for an open and a closed circle: receiving energy from above, ordering it for the benefit of the spheres below.

Martin Atwood held the title of Mercury. The scar the creature had given him healed quickly, and within a week he seemed rather proud of it, as if he'd won it in a duel. At the meetings of the Company he counselled investigation, exploration, analysis.

He owned properties all over London, each of them handsomely furnished, empty, and rather lonely. After Arthur left his house, taking Josephine with him, Atwood graciously put them up in his flat off Piccadilly. He promised that the place was warded against evil influences, which was more than could be said for Rugby Street. He lent Arthur the services of the maid, Abby. Arthur shook his hand and said thank you; but he was still not inclined to trust or forgive him.

III. VENUS

The Company had made a few tentative explorations in the direction of Venus, but had found the experience terrifying. In that direction the astral space became rapidly hotter and faster and brighter until one's thoughts began to burn.

If Venus had inhabitants, they might resemble Adam and Eve in the Garden; they were likely hermaphrodites, or shape-changers. Their homes would resemble forests in their elegance and complexity and vibrant living energy. Among the symbols of Venus were ivy, ambergris, and tin, and the fifty-forth and fifty-eighth Hexagrams of the *I Ching*. Its hours were favourable for the learning of secrets and the resolution of mysteries—and for love, of course, though "love" as the Company's philosophy conceived of it was a rather severe and mathematical thing, involving combinations of certain psychic energies.

In Josephine's absence, the role of Venus fell to Arthur. He thought that it was hard to imagine a less likely Venus. But Atwood assured him, smiling, that in magic the union of male and female was a very powerful principle.

IV: TERRA MATER

The title of Terra Mater belonged to a man called Samuel Jessop, who in everyday life was a Detective Sergeant in the Metropolitan Police. He was solid and square and bowler-hatted. Once a month he went by train to the seaside, where he tested his strength against the ocean by swimming out as far as he could until he could swim no more. "A little farther each time, Shaw. One day, who knows?" Apart from that, and of course his membership in the Company of the Spheres, he appeared to have no obvious eccentricities, and struck Arthur as surprisingly level-headed. He was a Methodist. Arthur liked him.

It was Sergeant Jessop who conducted Arthur's initiation into the inner circle of the Company, such as it was. A tap on the shoulder, hood on the head, and turned thrice around; afterwards, whisky and a cigar.

"In deference to your wound, Shaw, incurred in the line of duty, we'll excuse you the ordeals."

"Decent of you, Jessop."

"Don't tell Atwood. Something of a stickler, that one."

Sergeant Jessop gave Arthur a gift: a book, John George Hoffman's *Pow-Wows, or Long Lost Friend,* which he said was a very old American book, full of honest and old-fashioned Christian magic.

"Charms for healing the sick, and driving out evil spirits, and finding lost sheep. That sort of thing."

"I don't know what to say, Jessop."

"Atwood says it's a mean little thing, a waste of paper. But I've found it worth the study. Atwood's a clever chap, but there are things His Lordship doesn't know; up there and down here."

"Not so long ago, I thought I knew *down here* well enough. Now I wonder. Thank you, Jessop."

"I know that feeling, old chap. I know it well."

V: MARS

Mars, Atwood explained, had been selected as the Company's first destination not because of any particularly appealing feature of the planet itself, but because every journey had to start somewhere, and it was easier by far to go *down* than *up.* Nevertheless, Atwood was an attentive student of all the latest scientific discoveries regarding the red planet. He and Jupiter subscribed to *Nature* and to *Astronomer,* and collected sketches and photographs of the planet's surface. They considered their own methods of investigation to be very superior to mucking about with telescopes, but they were not too proud to borrow.

"Take Flammarion," Atwood said. "Do you know him?"

"The French astronomer?"

"None other. Flammarion holds now that the waters of Mars—he thinks he can see them—might be a different sort of thing from our water. A *sixth state,* he calls it, a *dense vapour, viscous, sombre, and dark.*"

"And?"

"So you see, the conditions, Shaw, may be very different. It's a different sphere of being."

"I know Flammarion. He says there's canals on Mars. Civilization. Is that true?"

"I doubt it. Remember, Mars is beneath us in the ordering of things; if it has inhabitants, they will be slower than us. Simpler, colder, stupider, and less energetic. Their recreations are likely primitive."

"So Josephine may be—"

"The Martian year," Jupiter interrupted, "is six hundred and eighty-seven days; astronomers have calculated it. So we may take that as a sign that the Sphere of Mars experiences time at roughly half the Earth's rate."

"A sign?"

"A sign."

They were like Humpty-Dumpty, Arthur thought. Words meant what they said they meant.

Thérèse Didot held the position of Mars. She was middle-aged, petite, pretty, and French. She appeared one sunny afternoon at the flat off Piccadilly, breezed past Arthur with a smile into the hallway, and told him that she had decided to make it her business to teach him a thing or two. In return she said that she wanted to know all about Josephine, and their engagement, and their plans for their wedding, and their hopes for their children. She said she was very fond of children.

"I'm afraid I'm not in a mood for conversation, Miss Didot."

Thérèse sat daintily on the sofa. "Then perhaps I will talk and you will listen."

Miss Didot smiled and looked around the flat. Her eye landed on the little shaving-mirror on the mantelpiece, which Arthur had purchased after discovering, to his irritation, that Atwood's flat had no mirrors. She *tsk-tsked*.

"I advise you to dispose of that, Arthur. All sorts of wickedness may be done by means of mirrors."

"Mirrors?"

"Please. Sit. I would like to help you, Arthur. It's been too long since I had the pleasure of teaching the young."

Arthur sat down on a chair by the table, in somewhat ungracious silence.

"How do you suppose I come to know Lord Atwood?"

"I have no idea, Miss Didot."

"I was his governess, when he was just a tiny thing. His mother was dead, poor creature."

"Hmm. I wouldn't have guessed. Hard to imagine him as a child."

"He was a very sweet boy."

"I don't see that this is any of my business."

"So, you see, I am a teacher. I am not the greatest or wisest of teachers. I cannot teach you enlightenment. I do not have it, and I do not know if you want it. But I can teach you some things that will be helpful in this world. May I tell you a story? It concerns mirrors."

"I suppose so."

"It also concerns a young man—no older than you are today. And I suppose this was not very long ago—not quite ten years, which does not seem so very long at my age. This young man was a talented magician— but then, his father was a talented magician, too; in fact, he was one of the stately old magicians of England. This young man's father lived in a big house in the country, which was very old, and had belonged to his father, and his father before him, and he knew every stone, and he knew every tree in the woods, and he knew every man and woman in the village of which he was the lord; and he believed in fairies in the woods, and devils abroad at night, and was very old-fashioned, in the way of English magicians."

She paused to smooth down her skirts. Then she glanced over Arthur's shoulder at the mirror behind him and tidied away some stray hairs. Then she smiled.

"And so the young man learned magic the way other boys might learn the alphabet, or playing with a ball. And because he was proud, and his father was proud, they struggled, and they grew to hate each other. And when he was a young man he fled; to London first, then to Paris. But Paris was not far enough to escape from his father's shadow. Because the young man wanted to be a magician, and in that world his father's shadow was very great, and very wide. Other young men in a similar predicament might have struck their fathers, or shot them. But that was not how this young man had been raised."

"You refer to Atwood, I take it."

"I am telling you a story, Arthur. He sent letters. From Paris, first, then from Berlin, then from Morocco. At first those letters were quite ordinary; he sent stories of his travels, just as any loving son might; stories of his studies, the libraries that he visited. He wrote that he had visited Rome, and that he thought he might become a Catholic, and sought his father's blessing—which was denied—and so on. Then the young man began to write of nightmares. He wrote that he had contracted a fever, and that ever since, he had been followed on his travels by nightmares. In those nightmares he woke under a night sky—no stars, moon-lit—and all around him were black men: a crowd of them, black as ebony, and black-eyed, and silent as statues, and the moon also was black. The old man, as it happened, had a peculiar horror of Africans; he did not like those stories at all!"

She glanced at the mirror over Arthur's shoulder, smiled, and adjusted her hair.

"Still the letters came. This young man was on the Grand Tour: they came from Madrid, from Switzerland, from Jerusalem and Istanbul. He wrote of his visits to the old libraries, the bath-houses, the mountains—and he wrote of his dreams. Each time a new detail added to the dream: a crow, a black lion, a crack across the moon, a man who held a horn in his hand. And the old man was no fool; of course he understood by now that magic was being worked against him, but it was too late, you see. Once you see, it is too late; because then if you were to stop reading, and the words kept coming, you would not know what was in them, and wouldn't that be worse? You would have no defence against them. They would continue in your dreams.

"The old man could not sleep. He paced. He wrote back, and his letters were full of hate and spite and the blackest curses. Because he was old-fashioned, he invoked the names of devils and angels; there was magic in them to singe a postman's fingertips! But not this young man, who put them directly into the fireplace, and then wrote of his travels in Italy. He left Rome—he wrote—and he went up into the mountains. On a path across a stream one evening he saw a man who was as black as a crow and had but one eye in his head. He fled. On the train that took him away from Turin, he saw the man again, from the window, at a station. Please, Father, please help me. Mockery! The old man went red in the face with fury, and clutched his heart. Mockery! The young man wrote of his dreams: a black eye, a veiled face, the sky itself like a black veil being pulled aside, to reveal the true stars beyond! He wrote that he was consumed with fever, and that he was writing from a hospital bed. He wrote in such a trembling hand that the old man had to get out his spectacles and pore over the pages to read them, as if he were reading the oldest of grimoires, made of ancient parchment that might crumble to dust if he breathed on it. The old man held his breath. *Father, help me, please,* he read. *A voice spoke to me in the mountains, and it will not stop whispering. It will not stop. Its voice is as black as the night.* And then one night the old man cried out, and when the servants came running they found him dead, stretched out on the floor, lying in a corridor beneath a black mirror."

She seemed to be waiting for Arthur to say something. He wasn't sure what to say. Her story struck him as revolting.

"But of *course* it was black," she laughed. "Do you see? It was night!"

She stood, looking pleased with herself, and straightened her skirts.

"Atwood killed his father; is that what you're saying?"

"That is one version of the story. There are others. I want you to understand what a magical war is—what it can be."

"That didn't sound terribly magical, Miss Didot. It sounded like an unpleasant trick to play on a confused old man."

She sighed.

Arthur stood to see her out, and observed to his shock that the shaving-mirror had fallen from the mantelpiece, and now lay shattered at the foot of the fireplace.

"Every mirror is an eye, Arthur; every eye is a door. Please do not replace it."

"Miss Didot," he said. "How did you do that?"

"Glass *wants* to shatter! The things of this world tend towards decay; the trick is keeping them whole. But since you ask, perhaps I will teach you a thing or two—since we must go to war together. Abby! Abby, my darling, will you fetch us some wine-glasses? Not good ones! Now, Arthur, sit, sit."

She reclined smugly on the sofa. "The shattered mirror, as it happens, is one of the symbols of Mars; so too are blood, and sand, and rust, and the sword. By these signs, Mars makes itself known in our sphere."

VI: JUPITER

The Company had never explored as far as Jupiter, and it was likely that no human consciousness could survive at those depths. Imagine a vastness of ice and storms, Atwood said. Something like a polar wasteland, something like an ocean, formless and always night. The waters, before God moved upon them and gave them life. Probably only very simple creatures lived in those vast ink-blue depths. They would be slow and ugly giants, like the dinosaurs, built to endure terrible cold and endless pressure.

The symbols of Jupiter included the whale, Behemoth, and Jörmungandr; the anchor, the empty throne, the barren womb. The hours of Jupiter were suitable for necromancy. The woman who went by that name was as secretive as a spy, and Arthur never learned a thing about her.

VII: SATURN

To imagine what it would be like to walk in the Sphere of Saturn, Atwood said, imagine a flat and endless plain of lead, beneath a sunless sky of lead. Nothing could live beneath that terrible grinding pressure; if there were inhabitants of Saturn they could be made of nothing but shadow, and their movements would be so slow as to seem almost timeless.

Arthur said that he didn't see why God should make such a dreadful place.

"Well," Sergeant Jessop said, after sucking thoughtfully on his pipe for a while, "he made Hell, didn't he?"

Saturn's hour was favourable to rituals pertaining to gross physical motion and the opening of doors. The role of Saturn was occupied by a young actress named Caroline Arnold, who liked to dress in what she thought of as Indian attire, and who believed that she could see ghosts and fairies. For all Arthur knew, perhaps she could. The experiment into which he'd blundered was the first time she'd joined one of the Company's rituals. She didn't attend the war councils of the Company, and so far as Arthur could tell she had no idea of the danger that they were all in. He advised her to quit the Company, for her own safety. She didn't listen.

VIII: URANUS

The still-greater depths of Uranus could not be visited, or perceived by human senses, sixth or otherwise, or described in words, or even imagined. Its correspondences were obscure.

The role of Uranus was occupied by Dr Donaldson, a theologian from University College. He liked to wear green. He grumbled and complained of aches. When not visiting the stars, he occupied himself organizing efforts for the relief of the fallen women in Whitechapel, and authoring a many-volumed dictionary of the language of the Angels. He didn't agree at all with Atwood's and Jupiter's theories of the Spheres, but he kept his own theories to himself, and Arthur never learned much about them, except that he thought that the worlds were arranged in something less like a tower and more like a rose.

At the Company's first war meeting, Dr Donaldson advised negotiation with the enemy. The next day the *Evening Standard* printed rumours regarding Donaldson's scandalous activities with the fallen women of Whitechapel. He immediately threatened to sue. Later that week, rumours appeared in the *Proscenium* and in letters to the *Daily News*, and the *Law Times* reported that Dr Donaldson's suit was sure to fail, the wickedness of his conduct being apparent to all fair-minded people. All of those publications belonged to Lord Podmore, so the members of the Company regarded this as a form of magical warfare, though it seemed to Arthur to be nothing more than old-fashioned slander. Magical or not, and true or false, within a week Dr Donaldson had resigned his position at the college, stopped answering Atwood's letters, and departed for America in disgrace.

IX: NEPTUNE

Logically, Atwood said, there must be some minimum possible quantum of energy, a constant point past which there was nothing but nothingness. That was the state of Neptune. It corresponded to no geometrical shape, not even to a single point, but wavered perpetually between point and absence, between being and nonbeing, between 1 and 0. Among its symbols were the right foot; Terminus, the god of boundaries; callipers; and the noose. Its hour was favourable to rituals of measurement, division, and navigation.

The fellow who occupied the role of Neptune was a solicitor by the name of Arnold Leggum. He was a Yorkshireman, and he looked rather uncannily like Mr Gladstone, but that was just a coincidence, signifying nothing. Two days after Dr Donaldson left for America, a wheel fell off Leggum's cab as he rode down Oxford Street, and he tumbled out of his seat and beneath the hooves of oncoming traffic. He died in hospital two hours later of a head injury, raving about stars and storms and a great black dog. Of course the surviving members of the Company believed that that, too, was the result of magical attack by their enemies. Arthur supposed they might be right.

"We have hardly begun to fight," Jupiter said, "And we are seven."

Gloom settled around the Company's table.

THE SIXTH DEGREE

{ *The Great Magical War of 1894–1895* }

Chapter Eighteen

Josephine remembered. For a long time there was nothing she could do but remember, over and over.

They'd gathered on a summer evening at Martin Atwood's house on Hanover Square. They sat around the great oak table in Atwood's library. The table was lit by many-coloured lamps, and the recesses of the library were full of distant and flickering shadows. It was dark. Josephine sat between Mercury—Atwood—and Terra Mater—Sergeant Jessop. Atwood's hand warm and soft; Jessop's hand hard and callused. They chanted. On the table in front of her there'd been a white card with a red hexagram on it. Red and black. A corona of flickering gold formed as she stared at it and followed the chant. She tried not to be afraid. Jupiter had praised her courage, her insight, her intuition. Atwood had said the same. It was dark. Well, what did her intuition tell her? She was excited. She was afraid. She didn't know what would happen. Her head was full of the Company's ritual, intricate and demanding and odd. She tried to concentrate. She thought of Arthur—safe now, thank God, if Jupiter kept her word. She felt light-headed with relief at the thought. She felt herself rising up, up through the darkness, as if she'd been unfolded inside out through the top of her head in a sudden dizzying moment; and then up through the star-painted ceiling of Atwood's library and past chimneys and washing-lines and pigeons and soot and clouds; and then up into the stars. It was dark. There was a pillar of light ahead of her, a nine-pointed star of light. The others were with her, invisible, silent now. The chanting was over; it was all a matter now of the mind, the soul, the perceptions. She *perceived* them; she didn't see them. It was dark, and Atwood was there, and Sun, and Jupiter, and Thérèse Didot, and Sergeant Jessop. Up through the darkness, their wills intertwining and leading one another. Down into the dark. Up and down were all the same thing. Colder and colder, slower and slower, emptier and emptier. Nine bright minds like fireflies drifting in the dark, joyful and terrified. Jupiter, a speck of violet light, led the way; then Atwood, sparking ruby-red; then golden Sun. They fell. There was a moment when they passed out of Earth's domain and into what lay beyond; it was like suddenly falling into cold water. They fell farther. It was dark. Jupiter's light began to rise, receding as Josephine fell. Josephine felt something lifting her, shaking her. Someone's hand on her arm. There was no arm. She had no arm. There was nothing but her mind, and the stars. She fought, not wanting to wake. It was dark. Atwood's light rose, and Sergeant Jessop's. Jupiter's light winked out. She was frightened now—she tried to rise again. Neptune was gone, and Thérèse Didot. She couldn't rise. She was alone. They were all leading one another and she was alone. It was dark and she was alone. Their light faded in the distance.

S he screamed into silence. Nothing moved.

S he remembered: the gathering on a summer's evening. In London. A sky of warm and pink-tinged clouds and the cry of street-sellers and the smell of horses. Atwood's man Lewis met her at the door and hurried her down to the library, where it was dark.

S he remembered: the words of the ritual. The rhythm of the chant, fading into silence. The thick sweet incense that had filled the room, making her head spin, making her laugh. The swirling of light, fading into darkness.

S he could see—it wasn't all darkness. There were a handful of stars in the far distance.

The bright stars. The pure aether. Everything was silent and still. There was neither heat nor cold. There was nothing to touch, and nothing to touch with. She couldn't move. She was alone. Without the others pushing or pulling her along, there was nothing to move with, and nowhere to go. No up and no down.

A mistake. An accident. Jupiter had said it was dangerous. Surely they'd come for her. She waited, and waited. There was no way of knowing how long she waited. They didn't come. She grew angry, helpless and humiliated and betrayed.

After a long time, her anger burned itself out. Terror took its place. Something had gone wrong. Another accident. Atwood and the rest of them might be just as lost as she was—or they might be sitting in their library, scratching their heads, wondering what had happened to her. They might never find her. She might never see London again, or Arthur, or her sisters or her mother or anyone else.

She was terrified for a long time. Eventually that passed too. She began to think.

S he'd moved.

T he stars had changed. She'd moved. When she was angry, she'd shook and burned and moved across the sky. When she was afraid, she'd fallen. Not very much, not compared to the vast empty distances she found herself in. But she'd moved. She wasn't helpless. It was possible to move. Anything might be possible. Those weren't stars. This was the realm of the spirit, and hers was strong.

Which way was home?

She willed herself to move. Nothing happened.

T he stars moved, slowly but ceaselessly. The spheres turned. Motion was the ordinary, essential condition of the heavens. It was her fear that kept her frozen. Her will, rather than moving her, kept her fixed while everything else flowed; so she tried to calm herself. She tried to drift, to think of nothing; she recited old poems, she remembered street addresses in London, she thought about her little office, her typewriter . . .

* * *

Was she moving, or was the scene moving around her? An unanswerable question. There was nothing to hold on to, nothing to measure against. The vision transformed itself; that was all she knew.

A cluster of lights came into view, moving and growing. Her attention was quickly riveted by a large red star in the distance. A dim far mystery of red against an unfathomable night. As she moved towards it, she felt a spell of overpowering fascination. It was Mars, the fourth planet, unexplored and unknown; irresistible, enchanting, magnetic; calling across the unthinkable void.

Atwood had spoken of natives. Men and women of an unthinkably distant country. Shelter; language; warmth and light. Civilization, perhaps.

The red light grew, faster and faster, as she felt herself rushing with the suddenness of thought through the trackless dark.

At the last moment she faltered. The red light of Mars grew ugly as she fell towards it, as it filled the sky; it darkened to a bloody, baleful purple. Wasn't that what everyone said it was: a dead world, a ruined world, a wasteland? The thought of what that might mean—not mere words in a magazine, read in a comfortable library in London, not just an amusing story in the newspapers, but the thing itself, looming before her! She was afraid to fall into it—afraid it would swallow her whole. She circled it, around and around, in light and darkness and light again. Two discs of light circled it with her, racing one after the other. The moons of Mars, or their spiritual shadows. Phobos and Deimos. One was ivory and rose. The other was bright red, like a furnace, and it scared her terribly, for no reason she could possibly explain.

She steered towards the ivory moon.

No sooner had she thought it than she burst through thin clouds, white but tinged with pink, and into cold air and faint sunlight. A landscape of white hills, coral colours, orange and gold and grey, rose-red rivers. A vast shadow—a chasm—a quarry—a crater. Within the crater, a city of ivory towers, some tall and thin, others domed and gilled like vast white fungus. She fell towards it, tumbling, helpless to stop herself. Fairy-tale towers rose around her. They curved as they rose, like horns. She fell past windows of rosy glass, casting no reflection as she went. Thin spiny plant tendrils dangled bulging flowers across the streets as if they were lanterns. There were sounds again, at last, and scents, and, astonishingly, a familiar sight: the streets and squares and bridges of this scrimshaw city belonged to the same species of fern-winged elf that had fallen unwillingly into Atwood's library. There were thousands of them.

She fell and came to rest in a room that contained two of the creatures—the natives—the Martians. The room was otherwise bare, containing nothing except some rows of blood-drop red beads on the floor, like a half-finished game of chess. The two Martians stood by a window that overlooked a river. They didn't notice her. There was nothing to notice. She was perception, without form. It was possible that she was going mad. Their fingers and wings were intertwined.

Nothing she could do could attract their attention. She could make no sound, touch nothing. She could not be seen.

She watched them. They stroked each other's wings. After a little while, she decided that she had possibly interrupted them in a moment of romance.

She left by way of the window—quite fearlessly, the fear of heights apparently a frailty of the body—and went out into the lunar city to see what she could see. In London it was midnight, and Arthur sat by her bedside in Atwood's flat, holding her hand, watching by the light of a candle on the mantelpiece as her breath rose and fell, rose and fell.

Chapter Nineteen

I: The Rite of Jupiter

Atwood called a meeting of the Company on a Wednesday night in August. By his calculations, the hour—an unsociably late one—was governed by the Sphere of Jupiter. Their meeting was in an upper room of Atwood's house, which he called his *scriptorium*. Martin Atwood, Jupiter, Sun, Thérèse Didot, Sergeant Samuel Jessop, and Arthur Shaw were present. They sat around a long table, with Atwood at one end and Jupiter at the other—all of them except Sun, who orbited the table at a steady pace, counter-clockwise. The tablecloth was violet satin, embroidered in silver with the symbols of Jupiter (the sphere, not the woman). Each person around the table held their left hand out, palm up. Jupiter uttered certain phrases over and over: *Nitrae, Radou, Sunandam; Noctar, Raiban, Zorami; et cetera*. On the table, in the middle of a pentagram, was a human skull; and between the skull and Jupiter was a six-and-one-half-inch lens in a circular gold frame. The lens and the skull had been positioned and polished with as much care and attention as the finest implements of a surgeon or an astronomer. Between the skull and Atwood was a candle.

Arthur's role was to hold up his hand without trembling—which was harder to do than it was to say—and to think of the dead. Any dead would do. He thought of his father and mother; his friend Waugh's brother, who'd died of an infection of the lung two years ago; patriotically, he thought of dead British soldiers in far-flung places; he thought of Mrs Wright, a neighbour who'd died last winter of pneumonia. Images of Josephine lying still in her bed came into his mind, and he struggled to push them out.

He worried that this was all terribly blasphemous. The Bible said nothing about trespassing on Mars, so far as he could recall, but it was very clear about leaving the dead alone. He'd never been all that devout—to his foster-father's endless and bitter disappointment, religion had always been something of a matter of convention to him, a fact that didn't require his immediate attention, like gravity, or the post-office, or America—but now he was starting to fear for the state of his soul.

He kept his misgivings to himself. The ritual continued. At each pass around the end of the table, Sun struck Jupiter gently on the back of her head. It was on the twentieth or thirtieth such blow that she suddenly stopped chanting, and began to speak.

~ *I'm dead.*

Her voice was both deeper and frailer than usual, and rather more Northern. She sounded a little like Arnold Leggum—the man who'd gone by *Neptune*.

"Yes," Sun said, still pacing.

~ *Bloody hell. No escape, then, is there? No bloody escape.*

"You are but a shadow, Neptune, and you will be gone again in but a moment."

~ *Bloody hell. Oh God. Oh God, help me.*

"Where did you die?"

~ *Hospital.*

"Which Hospital?"

~ *Bart's, I think.*

"How came you there?"

~ *I remember I was at the Oxford. The music hall, I mean. Chinese acrobats and a lady escape-artist. The things that woman could do! She could—*

"And afterwards?"

~ *Very nice if you like that sort of thing. Odd, I thought.*

"And afterwards?"

~ *Let me have my last happy memories, Sun, you miserable bugger.*

Sun scowled.

~ *All right! All right. Wheel came off the cab. Tipped out and head over arse on road. Cracked my skull. I remember a bloody great horse coming down on top of me, great big shining hooves like moons, loud as thunder. Crack, crack, crack. It hurts, dying does. Bloody broken teeth spilled out on the cobbles. Let you down in the end, don't they?*

Leggum had had a very fine set of false teeth, of which he'd been very proud.

Sun leaned forward. "An accident?"

~ *There was a black dog.*

"A black dog?"

~ *Or a wolf, or something like it. Big bastard, and loud, and bold as you please, runs out into the road. Frightened the horse. Rears up and bolts and the wheel comes off and out I spill.*

"And then?"

~ *Someone lifts me up and then everyone's talking about what to do with me. What's to be done. Awful, that is. No one can look at you. Let me go, I say, let me go, but they don't hear. Bloody driver's run off, mind. Moving again. In a bed. Someone poking at me. Women. Nurses. I'm screaming my head off, mind.*

"Describe these women."

~ *Hurts like bloody hell. Listen, Mr Sun, do you want to hear about what it's like to break your skull?*

"Describe these women."

~ *Do you want to hear what it's like breathing when your ribs are—*

"Describe these women."

~ *Just nurses. Gone now. There's a doctor.*

"What does he want with you?"

~ *He wants to know how I got here. Bloody nosy questions, same as you. I tell him go away, I'm dead. He says, no you're not, not quite yet. He wants to know about the Company.*

"What did you tell him?"

~ *Don't know. Can't think, can't stop myself talking. Bit of my bloody skull's broken—last words—oh, hell, my last bloody words. Stars. The thing, that thing we brought back. Atwood—where's Atwood? Listen, Atwood—*

"How long had you been in that hospital before he came to you?"

~ *Don't know.*

"How long?"

~ *Twenty-two minutes!*

"Describe him."

~ *Sitting down. Leaning close. Spectacles, tortoiseshell, round and clean. Black frock coat, don't know the tailor. Grey hair. No jaw to speak of. Four deep lines on his forehead, six when he's impatient, five when he smiles. Long beard, like the poet—what's his name, always in the newspapers? Green eyes . . .*

While she spoke, Jupiter stared at the lens, skull, and candle. Jessop slid a piece of paper in front of her, and put a pencil in her hand. Blindly she scratched out a series of sketches of the mysterious doctor of St. Bart's, in a number of different poses; precise but exaggerated, like faces seen in a fever or a fairground mirror.

Arthur shivered. The room had grown cold. The thing that possessed Jupiter wasn't a ghost, Atwood had said; only a shadow, a memory, a flicker of consciousness not quite extinguished . . . But it was ghostly enough to chill Arthur's spine.

~ *That's all. Then darkness.*

Very well. Sun rapped the table nine times.

Jupiter closed her eyes. She breathed in deeply and shuddered. Atwood tenderly took her hand and kissed it.

"Magnificent, my dear. Magnificent."

"Never again, Atwood. Never again."

II: The Rite of Mercury

The next suitable hour of Mercury was shortly after dawn on Friday. The Company took a train out of town together to a farm. The farmer was a tenant of Atwood's, a strapping sunburned rustic type who treated His Lordship with great deference, and asked no questions about the odd party he brought with him or the paraphernalia they carried out into his cornfield.

Jessop and Arthur rolled up their sleeves and got to work. They each carried a short plank, which they used to press down a wide circle in the corn. It was the last hot day of the summer, and before long they were both sweat-soaked and thirsty, red and itching.

The rite itself involved the slaughter of a dove. Atwood—who'd changed into a white surplice back at his tenant's house—cut the bird's throat and splashed blood at the circle's edge. Then he placed its body into a small black cabinet. The cabinet also contained a crown, a Jew's harp, a glass phial filled with spring water, a sheet of parchment six inches square, some matches, and a glass bowl containing a pinch of saffron. Atwood lit a match, burned the saffron, drank the water, wrote his own name upon the parchment forward and backwards, and then walked away without a glance back, out into the golden field and away over the horizon.

The rest of the Company waited. After a while they began to make small talk, mostly about the weather. Jupiter and Miss Didot had brought parasols.

The ritual didn't require six—Atwood alone sufficed. But he was anxious about exposing himself to his enemies, and so the rest of the Company were there to protect him in the event of—well, Arthur wasn't altogether sure what. He didn't know what form the attack of the Company's enemies might take, but he knew what they would say if he asked: *Watch for everything. Overlook nothing. Nothing is without meaning.* That was always their answer. He'd resented it at first, but had come to see it as good advice. While he talked to Jessop he listened for every shift of the wind, every insect that buzzed over the fields, every whisper of the corn; the footsteps of mice, the motions of birds overhead, the slowly inclining angle of the sun. His own increasing hunger. The itch on the back of his neck, and the tickle of sweat. The pretty ladybird that settled on Jessop's sleeve like a bright garnet cufflink. A stray grey hair on Jupiter's head. The constant shimmering glare of sunlight. In the middle distance there were haystacks. Everything was golden, fields and clouds both, the Earth indistinguishable at the horizon from the Sun, like one of those French paintings Josephine liked. Everything dissolved into points of light. There was a thousand times more in one single field than one could ever see and understand in a lifetime. Who needed other worlds?

Arthur laughed. Jupiter glared at him, and Miss Didot raised an eyebrow.

"Airy spirits," Sun said, waving a hand as if swatting at a fly. "Mercury is close, and you may find your thoughts are not wholly your own."

After a long while, a figure approached on the horizon. Arthur tensed, and started to get to his feet; but it was only Atwood. He'd been gone for perhaps two hours. When he came closer, Arthur saw that he was smiling, and he had a boyish spring in his step. He sat down cross-legged beside the cabinet.

Jupiter lowered her parasol, and said, "What is your name?"

Atwood grinned. Not his ordinary smile—it was wider and toothier. He didn't look himself at all, and when he spoke, his voice was high and breathy.

~ *I have no name.*

"What manner of thing are you?"

~ *Air and light.*

"Will you serve us, and go when we command?"

~ *I will. I will!*

"Do you know who we seek?"

~ *I know many things!*

"We seek the man who heard Arnold Leggum's last words. Will you find him for us?"

~ *I will!*

Atwood closed his eyes, and rocked back and forth. Everyone waited for perhaps forty minutes. When Atwood next opened his eyes, he was himself again, and he had learned the killer's name—one Dr William Thorold—and his address, just off Harley Street.

III: The Rite of Mars

Midnight, and the hour of Mars. The Company met at Atwood's house, in his library. In preparation for the ritual, none of them had eaten all day, or drunk anything but water, or committed any sin if they could avoid it.

They were joined by an aristocratic young fellow of Atwood's acquaintance, whom Arthur had never met before, and who seemed to be under the impression that the whole thing was a lark. Atwood seemed to be scraping the barrel a bit. Miss Didot sealed the door and the four corners of the library with water and salt. Jessop and Arthur and Sun and Jupiter and Miss Didot and Atwood and the new fellow each cut their left palm and intoned *Adonay, Elohim, Ariel.* They cut their right, intoning *Amon, Barbatos, Baal.* With blood and sand they marked out a hexagram on the table. Miss Thérèse Didot slaughtered a black crow, then quartered it, placing its parts at the points of that ugly star. She looked quite devilish as she did this, streaked with blood. Sun chanted. Sergeant Jessop brought in a brass bowl of water and placed it on the table. Miss Didot placed the eyes of the crow into the water, and then six hot coals. Lastly she screamed the name of Dr William Thorold and struck the water's surface with a knife.

Nothing appeared to happen. Afterwards the members of the Company stood around making small talk and congratulating one another on an impeccable performance of what was apparently a very difficult ritual. Atwood's footman Lewis came in with a bucket to dispose of clumps of bloody sand and bits of crow.

A rthur cornered Atwood in the hall after the others had left.

"What is all this supposed to accomplish, Atwood?"

"The consternation of our enemies. The erosion of their strength. Did you think it would be quick?"

"This is no use to Josephine! Muttering curses and cutting up crows— damn it, Atwood, we know who our enemy is."

"Only a madman or a fool would confront Podmore without proper preparation."

"Preparation. You mean delay. By God, Atwood—if you spent every night by her side, listening to her every breath. If you . . ."

He fell silent. Atwood looked at Arthur for a long time, then steered him into one of the many empty rooms of his house.

"Sit." Atwood gestured towards the chairs by the unlit fireplace. He fiddled with lamps. "There's more at stake than Josephine, you know. But I agree."

"What does that mean?"

"You mustn't breathe a word of this to the others."

"Of what? Why not?"

"The others are—traditionalists. They believe in rites and ceremonies. They'll do this sort of thing for ever. But you're quite right. We don't have time to waste, do we? The ordinary rules no longer apply. We must take firmer action."

Atwood leaned forward as he spoke, and watched Arthur intently. Lamplight made his shadow tremendous, uncanny. Arthur gave it a long look, half-expecting it to move, or speak, or do something dreadful as soon as he took his eyes off it.

"Can I trust you?"

"If it helps Josephine."

"Are you willing to what must be done?"

"What are you planning, Atwood?"

"My man Lewis is preparing my coach."

"At this hour?"

"I intend to visit our friend Thorold," Atwood said, "And to put some questions to him, man to man. Will you join me?"

Arthur was silent for quite some time.

"Thorold murdered our colleague Leggum, don't forget—and you may be quite, quite sure that he's done worse than that."

"Murder, Atwood?"

"Of course. Perhaps not by his hand. But you may be sure that it was no coincidence that Mr Leggum's horse bolted. If your conscience is troubling you, Shaw—"

"My conscience held its tongue through that diabolical ritual. Who am I to balk at a little burglary?"

"Good. Then I can trust you?"

"What do you intend?"

"It won't come to violence, if that's what you mean. I know Thorold by reputation. A mediocre magician. A good doctor. A quiet man. There were rumours concerning the death by poisoning of a business-partner. . . . Well, men of that sort are not brave when confronted."

"Men of that sort! I seem to remember a time that I hardly ever associated with murderers of any stripe."

"I beg your pardon, Shaw? You broke into *my* house boldly enough. Has your courage failed you now that it might be of some use?"

"Now, listen, Atwood—"

Lewis called out from the hall to let them know that the coach and the fourth of their party were both ready.

"Excellent," Atwood said. "Thank you, Lewis."

Lewis climbed up into the driver's perch with his lantern. Atwood climbed into the coach, and Arthur followed. A moment later, the fourth of their party hopped up, forcing Arthur to shift. He was horrified to see that it was Mr Dimmick.

"Dimmick! By God—what—"

Dimmick's grin was the same as it had been back when he'd worked in Gracewell's Engine, but the rest of him was greatly changed. He wore shoes and a hat, which made him appear somewhat less simian. His shoulders were still broad and muscular, but his face looked thin, as if he'd spent the last few weeks starving in a gutter, or tossing and turning in a fever. His cheeks were blotched with awful burns—grey in the darkness of the cab—and his left hand was wrapped in a dirty-looking bandage. He rested his long black stick on his knees.

"Ah," Atwood said, "of course, you've met; you were both Gracewell's employees. I have retained Mr Dimmick's services for tonight."

"He tried to kill me!"

Dimmick held up a hand. "No hard feelings, Mr Shaw! I got myself confused, that's all. All our hard work going up in flames. You just asked too many questions. Just a nosy bugger. That's all. Innocent man. See that now."

"Right. Yes. That's right, Mr Dimmick."

The coach started moving, and Arthur realised that he was stuck in it with Dimmick whether he liked it or not.

Dimmick nodded. "Thought on it long and hard, bandaged up in that bed. Let 'im go. Let 'im be. That's what I thought, in the end."

Dimmick leaned forward, putting his grinning face unpleasantly close to Arthur's. "Don't worry, Mr Shaw. No man in London better than me to have on your side in a fight. Ask His Lordship."

The streets were empty and they were quickly moving at such a gallop over the cobbles that it made Arthur queasy.

Atwood muttered over his hands, uttering the names of the stars and the angels and the Kabbalah.

"Atwood."

"Hmm?"

"Atwood—why *is* Mr Dimmick here?"

"Dimmick is here to ensure that all goes well."

"And how will he do that?"

"I would not say that Dimmick is a learned man. He has not developed his mind to any great extent—even Dimmick would admit that. But he is well-travelled, and he has developed his body. Boxing, and weightlifting, and the deeper arcana: *savate*, and *jujutsu*, and what-have-you."

Dimmick sat back smugly. "You and me, Mr Shaw, working for His Lordship again."

Arthur didn't think of himself as Atwood's employee, but he didn't want to argue the point.

"Mr Dimmick—what happened to Vaz?"

"Who? Oh yeah, him. Could be he got out." Dimmick shrugged, as if it was of no particular concern to him whether a man was alive or dead, whether he had or had not murdered him.

They rode for a while in silence and darkness, except for the hooves of the horses and the crack of Lewis's whip, and Atwood's mutterings, which Arthur took to be a form of ritual preparation. Dimmick absent-mindedly tapped his stick on his knee.

"This is awful, Atwood."

"He must needs go that the devil drives, Shaw."

"Devils. Quite right. Devils indeed. Now we're consorting with—listen, Atwood, why can't your Hidden bloody Masters help us?"

"Be quiet, Shaw. I have to prepare myself. You should be ready, too. No help will be coming from that quarter."

"No—I dare say not. There's no such bloody thing, is there? There's just you and Jupiter and Mr Sun; madmen the lot of you, and I'm the maddest of all for listening to you. I should take Josephine to a doctor."

"I'll have Lewis stop for you if you want to walk home. Otherwise, be silent."

Arthur stewed for a while in silence.

Lewis called muffled commands. The coach came to a stop.

Harley Street was silent. A weak moon, thick clouds. A light here and there in an upper window suggested doctors working late into the night over studies or experiments. The heat of the day was long gone. Something in the air threatened rain. Lewis stayed with the coach on the corner. He shuttered his lantern, rolled a cigarette, and hunched against the cold.

No lights in Thorold's windows. It was a dark and nondescript edifice of brick, indistinguishable at night from any of its neighbours, except that a plaque by the door identified Thorold by name and as a consulting physician at St. Bartholomew's Hospital.

Atwood gestured at the door, and Dimmick stepped forward, hunching over the lock, seeming to use his stick as a sort of crowbar. The door opened with a sickening crunch and Dimmick led the way inside.

To their right was a waiting room. Shelves of heavy tomes, presumably medical, and paintings of the sea.

A sound of footsteps, then a cough, somewhere in the darkness ahead. The glow of a light coming from under a door. Arthur froze, turned to bolt back out into the street. Atwood put a hand on his shoulder and pointed to the waiting-room. Dimmick took off his hat.

Light filled the hall. Thorold emerged from his pantry, nudging the door closed with one slippered foot. He cut an unimpressive figure, and at first Arthur took him for a servant. He was barefoot, in a nightshirt and cap, with a pair of large horn-rimmed spectacles. He carried a candle in one hand and a plate of biscuits in the other. He turned, dropped the plate, and stared in wide-eyed shock at the invaders, lifting up the candle as if he thought they must surely be a trick of the light, and a better angle might dispel them.

In the light of the candle Dr Thorold looked pale and clammy, as if he'd been awoken by a nightmare.

"You!" Thorold stared at Atwood. "You bloody lunatic, what are you doing here?"

"Thorold!" Atwood made a gesture with his left hand, holding up fingers like crooked horns. "Stop, Thorold. You're—"

Thorold blew out his candle, dropped it, turned, and ran. Atwood ran after him, but in the dark he stepped on the candle as it rolled underfoot, and he fell. Arthur stooped to help him up.

"Stop him! Stop him—Dimmick, where's Dimmick?"

Dimmick charged, jumping over Atwood, holding his hat to his head and brandishing his stick. Atwood and Arthur ran along behind him, through Thorold's parlour, where Arthur banged into a looming black grand piano, and Atwood was startled by his own suddenly moonlit white-faced reflection in a mirror. When they entered Thorold's study—a dusty, dark dead-end cluttered with books and papers, stuffed owls and weasels, jars and skulls and flasks of God-knows-what—Dimmick already had Thorold cornered, his stick under the old man's jaw. Thorold's spectacles had come loose from one ear and dangled precariously on the end of his nose.

"You *will* answer my questions," Atwood said.

Thorold glared. "This is common burglary, Atwood."

"Hah! Then you admit you know who I am."

"Of course I know who you are, Your Lordship. And is this creature Dimmick? I know him by reputation—but Good Lord, look at him. What a specimen. Leave my house, Atwood."

"You murdered a colleague of mine, and you're in league with my—my enemies."

"I don't know what you're talking about, Your Lordship. Of course I follow your work—we share an interest in the new science, after all. Mine is an amateur interest, but of course medicine occupies so much of my time. I knew your father, once upon a time. A great man—"

"Enough!"

Dimmick jabbed Thorold's chin and he fell silent.

"Now, answer my questions, doctor, and truthfully. By Mercury I command it, and Ishtar, and the Holy Ghost. Oriston, Soter, Eloy, Tetra-grammaton . . ."

Dimmick relaxed his stick to permit Thorold to remove his dangling spectacles. Thorold ignored Atwood's chant, glanced at Arthur, and asked who he was. Arthur said nothing.

Thorold polished his spectacles with his sleeve, muttering.

"I'll ask again. Who are you, young man, and why are you in my house, and why are you in league with Martin Atwood? What has he promised you? You have made a very foolish choice, my friend—Atwood's path will lead to your ruination as a magician and as a man."

". . . Zeboth, Adon, Elion, Tetragrammaton!" Atwood said. "Name your allies, Doctor Thorold."

Thorold quite casually tossed his spectacles to Arthur, who blinked in surprise and couldn't help but catch them. Instantly he found himself dizzy and stumbling—it seemed that the room had spun. He thought for a moment that he'd somehow tripped and fallen—where had that bookshelf come from, and where had the desk gone?

He realised with a sickening sensation that he was now standing where Thorold had been standing a moment before, and Thorold had taken his place on the other side of his study. It had only taken an instant, and now all four men in the room were moving again, but Thorold was too close to his desk to stop. He snatched up a small glass jar, and gulped most of its contents down before Dimmick's stick knocked it from his hand. His face twisted in pain and he fell to the floor.

Atwood shouted "Name them!"

Thorold sprawled, thrashing his naked hairy legs. He coughed out names: *Backhouse, Carroll, Sandys*. Atwood repeated his command and Thorold coughed out *Podmore*, and then laughed, and then roared senselessly, jerking and twisting as if his neck and his spine were breaking—as if he were being broken in the jaws of a great invisible cat—and his eyes rolled up in agony. His limbs shook and his hair stood up, thick and bristly.

Thorold jumped to his feet. He seemed taller now: long-limbed, wild-eyed, long-toothed. Long hairy fingers grabbed Atwood's shirt and lifted him, struggling and uttering futile words of power; then Thorold threw Atwood into the door-frame. Atwood cried out and slid onto the floor.

Arthur dropped Thorold's spectacles and looked about for a weapon. Nothing obvious presented itself.

Dimmick picked up a large glass jar and dashed it on Thorold's head. Dimmick's stick appeared to have been snapped in two somehow while Arthur wasn't looking. Blood and glass everywhere—Thorold staggered but returned to the fray, with vigour that would have been remarkable in a man a third of his age. He seized Dimmick by the throat and the two of them wrestled, reeling from side to side of the room, knocking books off shelves and shattering glass. Occasional moonlight illuminated them. Dimmick butted Thorold's head, drenching the scene in fresh blood. The doctor howled, lifted Dimmick, and hurled him bodily into a shelf. Dimmick fell to the floor and rolled in broken glass, swearing mightily.

Atwood crawled towards Arthur and crouched in the doorway at his side. He was winded, and bleeding from a cut on his head.

Thorold ran for the door—almost down on all fours now, loping—and Arthur tackled him. They rolled together, sliding on smooth parquet into the wall. Somehow Arthur ended up underneath the old man, whose eyes were yellow, whose breath was foul, whose teeth glittered. Arthur held on to a hank of his hair for dear life, scared to let go.

Dimmick struck Thorold on the back of the head with a candlestick, then hauled him off Arthur, grunting, *hup, hup, hup, you bastard, hup.*

Atwood, on his feet again, chanted some sort of gibberish, one hand commandingly raised. What effect this had, if any, Arthur couldn't tell. Dimmick and Thorold, bloody and tattered, bashed each other against one wall, then another. Then in the next sliver of moonlight Dimmick had somehow got up on Thorold's shoulders, the better to bash at his head and gouge at his eyes. Thorold bit Dimmick's wrist. They stumbled, writhed. Dimmick kicked Thorold's leg. Thorold howled and fell. Bone glinted. Dimmick kicked again, and again, and again. Then, as Thorold writhed on the floor, Dimmick went for the candlestick again.

Arthur averted his eyes from the final blow.

In the silence that followed, Arthur could still hear the echoes of the struggle—*thump thump thump*. It took him a while to realise that it was his heart.

Atwood re-entered the study.

"Well done, Mr Dimmick."

Dimmick swayed. "Sir."

"Fortunate that I was able to contain his power."

"Yes," Arthur said. "Well *bloody* done, all of us. God forgive us."

IV: The Hour of Venus

By Arthur's reckoning, it was now the hour of Venus, which was suitable for the calling up of spirits, the learning of secrets, and the resolution of mysteries.

They searched Dr Thorold's premises. Atwood had uttered some words that he said would delay the arrival of the police, or nosy neighbours. Arthur found bandages, and bound Dimmick's wounds as best he knew how, while Dimmick cursed at him. Atwood collected all the papers he could find in Thorold's study, and a handful of books.

"Thieving from the dead," Arthur said. "Good God."

"These may hold the key to the conspiracy. If you lack the will to do what must be done—"

"I swear to you, Atwood—" Arthur made a fist, then let it go. "Never mind. I'll search upstairs."

Upstairs, he found no evidence that Thorold had any family, for which small mercy he gave thanks. There was an empty maid's room, its window swinging open over the garden. No other servants. Thorold lived frugally for a man of his station. *Had* lived. He'd liked photographs, and paintings of dogs, and he had a large collection of books in French and German. He was—had been—untidy, in the way of scholars and elderly bachelors (not to mention wolves), and his rooms upstairs were full of heaps of papers and books arranged in ways that no doubt had made sense only to him, with cups and plates and old bits of toast interspersed among them. Medical papers. Accounts of expenses and income. A lecture on hospital administration. Some correspondence with the university. A quiet life, and no more than a moderately eccentric one. It did not seem like the house of a murderer, or like the lair of something worse.

When Arthur came downstairs again, Atwood was searching through the cabinets in Thorold's study.

"The maid may have fled by the window," Arthur said. "I wouldn't be at all surprised if she goes to the police. Atwood, are you listening?"

"Yes. What clues did you find to the nature of the conspiracy?"

"Conspiracy? Not a thing."

Arthur glanced through the door at the lanky thing that lay dead on the floor, and shuddered.

"I don't know," Atwood said.

"Hmm?"

"Doctor Thorold's transformation. I've never seen anything like it. Old magic, made new. . . . I wish we'd been able to save some of that fluid."

"Thank God we didn't!"

Dimmick slouched by the front door, smoking a cigarette. Arthur advised him to leave his bandages alone. Dimmick swore at him.

The door to Thorold's basement was locked. It didn't respond to any of Atwood's mystical passes and muttered incantations. Dimmick limped up, kicked it open, then went back to sitting and smoking by the front door.

At the foot of the stairs there were four cages, containing some dogs and a much-abused ape. Arthur thought it was a chimpanzee. Whatever it was, it awakened Atwood's mercurial sympathies. Tears came to his eyes, and he insisted on giving the creature a merciful death. A job for Dimmick, naturally.

There was another door, not locked. The windowless room beyond was full of a terrible bitter-sweet odour. Apart from the odour, the room contained bookshelves, cabinets, unlit gaslamps. In an alcove in a corner

Arthur found a collection of sketches and photographs of Augustus Mordaunt, the late Duke of Sussex, whose mysterious death on the night of the storm had kept the police busy for the past half-year, and the newspapers occupied in ghoulish speculation. Words in heavy gothic lettering circled the dead man's face: the names of angels and demons and fairies, drippings of wax and blood and tar. On the floor of the cabinet was a dagger, and a glass jar with a dried black fluid encrusted on it. This, Arthur supposed, was a clue. He called Atwood over.

"Ah," Atwood said. "Well, well."

"Can you explain this, Atwood?"

"As a matter of fact, I can. I suppose you know that the late Duke had an interest in the occult? For a very long time. I had approached him regarding the activities of the Company. He was very interested, though somewhat alarmed. He was terribly ill, you know. Who knows what we might find out in the spheres, I said—who knows what treasures, what powers, what medicines . . . He began to support us. With money, that is. Gracewell always says that the Engine should pay for itself one day, but in the meantime I find I have to shoulder rather more expense than I would like. I've had to sell off some properties. Anyway, there it is; you can see why my enemies would do what they did."

"By God, Atwood—is everyone in London a magician?"

"Fashion. Lately there has been a quite regrettable fashion. Men of power, greedy for more power over this world, take to the study as if it were a business."

"And you?"

"My sights are set higher. Knowledge, Shaw, not power."

Atwood scraped the wax and sniffed at his fingernail. He poked at the glass jar, being careful not to touch the fluid. He began to explain the ritual Thorold had employed, the forces he had summoned to inflict ill-health, fevers, bad luck, trembling, and falling. He paced the room, candle held high, guessing where Thorold and his co-conspirators had sat to perform this horrible procedure.

"A minimum of half a dozen, Shaw. A minimum. If only they'd left their cards, ha-ha. On the night of the storm—the very same night, while we were otherwise occupied—a blow from two directions at once. They are *schemers*, these people . . ."

Arthur stopped listening. He'd seen enough to suppose that whatever awful things Atwood was saying were true, or true enough. He felt that there should be a moment of silence.

So they'd solved the mystery of the Duke's murder, where Scotland Yard had failed; and the *Times*; and Arthur Conan Doyle; and a hundred psychics, letter-writers, and busy-bodies. But what now? They couldn't tell the police what they'd done. They couldn't tell anyone. No one would credit it if they did. So order and sanity couldn't be restored, and the mystery was unsolvable after all, and things would only get worse. He would have preferred not to know.

Atwood set the pictures on fire, and smashed the glass.

"Did you know?"

"Hmm?"

"Atwood—did you know? Is that why you wanted to come here?"

"We avenged two murders tonight. I would think your conscience could be at ease."

"Did you know?"

"The spirits gave me an inkling. Though I wish they could have given me more warning of Thorold's . . . tendencies. Let that be a lesson to you about spirits."

"And how does this help us find Josephine?"

"One less enemy." Atwood paced around the room in circles, stopping sometimes, as if imagining his enemies seated for their horrible ritual. "And how else should our investigation proceed? Nothing in magic is by the direct method. Yet now I begin—perhaps—to perceive the nature of our enemy. The shape of their circle. We have shed a little light upon the dark."

"We're back where we were."

"Then tomorrow we may begin again."

"It's Sunday tomorrow. I intend to go to church."

V: The Hour of Saturn

It was the small hours of morning when Arthur finally arrived back at the flat off Piccadilly. He entered quietly, took off his shoes and coat, and crept into the silent room where Josephine slept.

She wore a white nightdress. No blankets or pillows; not safe. The maid Abby had brushed out her hair. She grew paler every day of her absence, the way that dust will accumulate in an unused room. Arthur suspected she wasn't eating enough.

There were times when she twisted and moaned, as if she were having a nightmare; and there were times when she was calm, even smiling. When she smiled, Arthur told himself that it was a sign that all was well wherever she was, and that she was on her way home to him. When she moaned, he told himself that it meant nothing at all.

Abby was asleep in a chair in the corner of the room, her knees drawn up and her head on her arm. Asleep, she looked even smaller than she did awake—she was little more than a child, and, curled up in a chair, she looked doll-like.

There were tears on his face. He wiped them with his sleeve. The horror of Dr Thorold's house returned to him and his knees trembled.

He crept out of Josephine's room, and closed the door.

He couldn't sleep. He couldn't even think of sleeping. He lit a candle, poured himself a glass of Atwood's whisky, and paced. He examined the books on Atwood's mantelpiece: a family history, Lucretius, Milton, various Bibles, the *De Lapidibus* of Bishop Marbode, and the *Contra Celsum*. Baedeker Guides: *Paris and its Environs, Palestine and Syria, The Eastern Alps.* Far-off places he would surely never see. He stared out the window waiting for dawn to come over the rooftops. He cleaned his shoes. He took off his jacket and inspected it for tell-tale signs of the struggle at Dr Thorold's house. It was while he was brushing at a speck of dirt on his cuff that he noticed that a calling-card sat on the table by the door. Someone must have visited and left it with Abby. He went to examine it.

The card bore a design of an ill-tempered dragon coiled about what might have been a printing press. Beneath that was the name Henry Addington, Lord Podmore.

It gave Arthur a chill to see that name, and a worse chill to think that Podmore or his agents had been knocking at the door that night. The card hadn't been there when he left the house to attend Atwood's Rite of Mars, and that had been at eleven o'clock. It was now perhaps three or four in the morning. A midnight visit could hardly be a friendly one. But then why had Podmore left his card?

There was no note with it, no letter. Nothing was written on the back of the card. The paper was very finely glazed—in fact, it seemed polished, so that in the darkness of the hall it was somewhat dimly reflective. Curious, Arthur held it up so that it caught the faint light of the candle next door. He could see the shadow of his own face reflected in it, dim and wobbling. He lifted the card a little higher and tilted it. The reflection of the candle's light sharpened and brightened, and his own face became clear, as if he were looking into a mirror. Behind him, over his reflection's shoulder, stood four men. His reflection's eyes widened.

Chapter Twenty

Arthur dropped the card, and his drink. He turned to see that four men stood in the hall, quite impossibly, as if they'd stepped Alice-like from the mirror.

Three of them were young men in shirt-sleeves and caps, all of whom had the grey pallor and inky eyes that Arthur associated with Podmore's men. The fourth was older: fat, imposingly tall, black-bearded, in a long green coat. Stranger still, they had brought a long black cabinet with them.

Two men rushed him. He swung his fist and caught one with a glancing blow, but it did no good. They shoved him against the door so hard that the breath left his body, then forced him to his knees. At the fat man's gestured directions, they heaved him up and shoved him into the drawing-room and down onto Atwood's sofa. One man remained to menace Arthur with a knife, while the other two dragged the long black cabinet into the room, then went into the bedroom. One dragged Abby out and threw her in a tearful heap in a corner of the room. The other carried Josephine flung over his shoulder. The knife-man gave Arthur's collarbone a significant jab.

They heaved the cabinet up on its end and stood it against the wall. It was man-height, and extraordinarily ornate, made of polished ebony, inlayed with gold and ivory and pearl. The lower part of it was decorated with complicated, swirling designs that looked Arabic to Arthur's eye, while the upper part was crowded with Egyptian hieroglyphs. Podmore's men opened the lid, put Josephine inside it, and shut her away as if in a wardrobe. There was a loud *click* and a much louder *thump*. When the lid swung open again, the wardrobe was empty.

Arthur croaked. He felt faint. The only light in the room was the candle that was now in the fat man's hand, as he *tut-tutted* at Atwood's bookshelves. The cabinet loomed nightmarishly. The pale men moved through the gloom like burglars, like figments of a nightmare.

The fat man leafed through a book, shaking his head and muttering. Then he sighed, put it back on the shelf, pulled up a chair, and sat facing Arthur.

"Arthur Archibald Shaw," he said. "My name is Addington—Lord Podmore. I hear you are a newspaper man. A noble profession. I am a newspaper man too, in my way. I do not ordinarily make unannounced visits, or indeed poke my head outside my shell at all; but to make the acquaintance of young Master Atwood's newest associate I will make an exception."

He gestured at the man with the knife. "You there—find us something to drink. Mr Shaw will need to wet his throat. He has a great deal to tell us."

Arthur sat on the sofa. Thugs loomed. The wound in his side ached, for the first time in a long while. It had healed so swiftly, thanks to Sun's excellent ministrations, that he'd almost forgotten it, but the struggle appeared to have aggravated it again.

"Well, Mr Shaw. Is it true?"

Lord Podmore had placed the candle on the table. Now his head seemed over-large, floating in the darkness. There was something gross about him; he resembled a caricature that might have appeared in one of his own newspapers. His sallow skin appeared golden, his copious black beard oily and glittering, his eyes recessed in shadow. He had an air of irritation at having been called out so late at night.

"Your wife, Mr Shaw—is it true that Atwood and his fellows sent her among the spheres?"

"We weren't married."

"Ah." Podmore nodded. "My apologies. Sometimes my men err."

"The spheres—yes. So Atwood tells me."

"Well!" Podmore poked one of his men cheerfully in the elbow. The man scowled, and flinched from the contact like an unfriendly cat. "That would be a story, wouldn't it. Imagine it in the newspapers: *London bride-to-be visits the moon.* I don't suppose she disappeared on her wedding night, did she? No? *Was* it the moon, Mr Shaw, to which our friend Atwood dispatched her?"

It seemed to be a genuine question, expecting an answer.

"Mars, he says."

"Even better. The public love their stories of Mars. Wandering among the canals. The ruins of ancient glories." Podmore laughed. His men didn't. They prowled around the room, coming in and out of sight.

"What have you done with her? Where is she? What is that . . . thing?"

"That?" Podmore glanced at the cabinet. Its door was closed now; its ornament glittering in the dark. "That is the Cabinet of Osiris." He looked as if he expected Arthur to recognise it.

"What have you done with her?"

Podmore shrugged. "Your wife is with your erstwhile employer Mr Gracewell. Neither of them need come to any harm, but you understand that we must know what your new friends have done to her. There are a great many urgent questions. Matters of emergency, one might say."

"What do you want from me?"

"Answers, Mr Shaw. How do you come to be working for Martin At-wood's merry band?"

"Accident. Bad luck. The storm."

Podmore laughed. "Come on, Shaw. What did Atwood promise you?"

"Six pounds. Six bloody pounds a week."

Podmore looked confused.

Abby started sobbing and pleading to know what they meant to do with her. Arthur wanted to calm her, but he was too afraid himself, and couldn't find the words.

"You and you," Podmore said. Two of his men picked Abby up off the floor and threw her on the sofa beside Arthur. Her elbow jabbed his wounded side and he swore.

"I'm sure you will find this terribly difficult to believe, given your cur-rent unfortunate predicament, but we—*my* colleagues and I—have no evil intent. Atwood's lot, on the other hand, are terribly dangerous. We are act-ing in the best interests of London—of England—the Empire. The world, for that matter."

Podmore settled back into Atwood's sofa as if it were a favourite arm-chair at his club, folded his hands across his belly, and adopted the style of a man making an extemporaneous after-dinner speech. "And you are here quite by accident. I see that now. An innocent—a bystander—entangled in schemes of greater powers. And yet, this is such a time of crisis that no man can stand neutral. The Company of the Spheres must be stopped. *Delenda est.*"

Arthur reached under his shirt and poked gingerly at his wound. No blood, thank God. It felt swollen, and itched abominably.

One of Podmore's men stood at his master's shoulder. Another leaned against the Cabinet, and the third was somewhere behind Arthur, by the window. From where Arthur sat, he could reach out and strike Podmore; but what good would that do? They had Josephine. God only knew where.

"What do you imagine will happen, Mr Shaw, if the Company succeeds?"

"I don't know."

"Man was not meant to walk on the moon. Still less on Mars, or Venus, or wherever else Atwood might choose to gallivant off to tomorrow." Podmore paused, as if expecting laughter, then snorted. He rolled his drink around his glass. "I never did like that arrogant child, even before what happened to his poor father. He sought my support for his enterprise. I was appalled. Delusions! Lunacy! I blame that woman, whoever she is—they encourage the worst in each other."

He shook his head sadly, then he sent the man who stood at his shoulder off in search of something to eat. "Hungry work, the Mirror of Solomon."

Arthur took him to be referring to the trick he'd used to enter Atwood's flat.

"What do you know of the denizens of Mars, Mr Shaw?"

"Nothing. Nothing at all."

"Quite. Nor do I. Nor does anyone. Devils; angels; who can know? Unknown powers. Atwood believes he can master them. Perhaps. I consider his confidence unwarranted. God knows what sort of wrath he might call down—and not only upon himself."

Podmore's man placed another glass of whisky in his hand and some bread and cheese in front of him.

"Suppose he prevails—suppose the Company opens a route to the spheres. Imagine, before Columbus discovered the New World, trying to guess what wealth it might hold. Understand, Shaw, I'm not talking of goods or furs or silver or potatoes, I mean *power*. I mean the magical power that might be the Company's if they control the route to the spheres themselves. How could we permit that? And I shan't even speak of the trouble that infernal Engine could cause—training a mob of riff-raff in tech-niques they have no business knowing."

Podmore ate a chunk of the bread, and wiped his mouth with his sleeve.

"There is a delicate balance, Mr Shaw, and Atwood threatens to upset it. If we don't stop them now, someone else will—someone worse. Magical war, Shaw, with London as the battleground. The Germans are already here—so my men tell me. And God help us, what if the Americans get involved? Or the bloody Chinese?"

"Germans? Americans? Chinese?"

"Dear me, you are a naïf, aren't you, my boy? I am speaking of the magical societies of Boston, of Peking. I am speaking of the Teutonic Order and the Hyperborean Society of Berlin and worse . . ." Podmore shook his head. "So you see, Shaw, why your friend's ambitions must be stopped."

"He's no friend of mine," Arthur said.

"Good!"

"Will you let Josephine go?"

"Perhaps. If you help us. More is at stake than your young woman."

Podmore held out his hand, and one of his men placed a notebook in it. He leafed through the pages, muttering to himself. His men hovered. They seemed to be waiting eagerly for something awful to happen.

Arthur's wound throbbed so painfully that he doubled over. He stared at his feet, trying not to throw up, contemplating his situation. All this talk of Germans and Chinese was more than he could keep straight; it might be true or it might be fantasy. Podmore had Josephine. That was what counted. If he helped Podmore, Podmore might release her. But then what if he helped Podmore, and as a result Podmore prevailed over Atwood? Then who would rescue her soul? Body or soul, soul or body. If he saved her from Podmore, could she bring herself back from wherever she was? He didn't know what to do. His wound felt as if it might tear open.

Podmore rapped his knuckles on the table. The noise made Abby jump. "The names of your colleagues, Shaw."

"Sun. Mercury. Terra Mater. Mar—"

"Their real names."

"I don't know them all. Martin Atwood. Samuel—Samuel Jessop. But

Jessop is in the same boat as me, Podmore. He's hardly a leader of Atwood's group, he's really only a—"

"I know a thing or two about Sergeant Jessop, Shaw—we can discuss him later. What do you know about the woman who calls herself Jupiter?"

"Nothing."

"Remember: the young woman's life is in my hands."

"I can't tell you what I don't know."

"Who is the master of their Company, Mr Shaw?"

"Their master? Atwood, I suppose—or Jupiter, or Sun. I don't know what you mean."

"How did Mr Norman Gracewell come by the idea for his Engine?"

"I don't know. He's a mathematician."

"You believe he invented it himself? Without aid?"

"I don't know what you mean. You have him prisoner, sir—I suggest you ask him yourself."

"Oh, we have. He's terribly uncooperative. Says he doesn't remember. He doesn't remember rather a lot—most of '83 and '84. I'm sure you can imagine how that worries us."

"They have a book."

"A book?"

"They call it the *Liber Ad Astra*. It's where they write their secrets."

Podmore motioned for him to continue. He began to describe it, but soon Podmore was rolling his eyes.

"This is nonsense, Mr Shaw. Mere fog. Atwood has been wasting your time. Keeping you in the dark." Podmore sighed. "Would you like something to eat? I can see we are going to be here for a very long time."

By now Abby had stopped sobbing and was curled up in a corner of the sofa as if hoping to burrow into it and be forgotten.

Podmore yawned, and for some reason that casual gesture made Arthur furious all over again. He didn't see how the members of the Hyperborean Society or the magicians of Peking could be that much worse than Podmore.

"Now, Shaw, tell me about the operations of Gracewell's Engine."

"What do you want to know?"

"Everything, of course. Everything that you know. Can you reconstruct it?"

Arthur's heart sank still further. He had a vision of his future: working for Podmore, slaving over a third and still more inhuman iteration of the Engine, out in God knows where, with Podmore's uncanny thugs looking over his shoulder, nothing to keep him working but the promise that one day Podmore might return Josephine to him. He'd grow old. He'd go mad.

"Speak, Shaw. Answer the question."

It would be better to charge Podmore, hope to bowl him over, break free, and escape into the street. Worry about how to rescue Josephine later.

"Can't speak, Shaw, or won't speak?"

He felt Abby trembling beside him.

"Shaw, do you know what they are? My men, that is. Has Atwood told you?"

"No."

"I want you to understand who I am, and I want you to understand that I am a far greater magician than that upstart, so listen. Each of these men is an employee of one of my newspapers. I won't tell you their names. They don't know their names themselves, in their present state. They wouldn't know their own wives or children. And tomorrow they will remember nothing of tonight's events. Nothing of what they might do."

"Lord Podmore—"

"Lord, they know not what they do! A state of ecstasy. No doubt you've noticed their eyes—ink, Mr Shaw. They drink it. At my command. A condition of employment in the inner circle. It's a precious commodity, that ink; rarer than diamonds. It costs me great labour to extract it. The ink of newspaper stories, Mr Shaw. The nastiest sort. Murders and pogroms and babies dead in their mothers' arms and disease and sin and wickedness and horror. All the worst that London is capable of imagining. They're drunk with it, Mr Shaw. Positively tipsy. Whatever they do now, they'll forget in the morning. Nothing but a nasty story. Do you understand? Do you believe me? In their trance they have a certain gift of prophecy. A gift for bad news. The terrible things that they say come true—even if they have to make them come true themselves. Shall we ask one of them now, what happens to Mr Shaw? What happens if he won't speak? Eh? Shaw, are you listening to me?"

The wound in Arthur's side throbbed again, stunning him with pain. He put a hand on Abby's arm and squeezed so hard that she gasped in shock. With the other hand he pulled up his shirt. The wound was hot and swollen, straining against the stitches.

Arthur couldn't take it any more. He tugged at the end of one of the stitches and it came loose, unravelling like a shoelace. Almost at once he felt such a surge of relief that he hardly noticed Podmore getting to his feet. He tugged at another stitch. The pain eased more as the lips of the wound sighed gently open. Wondering why he hadn't thought of this earlier, he probed the wound. No blood. Longer and wider than he remembered. Another stitch unravelled. He reached inside the wound as if into a pocket and a sharpness pricked his finger. Something soft and warm and sleek brushed out past his hand, flapped out in front of Abby's openmouthed face, and up towards the ceiling.

His wound had hatched a bird.

It was black, and no bigger than a sparrow, except for a long, elegant, ribbon-like tail. Its breast was a brilliant ruby-red, and there was a touch of yellow on its sharp little beak, the beak that had pricked Arthur's finger. It didn't look English. Its call was clear and metallic. It circled the room, up near the ceiling, in a steady calm orbit, apparently not confused or surprised to be occupying a flat with Arthur, a shrieking maid, several silent thugs watching it with narrowed black eyes, and a furious red-faced newspaper-magnate-cum-warlock.

Something about it seemed to utterly infuriate Podmore, or perhaps terrify him. He threw his drink at it, and then a cushion. He stood on his chair and tried to catch it with his hands. He shouted at his men to *stop it, stop it at once!* One of them jumped up on the sofa; another ran to get a broom; a third jumped from the mantelpiece, missed the bird, and crashed onto the table, putting out the candle. The bird shrilled overhead. Its call was louder now, loud as a bell, as if it were crying *wake up, wake up, wake up.*

For a minute or two Arthur watched all this as if he were in the theatre, watching God knows what. Then he jumped to his feet, ran for where he thought the fireplace was, and scrabbled for the poker. He pulled Abby with him. Someone big moved behind him and he turned and swung the poker. He hit something; there was a thump and a howl of outrage. He swung again. Something cracked, and the grunt of pain was Podmore's. Abby stumbled and nearly pulled Arthur over with her, and the next thing he knew, Podmore was gone. Arthur swung the poker once more.

He seemed to be flailing at shadows. There were running feet and shouting and the shrill insistent call of the mysterious tropical bird.

Sun!—Sun must have done this, whatever it was, when he stitched up the wound. A measure of protection, to make up for the watch he'd reclaimed. Which was all very well, but it would have been better if he hadn't kept it a secret—there were enough bloody secrets!

Arthur ran across the room, swinging the poker wildly, pulling Abby behind him, until he found the Cabinet. It seemed taller in the darkness, much taller and heavier than it could possibly have been when Podmore's men brought it in. He bashed it with the poker until it opened. Terrible crashing and sparks. Bits of ornamental something or other depicting devils and angels and ibises and jackal-headed somethings fell off. The door swung open. No Josephine. White shadows tumbled out and enveloped him. There was a smell of dust and soap. He flailed at the shadows that covered his face; stumbled and tripped and fell and lay on his back as they fell on top of him.

Abby lit a candle.

Arthur was lying on his back under a small heap of dusty old clothes. There was broken china all around him. There was no looming and arcane Cabinet of Osiris overhead, only the wardrobe that had always been in the corner of the room, which he'd never bothered to open before.

He stood. Abby was in her nightshirt, breathing heavily. The room was otherwise empty. No thugs, no bird, no Podmore. The table was not broken. No sign of Podmore's half-eaten meal or the glasses he and his men had drunk from. Apart from the damage Arthur had done to the wardrobe, everything was as it had been before he picked up the card.

He ran into the bedroom. One thing had changed: Josephine's bed was empty. He threw open all the doors and looked out the window. She was gone.

He went back and shook the wardrobe as if she might tumble out of a concealed chamber, like a magician's assistant.

Abby was already half-dressed and packing up her things. He started to ask her if she'd seen what had happened, if she'd seen Podmore and the Cabinet and Sun's bird too. She shook her head. She wouldn't speak or look him in the eye. She finished packing and left.

His wound was closed. A pink bumpy scar. No stitches.

He poked around the flat for a little while longer. Then he began to imagine Podmore's men returning. Or Atwood and Dimmick, wanting to know what had happened. Thérèse, paying one of her visits. He thought of all the things he'd told Lord Podmore, all the secrets of the Company he'd spilled. He packed up a handful of possessions and any money he could find, and fled.

Chapter Twenty-one

By dawn, Arthur had decided that he had no choice but to return to Atwood, to confess his betrayal, to seek sanctuary and forgiveness, but when he arrived at Hanover Square, he found Atwood's house in ruins. Fire had shattered the windows and collapsed part of the roof. It was clear at a glance that the house was abandoned. The trees nearby were bare, and the square was littered disgustingly with dozens upon dozens of dead crows, and pigeons, and rats. Lord Podmore had obviously wasted no time.

Arthur turned and walked away, and walked for hours, until he hardly knew where he was any more. He found a cheap boarding-house room and a corner of a park to sit in until the evening; then he got drunk in a vile and noisy gin-palace. He told himself that he was drinking to get up courage—but for what? He didn't know. He had no plan. He drank with the diligence and patience of a man working out mathematics in Gracewell's Engine, and he staggered back to his room and fell asleep on the floor, where he suffered a terrible nightmare all night long.

In his nightmare, Josephine was lost on a vast blood-red plain, under a dark and shifting and shadowy sky. She stumbled in the gloom over sharp rocks. Something pursued her, something that was too huge and too dark to see clearly, something so huge that it seemed perhaps it was Mars itself. Arthur called to her to come and join him in his hiding place, but she could not hear him—or perhaps, he began to fear, she didn't trust him. He had failed her once too often. It was his pride and greed that had left them in their current predicament. He said as much to Atwood—in his dream Atwood was with him in his hiding-place, stroking his elegant little beard and chattering away about Albertus Magnus and Dr John Dee, and about the uses of vervain and mandrake root, and the thousand hidden names of Krishna, and the monsters (black and thousand-legged and hungry and squirming) that lived on Saturn. Gracewell was there too, drawing geometric figures on the walls of the cave. Sun stood behind Arthur, writing something on his back. Even Podmore was there, watching and taking notes. Arthur stood in the mouth of the cave and called out for Josephine. He called out all the names he could think of for her, until he was calling out nonsense words into a shrill wind that smelled of sand and blood and ruin. Josephine ran, and stumbled. The shadow loomed over her like the rising of a hideous purple-green moon, a sour and rotting thing.

He went to ground. The Company couldn't help him, wouldn't help him. If Atwood had survived the destruction of his house, he'd know that he had been betrayed. He would not forgive. Arthur was almost as afraid of Dimmick finding him as he was of Podmore. He hid from mirrors and covered the windows of his rented room with newspapers. He performed the few magics of protection against evil that he remembered from *Pow-wows*.

On Saturday afternoon he went out to Blackheath. He sat out on the grass by himself until it was dark, and all the holiday-makers and picnickers with hampers and nurses with perambulators and children with kites had gone home, and he was alone. Then he lay down on his back with his hands behind his head and waited for the stars to come out. It was a clear night and the sky was soon an unbroken spread of stars. Arthur thought he recognised Orion, and Cygnus. He could see the unwinking light of Mars in the southern part of the night sky, and he prayed. He willed himself to see Josephine. He strained to set his imagination free, like a hawk. He sought new modes of perception. He thought that perhaps, his need and desire being so great, he might somehow invent for himself methods that had so far exceeded the grasp of Atwood and Sun and Jupiter and all the combined minds of Gracewell's Engine. He focused his mind on the steady light of Mars, and he thought of its red plains, its two moons. He tried to imagine how Earth might look to someone standing on Mars; struggled to cast his imagination there, to forget his body, the damp of the grass, dogs barking, the dirt clumped beneath his shoulder. *Josephine*, he thought, *Josephine, help me, show me the way, show me where you are, stretch out a hand to me.* It didn't work. Nothing happened. He got very cold.

On Sunday he decided that it was high time he went to church again. He didn't dare go back to his usual place of Sunday worship, for fear that Podmore or Dimmick might be watching. Instead he went to St. James's on the Marylebone Road. It was a large and handsome structure. He chose it almost on a whim, dithered outside, and ducked in at the last moment. The congregation was numerous and bustling, the pews packed even on a beautiful summer's day.

The truth was that he was somewhat relieved to find that he *could* still enter a church. After all his dabblings in crime and sorcery, he'd been half-afraid that the congregation might sense his wickedness and cast him out. A bell might start ringing; lightning might strike him. Instead the sexton gave him a pitying glance and led him to a vacant seat at the very back of the church, beside two old ladies in black who stiffened as he sat down. A marble angel overhead spread its wings and looked down, stone-faced.

He supposed that he looked like a desperate man, a vagrant in need of shelter, a sinner in need of salvation. He was all of those things. He'd hardly changed his clothes in a week. He was jealously hoarding the money he'd snatched from Atwood's flat; he was afraid to visit a bank. The old ladies glared at him, and sniffed. He stared fixedly ahead at the pulpit as the congregation filed in, coughing, murmuring, and gossiping about business and children and holidays and politics and illnesses.

The congregation rose to sing "Creator of the Stars of Night." Arthur joined in, stumbling a little over the hymn's familiar words. If there were a Creator of the Stars, Arthur had seen enough to know that He could not much resemble the God Arthur had always believed in. He found himself trying to imagine the God that the native of the spheres might have worshipped, the God in whose image it might have been made. He simply could not see how it could be the same God that was known to St. James's Church on the Marylebone Road.

The minister stood at the pulpit. There was a hush in which every rustle of the minister's robes and the turning of the pages of his book could be heard, and then he coughed, and began his sermon. He held both sides of the pulpit in his hands and spoke firmly and plainly. His theme was pride, and he took as his text the temptation of Christ in the wilderness by the Devil. Arthur put his head in his hands and imagined the wilderness as the blood-red plains of Mars. He imagined the Devil, standing on a mountaintop, showing off all the ruined glories of the civilizations of Mars. He imagined the Devil with Atwood's face.

But it wasn't Atwood's fault; it was his own. Everything that had happened, to him and to Josephine. If he hadn't blundered blindly into Atwood's house! If he hadn't let greed and ambition blind him to the dangers of Gracewell's Engine! He thought of the men who'd gone mad in Gracewell's Engine, and wondered again what had become of them. *Rising out of the room*—how callow his ambition seemed now. His errors had multiplied and now it was too late to mend any of them.

The minister came to the end of his sermon, and Arthur realised that he hadn't followed most of the man's argument. Well, it was too late now. He stood again to sing. A collection went round. He fled.

It was bright and hot outside and he instantly missed his hat, abandoned in Atwood's flat. He didn't know where to go next. He stood, blinking in the sun, waiting there in the vague hope that some sign might show him what to do.

"Arthur!"

Someone was calling his name. His first instinct was to run.

"I say—Arthur! Is that you? Good Lord, Arthur, it is you! Wait—wait there! Are you—by God, you look an awful bloody mess. Is this your church now? I haven't seen you in weeks. God, my boy, if you've fallen on hard times you know you need only . . . What happened to you?"

By the time he had completed that speech, Arthur's uncle George Weston had caught up with him, and extended his hand to shake.

George Weston wasn't Arthur's real uncle. He had a number of uncles and aunts on his father's side, but they were all in the civil service in far-flung parts of the Empire—or possibly, these days, dead. George Weston was Arthur's foster-father's brother. The two Weston brothers could not, in Arthur's opinion, be less alike. George was good-natured, quick-witted, artistic, and generous. He had an energetic way of talking and a habit of tilting his head to one side and nodding as he spoke, as if he wanted to be sure that you agreed with every word before he offered another. He made a good living in publishing, writing humorous stories about boats. It was George Weston who'd first found Arthur work at the *Mammoth*. He was married to a very lovely woman by the name of Agnes; they had no children.

Arthur was utterly astonished to see him. He'd begun to think he might never again see any of the figures of his former life. He shook George's hand, not knowing what to say.

George studied Arthur carefully, nodding. "Hmm. Hmm. Is something wrong? Is—God, Arthur, is it Josephine?"

"Josephine," Arthur said, "is—she's very ill, George."

George started asking all sorts of questions about Josephine's illness, and insisting that he be permitted to visit her. He considered himself something of an amateur expert on medicine—he liked to write about doctors, and he owned a number of medical encyclopaedias. He meant his questions kindly, but they were not easy to answer.

"At the very least, Arthur, you must let me buy you lunch!"

It wasn't an offer Arthur could refuse. George's hand on his arm was firm. He steered Arthur through the busy street towards a nearby chop-house. Arthur settled heavily into a chair and George sat down opposite him. George had a newspaper and two or three parcels of shopping—mostly books—which he placed beside his chair.

George took another long look at Arthur. "Arthur, when did you last eat?"

"I don't recall. It's been rather difficult lately."

"I prescribe coffee, and plenty of it. And steak. And green vegetables, as many as possible."

He summoned a waiter, who brought coffee. It did Arthur a great deal of good, and it also gave him something to stare at while he lied to his uncle.

"A state of coma," Arthur said. "That's what they call it. The doctors say it's caused by an infection—an inflammation of the tissues of the brain. She breathes, she eats and drinks, but she cannot speak. Her mind is . . . elsewhere."

"What doctors? Where is she?"

"Oh—a multitude of doctors. I sought second opinions."

"But who? I know one or two good doctors myself. I know a chap who studies the brain. I . . ."

"They say she'll recover, George. They promise me. They're doing all they can."

"By God! I saw Josephine just a few weeks ago, didn't I? She was in fine health. How terrible. How terrible. You must be . . . Arthur, if you ever need any help, Agnes and I would . . ."

"Of course. Of course." Arthur sipped his coffee. It made his head spin.

By the time Arthur's steak arrived he was ravenously hungry, and he attacked it like a starving man. Perhaps he *was* starving. He really couldn't remember the last time he ate. Between mouthfuls of red meat and green vegetables he told George that he'd let the flat on Rugby Street, and moved into cheaper accommodations, because of the costs of Josephine's care. He confessed that he'd resorted to spiritualists and faith-healers and prayer.

"Of course," George said. "Of course. Well, Josephine has my prayers as well, and Agnes's, when I tell her."

"I should have come to see you weeks ago, of course."

"You certainly should have. Does your father know?"

"I honestly don't know. I don't recall writing to him; but I seem to have spent most of the last month in a dream, so perhaps I did. Perhaps. George—let's not argue. I want to hear nothing but good news, just for an hour or two. Ordinary life. Business. How's business, George? I see you've been buying books. I always liked talking about books with you. I miss it. What did you buy? Let me see, let me see. What's in the newspaper—good God, I haven't read a newspaper in—I don't know how long. Have you sold any stories?"

"Well—yes. To the *Strand*. And Longmans is publishing another set of the stories in just another—hmm, another month. Rather exciting, rather frightening, as always."

"Well done, George. Well done."

"What's more—can you keep this secret, Arthur? What's more, I think I may be in the running to be the editor of a new magazine. I might be able to find you work there, if you're interested . . ."

"Thank you, George; but I'm a bit busy at present."

"To be frank, Arthur, you look rather desperate."

Arthur chewed on his steak. "I dare say I do."

"Whatever happened to that job in Deptford?"

"The building burned down."

"Good God. You have been having bad luck. Did you break a mirror, or step on a black cat?"

"Not that I recall. Tell me about the magazine."

"Well, it'll be something of a salmagundi, at first—but all very humorous, of course, and the best quality. There's money behind it. Old Podmore himself is putting up half of it—you know, Lord Podmore—and then there's an American financier . . . Are you all right?"

Arthur's fork had stopped half-way to his mouth.

"We're thinking of calling it the *Phaeton*—the magazine, that is. What do you think?"

"Very fine. Do you—have you met Lord Podmore, by any chance?"

"Not yet; but, as a matter of fact, I'll be dining at the Savoy with His Lordship tomorrow night. The American gentleman, too. You know, he's a decent sort of fellow, Podmore. Not half the ogre his reputation suggests. A sharp businessman, too. You wouldn't want to cross him. He plans to outsell the *Strand* by the end of next year, and by God if I don't believe he can do it."

Arthur told him that it was a joy, and the best sort of medicine, to hear about a dear friend's good fortune; and that he wanted to hear all about the *Phaeton*, and all about the dinner with Lord Podmore at the Savoy tomorrow, including the courses, the guests, the hour, and whether they would be sitting in the big dining-room—where Arthur had heard you could see and be seen by royalty on a good day—or in one of the lesser satellite rooms, where you might have to make do with stockbrokers. A great opportunity. Good for George. Long overdue and well deserved.

Arthur ate like a horse while George chattered away, full of innocent enthusiasm. He felt a great deal stronger, and his mood began to turn around. Sunshine streamed in through the windows. Arthur's conscience troubled him a little, but he drowned it with coffee, plugged it up with steak and potatoes. He thought that he could probably, if all went well, ensure George's safety; but what he was planning would certainly be curtains for the *Phaeton*. A bloody shame. But he had no choice. If this wasn't a sign from Heaven, he didn't know what one would look like. The Lord watched over London, and the Marylebone Road, and stupid men like Arthur; and if that was true, then no doubt he watched over everywhere else too, wherever the sun's rays shone, wherever Josephine was. And He helped those who helped themselves. Arthur smiled and shook George's hand.

Chapter Twenty-two

A rthur took the train out to Gravesend the next morning. From there he walked out to Rudder Hill, where he found Mrs Archer in her cottage. The door and the windows were thrown wide open, the clutter had been organised into a multitude of neat piles, and she was packing as if to go on holiday—that is, her enormous son was packing cases, while she sat and barked commands.

Arthur said *hello* at the window. Archer's son rushed out scowling and grabbed him by his collar.

Mrs Archer emerged from her cottage, wiping her hands on her dress. "You. Heard what happened to Atwood. Atwood gone, Gracewell gone, all over—all debts cancelled, to my mind. Getting out."

"An alliance," Arthur gasped. "When last we met, you suggested an alliance."

"Hah! Who with? Who's left? You?"

"I can make it worth your while. I know who buggered up your stars, Mrs Archer."

"Eh?"

"Atwood said you were very old, and very strong. Are you stronger than Lord Podmore?"

"That boy? Hmm. Perhaps." She motioned for her son to put Arthur down.

"Yes or no, Mrs Archer?"

"Don't hurry an old woman. I'm thinking."

T he Savoy Hotel, which had opened only a few years previously, was currently among the most fashionable and exclusive establishments in London, boasting electric lighting, American elevators, the finest chefs that could be poached from Paris, and so on, and so on. Arthur's clothes were in such a shocking state that he would be lucky to be permitted to beg outside the gates.

He entered the courtyard by the carriage entrance, off Savoy Hill, slipping between two large black carriages and then following in the footsteps of a busy-looking footman, adopting the footman's purposeful stride: long-legged, youthful, a very particular combination of awkwardness and self-important swagger. Atwood had once told Arthur that walking in a man's shoes was half-way to being him. We are nothing but the sum of our motions, Atwood said. Atwood illustrated that theory by copying Arthur's gait as they walked side by side along the Embankment, then dropping suddenly to his knees, causing Arthur to stumble and knock his head on a lamppost.

Nobody looked twice at him as he crossed the courtyard. He might as well have been the young footman's shadow. Busy servants crossed his path as if he weren't there. Young lovers idling by the fountain glanced at him, untroubled, as if he didn't in the slightest blemish the beauty of the courtyard—which was all soft evening shadows, white brick, fragrant flowers, glinting pearls and turquoises. There were a thousand eyes on the balconies above and nobody cried out, *Who the devil is that?*

A magician is at home everywhere, Atwood used to say. A magician is at home among kings and princes; a magician is at home on Mars. That was easy for His Lordship to say.

At the last moment, just as the footman was about to go inside, Arthur couldn't resist an experiment. He reached up and scratched his head.

The footman stopped in the doorway. He shifted from foot to foot. He dropped one of the bags, took off his hat, and scratched crossly at his hair.

The footman stepped into an elevator and disappeared. Arthur strode directly through the ante-room, past fireplaces and two huge potted palms, into the restaurant, then across the big dining room to a table not far from the south-western quarter of the room, where Lord Podmore sat with George and two men Arthur didn't know. According to George, one of them would be an American stockbroker by the name of Frisch, the other a publisher by the name of Snaith.

They had not yet begun to eat.

"Podmore!" Arthur said. "What a pleasure to see you here. And George, and Mr Snaith and Mr Frisch."

A waiter in a white apron moved smoothly into view. Arthur commanded him to bring a chair, so that he could join his friends at their table.

"Arthur?" George said. He had a confused half-smile.

Podmore had been in the middle of an anecdote, or a joke, leaning back expansively with one hand on his enormous belly. Now he watched Arthur with curiosity, and perhaps just a sliver of wariness.

"I'm terribly sorry," George said. "This is Arthur Shaw. He's a friend of mine, and I'm afraid he's had a terrible run of bad luck lately—his fiancée is—ah . . . Arthur, now is not the time."

The waiter hovered uncertainly. He looked from Arthur to George to Podmore, who remained silent and still.

Arthur indicated to the waiter where he wanted the chair to be placed, across the table from Podmore. The waiter dithered. Arthur looked at him patiently. A magician is nothing more than a man who expects his orders to be obeyed, as Atwood was fond of saying.

At last Podmore nodded very slightly. The waiter breathed a sigh of relief and rushed off to find a chair.

Arthur considered that a draw.

Podmore nodded to Arthur. "Hello, Mr Shaw."

"Hello, Your Lordship."

Poor George looked confused, and very uncomfortable.

"Arthur! You know His Lordship?"

"I might ask you the same question," Podmore said. "But everyone seems to know everyone these days. Yes: Arthur Shaw and I have met. A bright young man. I was so terribly sorry to hear about Josephine."

"Your Lordship is too kind."

"You have mud on your shoes," Podmore observed.

"I had business out in the country," Arthur said.

George tried frantically to meet Arthur's eye.

Arthur had a good view of the restaurant, and in particular the entrance and the lobby beyond it. At his back—it gave him a certain confidence—was a pillar, broad at its base and surrounded by a little pyramid of shelves laden with fine china and bottles of dozens of kinds of liquor. Above the shelves shone a row of electrical lights. The pillar, every other pillar in the great room, and every wall, was panelled with ornately carved mahogany. Heavy carved beams partitioned the ceiling into

squares of gold and red. In the distance, a tremendous painting dominated the scene, depicting Captain Cook encountering unfriendly natives
under a stormy tropical sky. It was a Monday evening and the restaurant
was perhaps not quite at the height of glamour that it was said to reach on
Sundays, but it was still very busy: at the tables around them were dowager dames in pearls and rubies, and famous actors, and magnates of steel
and shipping, and no doubt a smattering of Balkan princes or globe-
trotting American heiresses.

Podmore reached for his wine-glass. Arthur noticed with satisfaction
that he was favouring his left hand—his right appeared to have been hurt.

The man on Arthur's right—a stocky middle-aged gentleman with a
thick moustache and rather rough-hewn features—opened his mouth and
proved to be the American, Frisch. "If you don't mind my asking, Your
Lordship, what's all this about?"

"I expect young Mr Shaw wants to talk about his unfortunate fiancée's condition—when last we met I indicated I might be able to help her.
I thought I might recommend him to my good friend Doctor Thorold, but
there's been some unfortunate news from that quarter too—had you
heard, Mr Shaw?"

Arthur extended a hand to the American. "Hello, Mr Frisch. I'm Arthur Shaw. I hear you're an American. Are you from Boston?"

"New York."

"I say. How exciting."

"It sure is, isn't it?"

Frisch seemed to sense conflict brewing, and found it amusing. The
other man, who had to be Snaith, was keeping his mouth shut, presumably because he didn't understand the situation and was anxious to not
somehow offend Podmore.

"Arthur," George said. "I don't know what—"

"George, I think it would be a very good idea if you left now."

"No," Podmore said. "Stay."

"George," Arthur said. "You've always been very kind to me, and I'm
very grateful, and I'm very sorry. I hope you'll trust me when I say that
it's very important that you leave at once. You too, Mr Frisch. Snaith."

"This is very silly," Podmore said. "You are causing a very silly scene,
Arthur. We were talking business. George, sit down."

The waiter brought a glass, and attempted to pour Arthur wine, but

Podmore glanced at him, raised an imperious eyebrow, and the poor fellow stumbled and spilled wine all over Arthur's coat.

"Quite all right," Arthur assured him. "Quite all right." He shrugged off the coat and gave it to the waiter to take away, and faced Podmore in his shirt-sleeves.

Podmore smiled unpleasantly.

By now people at adjoining tables were glancing over with curiosity and whispering.

Podmore dabbed at the corner of his mouth with his napkin. Then he smiled at Arthur and asked, "Is your friend Martin well?"

"I expect so," Arthur said.

"Hmm," Podmore said. "I must say, you're in good spirits, Mr Shaw. The last time we spoke you seemed rather—frankly, rather timid. Now here you are, barging into the Savoy, dressed like a savage, ordering Mr Weston and Mr Frisch and what's-his-name away from the table."

Snaith flinched.

"I confess," Podmore said, "I'd like to know what you think you have up your sleeve."

"All right," Frisch said. "Okay, gentlemen. That's enough beating about the bush. Is this business, or is this personal? What's going on here?"

"I'm here to make a proposal," Arthur said.

Podmore put his napkin down. "Well, let's hear it."

"I want you to give me Josephine, and Gracewell, without further unpleasantness."

Podmore laughed. Snaith—clearly a born toady—laughed too. *Oh God,* George said, putting his head in his hands. Neither Arthur nor Podmore listened to him. Podmore stopped laughing, stroked his beard, and stared with sudden ferocity into Arthur's eyes. It was all Arthur could do not to fall out of his chair. His skin prickled; he felt shame, terror, despair, humiliation. He was worthless, lower than a worm, a ridiculous scarecrow of a man . . . . He buckled under Podmore's telepathic broadside, under the thunder of psychic cannon. Podmore's eyes had become very large and round, and they seemed to shine with a horrible black light. Sweat trickled down Arthur's brow. His hand shook, and the veins beneath his skin seemed to bulge and writhe disgustingly—he was a loathsome, decaying creature. He felt a terrible urge to get up and run. He didn't. He'd survived Gracewell's Engine. Lesser men had gone mad. He knew what discipline was. He clutched his napkin-ring so tightly that his knuckles hurt. He silently recalled the symbols of the Engine, and recited the names and mystical properties of the planets, and the stations of the Underground, and some fragments of Josephine's poetry that he knew by heart, and some bits of Dickens, and whatever else he happened to have in his head.

A waiter approached the table bearing a silver tray, but stumbled as if he'd been struck in the head, and fell to his knees, spilling hot borscht all over the floor. Frisch ran to check his pulse and help him back to his feet.

Podmore looked down at the waiter. "Oh dear," he said. "Poor fellow."

Arthur took a deep breath. He felt as if he'd been beaten, but Podmore was sweating too. Podmore looked surprised—not afraid, by any means, but at least annoyed.

Podmore leaned forward, and whispered, "Is Atwood here? Sun? The women? Any of your colleagues?"

Arthur shook his head.

"No," Podmore said. "No. I would know . . . But you're not alone, are you, Shaw?"

"Oh God," George said. "Oh God, Arthur. You should go home—you're not well."

"Go away, George, please—it's better if you hear none of this."

"Arthur believes me to be a magician," Podmore said. "Of notorious reputation. He thinks I stole his fiancée. And he blames me for the burning of his friend Atwood's house—certainly an unfortunate incident. I hear that one Sergeant Jessop, a policeman, died in the fire."

George went pale.

"I'm sorry to hear that," Arthur said. "I liked Jessop. He was a good man."

"Well," Podmore snapped, "he shouldn't have worked for Atwood, then."

George sputtered. "Burning? Dead policemen?" He threw down his napkin and stood, with an expression on his face that suggested he was going to try to summon the authorities, if only he could think of the proper authority to call. Podmore barked *no* and he sat back down.

Podmore picked up his fork and stood it on its end. Snaith stood, stepped over to the shelf behind Arthur's head, and picked up a sharp knife. Moving by instinct, Arthur reached out and knocked over Snaith's wine-glass. Snaith slipped on spilled borscht. He lay on his back looking confused, as if he had no idea what had just happened or why he'd stood up in the first place.

They had by now attracted the attention of every other table in the restaurant. People were turning to stare.

A waiter approached, bearing another tray of soup. He trembled as he served them, then fled—rejoining a long row of waiters who stood by the wall, watching anxiously.

Arthur said, "George—I'm sorry."

He snapped the stem of his wine-glass, causing the leg of George's chair to snap so that he fell on the floor and hit his head on the chair behind him. The dowager dame who'd been sitting in that chair gave a little shriek, then got to her feet and left, taking her party with her. A couple of waiters quickly came and led George off, bleeding from the head, in search of first aid.

Podmore pushed his soup to one side. "Very well. Frisch—go. Snaith—go."

Both men stood at once, with the quick obedience of well-drilled soldiers, and left without a word. Frisch wore an expression of mild confusion; Snaith, relief.

"Well, Shaw. I see Atwood has taught you a trick or two."

"Give me Josephine, Your Lordship; Josephine and Gracewell."

"Did you come here to threaten me? I am *tremendously* insulted—not to mention inconvenienced—by this display. I doubt Mr Frisch will do business with me in future. People will talk—"

He looked around the restaurant, observed that he had an audience, and sighed. "I'll return your woman to you. I don't need her any more."

"And Gracewell?"

"I don't want to hurt you, Shaw. Every act of violence is a stain on the soul. It weakens; it corrupts. I do not want to go to war. I do not want to conduct myself in this unpleasant way. You may find this hard to believe, but I did not become a magician out of greed, or anger, or to play stupid tricks, but to purify my soul; and I still hold out hope of Heaven when I die. I will ascend then among the spheres in the usual orderly fashion." He sipped his wine.

"I've seen your thugs," Arthur said. "I know what they are."

"Do you? A necessity, that's what they are. A regrettable necessity. Because of people like Atwood."

"A regrettable necessity," Arthur said. "Quite." He glanced at the entrance to the restaurant, and shook his head. "I didn't come alone, Your Lordship."

Podmore slowly put his glass down, and turned his head. "Oh, good God."

He stood, resting his hands on the table.

Mrs Archer entered the restaurant, hanging off her great mute son's arm, breezing past anxious waiters, snatching a peach off a stranger's table.

Arthur glanced at his watch. She'd promised him half an hour to get George out of the way and attempt to negotiate. She was a little early. Eager, no doubt. Keen to see who was stronger, her or Podmore. She bit cheerfully into the peach.

They stared at each other across the restaurant. Podmore swayed a little, his knuckles whitening on the table-top. Mrs Archer stepped forward, leaning, as if into a high wind. In the straight line across the Savoy restaurant between the two of them, people flinched, choked on their wine, or suddenly found reason to wipe their mouths, check their watches, and head for the exits. Waiters bearing trays declined to cross that line, turning back towards the kitchen.

Podmore muttered under his breath, invoking names that Arthur had never heard before, even in Atwood's books. A phalanx of white-aproned waiters formed and marched across the restaurant towards Archer, with the apparent intention of forcibly removing her. Her son stepped forward, scowling, to block their path.

Archer narrowed her eyes. A grand-looking silver-haired lady got up from her chair and confronted Podmore, telling him that his newspapers were disgracefully unpatriotic. An actor stood and told Podmore that his newspapers' reviews of *Lady Windermere's Fan* had been damnably unfair and frankly philistine. A third and a fourth and a fifth person started clamouring at Podmore about something or other—Arthur could no longer make out what any of them were saying.

Podmore invited them all to sod off. Then he rapped his fork three times on the table, and said some words in Latin.

A beautiful and fashionably dressed young lady stood and pointed at Archer, laughed, and whispered *What on earth is she wearing?* The whisper was loud enough for everyone to hear, and it was joined by others, a choir of unkind whispering and laughing: *How in the world did someone like that get in here? Is she a beggar? What do you suppose she wants?*—all of it directed squarely, from every corner of the room, at Archer.

Arthur winced. It didn't seem to trouble Archer at all, or shake her confidence; as if she were the one who belonged there, baggy filthy old dress and all, and it was the Savoy's guests who were absurd; as if she belonged to an older and grander aristocracy than any of them. She bit the peach again, messily, contemptuously, laughing.

The whispering of the crowd continued, but new notes entered into it—confusion, followed by alarm, followed by outrage. It took Arthur a few moments to understand what Archer had done, and by that time it was far advanced.

What an aboluble dress that woman's wearing!

Borrible. Simply borribile. Borbulous! Halla dorl she?

Somebody should call for the integuments. Somebody should chamomile the grobes at once.

Worrabile? My dear, if the tidal—that is, the tumnal—the dolmen or ah dunce-cap, Adonai, I, ah, ah, ah . . .

Nonsense wafted from every table. The condition appeared to be rapidly worsening. Some guests, panicking, shouted and shouted; others clapped their hands to their mouths, afraid of what might come out. Husbands and wives looked at each other in alarm and disgust. They tried to swear and managed only to say *Albumarle!* or *Belladonna!*

Podmore banged his hand on the table and cleared his throat. Ladies and Gentiles, I urge you to remain camel. Calm. I urge you to remain calm. I think that most of you know who I argue—who I am—and that I abominate, ah, that I ballaton, that—a mere momentary hysteria. I expect that lorrabiles and goblins of your stamen, stature, gondolas, that is—I mean gentlematins, men, *men*, I—God darbat you, old woman—enough!"

All eyes were on him. He was beginning to sweat.

The lights burned out, and two behind Archer's head caught fire. The dark and the fire gave her and her son a devilish appearance. Arthur couldn't guess who was responsible for putting out the lights, Podmore or Archer or both of them. Someone screamed.

That was the signal for Bedlam to break loose. The dowager dame who had been complaining to Podmore about his lack of patriotism clawed at his face, drawing blood. He swore and shoved her aside. The actor started shouting. People were running to and fro. Arthur got up from his seat just in time to duck out of the way as a waiter swung a wine-bottle at him. Plates, bottles, cutlery, went flying, hurled in Podmore's direction, or Mrs Archer's, or Arthur's own, or at no one in particular. Arthur sheltered behind the pillar and listened to screams of rage and the sound of shattering glass and china and table-legs. It was as if a legion of devils had been admitted into the Savoy Hotel and placed within the diners at the restaurant, the way Christ put those devils in the country of whatchamacallit into a herd of swine. As a matter of fact, that might be exactly what had happened. Arthur didn't know. For a moment, he had an awful notion that the chaos might not stop in the dining-room of the Savoy—why should it? What if Podmore and Archer's struggle spilled out into the streets, and drove all of London mad? What if—

Someone jabbed at Arthur's face with a fork. He snatched a large silver tureen from the shelf and used it to defend himself, swinging it to and fro with both hands, laying low a peer of the realm with one blow, a French ambassador with the next.

Battle-lines formed, Archer's army against Podmore's, armed with knives and forks and spoons. A dozen aristocratic young men on either side of the battle formed a sort of non-regulation scrimmage, heads down, slipping and sliding in spilt food. Archer had climbed upon a table now and hiked up her skirts, and was directing her army with a silver ladle. Most of the waiters were on Podmore's side. Most of the women were on Archer's. Others were jerked this way and that as the two combatants struggled with each other.

A prominent surgeon nailed a waiter's hand to a table with a fork. A German Grand Admiral stabbed a Bishop in the eye with a spoon. China crunched underfoot. An Indian Prince hurled a tureen of hot soup at Podmore—a stockbroker intercepted it. The Duchess of Bolton attempted to strangle the young actress Miss Lily Otway with her own pearls. Some Italians fought bare-knuckle with some Americans. Archer's son pressed forward across the room, making slow headway against a tide of enraged waiters, in peril of sinking beneath them.

Podmore stood on the table, chanting something. Arthur bowled the silver tureen overhand across two overturned tables and hit Podmore on the back of his head. Podmore grunted and fell over.

The fighting continued for a little while, but without the same enthusiasm. Eventually people started slipping away, nursing their wounds, jabbering nonsense to themselves, embarrassed to look one another in the eye. Mrs Archer's son picked Podmore up, head-locked him, and dragged him red-faced and gasping out of the restaurant. Archer followed, laughing, stealing food as she went.

The lobby outside was largely deserted. Plants had been uprooted from their pots, paintings slashed and thrown in the fireplace, china smashed across the floor. Two white-jacketed members of the hotel's staff knelt on the floor, restraining a howling and kicking man. A woman in black sobbed on a sofa.

Policemen rushed from the courtyard.

"Don't mind us," Archer said. "Don't mind us."

The policemen continued into the restaurant, hardly glancing their way.

Arthur's uncle George lay face down on the floor by the fireplace. He was bruised and his jacket was torn. His head was bloody, and he appeared to have been trampled by fleeing patrons.

"He'll live," Archer said. "You didn't think we would go to war and no one would get hurt, did you? Now, hurry along, hurry along, before worse happens."

Once Lord Podmore had been brought around by smelling-salts, and sufficiently menaced by Mrs Archer's son, he proposed that, while surrender was obviously impossible—his associates would not permit it— they might perhaps be able to hammer out some rules for the conduct of the war. Indeed, he was willing to go so far as to say that kidnapping probably was, when looked at in the clear light of hindsight, somewhat beyond the pale.

"I can't speak for the Germans, though. I can't speak for the Chinese, or the Americans. By God, Mr Shaw, won't you speak to Atwood, and beg him to see sense, before it's too late. By God. Isn't it bad enough already? Look at this creature, Mr Shaw!"

Podmore pointed to Archer's son. "Look at this creature! Look at her, and that thing she calls her son—look what you've allied yourself with. Is it Christian, I ask you?"

Archer laughed and poked him in the ribs with her stolen ladle. "Get on with it, Your Lordship. Make your telephone call, or release your pigeons, or what-have-you."

Podmore summoned up what was left of his pride and led them down to the river. By this time the sun had begun to set, and there was a chilly damp fog by the river. He led them south to an expanse of muddy riverbank, where an abandoned landing, ruined by the storm, stuck out into the black water. He asked if he might be permitted to borrow a match from someone; and then he took a grimy old lantern from a rusty hook on a moss-green post beneath the landing. He lit the lantern and stood out on the edge of the water with its red flame held high. Archer's son stood behind him with a hand on his shoulder.

Out on the water there was a boat. Through the fog it loomed as big as an inter-continental steamer or a prison hulk. The setting sun made a road of fire across the water, and here and there red sun reflected from the boat's wet black mass, as if the whole thing were aflame.

Lord Podmore moved the lantern from side to side and up and down.

After a while something moved across the water: a black speck approaching on the flaming road. It slowly became clear that it was a rowboat.

The sun set behind the rooftops. The fires went out.

Podmore sighed and put the lantern back on the hook. By its light Arthur watched the boat approach. The rower was a nondescript middle-aged man with sandy hair and spectacles. Gracewell sat in the stern. Josephine sat beside him. For a moment, Arthur thought she was awake. He ran forward to meet the boat, splashing in the mud, until he came close enough to see that her eyes were closed, and she was leaning against Gracewell's shoulder.

"Podmore," said the man on the boat. He let go of the oars and rested his hand on the pistol beside him on the bench. "Podmore, what's the meaning of this? Is that—good God, is that—"

"Yes, yes," Podmore said.

"Shaw," Gracewell said. He seemed distracted.

"Please, sir," Arthur said.

"Hmm? Oh."

Gracewell passed Josephine over the side of the boat into Arthur's arms. Her skirts trailed in the muddy water.

"Good evening," Gracewell said. "It's good to see you again, Mr Shaw. I've had some thoughts. Very enlightening. A period of uninterrupted thought was just what I needed. Thank you, Mr Podmore."

He reached out and shook Podmore's hand, to Podmore's obvious surprise.

Arthur slumped down by the water's edge, with Josephine in his lap. His eyes were clouded with tears; he closed them, and for a moment he felt as if he were back on Rugby Street.

"Bloody mess you've made, Your Lordship," said the rower.

There was some sort of altercation then, or argument, or negotiation, between Mrs Archer and Podmore and the rower, but Arthur didn't listen to it. It ended with Podmore getting into the boat.

Arthur sat on the ground and held Josephine close, watching as they rowed off. Soon they were no more than a speck in the firelight, and then he couldn't see them at all.

"Greedy," Archer said. "Greedy old fool. Thinks London's all his, and nothing for the rest of us. Well then, why shouldn't my son seek his fortune in the colonies?"

She laughed and poked Arthur's shoulder. "Thinks all of England is his, his money and his newspapers and all of that. Thinks all its magic is his too. Well, there's older magic in England than his, and stronger. And perhaps one day your Lord Atwood will see that too. You just see that I get what you promised me. Young man? You just see."

Josephine felt thin and frail, underfed and unwashed. Arthur whispered her name, over and over, but she didn't hear him. She was faintly smiling.

Chapter Twenty-three

The lunar city was a beautiful vision. Josephine had never seen India, or China, or Greece or Rome, or, for that matter, Scotland or Wales . . . or even very much of England, really— but she *had* seen the ivory city on the rosy moon of Mars. If she found her way home—if she woke—*when* she woke—it would be her duty to describe it, to somehow find words for its sights and sounds and scents. Or would it fade on waking, like so many beautiful dreams? Would it tarnish?

She haunted every inch of it, hungry for experience. She could go anywhere, and see anything, and listen to whatever she wanted. She moved by pure will, pure perception. She had only to look at a place to be there. She explored every winding street, she drifted along the banks of the red river, she hovered at the fluted tops of towers. She became quite brazen about spying on the Martians, and soon she thought nothing of drifting in and out of their bedrooms, their churches, their business meetings (if that's what they were), or their Houses of Parliament (if you could call them that).

The lunar city lay inside a tremendous crater. In the west—sunsetwards— rose towering grey-white walls of rock. A rose-red waterfall plunged down the crater's edge, dwarfing the city's tallest towers, and a river ran through the city. In the east there was a lake. Flowers floated on it, so large that at first she took them for ships. Close by the waterfall there were quarries where the Martians hacked red gems from the white rock.

The city somewhat resembled an illustration Josephine had once seen in a magazine. It wouldn't surprise her if it had been *The Monthly Mammoth,* in which case the words beside the picture might well have been Arthur's. The illustration—which seemed to have very little to do with the words, which were about telescopes—showed the civilization of the canal-builders of Mars, as the artist imagined it, all spires and domes and wise bald men in robes. In fact, the city resembled that illustration closely enough—apart from the bald men—that she now wondered if the artist had somehow been granted a vision of it, or if the city existed only in her imagination, built from her memories.

What the city didn't resemble, in any way at all, was what Martin Atwood had expected to see. He'd spoken of slow-moving primitives, war-like savages, mere brutes. He'd imagined a spiritual realm slower and simpler and colder in every way than Earth, and ripe for conquest. None of that appeared to be true. Rather an alarming thought—she'd hoped Atwood's Company knew what they were doing, at least a little.

The city was built in stone, and for the most part in straight sharp lines, or in sharp-edged curves that resembled sails, or something carved by the wind. Between the towers and the domes, the streets were cluttered with buttresses and archways and uneven stone channels, as if they were an afterthought, merely spaces between the buildings, an unavoidable architectural necessity. Everything was built as if its makers did not take much account of gravity, or the ordinary rules of proportion or balance. The city's makers built sharp narrow spires where a London architect might rely on squares; and where the Londoner might embellish with pillars or gargoyles there were odd rills or flutings in the stone, or ornaments for which Josephine had no names—it was like listening to a foreign language that resembled English just enough to confuse and disorient. She kept seeing shapes in the stone that were momentarily familiar, that reminded her of staircases, or balconies, or, for that matter, leaves or faces or wings; a tower-top like a ram's horn or a parrot's crest; bone-white ghosts of pelvis or rib-bone, or wheels or ploughshares or windmills or sewing-machines . . .

Was this—the stuff this vision was made of—what Atwood's Company had called the *aether*? There was something a little insubstantial about it, a little alien. The city's stone was a little like marble in its richness of colour; a little like snow, glimpsed at sunset.

Everywhere there were flower-gardens—or perhaps they were farms—full of mossy, fern-like, tendrilly plants, red and gold and ochre and violet. Creeping plants, well suited to arid soil. A thin red gorse or furze grew on the walls of the towers, etching tremendous shadow-shapes into the stone. Occasionally, long flowering stalks or vines or sturdy tendrils sprouted from the walls, sometimes stretching from tower to tower to make hundred-foot-high bowers. All the flowers of the lunar city were pale, as if the city were a faded watercolour painting, or as if the city were always in twilight. In fact, everything in the city was pale, except for its vibrantly purple inhabitants. There was something oddly out of place about them.

They lived rather the way one imagined the Spartans had: in buildings of clean stone, without luxuries or clutter. Their city was pristine. No dirt, no rubbish in the streets. No horses. The city felt either terribly new, or terribly old, like something in a museum. They might have lived there for ten thousand years, or arrived yesterday.

They wore little in the way of clothes, just thin shifts of a rosy-white silk-like material. It did not seem immodest. She realised that it was those scraps of silk that she'd mistaken for fish-like scales on the poor creature back at Atwood's house. In fact, their skin, though blue, was otherwise not wholly inhuman. Earth people and Martians were clearly the work of the same Creator, except that It had seen fit to give only one of them wings.

She had no way of knowing how much time had passed. The days and nights seemed longer than on Earth, but she knew too little of astronomy to make sense of this. Free of the body and its needs, time passed slowly; but when her attention wandered—because she was nothing here but attention—great stretches of time could slip by in an instant. Sometimes that happened when she was thinking too deeply, or because she was struck by some odd moment of beauty; sometimes it was because she was afraid, or despairing, or homesick. The fits of vanishing terrified her. Who knew how many days passed on Earth each time? Each time hope of rescue grew fainter.

She'd caught only a brief glimpse of the unfortunate creature that had fallen into Atwood's séance. Its wings had looked to her like the leaves of ferns, or like silk ribbons—limp and tangled and helpless. On the ivory moon they looked very different.

No two Martians had wings of quite the same pattern or colour or shape. They were typically blue or purple or rose-pink, and thickly veined, and faintly translucent, like cloudy glass or a fine silk. They might come in three pairs, or four, or five or six or more; they might be straight as knives, or curved, or more complexly shaped. One could never quite grasp their shape or pattern, partly because they were rarely still, partly because they grew more and more complex the closer one looked. In repose, they might fold away like a fan. In flight, they resembled butterfly wings, or in another way a peacock's tail; at full extension the wings might dwarf the lithe and elfin Martians to which they were attached. The wings were beautiful—far more expressive than the Martians' thin faces. But they were wings only in the loosest sense, and for want of a better word. They didn't beat. They rippled and shifted. She didn't understand how they worked.

For the most part, Josephine had the highest tower-tops to herself: room after ghostly echoing room, and chasms of empty air. No birds roosted there. The flowering tendrils entered through the windows, but no insects attended them. There was no Martian pigeon, and for that matter no Martian rat or cat or fox. There was no life in the city except for the Martians themselves, the moss and the tendrils and the flowers, and one ghostly Englishwoman.

She saw everything, but she understood nothing. Did they really have bedrooms, churches, business-meetings, Parliament? She didn't know. Their principal industries appeared to be flower-farming and bead-making, the latter of which took place in a multitude of hot little workshops. She studied this as if she were preparing to make a report to Parliament on the progress of an African mission. She supposed that they made the beads out of the gems they quarried from beneath the waterfall, though she never did quite understand the process; at least, any more than she had ever understood how coal got to London, or how steel was made.

She gave their buildings names. She called one squat tower *Big Ben*; she named a *St. Paul's*, and an *Embankment*, and a *Shaftesbury Avenue*. A circle of red dirt with a white stone spire in it she christened *Piccadilly Circus*. A row of empty stone structures reminded her of the Egyptian Avenue in Highgate Cemetery. Something somewhat castle-like reminded her of St. Pancras.

For the most part, the Martians were silent. Their language, it seemed, was in the motions of their hands and fingers and wings, which they used like semaphore-flags. They were always in motion, never still even for a second. It was rather exhausting to look at, like a carnival. If a Martian were to walk down the Edgware Road, flapping his wings and waving his arms, he'd be committed to a hospital for the insane.

She wondered what had happened to the creature that the Company of the Spheres had caught in their library. Poor thing! Atwood and Jupiter and Sun and Sergeant Jessop must have looked like the most terrible monsters to it. She resolved that she would on no account let herself be captured that way.

As a matter of fact, *capture* seemed not to be a very great danger. Her greater concern was that she might never be able to attract their attention at all; and that without their aid, she would remain a ghost indefinitely.

At dawn and dusk the city's inhabitants stretched their wings, gathered on the highest perches they could find, and stared up at the vast face of Mars—which, viewed from the moon, was a disk the size of a cannonball, dark purple and dimly glowing, deeply etched with long dark lines. That appeared to be their one expression of what one might call religious feeling. To Josephine's eye there was still something menacing and terrible about the face of Mars, but these moon people looked up at it with longing.

There were other lights visible in the sky. There were stars, and at certain times, the second moon was visible, livid and furnace-red. The Martians averted their eyes from it.

Perhaps one of the visible stars was Earth. Josephine rose up to the domed top of the tallest tower in the city, stared at the stars, and willed herself to rise up and travel towards them. She couldn't. Gravity held her in the ivory city. Or perhaps she was just too scared to face the void again.

All her education had suggested to her that, should one find oneself granted a vision of the heavens, one might expect great spiritual revelations, poetic or romantic ecstasy, profound peace, brilliant insight. For a while she entertained the idea that she was in fact in Heaven; or possibly in Hell. It didn't last. Fear passed, ecstasy faded, and yet she didn't wake. The vision implacably persisted. She was less confident of the meaning of life or the nature of Creation with every passing hour. She was not enlightened or transfigured; she was merely lost.

Was she mad? Was it all a hallucination, a dream brought on by Atwood's incense (God knows what had been in it—*hashish* or opium or worse). It made no difference. It was real enough for her.

What she needed was to find someone clever to speak to among the city's inhabitants. Someone who might be able to see her, and understand her, and help her find a way home. Their equivalent of an Atwood, then, or a Jupiter. She went looking.

She'd been so amazed by the sight of the Martians that it only belatedly occurred to her how few of them there were. Most of their towers were empty, and none of them were crowded. London could have swallowed the population of the city twenty times over. They could all have packed into Limehouse, quite possibly without coming to the attention of the police. And the rest of the moon, for all that she could tell, might be uninhabited. At the edge of the city rose the grey-white walls of the crater; beyond that was wasteland, nothing but rocks and red moss as far as she dared to venture.

There was nothing in the city that particularly resembled an observatory, or a telescope, or a university.

It slowly dawned on her that each and every one of the Martians was a magician, or would have been considered a magician on Earth. They rarely touched anything with their hands, using their long fingers mostly for gesturing; but each of them could move objects with a glance, by will alone. The *Occult Review* would have called it *telekinesis*. Perhaps that was why they had so little in the way of tools, or furniture, or pots and pans, or other bric-a-brac. Man relied on tools made to fit his hand. The Martians did not.

She was delighted by that discovery for a while—the first few times she saw them do it, she thought she was imagining it. Then she began to despair. It was one thing to fling a few white rocks or orangey moss-flowers about, and another entirely to project a person from the Martian moons to Earth. And if *everyone* was a magician, that would only make it harder to identify the few truly powerful ones—if there were any.

They *did* have an army. She discovered that one long gloomy afternoon, when the red moon was unusually large in the sky—a sharp half-disc of red light that made the rest of the sky seem darker, as if it were threatening to storm.

The largest gathering of Martians she had ever seen formed in the mossy space that she'd dubbed Piccadilly Circle. That was a wide circular expanse of white stone, with a tall wave-like spire at its centre, roughly where the Angel would have been if it were the real Piccadilly. Martians streamed in from all sides, fluttering down from the tower-tops. She didn't know what signal had summoned them. Perhaps it was the red moon itself.

At first she thought they were gathered for sport, but she'd been watching them long enough to detect something grim in their manner.

Half a dozen Martians fluttered up and perched on ledges on the spire. They made wide gestures, as if conducting the activity of the others. The rest—hundreds of them—formed what appeared to be two battle-lines. Then they tore into each other. They had no weapons; instead they fought with their hands, and with their sharp-edged wings—which were complex and multi-segmented, like fans or ferns, so that they could strike with one part while the rest remained in dizzying motion. She supposed they were striking with their wills, as well, their *telekinesis*. The battle was impossible for her to follow—it was too fast, too chaotic, too alien—partly because all the Martians were the same bright colours, and partly because they didn't form *squares*, the way a human army might, but arranged themselves as halves of a circle, the front between them constantly moving around the circle like a clock-hand. They spun up into the air, a fluttering column over the square, like a whirlwind of leaves. Nobody seemed to be winning. They drifted out of the circle when they were hurt or too tired, and they drifted back in again, around and around. They bled pink. She was surprised; she'd rather expected blue.

It went on through the whole afternoon, and into the middle of the night, which seemed to stretch out for a week. It was every bit as futile and ugly and disappointing as terrestrial violence.

The red moon was big again the next day—in fact, it seemed to be getting slowly bigger. The fighting happened again. They seemed to be training; preparing for war.

She went back to the place where she'd first—what was the word? Awoken?

For no particularly good reason, she thought of that district—if you could call it that—as London Bridge. It was a patch of towers on the edge of a hillside that sloped down to the river, extending into a small peninsula that rather resembled a miniature Isle of Dogs—in fact, she might have called it that if she hadn't already used the name for a bend upriver.

Eventually she found what was probably, so far as she could tell, the room where she'd begun. It was small, curved, with a peaked ceiling. Creeping red flowers grew in the window. There were neat rows of beads on the floor in a corner. Narrow doorways led to three small side-rooms behind curtains of black beads, the kind she imagined one might find in an opium-den.

Two Martians lived in those rooms. They were the two she'd seen embracing when she first arrived. There was nothing particularly special about them, so far as she knew. It seemed to her that they were young, and she thought of them—for want of a better word—as married.

Both had long elfin faces, eerily beautiful, with narrow mouths and inscrutable silver eyes. Both had long thin arms tight with corded muscle. One was very slightly larger than the other, and had more vivid colouration. The other had somewhat more extravagantly complex wings. She supposed that one was male, and the other female, but she had no firm idea which was which. Rather arbitrarily, she dubbed the more-purple one *Adam* and the complex-winged one *Eve*. And then she settled in to haunt them.

For the most part the Martians ate communally, like schoolchildren or soldiers—and sparingly, picking at fruit and fungus and the sharp spines of red leaves. Meals fit for hummingbirds. They argued vigorously as they ate, about God knows what. Like Athenians; a disputatious people. They drank a red wine—there was no other word for it—which had the scent of a stronger and fiercer wine than any Josephine had ever encountered on Earth, a wine that poets might write about, that might drive Bacchae to flesh-rending frenzy. Adam and Eve drank it, then fell about in what might have been ecstasy or laughter or dancing—and what quite often turned into playful fighting, or possibly mating. It was hard to be sure—their wings touched, the frilled edges shimmering and trembling, forming a discreet curtain. The first time it happened, Josephine fled at once. Afterwards she peeked—at first with a mixture of fascination and deep embarrassment, then with a certain scientific detachment. If she was to understand them, she had to know everything. They were, after all, not human. She remembered following her father about on his visits to the farmers of his parish and glimpsing the coupling of farm animals. Strange, the things that could make one homesick.

O ne day she panicked, waking from memories of London, to find that Adam and Eve were both gone. They'd left while she was drifting— but only to move to some upper rooms of their tower. They had few neighbours, and few possessions, and appeared somewhat nomadic.

A nother thing Josephine learned was that the rows of beads on the floor, which she'd taken for a chess-like game, were writing; or rather, something half-way between writing and a sort of psychic phonograph. Martian language was mostly motion. They moved the beads with their wills, imparting to them patterns of motions that could be repeated endlessly. It was rather like automatic spirit-writing, or a medium's planchette. She learned that there was a particular pattern of floating motions that Eve liked. Martian scripture, perhaps, or music, or a favourite novel.

D ay by day, Adam and Eve grew less strange to her. She recognised their habits, their little courtesies to each other, their signs of affection or irritation. She learned their quirks of personality. Eve was passionate and quick to anger. Adam was slower, cooler-headed. She began to think of them rather the way one thinks of the couple who live at the end of the street, who one doesn't know by name, but who must surely be rather the same sort of person as oneself.

Their routines were erratic, by the standards of Londoners. They had no fixed or regular employment. A day on the white moon was like at least a dozen days in London. Sometimes one or both of them went to work: sweeping some patch of street, or tending flowers, or making and sorting beads in a low-ceilinged workshop next to a red fire. Sometimes they had tremendously long fits of inertia, and what she took to be melancholy. Sometimes they went to a place just across the river, where they stood for ages in a long low building shaped like a wave of white stone, in front of twelve smaller Martians. These were the first children Josephine had seen; they reminded her irresistibly of large butterflies. Adam and Eve stood on a low stage and talked to them all day. Teachers, then, or possibly priests.

Like priests or like scholars they seemed to talk a lot, and argue constantly, about nothing in particular. A disputatious people. Sometimes they fought. Their arguments seemed to get fiercer and more bitter as the red moon steadily grew larger.

After a while, it seemed to Josephine that she'd learned all she could from them, and perhaps it was time to haunt some other household.

She might drift from house to house for ever. Why not? She might out-last Adam and Eve—bodiless, she might live for ever! That was a rather ghastly vision of eternity. In fact, it made her so afraid and unhappy that she was unable to concentrate her attention on anything for a while, and some great unguessable span of time passed in the blink of an eye, as if she'd ceased to exist. She only knew that time had passed because the city appeared to have undergone some sort of storm, or a small earth-quake. Many of the long vines and tendrils that hung across the streets had been cut through, exposing raw pink fibres. Dead flowers lay in drifts. There was damage to the stonework, and quite a number of the Martians sported fresh wounds. Adam's wings were torn on his left side, and he had been slashed from forehead to mouth, right through one of his beau-tiful silver eyes. Their classroom was down to ten children. On the other hand, the baleful red moon had dwindled to a pin-prick again, and the fighting in Piccadilly had stopped.

She could see, and hear, and even smell. Why, then, shouldn't she be able to *touch*?

It was faint at first, but after long trial and effort, and deep introspec-tion over the difference between *sensation* and *imagination*, she found that she could sense differences between surfaces. The white stone was soft, a little like firm india-rubber. The mossy plants tingled. The wings of a Martian were sharp, and somehow silky and rough at the same time.

And if she could touch something, then why shouldn't she move it?

It took days and nights of practice and study and frustration. It was like learning to walk again, or speak.

Adam and Eve came home, leaping up to the ledge outside their rooms, landing crouched. Adam, wounded, stumbled; Eve helped him. They groomed each other's furled wings with their long violet fingers. By now that no longer struck Josephine as odd; in fact, it struck her as touchingly domestic.

When they stepped into their room it was with great joy that she finally lifted up all of the red beads at once, hundreds of them, and set them spinning madly around one another.

Adam recoiled in horror and stumbled against the wall. Eve shrieked, snapped her wings wide open with the sound of a gunshot, and fled from the window, pulling Adam after her.

———✦———

Chapter Twenty-four

For a moment Josephine wasn't sure what had happened. Then she let the red beads go and moved to the window. Adam and Eve were already almost out of sight, gliding with their wings outstretched high over the surface of the wine-red river, shining in the moonlight—no! Not moonlight, of course—*Mars*-light. They curved right together, Eve leading the way.

Following them, Josephine felt for the first time that she was truly flying. The sensation was exhilarating. They couldn't escape her, turn and wheel however they liked. She pursued them effortlessly. She was stubbornly determined to make herself known to them.

Adam faltered, slowly descending towards the water. Eve rose higher. Watching Adam settle on the riverbank, Josephine lost sight of Eve for a moment. When she next saw her, Eve was climbing like a squirrel up the side of one of the tall pillars that ran along the Embankment. When she reached the top of it, she stood with her wings outstretched and began a rather eccentric dance. Josephine watched with amusement.

With Mars-light at her back, Eve cast tremendous shadows over the city below. Martians going about their business looked up in alarm. Blue silver-eyed heads poked out of windows. Then, from a thousand windows, a thousand sets of wings took to the air. Eve's dance had been an alarm, a battle-signal. Suddenly the city was in a panic.

Eve! The name was ridiculous now. There was no longer anything familiar or domestic about her—*it*. In fact, it was rather terrifying, stretched up to its full height, jerking frantically.

Josephine was frustrated, and angry, and frightened, and humiliated. She supposed she shouldn't have expected them to be *pleased* to be confronted by a ghost in their house. Even so, this reaction seemed out of all reasonable proportion. The whole city was on the alert now—it had taken only moments. The silhouettes of the towers bristled with winged sentries. There was a terrible sharp rustling noise, as of a field at night filled with a thousand grasshoppers. In the distance, she saw a mob gathering at Piccadilly. A mob, or an army. The silent alarm kept going, as other Martians took to the tower-tops, relaying Eve's message. Shadows and flashes of light flickered across the city.

Something was wrong. She hadn't understood the Martians or the city at all.

There was nothing cosily domestic about the Martians, nothing comprehensible. There never had been. Loneliness and longing for home had confused her. They were a legion, a riot, a swarm, a host of angels or devils. The city bristled and roiled beneath her, and its inhabitants hardly seemed like *people* at all, but like one enormous animal; like a hive of maddened bees, terrifying and terrified in equal measure; or like some horrible eruption of nature, a whirlwind or a tidal wave.

Deimos and Phobos, the moons of Mars; Terror and Panic, the sons of War. Which one was it she'd landed on? Either way, it was well named.

Eve leapt from the top of the pillar, gliding down in a wide circle out over the water, then curving in again, north of the river. She was nearly gone from sight before Josephine could think to follow her. A sudden headlong plunge, a reckless acceleration no locomotive on earth could match, and Josephine was down amongst the towers, crowded on all sides by Martians, all of them tensely alert for whatever it was they were alert for. Ahead of her, Eve was distinguishable from the crowd only because of the speed and purpose with which she moved. Eve cornered sharply, then dropped to the ground, running at full tilt, long-legged, north and then left and then right, then leaping up to the window of her school—or what Josephine had foolishly thought of as a school; God knows what it really was! The infants were there, running and fluttering about in a panic, and Adam was there already, trying to herd them. They were trying to protect their children from her.

It was terribly, touchingly human. She looked at the Martians again and once again saw ordinary men and women and children. What sort of monster did they think she was?

In a fit of frustration, Jo soared up onto the schoolroom's little stage and sent all the brightly coloured beads in the room flying, a chaotic explosion of red and black and gold and white, shooting off the walls in a hundred thousand different directions. Then, as Adam and Eve led the infants out to safety, she sank down in despair. Outside, she could still hear that strange sharp rustling, the sound of a thousand terrified and angry Martians.

Despairing utterly, she ceased to perceive anything at all, not even the passage of time.

The next thing she knew, she was still in the schoolhouse, and a single Martian was creeping towards her.

She'd expected a furious mob; or possibly that the anxious and panic-stricken creatures might simply declare the schoolroom haunted, taboo, and never enter it again. This was an unexpected approach.

It came in through the door at the far end of the room and approached the stage where she waited. It moved slowly, patiently, cautiously, pausing repeatedly to look all about the room, as if it thought it might spot her hiding in the eaves, like a spider in its web.

This creature was very old—the Martians were human enough that she could be sure of that. Its wings had a dry and brittle look to them. Its colours were faded. Its long face was wrinkled like a monkey's, or a hob-goblin's, with a narrow dark mouth. It was scarred, too. The elderly ones were generally scarred—because of that horrible fighting, she supposed—but this one had had an unusual run of bad luck, or was unusually clumsy. One of its eyes was the black of tarnished silver. Its wings were frayed. Its back and chest looked as if it had been whipped.

The name Piccadilly popped into her head, and she thought of that as the old creature's name from then on. She had to call it something, after all.

It quite clearly wanted to talk to her.

She let herself feel cautiously hopeful. Perhaps this was a leader or a wise man; a wizard or a king or a scientist; or a policeman, at the very least.

It crouched, elbows on its knees. It was very still, except that its gaze sometimes shifted about the room. It quite obviously didn't know where she was, or, for that matter, *what* she was.

She wasn't at all what it had expected. It was surprised by her. Its fear was subsiding, and now it was intrigued.

How did she know that? She certainly hadn't read all of that from its eyes, those silver spoon-like discs with their tiny slitted black pupils, or from the quivering of its shoulders and its ragged wings. But she knew it.

She realised that it was *talking* to her. Telepathically, as the psychical researchers of London would have said. It was putting thoughts in her mind. She recoiled. It was an unwelcome intrusion—a violation. There was nothing left of her but her thoughts.

The creature started to its feet. Its wings expanded. Suddenly it was poised to flee again.

She tried to calm herself. Its mode of communication was strange and unexpected, but that was all. She could hardly expect it to have the manners of an Englishman. It meant her no harm. She felt that very strongly—or rather, it was *telling* her that it meant no harm. It was very afraid of her.

She was suddenly terrified at the thought that it might flee, leaving her alone again.

It was asking her what she was. There were no words in what it said, just the question. It had expected her to be something different. Something awful. What had it expected? She asked it: *What did you expect?* In answer, she got a jumble of incomprehensible images: something night-black, vast, a cloud of dreadful smog, a black eye, a crack in the earth, the darkness of Hell itself.

A devil of some kind. *The* Devil, perhaps. A disembodied spirit, here on the Martian moon, was not an amusement for spiritualists or a thrilling ghost story or fairy tale; it was a real and vivid horror. She felt certain that this was not a mere superstition, that the Martians feared something that they had actually experienced, something as real as a tiger.

Piccadilly was shaking. She did her best to communicate that she was peaceful, that she was not an enemy to Piccadilly or his kind—and suddenly she found herself thinking of him as *him*. He wasn't a monster. The thing he feared, the thing he'd mistaken her for, that was a monster. He was a frightened old man.

There were things Josephine could sense that Piccadilly didn't mean to tell her, but revealed anyway. The first thing she read in his mind was that he wasn't alone. There were hundreds of others, waiting outside. They were perched all along the spine of the roof like crows on a wire. They were waiting outside the door like a besieging army.

She reached out her mind and listened for them, for their thoughts, as they waited out there in the dark. It wasn't hard; in fact, as soon as she tried, they crowded in on her. There were so many of them that they made a racket. They were ready to hurl themselves at her and destroy her, even if it meant their deaths, if she turned out to be the devil that they feared. They had sharpened their minds for battle.

Atwood and Jupiter had said she was *sensitive*, but the intensity with which she sensed the mob outside and her communication with Piccadilly were quite unlike anything she'd experienced before. An effect of her current disembodied condition, perhaps, or something in the air on the Martian moon; or just one of the things in her dream.

Her more pressing concern was that an army was waiting to destroy her, if she didn't quickly convince Piccadilly that she was harmless. A mob, waiting to bludgeon her with their thoughts; what would that be like?

Another thing she read in Piccadilly's mind was why he'd been chosen to confront her. He wasn't a scientist, or a leader, or a policeman. He wasn't especially wise, or clever, or strong, or brave. It was just that he was old—it seemed to her that he was *unfathomably* old, by the standards of human beings. He was dying. His mate and his children were dead, lost to war, or disease, or bad luck, or time. He was expendable. He hadn't wanted to confront her—he hadn't volunteered. It had been *proposed* that he should go, and he hadn't wanted to say no. It would have been embarrassing for a Martian of his age to say no. He would rather face the Devil itself than face embarrassment in front of his neighbours. Not so different from an Englishman after all, she thought; and she felt a pang of genuine sympathy for the poor old creature. He must have sensed it, because his eyes widened in surprise, and then his shoulders and wings relaxed a little.

Quickly, she tried to tell him what she was. She tried to communicate an image of herself, of her body and her face, but that seemed merely to confuse him, as if she were babbling nonsense. She tried to tell him where she was from. She called up images of London, fragments of the city: a view of the Thames, the house on Rugby Street, Regent's Park, factories and trains and stations, meat-markets and Atwood's mansion and Mr Borel's stationery shop and her typewriter all jumbled up together. Piccadilly was alternately alarmed and delighted, appalled and amused, impressed and confused.

He was on surer footing when she tried to tell him about *space*, and about the stars. He knew—the Martians knew—that they weren't alone in the universe. They knew that moons and planets other than theirs were inhabited, and if they'd never encountered an Earthwoman before, that was merely an accident, rather the way Josephine had never encountered an Egyptian. He was confused by her mode of transport, but not incredulous.

She tried to describe her fall, out of the darkness of space and towards the great dark face of Mars. She sent him an image of the two moons, white and red. In response, he sent back a jumble of confusing images. In his mind, the ivory moon was light, with welcoming wings. The red moon was Hell.

As soon as she thought that, the name *Angel* came into her mind for the ivory moon. A moment later, the name *Abyss*—the red moon—made itself known. She was quite certain of the names, as if she remembered them from a book she'd read in childhood.

Piccadilly was tense. If he were an Englishman, he would have been frowning.

Abyss. Was that where their enemies were from? Was that what they'd thought she was—a devil from Abyss? She probed his mind further. No, there were two kinds of enemy. A war on two fronts. The twisted folk of Abyss, and the devils that ruled the face of Mars. That was how he thought of Mars: a huge face, the face of one of his people, solemn as a saint's, but bloodied and scarred and blinded. The name in his language for Mars: *Vast Countenance*. God and home and mother and father all at once. They were exiled from it—driven to the moons by some unimaginable disaster, some incomprehensible atrocity. Flight; a fall. They were out of their proper place, driven from their proper course. The inhabitants of Angel were exiles, refugees, flotsam; driven from the surface of Mars, exiled from the Vast Countenance. Josephine reached for more, bombarding the old man with questions, hungry for names and words and history and explanations. She realised, almost too late, that she was terrifying him—that he'd got to his feet and was crouching, ready to leap—that the army on the roof was about to throw itself at her.

She withdrew from his mind, retreated, made herself small and quiet and harmless.

Slowly he settled himself again, drawing in his wings. The army outside relaxed. Cautiously, they resumed their conversation.

After a long while, a few of Piccadilly's fellows came creeping in—frightened at first—to discover what she was. Soon she had an audience.

Chapter Twenty-five

When Arthur finally tracked down what was left of the Company, he got a cold reception. They were hiding—*planning*, Atwood said—in Sun's house. It was a nondescript building near the Albert Docks. Inside, it was finely appointed, full of odd statuary that looked, to Arthur's eye, only half-finished. He tracked it first by memory—he recalled Thérèse mentioning a visit to Sun's house by the docks; and then by asking after a well-to-do sort of Indian gentleman—a merchant, perhaps, or a nabob, or something of the sort; and lastly by means of Mrs Archer's inquiries among the pigeons, the rats, and the crabs. He went alone. It was Dimmick who answered the door, and the next thing Arthur knew, he was being wrestled through the hall and thrown onto the uncarpeted floor, where Atwood and Jupiter stood over him and accused him of various forms of treason, oathbreaking, vile cowardice, and desertion. *Gracewell*, he said. *Gracewell . . .* Dimmick—without malice, but in a professional sort of way—gave his leg a kick. *I have Gracewell . . .* Sun put a hand on Dimmick's shoulder and said, *Hear him out.*

Atwood helped Arthur up. "Gracewell?"

"I have him."

"By God. You're not joking, are you, Shaw? Well, well. Perhaps I've misjudged you. For Gracewell, one can forgive a little treason."

"Podmore and I—well, I saw to it that Podmore let him go."

"How? Why?"

"More to the point," Jupiter said, "where *is* Gracewell?"

He was in the care of Archer and her son, in a boarding-house. That sent Atwood into a rage all over again. Dimmick, who'd started rolling himself a cigarette, put it behind his ear and waited for instructions. *Archer! Shaw, are you mad?* And that wasn't the worst of it.

Arthur explained what he'd promised her for her assistance. Atwood positively exploded when he heard her terms: nothing less than full membership in the Company, access to its books and records, a full one-ninth share in all profits and proceeds of any expedition to Mars—

"How dare you, Shaw? How dare you—who do you think you are to make such a promise?"

—and full participation in any such expedition, should there ever be one.

"We have no choice," Jupiter said.

"We must have Gracewell," Sun said. "I see that you fear this woman. But I also recall that you once promised you could control her, if it was necessary."

"I *see*," Atwood said. "Then I suppose you should do as you please, Mr Shaw, if you think you know best."

He stormed off in a sulk, as if he planned to send a telegram to his Hidden Masters in Tibet and complain of insurrection.

The capture and recapture of Norman Gracewell were just the opening moves of London's Great Magical War. It continued through autumn, and on into winter.

Mrs Archer (gloating happily) took on the title of Terra Mater. Sergeant Jessop, the previous holder of that title, was dead—Podmore hadn't lied about that. No members of the Company attended his funeral.

Thérèse Didot had suffered too. She wouldn't say how, but her hair had gone grey.

When asked about the bird that had saved Arthur from Podmore's men, Sun merely smiled, and said that he was sure Arthur would have an opportunity to repay his debt in due course.

They rebuilt Gracewell's Engine.

Gracewell refused to speak about his confinement, except to say that it had given him a lot of time to think. He was thinner, and quieter, and he no longer looked anyone in the eye or made conversation. He wouldn't shake hands, and he hardly ate. He took cocaine and worked all night without rest. His third Engine was superior to the second, cheaper and more efficient. It had to be—sensitives were becoming increasingly hard to find in London.

They built the third Engine just a few miles from Gravesend, not far from Rudder Hill. Since Gracewell had become quite incapable of handling ordinary responsibilities, Arthur took on the job of organizing construction. The building was a sprawling ugly thing of timber and concrete, hastily built and prone to collapse, at the end of a trail through the woods. They told the locals it was a clerical office for the Europa Shipping Company. Mrs Archer said that she liked being able to sit on the bench outside her house of an evening and look down from the hillside onto the Engine, buzzing away in the wooded valley below.

One moonlit midnight at the end of October, a black storm brewed up over the sea and rushed inland, where it drove the trees of Rudder Hill so violently that some of the locals (staggering home from the pub) claimed to have seen the trees themselves get up and march downhill, thrashing their heads in a frenzy. By the morning, a good part of the western side of the Engine had been reduced to rubble, and there were drifts of leaves and broken branches everywhere. It was obviously the work of the enemy. Archer claimed that if it wasn't for her protection, it would have been worse.

The week after the incident at the Savoy, Arthur visited George in the hospital, where George lay with his head and his ribs bandaged while his wife, Agnes, fussed over him. George didn't recall very much about the incident at the Savoy, except what he read in the newspapers. He snapped at Agnes and spoke of suing the Savoy, which was unlike him— he'd never been the litigious sort. In fact, even after he was out of the hospital and walking around again, he seemed rather a different person. The doctors said that blows to the head could have that effect. They didn't know if it would last—the brain was largely unexplored territory to modern science. In the meantime, George, who'd always been slow to anger, now had a vicious temper. He'd always been quick to make a joke; now he was humourless. He stopped writing his stories. The newspapers convinced him that it was the electrical lighting at the Savoy that had caused the episode of hysteria, and he became obsessed with the study of electricity. At Agnes's suggestion, Arthur tried to invite him out to Gravesend to get his mind off things, but he refused to travel. He said it was dangerous to go outside. He was afraid of electrical currents, baleful astronomical influences, nameless forces.

* * *

It was a year of storms and other strange events.

The Company negotiated rules of engagement with Podmore and his allies: magic, but no guns, or knives, or burglary, or other activities that the Metropolitan Police would recognise as ordinary crime. That left a great deal of room for creative unpleasantness.

The incident at the Savoy, in which two people had died, was generally considered to be an episode of mass hysteria. There was a common theory that it was due to the pernicious effects on the brain of too much electrical lighting and the sudden acceleration of elevators. There were lawsuits against the Savoy and against the London Electric Supply Corporation. There were diplomatic difficulties arising from injuries sustained by a minor Italian Prince, and injuries inflicted on a Bishop of the Church of England by a German Grand Admiral; but whoever's job it was to smooth things over smoothed well, and by the end of the year the lawsuits had been settled and peace between nations maintained.

There were riots in London. The mob took exception to something unpatriotic printed in one of Podmore's newspapers (though no two members of the mob could agree on what exactly had been said, or what was wrong with it). They set fire to one of Podmore's warehouses, and feathered a delivery boy, and heaved expensive printing equipment into the river. Another mob (with a certain overlap in personnel) assaulted Sun's house, which—rumour had it—hosted immoral practices and was a prison for unfortunate young women. A curious sensation of vertigo swept through the mob before they'd broken more than a couple of windows; a sensation that left them reeling, vomiting, clutching at lamp-posts for fear of falling into the vast night sky above. This was generally blamed on a gas leak. A few of the ringleaders turned up the next morning on nearby rooftops, hanging on to chimneys for dear life. Sun's house survived, but his psychic exertions left him bedridden for a week. The mob, Atwood observed, could be a dangerous weapon, especially when one's opponent owned the newspapers.

Dr Sandys, the King's College theologian, hung himself in his kitchen. Archer was quick to claim credit.

Ravens amassed in the sky in great numbers, forming noisy black thunderclouds. Rats swarmed up out of the Underground. The vermin of London went to war. Their struggle lasted all through autumn, but ended inconclusively. Every morning there were dead birds and rats in the streets, on rooftops and window-sills, tangled in laundry. The newspapers concluded that the unusual weather of the past year had driven the wretched creatures mad.

In October, a Mrs Ada Carroll, a known associate of Lord Podmore, lost her house to a quite extraordinarily aggressive infestation of termites; but Mr and Mrs Carroll were noted amateur Egyptologists, and the popular theory was that they had probably brought back some sort of virulent strain of insect in an urn or a sarcophagus. Some friends of Lord Atwood's in Parliament proposed an investigation of the Carrolls's trade in antiquities.

The new rules of engagement left Dimmick mostly idle. He took to drinking and fighting down by the docks. He suffered no significant injuries, apart from a broken nose and a lost tooth. He grinned and told Arthur that he should see what he'd done to the other fellows.

The Company of the Spheres recruited a woman called Sadie Paget, but she didn't last. One September evening, as she sang by the piano in the Queen's Head, the instrument improbably (a dropped match?) burst into flames. She left London in a panic the next day, her hands bandaged. Arthur never even met her replacement—a young painter who styled himself *Parsifal*. When Parsifal left the Company (for the madhouse), Dimmick took his place. Scraping the barrel, rather, Arthur thought; but though Dimmick's magical talents were somewhat questionable, and his morals worse, he was undeniably brave.

Arthur didn't pay too much attention to the ins and outs of the war, to who was on whose side, to the daily news of alliance and outrage and plot and counterplot. He moved out of London, glad to say good-bye to the city's growing atmosphere of unease and discord. He bought a ramshackle little house outside Gravesend, not far from the new Engine, where he worked all day and half the night to keep the thing running. He installed a hand-cranked telephone and hired a housekeeper and a nurse to take care of Josephine. They whispered behind his back; thought he was mad, poor fellow. Mad, but rich. He had the backing of the general fund of the Company of the Spheres, so money was just about limitless. It was time that was scarce. Every day Josephine seemed fainter, paler, weaker. He had almost forgotten the sound of her voice.

The third Engine was staffed—at its height—by fifty individuals. Some of them had been in the second Engine, and a few had been in the first. They generally looked at Arthur with a certain dread and awe—Gracewell's mysterious enforcer; the great, gaunt, never-sleeping giant of the Engine; the man who knew the terrible secrets of the Work. He was rumoured to perform all sorts of odd rituals, and to keep his wife in an enchanted sleep. It amused him, in a bleak sort of way. He told a select few of the workers about his confrontation with Lord Podmore, and he showed an even more select few some tricks he'd learned from Atwood and Miss Didot, like glass-breaking, table-rapping, some small sleights of will. His small legend grew. They were afraid of him, and rightly so. He was not a cruel master, but nor was he especially kind. Time was of the essence. The Work remained hard. It was his policy that men on the verge of madness should be relieved of duty before they succumbed. A humane policy, under the circumstances; Atwood considered it folly. It didn't always work.

On nights when he couldn't sleep, or when the Engine was idle, he took long walks. He took up stargazing. He was menaced once or twice by a black dog, or a pack of owls. He was quick with a prayer or a charm to drive off evil spirits.

The Company expanded their ambitions. They refined their mathematics. Fortnightly, Arthur caught the train into London to join their experiments. Archer threw herself cackling into their business, and got her hands on the *Liber Ad Astra* over Atwood's objections. She said she didn't think much of this modern stuff—thin-blooded, she called it. She had *ideas*, which, much to Atwood's disgust, turned out to be good ones. The Work progressed rapidly. Each successive expedition into the void progressed further. Each time the face of Mars loomed larger before them. They began to plan an expedition.

It was Arthur and Atwood's habit to communicate weekly by telephone, to discuss the Engine, the experiments, Josephine's condition. In November, Atwood informed Arthur that the Germans had indeed arrived in London.

"How do you know?"

"It was in the newspapers. Professor Bohm and Professor Bastian of Heidelberg University arrived in London on the *Lady Margaret,* and are staying at the Grosvenor."

"And who are they, Atwood?"

"They are scholars. But they are also—and this is known only to those who know this sort of thing—members of the Hyperborean Society."

"And what's that?"

"The *Society*, Shaw—I'm quite sure I've told you. Honestly, you should pay attention to these things if you plan to move in these circles. You can't hide in the country for ever, Shaw—burying your head!"

"I don't see why not. Someone has to keep the Engine running. Well, so they're Hyperboreans; good for them. What are their plans?"

"Professor Bastian intends to lecture on political economy at King's, and Professor Bohm intends to visit the British Museum. That's what the *Times* reports. Bastian is terribly famous among the sort of people who like that sort of thing—economics, I mean; quite incomprehensible to me, I'm afraid. But both of them are up to their necks in the left hand path. Well, I suppose one can't be up to one's neck in a path—but the point is, their motives are without doubt ulterior. And we must assume that their allies will follow; or are already here."

"Podmore said that the Germans would intervene. I suppose he was right."

"We won't let the Germans stop us."

"What will they do?"

"Their worst. At least they haven't brought in the Americans—yet—so far as I know. Or the Chinese. I expect they'll do something dreadful. We will weather it. I'm more concerned about Archer, frankly."

Arthur didn't bother to respond to that. Atwood regularly complained about Archer—her repulsive habits, her base and primitive and unfashionable superstitions, her crude and vulgar conception of magic, her open and aggravating contempt for the Company's philosophy.

There was a long pause, during which Arthur pictured Atwood staring silently up at the ceiling, lost in thought. He wondered where Atwood was. The man had half a dozen flats, and he moved among them frequently, to confuse the enemy.

"Lord Podmore strikes at my investments," Atwood said.

"Floods; fire at the mill. Funds are short. The Engine is damnably expensive."

"God. Flood and fire. Will there be anything left when we're done?"

"Don't be dramatic, Shaw. There will be enough to run the Engine. I'll spend it all, if I must. Money is an illusion."

"There speaks a man who's never lacked it."

"It'll last. It need last only another month."

"A month?"

"Or thereabouts. We're closer—every time we get closer. We can see the shoreline. Are you ready? Are you eager?"

Atwood had set down a regimen of daily exercises for the members of the expedition—rehearsals for the ritual and meditations to prepare them for cold and darkness, hunger and fear, and whatever awaited them among the spheres. They were quite exhausting.

"Eager as ever, Atwood."

"Good. Good man. Closer and closer. It's hard to find good men, Shaw, hard to find the right men for this sort of thing. But we will. When will you get us the latest calculations, Shaw?"

"I'll send a man up to town tomorrow."

Atwood's plan extended no further than Mars. He seemed convinced that if he could achieve that goal—if he could plant his flag on Mars—then he would be guaranteed victory. He would prove his pre-eminence among magicians. From the vantage point of Mars, all the world and its secrets would be laid bare before him; his enemies would acknowledge his greatness and scatter. Arthur's own plans extended no further than finding Josephine. After that, he supposed they'd flee London together. South America, perhaps. He didn't know. He'd started hoarding money, skimming from the expenses of the Engine, saving for a disaster that he was certain would soon materialise.

After a long silence, Atwood said, "Is she . . . ?"

After another long silence, Arthur said, "The same as ever."

"Ah. Well."

"Well."

"Ever onwards, Shaw."

"Ever onwards, Atwood."

Arthur hung up.

He arranged for a messenger to take the Engine's latest calculations into town; but the unfortunate fellow was lost when his train derailed, along with a briefcase full of important papers and a dozen of his fellow passengers.

The work continued for more than another month. There were unforeseen difficulties, as anyone might have foreseen there would be.

Arthur spent the Christmas of 1894 alone in his little house on the edge of the woods at the foot of Rudder Hill. He had a fire to keep him warm, cold ham, a bottle of wine, and plenty to keep him busy. He spent two hours in the morning on his exercises. In the afternoon, he had calculations to work through for the Engine—problems of organization and the efficient flow of numbers through the great machine. He worked until the numbers danced in front of his eyes.

At midnight, he put down his pen, lit a lantern, and went out into the garden. He followed a path through the woods and half-way up Rudder Hill, to a place where he could blow out the candle, sit and watch the stars, and wish Josephine a merry Christmas.

Chapter Twenty-six

The Company of the Spheres came together towards the end of March 1895, at an evening hour governed by the Sphere of Mercury, to embark on what was expected to be—God willing— the expedition that would at last cross the void and touch the face of Mars itself. A first tentative exploration. A proof, God willing, that the thing was possible, that it wasn't madness.

They met in a warehouse in Deptford, not far from where Gracewell's second Engine had once stood. The floor was painted with star-maps, and the windows were full of candles to ward off the prying eyes of the Company's enemies. Mr Dimmick had hired some toughs, just in case, to be look-outs on the street outside. Two of them halted Arthur as he approached, stepping from the shadows and giving him quite a fright. He snarled ill-temperedly at them, shoved past, daring them to lay hands on him. They thought better of it.

He was already on edge, and late. In fact, his train had been so severely delayed and so slow, and the staff at the station so rude to him, that he'd begun to suspect the hand of the enemy at work. He was also tremendously anxious about Josephine. He'd left her behind that morning in the care of a nurse, having made arrangements with a lawyer to see to her in the event that—well, it was better not to dwell on what might go wrong. The expedition was not expected to take more than a matter of hours, but of course one never knew. He'd told the lawyer and the nurse he was travelling to Switzerland to consult with a specialist in the treatment of sleeping sickness.

As he entered the gloom of the warehouse he had a moment of panic and considered turning, running, and booking a journey to Switzerland after all. Mountain air, cold springs, and rest cures might be precisely what she needed . . .

"Shaw!" Jupiter's voice, echoes booming from the rafters, dispelled all thoughts of Switzerland. "Come in. You're late."

"Trains," he said, folding his coat on a shelf by the door.

"The spheres won't wait for the trains, Shaw. The hour is almost upon us."

Inside the warehouse, preparations were under way. Thérèse Didot was striding around placing and lighting paraffin lamps. Sun, his sleeves rolled up, was painting a great complicated magic circle on the floor, while Jupiter consulted the calculations and barked instructions. Atwood was meditating. A number of men Arthur didn't recognise were talking, smoking, and bustling about, moving boxes. There was a great deal of fussing, as there might be backstage before an opening night at the theatre, or the launch of a luxurious sort of ship. Nobody knew exactly what to expect, so they prepared for all manner of conditions.

Nine men would go on the expedition. Atwood insisted that—should they reach Mars itself—the dangers and privations that the expedition was likely to face were so great that it would be *disgraceful* even to consider sending women, especially after what had happened to Josephine. In fact, Atwood had confessed to Arthur that he and Jupiter had adopted this policy mainly in order to justify excluding Mrs Archer, whom they both mistrusted—and, in Atwood's case, at least, loathed. The policy had quickly taken on a life of its own, and had come to seem a very important moral principle.

Having by this somewhat accidental method convinced themselves that the expedition to Mars was essentially a military one, Jupiter and Atwood had gone out and hired ex-soldiers and sailors. The soldiers' names were Frank, Payne, and Ashton; they were hard men, weathered by travel to remote and unfriendly corners of the Empire and prepared for danger. They joked and cursed and lounged against the wall, and only the methodical way they smoked betrayed, perhaps, a touch of anxiety. Ashton shook Arthur's hand and said, apropos of nothing in particular, that all this pagan bloody magic didn't scare him these days, not after some of the things he'd seen and done in Afghanistan. Then he walked off without further explanation, pacing the circle's bounds anxiously, as if checking it for leaks.

Atwood's brief attempt to exclude Sun had failed. He had never been able to offer any sort of argument for this position, other than some mumblings about the necessity for someone to stay behind to prosecute the war, in case they were gone longer than expected; but that was a role that Jupiter and Miss Didot and Mrs Archer considered themselves more than capable of fulfilling. It was hard not to suspect that Atwood was merely jealous of Sun's place in the history books; that he did not want to share the first exploration of Mars with any other magicians whom posterity might mistake for his equal. In any case, he had been resoundingly out-voted. Atwood and Sun were to lead the ritual, to navigate the expedition's course through the aether. Equally importantly, they were to perform the ritual that would—after a brief reconnoiter of their point of arrival—bring them back home. They had both been practicing their parts for a month.

Arthur was to join them. No objection from Atwood. His motives were pure, His Lordship had said; let bygones be bygones. His place in the cir-cle was marked out on the floor, a dense knot where several lines of painted power converged. Dimmick was going too, over Arthur's strenu-ous objections—just in case, Atwood had said, just in case a firm hand was called for. And Archer's son was to join them—though Atwood didn't like it, it was the price of Mrs Archer's assistance. The son sat silently on the floor in a corner of the room, eyes half-closed, apparently entirely unperturbed, while his mother fussed over him.

Lastly, there was a dark young man at the far side of the room, with a bent nose and a thin beard, smoking and watching the proceedings with an air of amused disbelief.

"Our ninth," Atwood said, rising from his meditations. "A former em-ployee of Gracewell's—he has some small magical talent, and comes rec-ommended by Dimmick, who says he has a fighting spirit. More importantly, he's a sailor, used to long voy—"

"Good Lord."

"Good Lord what?"

"It's Vaz—as I live and breathe, it's Mr Vaz!"

Arthur almost ran across the circle—Payne snapped at him to *watch out!*—to take Mr Vaz's hand and shake it, while Vaz, equally astonished, let his cigarette fall from his lip.

"Good Lord, Mr Vaz. Good Lord. I thought you were dead. I thought you'd died in the fire."

"I thought *you* were dead, Mr Shaw! That was a terrible night, wasn't it? It was. It was! I had not thought to see a friendly face here."

"Good," Atwood said. "Good. A good omen, no doubt. The closing of a circle. Do you see, my dear? Do you see?" He walked over to Jupiter.

"I see, Atwood."

To Arthur's surprise, Atwood took Jupiter's hand and kissed it tenderly, then they embraced as if they were husband and wife and Atwood were about to go off to war.

"Places," Jupiter said, extricating herself and clapping her hands. "Places, gentlemen." She checked her watch. "The hour will soon be upon us."

The members of the expedition arranged themselves in the positions that Sun had marked for them on the floor: a complicated nine-pointed star. Thérèse Didot lit incense, and soon the room was filled with a dizzying sickly sweet haze.

In the centre of the circle there was a heap of boxes, packs, sacks, ropes. The paraphernalia of a polar expedition, heaped up like a Pharaoh's grave—the treasures of this world, waiting to be translated into the next. This was a precaution. Not knowing quite what to expect, or in what form they might arrive on Mars, Atwood had insisted that they be prepared for anything.

The chanting began, and it went on for some time. They rehearsed, over and over, Atwood or Sun or Jupiter stopping them again and again. The music of the chanting rose and fell. Archer's voice was the loudest, harsh and rasping. The words didn't matter, not in Arthur's opinion; it was the sound, the rhythm, the state of mind they created. But Archer saw things differently, and who knew what Atwood or Jupiter really thought.

Outside, night winds battered at the eaves and shadows passed across the windows. The warehouse was lit by paraffin lamps and a large number of candles, some of which dripped wax from the rafters. Atwood owned the warehouse, and it crossed Arthur's mind to wonder if he was insured against fire. Then he put those thoughts out of his mind, sat on the floor, and performed the meditations assigned to him. The hexagram. The red plains. Sand. The sword. Josephine's face appeared unbidden before him. He dismissed it.

Rehearsals bled imperceptibly into the real thing. The big show. The chant rose and fell, around and around. It revolved towards a dizzying peak. It was hard to remember precisely when it had begun. Smoke and incense filled the room, so that Arthur could hardly see Payne, the man next to him. Vaz was nothing but a smudge in the distance. Archer and Jupiter, walking around the circle and chanting, were strange monsters in the smoke—the coloured lamps they carried like eyes, like moons.

Sun was the first to go. He swayed and his chin fell on his chest and he slumped over sideways. Arthur's heart leapt. If all had gone well, Sun would soon be opening his eyes in another world. A translation, a transformation, a transmigration of the soul, perhaps not unlike death.

Atwood went just a moment later, falling elegantly backwards as if in a faint. Payne went shortly afterwards, with rather more of a *thud*.

Five minutes later—it felt like hours—Archer's son went. He grunted and dropped his enormous head and swayed. He grunted again, and shuddered all over, then opened his mouth and roared. Black mud poured from his nose. He clenched his fists and tore at his thin black hair. Archer stopped chanting and screamed, *No, no, my boy, my boy, what's happening to you, what have they done, what have they done?* His shoulders quaked. His eyes were bloodshot. He appeared to be having a seizure. Archer dropped her lamp and screamed, her hands to her mouth. Something in her eyes suggested that she had made a terrible mistake. As her son fell forward, blood streaming from his nose, she threw herself upon him, sobbing and shaking him.

Arthur had no idea what had happened or why. An error in the calculations? Something they'd failed to consider? The cause hardly mattered now. Archer's son appeared to be dead. That was a disaster. The ritual, all of Gracewell's calculations, assumed nine.

Jupiter and Miss Didot glanced at each other, then continued their pacing and chanting, stepping over Archer as she sobbed and wailed. Vaz tried to stand, but Dimmick seized his hand and pulled him down again.

It was too late to run. If Arthur quit now, leaving the thing undone, then anything might happen. Atwood and Sun might be stranded—the whole thing might fall apart.

Arthur sat and furiously strained for calm, for patience, for the dreamlike peace that was conducive to projection. His head spun. Archer sobbed. Wind and rain beat against the windows. Jupiter chanted the names of the planets. Miss Didot chanted the names of devils and angels, the ninety-nine gates, *Agares* and *Vassago* and *Marbas* and *Valefor*. Vaz and Frank slumped over on the floor—dead? Sleeping? Successfully voyaging through the aether? He didn't know.

Arthur sat on the floor. It seemed to him that he also stood, swaying. He was in two places at once. His head was now very far from his feet, as if he'd stretched, like Alice, as if he were rising up through the roof of the warehouse. Beneath him, Jupiter's and Thérèse Didot's lights revolved through the gloom. Archer's dropped paraffin lamp had started a blaze on the floor—the flames licking at the great heap of provisions in the middle of the circle, which threatened to burst into a pyre, and at the shoes of the recumbent body in a tweed jacket that he recognised, before the lights dimmed, as his own. But now there were lights above him, too, and he rose towards them. He held in his mind the images of the ritual: the hexagram, the sword, blood and sand. There would be ninety-nine gates to pass through. It seemed to him that the warehouse below him was full of swirling red sand, swallowing the lights. And was it his imagination, or had he glimpsed, at the edge of vision, a dozen strange men creeping through the alleys towards the warehouse, moving with sinister intent—Germans, perhaps, or Podmore's men, or possibly the Americans Atwood dreaded? Well, it was too late to warn Jupiter now. That was her problem. He could hardly hear the chanting now. There was nothing to guide him but his own will. Ninety-nine gates; he had committed the signs and names to memory. He passed through a hexagram of red light and became a ray of black light, streaming into the void. The gate named *Apep* was a ring of angels that shouted as he passed. Rising up and falling at the same time. Faster and faster, hotter and hotter; colder and darker and deeper. He faltered, almost, at the ninety-second gate, *Da'ath*, which took the form of a great revolving pentagram of ice; and at the ninety-ninth gate, which Atwood had named *Yaldabaoth*—the shape of it was indescribable. He closed his eyes in horror and it was only his will and his memory that carried him through, deeper and deeper into utter darkness.

Wind buffeted him. He stood firm.

Sand. Sand and dust tickled his face, blew about him, getting into his mouth and his nose.

He coughed, spat out dust. He opened his eyes.

A red plain stretched before him.

A jumble of images assaulted his vision. Inkblots—no, clouds of violet dust on the horizon. Rocks underfoot. Cold wind. A vast sky. Alien light. Some of the clouds were mountains, impossibly tall and thin.

No Josephine. Of course not, of course not, of course not. No smile, no welcome at all—in fact nothing, nothing as far as the eye could see. A dead world, an empty world.

Somewhere behind him, someone was saying, *It exists, it exists*. It sounded like Atwood. *It exists!*

He rubbed at his eyes.

His eyes! His hands, for that matter!

He patted at his arms, his chest. Solid. Flesh and bone. He was still wearing his tweed jacket. He didn't know quite why the jacket should seem so extraordinary to him, but it did.

His head spun. He swayed and stumbled. Atwood's voice called out *Look out there!* and Vaz called out something that sounded like *Hey!* It had hurt when he landed, knocked the breath right out of him. His breath! Arthur laughed. He lay on his back and looked up into an impossible sky, a deep dark inky starless violet, shifting and turbulent with dust-clouds. The moon—no, two moons, one red and one the other marble-pink—it was dizzying to think of them—two moons chasing each other around and around that sky—a sky that was a thousand times wider and darker and wilder than any sky that was ever seen over London—a vastness as huge and as terrifying as the face of God.

THE SEVENTH DEGREE

{ *Angel and Abyss* }

Chapter Twenty-seven

If there had been newspapers in the ivory city, they would have been utterly preoccupied with the Earthwoman Question. One day there would have been editorials urging that she be investigated, the next that she be deported; demanding that she be vivisected, or given the keys to the city, or exhibited on stage, or hauled before the courts, or condemned by the Church, or prohibited by Act of Parliament, or sent off on a tour of the provinces. She'd have been mocked in cartoons. (How does one caricature a invisible ghost? They'd have found a way.) All the experts would have weighed in; and even the common Martian in the street would have had his say, writing letters calling for Something to Be Done. Or, at least, that was how it all seemed to Josephine. What was certain was that the Martians of the lunar city were fascinated and horrified in equal measure by the news that they had a ghost in their midst, a spectral interloper from the mysterious Blue Sphere.

Now that old Piccadilly had shown her how, she couldn't help but hear their thoughts. There were so many of them, and they were so loud, like a swarm of crickets. She sensed emotions, images, longings, fears. She couldn't help but try to communicate, sending images of the Earth and London to and fro across the city, causing confusion, ecstasy, panic, and sometimes fits of agitated swarming that might be what passed for riots on the white moon.

Her—what was the word? her *ghostliness*—had some special meaning for them, something that was horrifying and revolting and compelling in equal measure. It had something to do with their flight from Mars, and with whatever horrible evil Piccadilly had feared. And apparently Martian newspapers if they had them—were no more reliable than terrestrial ones, because the news quickly got around that *all* Earthpeople were ghosts. Frightened crowds demanded answers, pointed up at the sky, at the tiny blue dot that was the Earth. She tried her best to correct their misunderstanding, but without a great deal of success. She tried to describe the human body, but they appeared to think that she was making a joke.

The crowds urged her this way and that, and important-looking people came to lead her here, or there, or elsewhere, to be studied and talked to and threatened and cajoled. She demanded that Piccadilly be allowed to go with her. In part, that was because she had begun to trust him. In part it was because she pitied him, and she didn't care for the way he'd been treated, and she felt that if there was fame and honour to be won among the Martians for subduing the Earth ghost, it properly belonged to Piccadilly. In part it was because he was the closest thing she had to a friend. He went before her into the crowded squares, shouting as if he were her prophet or holding up a red light to clear a path, like a philosopher in the marketplace. Squabbles arose around him, squalls of argument and excitement and motion. She had no clear idea what he was saying, but the role seemed to agree with him: as time went by he stood a little taller, his wings shone brighter. She felt drunk. She kept wanting to laugh.

By the time she was presented to their Parliament, the thrill of it all had worn off. She was tired of being prodded with questions, tired of being the object of fear and wonder, tired of understanding nothing, and rather afraid that she might simply disappear under the crush of attention. She wondered if that was what being famous was like back on Earth, and if so, why anyone would want it. All she could say to the Elders of Parliament was that she wanted to go home.

Parliament was her own word, of course. She didn't know precisely what they were, this little roomful of elderly Martians. All she knew was that Piccadilly was eager to impress on her their tremendous, paramount importance and dignity. So far as she could tell, most decisions in the lunar city were made by the *demos* as a whole, by casting of beads after the Athenian fashion—subject, no doubt, to the influence of certain great orators or generals or philosophers. Meanwhile, decisions of great importance were reserved for a caste or class or council of leaders, consuls, dictators—who were, perhaps, chosen for excellence of birth, not by the popular vote, and who therefore resembled Lords more than Commons . . . She didn't know. She suspected it was hopeless to try to understand the Martians in terms of terrestrial institutions—not least because she didn't understand those terribly well either. She certainly hadn't been able to explain Parliament to Piccadilly.

Regardless of what one might choose to call it, the highest authority of the city took the form of nine mostly elderly Martians. There was nothing obviously grand or powerful or dignified or important about them. They wore beads and scraps of silk, just like everyone else; in fact, it seemed to Josephine that they were, if anything, a little shabbier than the average. It seemed to her that they were mostly women. She couldn't quite say why—something about their manner suggested that they were matrons of their kind.

This innermost sanctum, this deepest penetralia of the lunar city, was a crowded little room that Josephine had initially taken for just one more of the hundreds of the bead workshops that could be found all across the city. In fact it *was* a workshop: there were tools, and work-tables, and scraps, and shavings, and clutter. There was an intense red fire in one corner of the room.

Three of them came shuffling forward, staring in various directions, as if hoping to catch a glimpse of her. The rest continued bead-making, working drills and needles with their fingers and their minds. First among bead-makers, Josephine thought, or stewards of the Bead-Makers' Union. Or perhaps the beads had some greater significance than she'd guessed—something military, something sacred.

She let them feel her desire to go home.

The matrons wanted to know all about Earth, and she told them what she could. By now, she'd conjured up the same images of Earth so many times and for so many questioners that they no longer seemed quite real, even to her. Under the endless pressure of questioning, questioning, questioning, she was starting to forget what was real and what wasn't—if anything here were real—if indeed there even *was* a *here*. Sometimes London seemed like something she'd read about in a book, or recalled from a dream. Were there *really* green trees, and blue skies, and a black and sooty city of pink wingless apes?

She felt herself drifting again, into one of those states of vanishing in which hours or days or months might pass in the blink of an eye. She willed herself to remain present. This room, these ancient old dried-flower Martians, were real and solid things. She concentrated on one in particular, the foremost and perhaps the most ancient of the three, a creature whose wings were little more than withered petals, and whose face—unusually broad and round for a Martian—was etched with wrinkles like veins in quartz.

Piccadilly stood in a corner, shifting nervously from foot to foot, like a pigeon.

They bombarded her with questions that were at first confusing, but which she soon began to sense were of a military nature. They wanted to know about the military capacities of Earth. They seemed to have in mind an alliance between the forces of Earth and the forces of the white moon against a common enemy. She supposed it had something to do with the red moon of Mars, and with their exile from the face of Mars itself. She was rather terrified by this responsibility, and tried her best to explain that she had no power whatsoever to commit Earth to anything. They found that hard to believe, or perhaps to understand. Their military line of inquiry was confused by the fact that they appeared to have London mixed up with the Earth, and policemen mixed up with soldiers, and they had no concept of a rifle or a cannon or a gunboat, or even of swords or cavalry. Her thought of *cavalry* confused them even further, as they seized on the image of an armoured knight out of Arthurian legend; and then Josephine thought of dragons, and then of "Jabberwocky." That caused the matrons great consternation. Suddenly, their images of London were full of dragons coiled around Big Ben, and Jabberwocks running wild in the Royal Botanic Gardens at Kew, while horses rode gleaming knights into battle . . .

Jupiter, she was sure, wouldn't be making such a terrible mess of things.

The matrons' next question came so clearly that she almost heard it as words: *Who is Jupiter?*

A hard question to answer. She tried to tell them about Jupiter, and about Martin Atwood, and Sun and Sergeant Jessop and all the rest of them, and about Atwood's house in Mayfair and the Company of the Spheres. She called up an image of Atwood's library, the lamps on the table and the star-maps and the mad symbols painted on the floor. That excited the matrons greatly. They wanted to know all about the Company's methods of travel. The notion of *leaving the body* fascinated and appalled them. For the first time, she thought they clearly understood what had happened to her.

They wanted to know if more Earth people would come, or if she was alone.

Well, would they? She didn't know. In recent days she'd stopped hoping that Atwood and Jupiter would appear to rescue her. Perhaps they'd never intended to rescue her at all. Perhaps they'd tried but couldn't find her. She still held out a vague hope, contrary to all reason, that Arthur might somehow find out what had happened to her and follow her; but that hope was fading. She'd begun to accept that if she was to find her way home, she'd have to do it herself. In fact, the thought of Atwood and his Company suddenly descending from the heavens was rather worrying. One ghostly Earthwoman had created a panic—what might the Martians do if nine of them appeared in their midst?

An image of the Company at war with the lunar city entered her mind. The matrons tensed.

She uttered a quick silent prayer. That set off a further round of shock and alarm and questioning. They appeared to take her prayer for a sort of magic spell. They found her notion of God highly distasteful, and, once again, her attempts to explain only seemed to make things worse: the Holy Ghost alarmed them; Hell seemed to confirm some deep and awful suspicion; the incarnation of God in a mortal body was half-comic, half-fascinating.

The matrons started to argue. She left them to it, trying to think of nothing at all. The three conversed among themselves, fingers fluttering and wings flickering, for a very long time. Meanwhile, the rest continued shaping and drilling and inspecting beads, threading them or moving them from one pile to another, and only occasionally pausing to express agreement or disagreement with this or that. They weren't a Parliament, or bishops or lords—they put Josephine more in mind of the Fates, weaving while they dispensed the destiny of kings and queens and nations. She named them accordingly: Clotho, Lachesis, Atropos; spinner, measurer, cutter.

With a sudden clatter of wings the Fates reached a decision.

Piccadilly stiffened, as if readying for a blow. Then he approached the table where the Fates worked. He had been summoned to testify. His wings were tightly furled and his back was bent. If he'd been an Englishman, he would have been on his knees.

He stood at the foot of the table, by the fire. He spoke quietly—that is, his motions were subdued, the colours of his wings faint. Josephine understood none of their questions to him, or his answers.

At last, Clotho reached out her fingers and entwined them in Piccadilly's. A gesture of peace—a benediction. Piccadilly ceased trembling. Josephine thought he would have wept if he could; laid his head in Clotho's lap like a child, weeping in gratitude, and love, and fear. Clotho, still and crystalline, glittering by firelight, resembled a pagan idol, carved from gemstone.

A moment ago, while they were getting confused about London, the matrons had seemed a little ridiculous. Now, in their own sphere again, among their own subjects, they moved Josephine to awe.

Clotho rose to her feet. With a thought, she indicated that Josephine should follow her. Then she went out into the street. Piccadilly, trembling, stood and went with her. The rest of the Fates turned their attention back to bead-making.

Josephine followed Clotho and Piccadilly alongside the rose-red river, through streets of white stone shadowed by towers. She was at first surprised that Clotho would venture out into the city alone, without a bodyguard or retinue, without secretaries or footmen or maids-in-waiting. Then she saw how passers-by looked at her, and understood that the whole city was Clotho's bodyguard, and retinue, and everything else she could need.

Their route took them away from the river, and towards a part of the city where the buildings were for the most part uninhabited. Great white dusty mausoleums, in the shadow of the wall of the crater; cold, gloomy, and remote. In the sky, the face of Mars was deep indigo, almost invisible against the blackness, and the red moon was a tiny splash of blood.

Clotho gave no explanation. Piccadilly appeared lost in his own thoughts, sad and hopeful at once. Was it possible that they had some way for her to go home—that they were taking her to some sort of port or gateway? They'd fled the face of Mars for the white moon; they must have some way of travelling between the worlds. Piccadilly's mood was odd—was he sorry to see her leave for her own world? Perhaps. On the other hand, it occurred to her that she might be bound for imprisonment, or execution. Her audience with the Fates had had something of the quality of a trial, and it was not at all clear to her that the verdict had been favourable.

She supposed she had no choice but to trust them. It was that or go back to haunting the cracks and corners of the city, perhaps for ever.

Clotho led them along a wide road—it had the air of a triumphal avenue, but it was silent and empty—and deeper into the gloomy districts at the city's edge, until finally their road came to an end, dissolving into a wide expanse of rocks and rubble at the base of the crater's wall. By now, they were entirely in shadow. The wall occluded Mars-light; at its foot there was near-total darkness. The rocks there were bare and lifeless, free of the red moss that throve everywhere else in the city. Only a faint light from the towers behind them lit their way as Piccadilly helped the ancient matron over the rough ground.

There was a cave—a deep crack, thin but tall, in the rough white rock of the crater's edge. It was utterly dark inside. With a wave of her fingers, Clotho made a small flame in the palm of her hand, revealing a plain tunnel of stone, rough-hewn, low-ceilinged, leading down.

Josephine was far beyond being surprised by mere fire-starting; it seemed no odder than striking a match. The tunnel was nondescript; but Piccadilly was trembling, and even Clotho had an attitude of quiet reverence.

The tunnel led only a little way into the underground before opening out into a great hall. Rough rock underfoot gave way to smooth and glistening paving stones. Nine-pointed pillars rose up into the darkness. The ceiling and the far walls were too distant to make out without abandoning Clotho's little circle of firelight, which Josephine had no intention of doing. She was suddenly conscious, as with a persistent itch that she'd been reminded of, that it was utterly freezing down in that subterranean darkness. No wonder Piccadilly was trembling.

For as far as she could see, the hall was full of the dead.

Piccadilly appeared frozen. Terror and uncertainty and sorrow radiated from him. Clotho stared fixedly forward, as if waiting for Josephine to do something.

With a jerk, Piccadilly started moving again, rushing forward, moving amongst the dead almost frantically. Clotho's light followed him.

Row upon row of Martians lay on the floor of the vault; row upon row in neat parallel lines converging in the darkness. Firelight glinted off folded wings. Curled up like sleeping children, knee-to-chin, they were surprisingly small, surprisingly vulnerable. As Piccadilly led them farther and deeper into the vault—hunting left and right, tracing his steps from memory—there was more and more dust gathered on the bodies. Some of them had been there for a very long time. Like Arthur and his knights, waiting to be woken; or like butterflies in a case, row upon row upon row, pinned and dried and dead . . .

But not quite dead; or at least, not all of them. Sometimes, as they passed, a pair of folded wings would shift slightly, the frilled edges rippling, as if glad of the touch of firelight. Fingers twitched. Chests rose and fell, almost but not quite imperceptibly. Not dead; sleeping. Hibernating, perhaps. Dozens and dozens of them. Young and old, male and female. Some terribly scarred, some not.

Piccadilly stopped. He crouched beside the sleeping body of a young female, and gently touched her wings.

Then he and Clotho waited, as if they expected the body to wake, or Josephine to wake her. To breathe life into her.

For a moment Josephine despaired, thinking it was just more confusion, another misunderstanding; they'd taken her for a real angel, and imagined she could heal the sick, wake the dead . . .

Then, all at once, she understood what they were telling her.

This was Piccadilly's—what? Child? Wife? Friend? Child, she thought. Her mind and her spirit were gone. All of the dozens or hundreds of sleepers in the great hall were the same. They were empty; their souls and their minds were gone. Casualties of war. What war? That hardly mattered now. She could make no sense of the visions Clotho and Piccadilly were sending her. The red moon, whirling around and around; the clash of armies in the sky over the white city. She didn't understand. What mattered was that they were offering her a body to replace the one she'd left behind in London.

Piccadilly trembled.

What sort of sacrifice was this? Agamemnon sacrificed his daughter for a fair wind, didn't he? What had Clotho promised poor Piccadilly? Or, more important, what was Piccadilly asking of her? For her to be one of them? For her to be *what* to him? To fill this empty vessel with her spirit. A manifestation; a materialization; a conjuration, stranger than anything Mrs Esther Sedgley had ever imagined. A metamorphosis. Waking on another world like a Princess in a fairy tale, among elves and fairy folk, in the magic places under the hill, on the far side of the moon!

The body in question was short for a Martian, but with long and bright and very finely edged wings. It was mostly indigo, dark for a Martian—the same sort of shade as Piccadilly, in fact. It was pretty. It was monstrous. It was fascinating and revolting.

Could she enter this body? Was it possible, this unprecedented metamorphosis or resurrection or reincarnation? Did Clotho know, or was she guessing? Was this a matter of ordinary medicine on the moons of Mars, or was it a wild experiment? She'd had enough of wild experiments. Should she do it? Would she be able to leave again?

If she refused, what would become of her? Alone for ever, ghostly, drifting, dissolving into nothingness . . .

With a sensation of giving herself up to a dream, Josephine moved towards the body and studied the blank silver eyes. For an instant they were like a mirror, in which she saw herself seeing herself. Then the next thing she knew there was a cacophony of sounds and sensations, an incomprehensible torrent of pain and joy and terror and feelings she couldn't name. The sensation of her wings opening! The world seen through wide silvery eyes. Colours were a hundred times brighter, as if she'd been seeing through a fog all this time. Piccadilly was bright as a parrot. The transformation of her perceptions that had been taking place slowly during her time on the moon finally rushed to completion. She saw Piccadilly for the first time without any suggestion of the *creature* about him, but simply as a rather dignified old man—an old soldier, something rather like a retired Major. Clotho had the plain grandeur of an abbess.

Josephine stood. It seemed to her that she was making some sort of noise. She fell over immediately, in a tangle of unfamiliar limbs, knees and elbows striking stone. Pain was a joy.

Chapter Twenty-eight

M r Vaz, his head and shoulders already thickly layered with dust, sat on a rock and muttered about Hell and damnation. Sometimes he lowered his head until it was almost on his knees, so that he appeared to be praying; he was in fact struggling for breath.

"Lord Atwood has brought us to Hell," he said. "What else would you call this? He has damned us."

Atwood wasn't there to hear this indictment of his character. He'd gone off to the edge of their camp some hours ago, to confer with Sun on their predicament.

Dimmick squatted on his haunches, idly scratching with his knife in the dirt, staring into the distance. There was a haze in the air—dust, and something oddly twinkling that was not dust. It appeared to be twilight; at least, one would hope it wasn't what passed for daylight on Mars. At the far horizon a row of tremendous mountains met a sky of black clouds, streaked with nightshade and lurid foxglove—a venomous sky. Clouds had covered both moons, the rose and the red. Thank God—it had induced a certain odd vertigo, to see those two moons chasing each other across the heavens.

Between the expedition's hasty and makeshift camp and the far horizon there were no signs of civilization, or greenery, or life. Green was an unknown colour here.

"Hell," said Mr Vaz.

"Shut up," Payne said.

Dimmick stood, and sheathed his knife. "Let him talk. He's right, ain't he? Call it what you like—this is Hell."

Vaz laughed, then started to cough.

Dimmick paced the boundaries of the camp. He was soon no more than a lumbering shadow in the haze. Among the many odd properties of the haze was that it distorted vision, unpredictably, like sea-water. He had no destination. He was keeping busy. Something in the atmosphere made joints stiffen quickly.

They'd been on Mars for perhaps half a day—it was hard to be sure. Nobody's watch had survived translation. They had not yet glimpsed the sun. They'd moved no more than a half-mile from the place they'd arrived, and set down what Atwood called a camp in a circle of rocks in the lee of a tall sweep of rock that gave no shelter from the cold. They grumbled, paced, quarrelled, prayed. Moods of religious horror passed over each of them from time to time, then moved on, like the shadow of a cloud, leaving them cold and drained. There was something unnerving in the air, something a little like the stillness and pressure that on Earth would precede a storm, but here seemed to precede nothing at all. This was a dead world.

They'd arrived—*manifested*—in various states of weakness, disorientation, and dismay. Atwood and Sun had been up on their feet limping around within half an hour or so, but Arthur had been unable to stand for at least an hour, and one or two of the men had taken it worse. Like drowning, Vaz said, seeming to speak from experience—or like the sensations produced by the Work of Gracewell's Engine. Just the thought of it—*I am on Mars*—was so strange that it made one's legs go weak.

There were eight of them. Archer's son had not appeared, and it seemed likely that he would not. It was better not to think about what had happened to him—what might still happen to the rest of them, for all anyone knew. Martin Atwood and Sun were off by the edge of the camp, pacing, deep in conversation—there was an occasional violet flash as Atwood lit a cigarette. Dimmick was now kicking desultorily at rocks. Vaz was doubled over coughing. Then there was the military contingent—Messrs. Payne, Frank, and Ashton.

Ashton was unwell. According to Payne, Ashton claimed to have learned magic from the feet of the Secret Mahatmas in Tibet, after deserting from the Army in India. Whatever secret learning he might or might not have acquired, it didn't seem to have done him much good. He'd survived the transit, but only by the skin of his teeth. He lay on the ground, green at the gills and moaning softly, with his jacket wadded up as a pillow under his head. No one knew what else to do for him.

Frank and Payne and Arthur investigated the supplies.

The supplies had caught fire back in London, when Archer dropped her paraffin lamp; but now they were here. That was another thing that was best not thought about too closely. Otherwise one might begin to wonder if this really *was* Hell—if they weren't, in fact, dead, and surrounded by the ghostly shadows of their former lives. But no good came of thinking that way. One could glimpse horror in a can of soup. The important thing was to keep busy. Arthur and Payne and Frank were conducting an inventory. "Keep warm, chaps," Arthur said. "Keep moving, that's the thing. Spirits up." Frank and Payne, never a talkative pair, worked in grim silence. Wise of them, Arthur supposed. The thin air made talking hard work. Of course they were used to mountainous territory.

After a while, Vaz came and joined them.

"Are you well enough, Mr Vaz?"

"Better to work than to think, don't you think, Mr Shaw? Wasn't that always our method back in Deptford?"

Not all of the articles the Company had gathered had survived the transit; and some that had survived the transit had been lost, scattered all over the dunes as they moved to their current camp, through the dark and the wind, in a state of fumbling panic.

There were three small folded tents, but one was torn beyond hope of repair. There was needle and thread. Three spare pairs of boots and a dozen pairs of socks. Three loaded Martini-Henry rifles. Six knives of varying sizes. Four walking-sticks. Four camp-stools, of which three were broken. A superfluity of spoons. Nine compasses, all of which spun uselessly, apparently unable to find north. Perhaps Mars didn't have a north. Payne lost his temper and stamped on one. Tobacco. Three belts, two coats. Not nearly the right sort of clothing for the cold; they should be wrapped up like polar explorers. Two pairs of binocular field-glasses. A canister of paraffin, for the hurricane lamps, and a tin of creosote, for use as an antiseptic. Tonic of iron and strychnine (one bottle). Isinglass plaster, for open wounds. Opium, for diarrhoea. Opium for nerves. Cocaine, to maintain energy. Mescaline, and a small quantity of hashish, and God only knew what else; Atwood had packed such a quantity of drugs that it seemed to Arthur he might just as well have stayed home and taken his drugs and dreamed of whatever he wanted to dream.

Food, water. Condensed milk, beef tea, hard tack, pea soup. Two shovels. Two short and narrow sleds, of polished hickory with steel-shod runners, and with the initials *M.A.* carved into the side. What Arthur wouldn't give for a pack of dogs to pull them! But of course no animal could have performed the ritual. Perhaps you could train a parrot, Arthur joked, though no one laughed. Cruel anyway, he supposed. Ice-axes: four. Tin-openers: four. One pistol.

Untrustworthy; it was hard to spark fire in the Martian air. One theodolite. One aneroid barometer, which appeared to be broken. Three first-rate telescopes and two boxes of lenses, cleaning supplies, and other spare parts. Eighteen boxes of John Redding & Co. matches, which were slow to light, quick to burn out; but at least they could smoke, a little. A bottle of champagne. *Thank you very bloody much, Your Lordship,* Frank said, *that'll be a lot of bloody use.* Four thin blankets.

Their climbing supplies were gone. Ditto their dynamite.

Maps, but not useful ones. A map of London, a map of England, two maps of the world—Earth, that is . . . well, perhaps they could trade them with the natives. Two copies of the Bible and one of the *Collected Dickens.* Assorted toy soldiers. Powdered chocolate, snuff, and a tin of Lyle's Golden Syrup. The snuff-case burst when Vaz picked it up, and he staggered off coughing again. Two pocket-watches, and one Modell 1890 folding knife. A case of fine artist's paper, and another case of paints and variously coloured pencils. All intact. Frank confessed, somewhat embarrassed, that it had been his ambition to produce maps of Mars, or perhaps even watercolours. Seemed stupid now, he said. Magical supplies, sometimes hard to tell apart from the trading goods. Herbs and candles. Opium. A knife, thrice-blessed and edged with silver. *Et cetera.* Ritual paraphernalia—the painted cards, the metronome, the coloured candles. Pages and pages of calculations and observations; tables and logs.

It was madness, that heap of clutter, all quite shockingly unnatural under that alien sky, that sinister light. Even saying the names out loud seemed blasphemous—*Remington, Lyle's, Taylors, Benson & Hedges.* They worked through the night, laying out little piles, as if—Arthur thought—they were making a magic circle to keep out the darkness.

With every moment that passed—with every moment that Atwood and Sun didn't return—Arthur's foreboding deepened.

"Shaw," hissed Vaz. "Shaw—what are we doing?"

"I don't know. Keeping busy."

"A vision of the heavens, Lord Atwood said. An opium-dream, I thought. Well, I will take His Lordship's money. Since the fire I have been hard up, and London can be an unfriendly place."

"I'm sorry, Mr Vaz. I did look for you, after the fire. How did you escape?"

"By the window. It's the ordinary method, I think."

"Well, I'm glad."

"And now here we are."

"Yes. I hope Atwood's paying you well."

"Well enough. My services are not cheap, I said—not after what happened at Mr Gracewell's. Money is nothing, he said. I said that it was not nothing to me. He said, if you come with me on this voyage, Mr Vaz, you will never want for money again. The world and all its riches will be yours, if you still care for them. What would you want with money, he asked; all the money you could dream of, if you could have it? What would you say, Mr Shaw?"

"A place by the sea, with Josephine. Leisure; peace."

"A ship, I said; a ship of my own."

"Yes. You told me. It sounds very nice."

"A fleet of ships, his Lordship said. Why not a fleet? If you want them. Why not? I believed him. Perhaps I still do. He never denied the danger. But I am not a coward. Mars, he said."

"Yes."

"Is it true? You seem to know Lord Atwood. Is it true?"

"In a manner of speaking. It's rather metaphysical."

"Metaphysical?"

"Spiritual."

"Spiritual? I am cold, Mr Shaw, and hungry. Does the spirit suffer from cold, or hunger?"

"Shut up," Payne interjected.

"If this is a dream, Mr Shaw, why can't I wake from it? What will happen to us here? What does Lord Atwood have to say for himself, now that we're all here?"

"He's right," Frank said.

Ashton moaned.

Dimmick returned from his wanderings. "Nothing," he said, then sat in silence on the ground, toying with his knife.

Arthur looked around for Atwood. He was off in the distance, huddled with Sun. Typical. Swanning off, leaving Arthur behind with the men—who were probably on the verge of mutiny. And who could blame them? He felt more than a little mutinous himself. Jumpy; paranoid. The cold was getting to him, and the weird light, and the awful sensation that someone, somewhere, was whispering, senseless and almost inaudible words carried on the cold wind.

Well then. He made a small speech. Importance of morale. Keeping busy. Not the British thing (nor, he supposed, the way of Mr Vaz's seafaring folk) to panic in adversity—now was it? Their return was a simple matter of calculation—of will. Atwood would see to it. Naturally. No cause for doubt. They'd soon be home, back in London, returning in triumph. The thrill of scientific exploration. The glory. First eyes to see. *Et cetera.* Even to him, it sounded cheap and threadbare. Frank and Payne eyed him with open contempt.

Vaz found needle and thread and set about mending the tents. Arthur went off in search of Atwood. Behind him, Ashton started to whimper softly, like a child gripped by a nightmare, but the wind quickly swallowed the sound.

At one edge of their camp—call it *south*, why not—there was a rough circle of stones. They swam out of the haze as Arthur approached, looking at first rather like tree-trunks—tall, thin, jagged. If some natural process had deposited them, it was not one Arthur was familiar with. On the other hand, if they were the work of Martian Man, they looked at least as old as Stonehenge, and there was no sign of their makers now.

Sun sat on the ground with his back against one of those stones. His legs were outstretched and his eyes half-closed. He looked the very picture of confidence and relaxation. Like Buddha, Arthur thought, asleep beneath the whatever-it-was tree.

Atwood paced, still smoking. At that rate, he'd exhaust his supplies in no time. He tensed as he saw Arthur approach, then relaxed.

"Shaw."

"Atwood. Sun."

Sun opened his eyes. "Join us, Mr Shaw. Lord Atwood and I are discussing our situation."

"So are the men," Arthur said. "Frank and Payne are close to mutiny."

Atwood shook his head. "I don't have time for that sort of idiocy. Where would they go? You read too much romantic fiction, Shaw."

"Ashton's unwell."

"The terrain is inhospitable, I'll admit. But, for God's sake! The man was in Africa."

"Well, Africa wasn't so bloody—" Arthur didn't know how to finish that sentence. He waved a hand, to indicate everything in sight that was unearthly about the surface of Mars.

Atwood wore something that vaguely resembled a military uniform—or at least the splendid regalia of some unknown Guards regiment. He wore a pistol at his waist. He was having a great deal of trouble relighting his cigarette. He cursed the thin Martian air.

Sun closed his eyes again. He appeared to be meditating.

"Well, Atwood?"

"Well what?"

"I've been taking an inventory of our supplies. I supposed you were thinking. Putting your genius to work. What have you determined? What happened?"

"Archer! Didn't I tell you? Didn't I say it would be disaster to invite her into our circle? Didn't I warn everyone? Her and her bloody son. That—*thing* she calls her son."

"What are you talking about?"

"The ritual, Shaw. Botched. I should have seen it! That thing, Shaw—scarcely human. One shudders to think how she made it. Mud and clay and bone. God! Soulless, you see—pure will. *Her* will. No wonder, then, that the ritual tore it apart. Cut its strings. Left it empty. No wonder it couldn't survive the transit. And so, the whole sensitive experiment—botched! I could almost suspect she planned the thing. I could almost suspect she's in league with the bloody Germans. I hope Jupiter cuts off her ugly old head."

"Speaking of Germans, I think I saw a pack of them sneaking up on the warehouse. Or someone up to no good, anyway."

"Yes. I know. Jupiter and Miss Didot are more than capable of dealing with them, I'm sure."

"Give me a bloody cigarette, will you, Atwood? God. Let's see. Eighteen boxes of matches, counting the gifts—twenty matches to a box, does that sound right?"

"It doesn't matter."

"Of course it matters, Atwood. Our supplies are limited. I don't know how long they'll last. I don't know how long they'll need to last. Well—what's the answer?"

"Don't be a fool, Shaw." Atwood reached out and pinched Arthur's shoulder. "Not flesh, not fat, not bone. Not really. Don't you understand? This ill-fitting fleshly suit of yours, it's made of nothing but your thoughts—your memories—your soul. What the Tibetans, wiser than us in these matters, call the *tulpa*—the thought-form."

Sun opened his eyes a crack, and looked at Atwood with what seemed to Arthur like suspicion.

Atwood tapped his head with his fingers. He looked somewhat wild-eyed, as if he were struggling to convince himself of an impossibility. "Thus we are condensed from the stuff of the aether—*poured* as if into a vessel shaped by our will, a palpable materialization of the spirit. And so we bring with us the trappings of our daily life. The weaker minds will find it hard to say good-bye to them. Will find it hard to understand. To purify—to cut away what's not needed. So, for the comfort of the men, no harm done. Morale. I don't care what your inventory reports, Shaw. The true adept needs no food, no water."

"True enough," Sun said.

"Let's see you throw away your bloody cigarettes, then, Atwood."

"Calm down, Shaw. Keep a level head, for God's sake."

"Answer me, then. What do we do now? How do we get home? Atwood? You promised we'd be here only an hour. We were to come here, show it could be done, and go back."

They had tried to perform the ritual in reverse, to relinquish their grip on Mars and pass backwards through the void, to wake in London. It didn't work. They remained stubbornly Mars-bound.

"That *is* what Lord Atwood said," Sun agreed.

"We've been here all night. What's happened? *Botched*, you said. What do you mean by that?"

Atwood smoked and stared at the horizon.

"We do not know the way home," Sun said.

"I beg your pardon?"

"We are too deep. We cannot merely wake, as if we were in a dream. We are *here*, Mr Shaw."

Arthur looked up. The sky was a haze of dark cloud.

Sun shrugged.

"I see."

Arthur smoked his cigarette down. He felt, frankly, a little numb. His hand shook—if it *was* his hand. It was almost a relief, after hours of foreboding, to have his fears confirmed. He could almost laugh. He'd done his best to save Josephine; no one could say he hadn't given it his best go, could they?

"Trial upon trial," Atwood said. "That is the magician's path. We will be the stronger for it."

Not for the first time, Arthur considered hitting him. Instead, he slumped down beside Sun.

"Damn it!" He stood again. "We need a destination. Something to keep us busy. If we sit here much longer, we'll go mad."

"I quite agree," Atwood said. "Well said."

"Lord Atwood and I have spoken," Sun said. "We have a plan. In fact, we have *two* plans; we are spoilt for choice, Mr Shaw."

"The stars," Atwood said. "We need to begin again. To plan our course home. We must find high ground, from which to observe the stars."

"I see. Or?"

"Or we go in search of the natives, and seek their counsel."

"What natives?"

"Keep a level head, Shaw. Remember that we caused one to materialise in Mayfair. They're around somewhere. We have simply had the ill-fortune of arriving in a desolate area. If you woke up one cold misty morning on a Yorkshire moor, would you conclude there was no life in London?"

"That one didn't seem inclined to assist us."

"Well. We have rifles."

Arthur stared out into the night. "And Josephine?"

Atwood shrugged. "Ask the natives."

"Where, then? North, south, west? Where is north? I suppose we'll have to mark our route by leaving bread-crumbs, or get lost going in circles."

"Hmm. I thought we might cut markings in the rocks, but the principle is sound."

Sun opened his eyes again.

"While you were tallying our supplies," Sun said, "His Lordship and I performed the Rite of Mercury. We inquired of the spirits of the air where we might wander, to and fro and up and down on the face of Mars, in search of shelter. They did not answer us. And so, either the spirits of this world are silent; or dead; or they do not hear the voices of men, and will not obey our call. Isn't that right, Lord Atwood?"

"You know everything that I know, Sun."

In the distance, there were signs of dawn. It was cold, and blue, and electric. It lit the edges of a tremendous cloud that swept up over the far mountains and poured up into the sky, like ink swirling in water. Dust; a thousand tons of it, a thousand miles away; dust and lightning and needle-sharp mountains, ten times taller than the Alps.

"Good God," Arthur said.

Atwood put a hand on his arm and smiled. "Think of this, Shaw. You have seen Mars. And whatever befalls you, you will always be a man who has seen Mars. And you're worried about counting matches!"

"Yes. Well. I don't like the look of that cloud; I vote we go another way. Sun—what do you say?"

A horrible wailing broke through the silence. The haze muffled it, made it seem to come from all directions at once. It was some moments before Arthur was able to recognise it as human.

Sun was already on his feet and running back into the camp. Atwood and Arthur followed.

They found Ashton lying on the ground, wailing and thrashing. Vaz held one of his arms and Payne held the other, while Dimmick restrained his head, none too gently. Frank had retreated to a distance of about ten feet and stood there pale and shocked, with a rifle in his hands. Ashton's face had gone bright red. His eyes were bloodshot, and staring wildly at nothing. He was quite clearly hallucinating. It was very hard to make any sense at all out of what Ashton was shouting: for the most part, he was simply shouting *No* or *Stop* or *For God's sake!*

Sun knelt, shooed Dimmick away, and held Ashton's head in his hands. Instantly, Ashton went still, though he continued to whimper and moan:

Please, please no. Sun inspected Ashton's eyes and appeared to be listening to his breathing.

"The effect of our translation, no doubt," Atwood said. "Disturbed the brain. I blame myself—he clearly wasn't up to the challenge. Poor fellow. We should all be glad that we survived unscathed."

Sun placed a hand on Ashton's forehead. The whimpering grew quieter and quieter. Then, even that ceased. A thin trickle of spittle emerged from the corner of Ashton's mouth. Sun closed the dead man's eyes.

Atwood gestured at the corpse. "Mr Vaz, Mr Dimmick—please bury the fellow, and find some way to mark his grave with appropriate honour. First martyr of the first expedition to Mars! Then, please prepare to march."

"Where?" Payne said.

"Homewards, Mr Payne. Rest assured. Mr Sun and Mr Shaw and I have consulted on the matter, and determined our destination."

Sun glanced at Atwood, then at Arthur. Then he folded Ashton's arms, and stood. The suspicious exchange of glances did not appear to be lost on Vaz.

Atwood went and sat on the ground some distance away, and closed his eyes. The wind spun dust at his feet.

Arthur approached him. "*What* destination?" he whispered.

"Go away, Shaw. I need to think."

Chapter Twenty-nine

J osephine was lost for a long while, adrift in the extraordinary sensations of this new body. There was a strong, steady pulse in her breastbone, where she supposed her heart was. It was slower than a human heart. At each cycle of the pulse, the wings—*her* wings—throbbed with something like electricity, something like the pressure of an approaching storm. The things that a Martian tongue could taste were for the most part simply indescribable in the English language. Sweetness—something like brackish rose-water—their thick resinous wine—other things she couldn't name. She was confused at first by the sensation of hunger, mistaking it for sorrow. Her long legs were unsteady. Her fingers were quick and sensitive but weak. Her vision was all colours and motion.

The body, she learned, holds its own memories. She'd never had cause to notice that before, her body and her memories having previously been well fitted to each other, like the sort of husband and wife who finish each other's sentences. Now she saw how the legs remembered how to walk, tottering at first, like an infant—she was so tall and thin and top-heavy!— and how the wings knew that it felt good to unfold, to stretch, to let whatever electric forces played across them have their way. Her first experiments with flight were a failure. Well—it would come. The body had quite definite opinions, expressed in the gut and in the skin, about what was good to eat; and about good and bad manners, and who had a trustworthy look to them and who did not; and who was handsome and who wretched, who to pity and who to bow to. Most important—and this occupied all her thoughts for who knew how long—the body remembered *language*.

The language of the Martians had three parts. The ground-note of it came from the motion of the wings, in whose whir and thrum she could now perceive subtle variations: this carried crude meaning. The shifting colours of their wings and the motions of their long expressive fingers carried accents, tones, commands, subtleties, and ironies she never fully mastered. Lastly, their telepathic expression served somewhat the same purpose as shouting, or pounding the table, or *harrumphing*, and was considered rather bad manners in ordinary conversation.

The body held its old habits. She babbled, over and over, repeating words and signs she didn't understand—until, slowly, she began to understand them. Names came to her, unbidden, forming themselves on her hands—the names of people and places, the names of concepts that she didn't yet comprehend. She watched her own hands moving, as if they were performing a Punch-and-Judy show for her, or they were a conjurer's hands, performing arcane passes. Sometimes a wave of horror passed over her, and it seemed to her that those hands were an alien thing, something like an insect's waving legs. That was less frequent as time went by. They came to seem like the strong and elegant and expressive hands of a healthy young woman; like her own clear and pleasant voice. She hardly recalled what Josephine Bradman's fingers had looked like. Short. Pink. Rough from needlework, callused from typing. Always black with ink or red from cheap soap. Impossible to picture.

She'd been moved to a room in a tower on the edge of the city. She didn't quite recall how she'd gotten there—it had been during her strange second infancy, when it had been hard to understand what was sense-data and what was a dream. There were no crowds, and few visitors. She vaguely recalled that Piccadilly had visited her once, when she was still mute, still confused; he'd seemed sad. Now he was gone. She supposed that visitors were kept away at Clotho's orders, to spare her from poking and prodding and gawping. Seven tutors lived with her, and fussed over her, and worried about her health, and taught her what the body couldn't about language, and bothered her with questions about the Blue Sphere—which was what they called the Earth.

Time passed. She didn't know how long. She told the tutors that the days of the moon seemed longer than those of Earth—and they thought that was very interesting, but they could devise no experiment for testing the proposition.

The tutors measured time primarily by the shape and size of the red moon. They explained that the white moon Angel and the red moon

Abyss both revolved around the Countenance of Mars, but they followed different courses: Angel was slow and steady, while Abyss followed a wild elliptical orbit. At times, Abyss was so utterly distant as to be almost invisible; but it slowly came closer and closer, until it overtook its twin and dwindled again. Nine revolutions around Mars completed this cycle and began it again. Since the exodus from Mars and the settling of the lunar city, this had happened some thousand times, or one thousand one hundred, or more—the tutors fell to squabbling over the precise number. To the Martian philosophy, in which there appeared to be little distinction between a thing's *motions* and its meaning or essential nature, the revolutions of those heavenly bodies were of great astrological significance.

Since she'd begun watching the moon, it had grown from a blood-red pin-prick, like a match struck in the room next door at night, to a flickering flame like the light of a red lantern.

The language of the lunar city could be described, without *too* severe a confusion of concepts, as a sort of lingua franca. That is, it was a common tongue—but *tongue* was itself a confusion!—made up of the hundred languages of Old Mars. There'd been more Martians back then: a hundred nations, instead of one lonely city. In various different languages, the names of her tutors were Blessed One, Morning, Mercy, Strength, Born-on-the-Quiet-Moon, and Beloved. The other two were named for a kind of plant that didn't grow on the moon, and a kind of mythical creature that was simply impossible to express in English. She privately dubbed them Hyacinth and Silenus.

They cohered slowly in her understanding. They were frightening, at first—a numberless swarm encircling her, prodding her with questions, with incomprehensible signs. It was a long time before she could see them as *tutors*—as seven fussy old men and women who delighted in language-games, grammatical quibbles, antiquarian trivia, mathematics, arid philosophical puzzles. They were tall and stately, thin and stooped, their wings like glorious Byzantine robes. Like most Martians, they found it hard to keep still. At any given moment during their lessons, two or three of them would be pacing around and around the edges of the room, circling one another in quarrelsome orbits, sometimes bumping into one another, distracted by their own lecturing. Several of them drank to excess at times, and fell asleep leaning in a corner of the room. Scholars were the same everywhere throughout the universe, she supposed. They questioned her constantly regarding the Blue Sphere, and they took notes, but their attitude suggested that they knew best, that the things she told them were interesting curiosities, but not strictly reliable; rather the way a roomful of missionaries might politely but not respectfully listen to an African describe his theories regarding the cause of thunderstorms. And sometimes she thought that perhaps they *did* know best. Her own memories of London were starting to seem very strange to her.

The floor of the room and all the shelves that lined the white stone walls were cluttered with heaps and towers and pyramids of red and black and golden beads, each of them a book or a hundred books of philosophy or poetry or science or tactics, all of them buzzing or shifting from time to time as the stray thought of a passing tutor set them in motion. There were no mirrors, much to Josephine's annoyance. They didn't have mirrors on the moon. In fact, the very idea of a mirror upset them—they seemed to see it as a form of black magic, the separation of soul from body. They questioned her on the subject for hours.

They started to go for long walks, the eight of them drifting through empty streets out on the edge of the city, under the light of the red moon. They travelled in long, looping circles with no particular destination in mind, arguing and debating, questioning, refining grammar. Sometimes the tutors came to blows—leaping and fluttering up to perch on windows and clatter their wings in outrage. As the days went by—and as the second moon approached—the tutors seemed to grow agitated. They became more quarrelsome. The ones who drank too much drank more. Josephine felt it too. The room felt confining. They yearned to fly.

Her continued inability to take to the air worried them. It struck them as unhealthy, insane, infantile; a form of paralysis. She protested that she needed more time. In fact, the thought terrified her. To fly, to respond to the urgings of her wings and take to the air, would be too utterly inhuman; it would be a way of going native. It would be to accept, once and for all, that she would never return to London.

She asked them, again and again, if there was a way of going home. They pled ignorance. In fact, they pled ignorance when it came to more or less all the questions that interested her. What was the red moon, and what would happen when it came closer? They wouldn't say. What had happened on Mars that had driven them to exile in the lunar city? What had they all been so afraid of when she'd first shown herself—what were the devils Piccadilly had feared? They changed the subject to matters of philosophy. They corrected her grammar, fell to squabbling over linguistic obscurities, and then, when their squabble was over, they pretended to have forgotten her question. Finally they told her, frankly, that she wasn't ready, that there were things she simply wasn't prepared to understand. As if they thought of her as a child, or an invalid. Or as if they feared she was a spy, and they were keeping secrets; on Clotho's orders, no doubt.

One evening she had a visitor. She sat in the window of her room, looking out on white stone stained red by the light of Abyss. Hers was the highest tower for some distance around, and so she had a view of an expanse of rooftops, domes, arches, buildings that looked unfinished, buildings that had begun to slowly crumble. All empty. Behind her, the tutors were engaged in philosophical disputation. Silenus and Born-on-the-Quiet-Moon were at the point of coming to blows over a difference of opinion regarding the distinction between the accidental and essential properties of substances. She'd started the dispute by mentioning Atwood's theories regarding the aetherial composition of the heavens, but it had long since turned to realms of Martian philosophy that she could no more comprehend than a cat could read Greek. She was staring out the window and recalling, vaguely, the monograph she'd been typing at the moment of her—her *translation*. One hundred and fifty pages of metaphysical hair-splitting, for a Mr Potter, a railway clerk. Had she put it in the safe before setting out for Atwood's house, or was it still on her desk—three-quarters typed and likely never to be finished—on the corner of her desk that caught the morning sun, beside the typewriter, beneath Mr Borel's stationery shop, on Rugby Street in London in England on Earth?

Lost in these thoughts, she didn't at first notice the shadow of wings approaching over the rooftops. Then she recoiled, jumping back from the window as suddenly her visitor rudely appeared in it, closing his wings with a *snap* that silenced the tutors, who turned as one to stare.

It was a male; he was small, dark, with a still and inexpressive face and exceptionally large and beautiful wings. He was obviously unexpected. It was equally clear that her tutors knew who he was, and that he was something of a celebrity. It was rather as if the Duke of Sussex had suddenly walked unannounced into a dining-room full of disputatious dons, or as if a group of village deacons had received an unexpected visit from the Archbishop of Canterbury.

He opened his wings again and said ~ *Peace. Be still.*

The tutors all buzzed at once. Josephine couldn't understand what they were saying, except that it seemed that some of them were expressing their respect, and some of them their displeasure at the interruption, and some of them demanding to know the stranger's business.

~ *Peace,* he repeated.

A conventional greeting, made with the hands alone. It meant little more than *hello.* He was ignoring the tutors, and studying Josephine. His expression was unreadable. Something about him suggested that he was the sort of person who expressed himself through action.

~ *You are the woman from the Blue Sphere.*

~ *I am.*

~ *I didn't believe it. I had to see it for myself. You are very strange. The Blue Sphere! A harder journey than any I have ever dared. You don't look strong enough.*

Silenus clamoured for his attention, telling him he had no business there, threatening to summon the authorities.

~ *I go where I will,* he said.

Josephine gestured into the room. ~ *Come in. Be my guest. Please. No one comes here.*

He remained very still, and continued to study her.

~ *What are they teaching you?* He gestured at the tutors.

~ *Philosophy,* Josephine said. *And words.*

~ *You speak well enough. What do you make of our philosophy?*

~ *I don't know.*

~ *Is that what you'll tell them in the Blue Sphere, when your way takes you there again?*

~ *I don't know the way back.*

~ *Stupid to come here, not knowing the way back.*

She turned to the tutors and asked, ~ *Who is this?*

They told her his name—it meant something like *Second Child.* An odd name. The way they said it suggested something rather dashing. Here in the lunar city, where children were scarce, perhaps it meant that he was lucky, or at least improbable. It carried connotations of a heavy and rare duty. A hero's name.

~ But who is he? What does he do? In their language, the words for *doing* were also words for *going*. The tutors started talking about great journeys, from which she understood that he was a sort of explorer.

~ I am of no great distinction, he said. *None of us here are of great distinction. I was born on this grey moon, many hundreds of revolutions after the flight from Mars. We are not what we were.*

Some of the tutors agreed with this sentiment, expressing what appeared to be quite conventional lamentations for their fallen state. A couple of the tutors patriotically objected on behalf of the lunar city, which, though falling far short of the lost glories of Mars, nevertheless prevailed, resolutely, against all adversity.

He turned to them for the first time, and interrupted before they could start to squabble. *~ I have seen the face of Mars*, he said. *I have cast my shadow on it. I have seen the ruins, and I know what we were, and what we lost.*

Josephine said *~ You have seen Mars?*

~ I am not clever, or beautiful, or learned, and I do not even say that I am especially brave. But my wings are strong. I fly well. Some say I fly the way we did when we flew over Mars. Once, long ago, our great-great-grandparents came here, across the dark. Now only a scattering of us are strong enough for that. We are not what we were. We have forgotten how to fly, because we have nowhere to go, except round and round in our little rooms, talking and talking.

The tutors took offence.

Josephine said *~ How?*

~ There are ways. A better question is: how do I come back? I'm strong. One day I won't be strong enough, maybe.

~ Is it dangerous?

~ Yes. But we go only when our moon is closest to Mars. We go to learn the things that we have forgotten; to bring back what we can.

Privately she named him *Orpheus*.

The tutors interrupted to say that this fellow's work was of course very admirable, in a way that seemed to suggest that he answered to them, that he was a sort of go-fetch-it for the scholars of the lunar city, dispatched in their service to bring back fragments of the old world, sights and sounds and memories, curios and bits of old rock . . .

Orpheus ignored them, and continued to stare at Josephine. ~ *Is it dangerous? Yes. There are terrible things down there. Are you one of them?*

~ *I don't know what you mean.*

~ *The way you move is strange. The way you speak is strange. What are you? You are not her. She stopped, you started; moving in her body, but not her.*

~ *Who was she?*

~ *A dead woman. They haven't told you who she was? They should tell you. Did you ask? Is this a normal occurrence on the Blue Sphere?*

~ *Certainly not.*

~ *I would have forbidden it, if anyone had asked me.*

~ *Do they have to ask your permission?*

~ *No. But I would have stood in their path. You frighten me. I have survived sixteen crossings, there and back again, and I know when to be afraid.*

~ *What is it that you're frightened of? You come here and you jump in through the window and you tell me you're afraid of me—as if I asked to be here! And they keep me shut up here on the edge of the city and they won't tell me anything—*

~ *I hear that you worship a ghost, you people in the Blue Sphere— that you have an invisible god, who watches from above and casts people into fire—a horrible thing!*

~ *No—you have it wrong.*

~ *You walked on the ground, and looked up at the stars, and made a god out of nothing. We looked down and saw the face of God beneath us. But now it is dead.*

He hopped down from the window, scattering the tutors, and settled on the floor in the middle of the room. He began to tell a story.

A half-dozen generations had come and gone since the flight from the Countenance of Mars. They were long-lived, and slow to breed; slower, since their exile. On the Countenance, things had been very different.

There were no cities there. There were vast red plains and sharp, cloud-piercing mountains; there were black forests of tower-tall trees, whose roots fed on subterranean lakes a mile deep. You could sleep in the heights of those trees, curled up among the vines. You could lose yourself in a maze of mountain peaks and be alone with your thoughts for years at a time. The people of Mars crossed the red plains in flights, in flocks, in tribes and families and great shifting nations-on-the-move, their shadows streaming far beneath them. They flew, on sunlight and wind and aetheric currents.

(The tutors interjected, to debate the nature of *aether* all over again).

They were always in motion. They had no settled abodes, and needed none. Their nations had no borders. A nation of the people of Mars was not a place, but a route across the world, a pattern of migration. Each nation was an idea, an argument, a philosophy. The people came and went as they pleased. There were a hundred nations, a thousand flocks and tribes, uncounted millions of lives.

They built. They were nomads, but not primitives. They beautified the face of Mars. They made lodges, temples, libraries. They left signals, markers, border-stones, records of their constant travels. They built with their minds, with their hands, with clever tools and lost arts. A nation that migrated through the cold north built factories. The Nation of the Eye—migrants between the deserts of the equator and the great western mountain—carved stone, and carved the mountain-tops. The Nation of the Strong Lungs, who hunted through the forests of the south, worked trees and vines, roots and fungus.

The hundred nations of Mars made war—ceaselessly, joyfully, for sport or to settle philosophical differences. They were long-lived, restless, energetic, fearless. Airborne migrant nations clashed over the plains and the mountains, seizing prisoners and trophies. The Nation of the Three Questions fought the Nation of the Pinion for a thousand years, around and around the cool and windy southern pole. At first, they fought to resolve a difference of linguistics. Soon it became a matter of honour, and then something that defined them. Neither nation could win. Families, flocks, and tribes changed sides, learned new languages and ideas, switched colours, maintained the balance of power.

That was the world Orpheus' great-grandparents were born into. They had belonged to the Nation of the Pinion, and the Nation of the Breath, and the Nation of the Broken Claw, and other nations that no one now

remembered. They had been warriors, thinkers, explorers, migrants, art-
ists of flight. Some of them survived the flight; not all.

The tutors now began to show off, reciting their own hybrid and
tangled ancestries, recalling the names of ancient Nations of Mars, like
the Liars and the Hindwing and the Heart, and their attributes. It quickly
became clear that there was hardly a single fact that they could all agree on,
except that among all the nations of Mars, it was the Nation of the Eye that
was most extraordinary. For example, the people of the Eye were the most
jealous of their territory; the highest mountain of Mars was theirs. Their
scholars cared little for philosophy and hardly at all for art, but instead studied the stars, watching the skies from their cold high peaks. It was their
scholars, looking sunwards, who discovered the existence of the Blue
Sphere; and whose investigations in the other direction, out into the dark,
revealed the vast Purple Sphere, and beyond that the distant and dreadful Black Sphere.

What precisely was wrong with the Nation of the Eye? On that, the tutors and Orpheus couldn't quite agree. They diagnosed a variety of philosophical sicknesses—some of which Josephine thought she understood,
and some of which would seem wicked only to a Martian. As Orpheus
talked, she pictured the princes of the Eye, sometimes as a single one-eyed
giant, and sometimes as if they were the grey sisters in the old fable, who
shared one eye between them. They were scholars: they studied the spheres
and wished to move as they did, in perfect revolutions about a still centre.
They ceased their migration, settled on the peak of the great western mountain, and remained there for years. Those who would not settle were driven
out—a wicked thing—or held prisoner—a wickeder thing—or killed, which
on the whole the tutors seemed to consider the least wicked possibility.

They built fortifications. They closed the mountain to outsiders.

There was war, of course. This unnatural and depraved conduct
aroused, as was right and proper, the outrage of other nations. The nations of the Pinion and the Three Questions came all the way across the
red desert from the south to go to war over the foothills of the mountain.

In time, the war grew bitter. The Nation of the Eye could not be fought,
could not be reasoned with. Their warriors had a terrible new strength.
They had new weapons, new techniques, that could strike armies from
the sky.

The great western mountain was the tallest thing on Mars by far, and because they held it for themselves, the Nation of the Eye declared themselves the natural rulers of Mars. They began to conquer. They made their scholars into generals, into princes. They destroyed the armies of the Pinion. They claimed authority to direct the migration of lesser nations. Something more than an insult; almost an atrocity. They razed the forests that were the hunting-grounds of the Strong Lungs. They seized the factories of the cold north.

They built prisons.

On the top of the great mountain, where the air was thin and the currents weak and only the strongest could fly, the Nation of the Eye built strange towering structures—temples, perhaps, or weapons, or devices for observing the night sky. Heroes of the nations of the Hand and the Pinion raided them, razed them; they were rebuilt.

What was the cause of this strange behaviour, this national sickness of soul? Some of the tutors attributed it to sin, or to an unfortunate side-effect of excessive study of the natural world, unleavened by spiritual pursuits. Two of the tutors attributed it to the influence of the stars, or unfriendly entities that dwelled among them. Orpheus said it didn't matter.

How long did this war last? On that point, there was general disagreement, which quickly turned into a squabble. A matter of years, said Born-on-the-Quiet-Moon—things changed swiftly on Mars. Generations, said Silenus—the nations did not surrender easily to the Eye, and the Eye was not easily defeated. According to Hyacinth's mother's tradition, the decline of Mars had taken a thousand years.

What was the secret of the Eye's strength? On this point, the tutors were uncharacteristically close to agreement. The scholar-princes of the Eye had called down aid from the stars. Or perhaps it was better to say that they had called something *up* from the lower and darker spheres of the Cosmos—from the Purple Sphere, that vast world of storms and oceans and great proud beasts—or more likely from farther down in the Black Sphere—a world of cold and dark and howling ghosts—or perhaps from farther still, from indescribable and incomprehensible depths. In the fortresses of the Eye (so reported the heroes of the nations who'd escaped them) there were ghosts, darknesses that moved and whispered, chained shadows, freezing fogs, moods of sorrow and despair and hate that stalked the halls looking for a body to take hold of, rooms that held nothing but disembodied pain, thrashing at stone walls. All these dreadful things powered the Eye's engines of war. Who was master, and who was servant—the scholar-princes of the Eye, or the things they'd called up? It was hard to say. Perhaps the question had no meaning.

All the nations of Mars united against the Eye. All their disputes were set aside, for the first and last time in the history of Mars. In the end, they threw themselves in their millions at the mountain, and they drove the Eye back, and they destroyed the Eye's fortifications and temples, and they littered the mountain's slopes with ten thousand dead. Slowly—or quickly, depending on which of the tutors was right—the Eye's power faded. One by one the scholar-princes were hounded from their fortresses and put to death; and Mars died not long after.

What happened, in the end? The tutors were uncertain. In the last days, the survivors had made few records, and what they had made was mostly lost. Orpheus, who'd seen the aftermath, said that perhaps it was better not to know. It was likely that the ghosts that the scholar-princes had called up had escaped. Perhaps, having opened the way to the deeper spheres, worse things now came boiling up, eager to remake Mars in the image of their own hells. Or perhaps the scholar-princes themselves had learned, as their empire fell, to take leave of their bodies, to become pure spirit. In any case, the darkness that had hovered over the mountain of the Eye now spilled down onto the plains below. Great rivers of fog and ash and shadow ran slowly but implacably across the plains, devouring whatever they touched. They poisoned the water, they blackened the sky, they turned forests to ash, laying waste to whatever had survived the war. Those who crossed their path went mad with fear, with hunger; or fell from the sky dead. They were too heavy, too terrible. Mars could not tolerate their presence.

There was nowhere to run from them; you could flee twice around the world and still run into them. Those who survived turned inwards instead. Refugees of a hundred scattered nations came together under a black and choking sky and pressed forward into what had been the territory of the Eye. In Orpheus' opinion, they hoped only to hasten their deaths. Silenus was of the opinion that they had been seized by a holy wisdom.

~ *What they found there,* Hyacinth said, *is best not spoken of. But since our guest has begun the story, I will end it as well as I can. In the* abandoned fortresses of the Eye they found the secret of the crossing, and they set out from their tower-tops into the dark and the space between worlds, where there was nothing for their wings to drift on but moonlight. Some died, and some were lost, and some came to the white moon. This city was here when we came, and it was empty. We do not know who built it.

~ *I have seen dead Mars with my own eyes,* Orpheus said. *I have seen the storms and the darkness. I have heard the whispering. I have fought with the few savages that still exist in the ruins living a half-life of madness and hunger; fought them for scraps. I have felt the fingers of ghosts clutch at my soul.*

The tutors watched warily. The light of the red moon was very bright.

~ *I thought that if I told you, I might see—I might see what you are,* Orpheus concluded. *But I still don't know.*

Josephine said nothing.

Orpheus moved back to the window in a single, elegant open-winged leap, and crouched there. He stared; she felt him probing at her thoughts. ~ *We came here as strangers—lost. We care for the lost. That was always our way.*

~ *Thank you.*

~ *But if you are our enemy . . .*

He leapt from the window, and as Josephine staggered back, he swooped on her. She had no time to be afraid. She lashed out in anger, with her will, and he spun aside, striking his wings against the wall and landing crumpled in a corner.

The tutors scattered to the corners of the room and readied themselves for further violence.

Orpheus stood. ~ *You're strong,* he said.

She was. She was clumsy, perhaps, and she was lost, but her mind and her will were strong. She was too angry to be surprised. Hadn't Atwood said she was strong? Hadn't Jupiter?

Orpheus paced, muttering to himself.

~ *But what does that mean? I don't know what to do. I'm afraid. Something must be done. I can't stand still.*

He rushed to the window.

~ *Wait,* she said.

He turned back to her.

~ *Yes?*

~ *Wait. The fortresses of the Eye—do they still exist? Have you seen them?*

~ *A dangerous question.*

~ *Have you?*

~ *Of all the dark places on Mars, those are the worst. We do not go there.*

~ *They knew how to travel between the worlds. Perhaps they had a way to travel to the Blue Sphere.*

~ *If they had, they would have already laid waste to it.*

~ *Let me go with you.*

The tutors rushed forward and began to interrupt and argue and panic. She swept them aside.

~ *You're strong,* he said. *But I doubt you are strong enough. And I don't trust you.*

~ *But—*

~ *Perhaps when we know what you are. When another revolution has come and gone; or a hundred of them.*

~ *That may be a long time in my world. I think we are shorter-lived than you. Everything may be gone.*

~ *In time, everything will be gone.*

He leapt from the window, spread his wings wide, and rose into the night.

Chapter Thirty

Orpheus was gone before she could think of chasing him. Josephine rounded on the tutors. *~ I must go with him.*

Impossible, they said, fluttering around her, enclosing her, patting and stroking her wings to soothe her.

~ You can't hold me here. A prisoner. It's wicked—it's wrong—you said so yourselves.

They argued. Silenus seemed hurt, outraged; Hyacinth, amused. They explained to her all the reasons why it was very important for her to stay where she was, for her own good, and for the good of others. A buzz of motion and colour. She closed her eyes and they continued to argue in her head. She pushed past them, knocking Born-on-the-White-Moon to the floor, and fled, out of the room and up narrow winding staircases (too narrow and too steep; made for whoever or whatever had built the city) into the upper empty rooms of the towers. She wanted to weep in frustration, to stamp her feet. She wanted to laugh. She felt like a child.

She paced the room. It was empty, dusty. White stone was lit pink by the light of the red moon. The ceiling was arched in an odd off-centre way. Two arched windows looked out over empty buildings. An empty room in a ruin. The tutors, wisely, didn't come after her—if they had, she might have thrown them downstairs. She knew now that she was strong—stronger than them. Not that it had done her much good; it was her strength that had brought her into Atwood's Company, and it was her strength that had brought her out here, but she was still lost. Strength outstripped wisdom. She felt both powerful and helpless; she felt furious.

She thought of the story Orpheus had told her. The scholar-princes of the Eye—she pictured a nation of Atwoods, a nation of Jupiters. The ruins of their fortresses—she pictured Atwood's house in Mayfair, the books on his wall, the paintings, the star-charts, all the paraphernalia of his magic. She couldn't imagine the danger being worse than what she'd already faced.

Hours went by. The light of the red moon waxed. It was coming very close now. It seemed to accelerate as it approached—an illusion, no doubt, the way dawn seems so slow at first and then so sudden. She could feel its approach: in her bones, in her fingers, in her wings. Contradictory sensations, wild tidal forces pushing one way and then the other. One moment there was a sense of horrible impending pressure, the next a sense of lightness, as if you might take off, pulled into the sky towards the moon. One moment there was fear; the next, anticipation.

Who'd built this city? Who'd built this room, and what was it for? They were gone now; but they too must have their history, must have lived and loved and fought and died long before Mars fell, long before Greece or Rome. Their language was lost. Their city was a refuge for strangers. London wouldn't last so long if Londoners abandoned it. St. Paul's might stand for a century or two, and the British Museum, but the house on Rugby Street would be dust in a generation or two. One day London would be gone—or in a thousand years, which was not so very long from the perspective of the universe. Things stranger than she could imagine might settle in the ruins. A parade of improbabilities, green and red and blue and yellow, men like Egyptian gods, with the heads of elephants and parrots and dogs and bumble-bees—taking the place of Londoners, and the Londoners gone who knows where in their turn. A great parade, an endless series of heavenly revolutions, coming and going, passing from sphere to sphere—a universe of vast and eternal flux . . . She felt dizzy. There was something in the air.

The tutors came up the tower. Hyacinth bustled in first, self-importantly, asserting authority by her very posture. But before she could speak, Josephine demanded ~ *I have to go with him.*

~ *Impossible. That you would even ask!*

~ *I'm not afraid.*

~ *You should be.*

~ *I have to find him. Go away. Go away!*

She shouted with her mind until Hyacinth recoiled, hopping downstairs. If she'd had skirts, she would have hiked them in a panic.

A horrible notion entered Josephine's head. When she'd first arrived on this strange moon, she'd hoped every day that Martin Atwood or Jupiter might suddenly appear to rescue her. Now she wondered if perhaps they *had* come after her; but what if they'd looked for her on Mars itself? What if they'd instead found the ghostly horrors Orpheus had warned her of? Even Atwood didn't deserve that. And what if Arthur had followed her to Atwood's house? What if he'd ended up in the same danger? They might even now be sitting down around a table in Mayfair, Arthur and Atwood and Jupiter and Sun, all of them hand in hand and ready to venture into the void, towards the haunted surface of Mars.

Next it was Silenus who came to lecture her, but she saw him off too. Then it was Mercy's turn. The two of them argued for hours, and when she pushed Mercy, Mercy pushed back. All the while the red light grew brighter, and her mood became wilder, and the tutors became angrier; until at last she pushed them all aside and ran up the stairs to the tower's highest window.

An archway opened onto a curving, sloping platform—there were a series of them around the top of the tower, rather unpleasantly reminiscent of the gills of a mushroom. She stood uneasily out on the topmost platform. There was little wind—even now, with the red moon bearing down close and the feeling of a storm in the air, the city was still and quiet. Behind her, she heard the tutors coming up the stairs. The tower rose above her to a horn-like point. Nearby towers resembled nails, church steeples, pyramids, honeycombs. As far as she could see, she was alone. She unfurled and stretched her wings. Always a strange sensation. Muscles moving where no muscles should be.

Before she could think twice or lose her nerve, she stepped out to the platform's edge and stepped off, snapping out her wings as wide as they would go. At first she felt nothing, nothing at all as she fell through the thin lunar air, nothing that would halt or slow her descent. Then she felt instincts coming swiftly to life, a warmth creeping through the edges of her wings, and those strange unwieldy things began to move of their own accord, not beating but stretching, contracting, arranging their complex fronds and entanglements so as to catch not air but *light*: the faint light of the sun, reflected from the surface of Mars, and the thick light of the red moon. Her fall slowed, then she began to rise. In a matter of seconds, the tower was far behind her, and the city was a blur below. She didn't know where she was going. The tutors would pursue her, she supposed, and so she turned towards the heart of the city, where she might lose herself in a crowd. That was her last coherent thought for some time: a thousand new sensations cried out for her attention, and she was lost in them.

Not air, but light, or forces more fundamental than light. Astronomers might talk—in that way they had, that made the universe sound rather ugly and cluttered—about rays, and spectroscopic something-or-other, and solar winds and so on. Or perhaps Atwood might have a better idea—perhaps the forces at play were more his sort of thing, telekinesis or the Odic Force or astral light or pure *vril*. Perhaps the conditions were peculiar to the Red Sphere. It was absurd and impossible to imagine bright blue Martians fluttering like a swarm of summer butterflies through London smog. Everything had its proper place. Hers was here, now, under the light of the red moon, high over the white city.

She swooped and turned between the towers, swiftly, effortlessly. The wings were weightless, buoying her up. When she tried to turn to see them behind her (so huge!) the result was that she rolled and fell, tumbling, laughing at the speed and the danger until she was able to catch herself on a thick rolling current of light and rise up again, soaring over a great grey dome. Something followed her across the stone below. It wasn't until she was far past it that she realised it had been her shadow.

The tower-tops were above her now, and she could see pedestrians on the streets below. They were all looking up. At first she thought they were looking up at her, but of course there was nothing remarkable about what she was doing. Not here. Here, flight was no more remarkable than riding the omnibus. They were looking up at the red moon.

In the heart of the city there were crowds. It was an out-of-doors sort of evening on the moon. Martians leapt from window to window between the towers, and she was frequently forced to swerve to avoid collision—now *that* caused them to stare at her! They were negligently careless of collision, like Londoners striding out into traffic.

Long tower-shaped shadows unfolded beneath her and folded away again. There was pollen in the air. The flowers were upturned, open, expectant. Red light flickered on polished stone. From the air it resembled campfires; the armies of Greece beneath the beetling towers of Troy. Martians staggered through the streets, drunk on red wine—had they been Londoners, they'd have been arm in arm and singing. Others perched like gargoyles in windows or on rooftops—no, more like cats on the hunt, watching, and waiting. Beneath her the streets opened into a square where packs of Martians fought, charging and swooping at each other, skirmishing, cutting and parrying with their wings. Was it a riot? Some Dionysian carnival, a night of madness? No—on closer inspection, they were sparring—readying themselves. She felt an urge to join them.

The thrum and whine of their wings made messages.

~ *Good luck!*

~ *Be ready!*

~ *Follow me! Follow me! Join us!*

A flock of Martians surrounded her, beckoning. They had no idea who she was, no idea that she was not truly one of them. The thought was delightful. What were they doing? Where were they going? She followed them for a while, drifting from window to window of the high towers, where the flock perched, clamoured, rattled their wings, urgently beckoned out into the night. They were raising the alarm, rousing sleepers, rallying the city's defenders. Against what? She hardly cared. Her thoughts were not entirely her own. She moved with the crowd, angry and joyful and wild—hardly even remembering why she'd fled the tutors' tower, or what she was looking for; just one of the defenders of the ivory city against whatever was coming.

The flock wheeled around a horn-shaped tower—she didn't see the signal and nearly turned too late—and then passed through another flock passing in the opposite direction, a thrilling cacophony of wings and signs all around her. Wheeling and banking again, she found herself in a part of the city that she knew. Old Piccadilly lived there.

She said ~ *This way!*

The flock ignored her. Whatever authority they recognised, she didn't have it. She split off from them. They didn't seem to mind, or even notice. She searched from window to window along the street until she found her friend's window. She knew it was his because he was standing in it, leaning out to watch the preparations below. He staggered back as she approached, as if he'd seen a ghost—which, in a way, she supposed he had.

She entered through his window and stood before him, breathing heavily, her wings trembling with excitement.

P iccadilly occupied a room on the middle floor of a mostly empty tower, in a street of no particular significance. The room was as spartan as any other. Piccadilly had retreated from the window to stand in a dusty corner. He was trembling; he looked terribly old. In his sudden retreat from the window he'd spilled a crystal decanter of red wine.

There was something about him that was not so different from a pensioner in London. An old man forgotten in a dusty room. Threadbare wings. The drink. Memories of the dead.

She stepped forward. His wings opened in surprise and alarm, as if to shield himself.

~ Why are you here? Now? Tonight?

~ I don't know what's happening, she said. Everything's moving— everything's moving, so suddenly. I don't know what's happening. They taught me grammar, and philosophy, and science, and nothing I needed to know.

~ How did you find me?

~ Luck. I didn't know I was looking for you. I thought I was looking for someone else. Can you help me? Will you help me?

~ Of course. Why now—I saw you at the window and asked, why now? But this is the night of the red moon, and everything is chaos. Anyone may find themselves swept up and whirled anywhere. Why not here?

~ I escaped.

~ That was a good place. That was where you should be. They said they would teach you. Make you strong.

~ At first, perhaps. But then all they did was ask me questions.

She saw that he was drunk. His lips were stained red.

~ I was glad when they took you away. I couldn't look at you. It was harder than I expected. I'm sorry. Shall we talk now? After all these months? Now, on the eve of the red moon? Yes. I shall not last through another one. That's well enough. I have lived to speak with an angel, and to see the dead wake. And for a little while, I was the leader of a school, and people listened to me because of it. That will do.

~ Who was she?

~ No one now.

~ How did she die? What happened to her?

~ You'll see. Very soon now, you'll see. You'll see what they do.

~ They?

~ Our brothers and sisters of the red moon. They didn't tell you?

~ No.

He went to the window, stiffening as he passed her. She wanted to throw her arms around him and hug him, the way she would have hugged her father when she was a child. But she didn't know how the old Martian might react, what that gesture might mean to him. And then it was too late—he was standing at the window.

~ They should have told you, he said. *Perhaps they were afraid to tell you. Afraid of what you would remember—afraid of what she would remember. Do you remember?*

~ I don't know—I feel afraid, and angry. Our brothers and sisters of the red moon—brothers? Sisters?

~ Have they told you how we fled Mars?

~ I don't understand.

~ The way was hard. Only the strongest survived. And some were lost. Some drifted. Some fell to the red moon. Isn't that how it is? We are blown here and there. I am old enough to know. Why did you come to me, of all people? I could ask, but why not?

~ And what happened to them on the red moon?

He shrugged. *~ A hard world. Harder even than ours. It moves too quickly, and it drives them mad. They have no good leaders and they have forgotten how to live. And so they steal from us. Whenever the red moon comes close enough to cross.*

~ To cross?

~ They have ways. Perhaps they remember some things we have forgotten. When the moons are close it's almost as if we are one again. And then there are currents, and they can cross.

He stood at the window and looked up.

The moon was huge in the sky, occluding the face of Mars. The air throbbed with its presence.

On the red surface of the moon, a scattering of black dust—a faint shadow, like soot on a lamp—grew slowly at first, and then faster, becoming a curl of smoke. Then, moments later, a flock of distant black dots, which next became cross-shaped, a thousand tiny letter X's—as big as flies, as big as bats, as big as birds; wings like a fleet of sails along a red river. Black sails swept along by lunar currents. An armada, sailing on a river of red light.

They were hateful; they were the enemy. It was a strong, clear, joyful hate, a good hate. It was no sin to hate, not here.

The city rippled its wings, tensed its muscles.

The enemy's final descent was so fast, so sudden, that Josephine didn't realise they were *there*, in amongst the people of the city, indistinguishable from them, until she heard fighting. The snap and crack and slash of sharp wings. Falling and running and hissing. The noise came from above and from below. Something sliced through a tendril overhead and it fell like a cut washing-line. Flowers scattered, some drifting in through the window.

In the next moment, one of the enemy landed in the window. Josephine leapt back. Piccadilly was too slow. A wing lashed out and struck open his throat.

Chapter Thirty-one

The killer leapt across Piccadilly's body and into the room. It crouched, reaching for the spilled decanter, which leapt from the floor into its harpy-claw hand. The killer lapped at the red dregs, then dashed the decanter against the wall. It glared at Josephine and hissed.

She realised with horror that it was trying to speak. To threaten, gloat, mock. The people of the red moon Abyss spoke with their voices. That struck her as barbaric, disgusting, an animal behaviour. They could hardly communicate very much that way—hooting and hissing. No wonder they'd descended into barbarism.

The killer's outstretched wings blocked her view of Piccadilly's body, but not his blood: red, thinner and paler than the blood of an Englishman, and an extraordinary amount of it. In the instant he'd died, his wings had stiffened, snapping beneath him when he fell. Somehow that was more gruesome by far than the blood.

Josephine noted sorrow, and anger, and fear, as if they were outside of her, filling the room.

She retreated to the wall. The killer's eyes shot to the door and back again. It tensed, ready to jump, and she tensed to meet it.

To meet *her*. The killer was a woman. Little more than a child—tiny and half-starved. Wings dull, mottled, and mute; bony chest so thickly scarred that she looked scaled. She wore a belt around her wasp-thin waist, braided from something bright. It resembled snakeskin. A Fury, dripping with blood, wild-eyed.

There was no possibility of communication, and nothing to say. Josephine, who'd never in her life lifted a hand in anger against anyone, was as eager for confrontation as the killer was.

The belt, she realised, was made of the bright fibres of severed wings.

The killer's own wings shifted. Veins darkened and lightened again as muscles tensed and blood pulsed. Their sharp, fern-like edges rippled. Dull meaningless patterns formed and unformed.

The killer was playing with her, feinting. She felt it probing at her mind—a nasty vicious whispering, looking for weakness—trying to confuse and distract her, to panic her.

Jo looked away, and down at her feet.

The killer leapt, and Josephine leapt a half-second later. They met somewhere near the ceiling, slashing and clawing at each other. Their wings scraped together with a terrible screech.

The killer was surprised. Her dead eyes lit up for a moment. The killer flicked her wings, rolled upside down, and leapt off the ceiling—an elegant motion that Josephine couldn't possibly mimic, so instead she fell, clumsily, which was perhaps for the best: her clumsiness confused the killer, made her unpredictable. The killer lashed out with the long edge of her wing, but missed wildly. Josephine circled and struck; they clashed, then passed each other. Cuts bled on Josephine's face and leg. The killer was unwounded. The killer hissed; Josephine was silent. A claw reached for Josephine's eye—she swung her head away. She parried, sharp teeth scraping her wing. It was an extraordinary, agonizing sensation. She stepped back and the killer followed. Wings struck against wings, cutting and parrying, a flurry of violent colour and light and motion. She parried by instinct. Then, suddenly, her wings and the killer's wings were enmeshed, interlocked, and they were struggling together, both trying to pull free. The muscles of her back screamed and nearly tore with the effort. Then Josephine's wings were free and for a moment she was airborne, her wings brushing against the ceiling, while beneath her the killer took an unsteady step forward, screamed, and stumbled. Jo wasn't sure why at first; then she saw that the killer had cut open her foot on the broken decanter. She struck quickly before the killer could stand again.

The anger went elsewhere, but the sorrow was still there in the room with Josephine, choking her.

There was nothing she could do for Piccadilly. She didn't know what they did with their dead. She hardly knew who she was or where she was. She felt drunk.

✳   ✳   ✳

S he crouched in the window, knees drawn up to her chin. Wherever she looked, she could see fighting. The raiders of the red moon had infested the whole city, it seemed. There was no clear plan to the violence. They killed, they looted. Packs of the white city's defenders fought the pirates in the street below; flocks circled each other in the sky, wings lit by red moonlight. She could tell the raiders of the red moon and the city's people apart by her anger; it was like a sixth sense, or possibly a seventh or an eighth. Her wings were trembling with sensation, and her mind was full of shouting and screaming.

J osephine leapt from the window and into the air, cutting at the back of one of the pirates, who fell from the sky behind her as she sailed on, landing in another window, on a distant tower. She collected herself, looked about, and leapt again.

T his time she was in mid-air when something slammed into her, knocking the breath from her lungs and buckling her wings. She fell.

She caught herself half-way to the ground—a treetop's distance from the stones of the white city, had there been trees, or the height of two or three lamp-posts, had there been lamp-posts. Wings outstretched, muscles aching, she sailed slowly down. She crouched with her hands and feet and forehead touching cool stone. She didn't know where she was. Two short flights had brought her to an unfamiliar part of the city, a wide avenue between white honeycomb towers, cluttered with stone arches and buttresses, and cut through with channels that once—in the days of the city's long-lost makers—might have held water, but were now merely obstacles, complex terrain to be fought over.

Something had knocked her from the sky, but no one had touched her. It had been a blow of pure force, pure anger.

They fought not just with their bodies but with their minds, with what an English occultist might call *telekinesis* and *telepathy*. Here the mind was a weapon, an ordinary technology of war just like gunpowder or cavalry on the Blue Sphere.

She remembered those empty bodies in the vault Clotho had led her to: withered husks, hollowed out by the enemy's weapons . . .

Two of the pirates came charging up, half-running and half-flying, moving from a dog-like crouch to an eagle's swoop and back again so fast that she could hardly make sense of what she was seeing. She tried reaching out with her mind, as if stretching beyond the edges of her wings, and struck one of them—the one that was at that moment in flight—so that it spun through the air and broke its wings against one of the stone arches.

The other pounced on her, slashing with its wings. Someone parried. A stranger's bright wing. A comrade, a fellow warrior of the white moon—a male, dark and handsome, one-eyed, who cut, parried, spun and ducked, then leapt high and struck down at the pirate, splitting open the pirate's thin skull with a kick of his heel. Before she could thank him, he was off again, crouched low and wings high, running back into the melee.

The scene before her was incomprehensible: the jumbled angles and arches and smooth channels of the street, the constant blur of motion and violence, screaming and clashing, bodies thrown this way and that. And at the edge of her awareness, the enemy's minds, prowling and looking for weakness . . .

She showed none. She leapt, lifted herself to the top of a white stone arch, and leapt again, sailing down into a deep channel, its sides slick with blood, where three of the pirates wrestled with two of the city's defenders. They turned to face her and she struck at them . . .

T he red moon was so close she could feel its pull. The air tugged her unpredictably this way and that, and sometimes she hardly knew which way was up and which was down. The architecture of the city ceased to make sense. She moved where she was pulled. A strange mood took hold of her. There was anger in it, and a wild joy, and something else: a sense of the smallness of her own life, blown here and there between those two vast whirling giants . . . but also a sense of its preciousness. It was worth spending, but not cheaply.

The pirates were everywhere. Soon her wings were ragged and she was bleeding from a dozen places on her face, her chest, her arms and legs. She'd hurled a half-dozen pirates from the air, sending them crashing to the stones below. She'd pinned a hissing and shrieking male, a big one, one-eyed, against a white wall, under red light, while two women of Angel cut at him—cut him to ribbons. She saw the pirates at the window of a school, pulling children out by their spindly legs. She saw them lifting fistfuls of beads, useless trophies, the words destroyed for ever as soon as the pirates touched them.

The pirates fought like wild things. The city's defenders were organised, well-prepared. There were signals and alarms all over the city. The shadows of signalmen standing with their wings outspread on high places, urging the city's warriors this way or that. Flocks formed, aerial formations, loose waves and tight phalanxes. There was a curt language of war, quite different from the city's usual elegant mode of communication—a language of jabbing, slicing, orders, alarms. Josephine knew none of it, but on some deep level the body itself remembered, and obeyed. She fell into line; and the line swept across the city, growing wider and deeper, until somewhere it left her behind and she was alone. Then, before too much time passed, another great bright wing of warriors came from above and behind and between the towers and swept her up again.

There was organization among the pirates, too, but looser, wilder, and always in flux. They were skirmishers, raiders, looters—they avoided resistance, fled from open battle, and looked for weak or solitary victims, unguarded treasures, opportunities for ambush. It was impossible even to guess at their number.

They had leaders, of a sort. Big brutes, who drove their warriors before them by force and with an awful piercing whistle; and wiry little ragged-winged old women whose eyes were bright with malign telepathic power; and desperate creatures who looked to Josephine like devils. They broke, fled, sacrificed their warriors to escape, evaded capture again and again.

There'd been one big brute in particular, who Josephine saw at the quarry, and again beneath the spike in Piccadilly Circus, and again on the mushroom-domed roof of a great tower at the bend of the river, and finally leading the retreat. He was a giant of his kind. He was thin, as they all were, with wiry arms and a narrow waist, but extraordinarily tall and long-limbed. His left hand was a stump, his chest deeply scarred, and one of his eyes blind; but his wings were pristine, unwounded, as wide and bright and beautiful and complex as a cathedral's stained-glass window. Otherwise, he was ugly; fierce, a wrecker and a looter, a cleaver of skulls and a ripper of wings. The second time she saw him, she tried to get close to him. He saw her, gliding down. His good eye was cunning. She reached out with her mind, knocked the brute's hand from his victim—and then he was gone, leaping up from window to window and out of sight, his mob following behind him. After that she kept a look-out for him.

When she saw him again, she charged. At that moment, she was alone;

unwise. The brute retreated and three of his men moved smoothly to her side, cutting her off from her allies, and she was instantly alone and afraid. This was up on the huge dome-like roof of a top-heavy tower overlooking the river. She moved left, right, as the three pirates lunged at her, and fled for the edge of the dome. They shrieked and whistled at her. She stumbled and went down to her knees. She felt them scratching at the edge of her mind.

One of them was strong. He forced his way into her mind. It was like when Piccadilly had tried to speak to her, months ago, except that, where Piccadilly had been gentle and nervous, this creature was savage.

The pirate's assault on her mind was wordless, but it filled her mind with visions of blood and violence, and of the horrors of the red moon Abyss. She saw a world of constant hunger. It hurtled through the void at such terrible speeds that its inhabitants were driven mad. There was hardly air to breathe. She felt her throat close. For months at a time there was no light, no flight. She saw the weak starving, choking, left to die. Darkness towered, threatened to overwhelm her. She shrank before it, small as a candle flame. She flared.

The pirate tumbled from her mind. He stumbled, suddenly weak-kneed, his wings trembling, and fell from the edge of the dome.

She fled.

She crossed paths with another pack of raiders, down by the river, as they retreated. They looked at her first with loathing, and then with fear, and then launched themselves upwards, leaping from window to window, clambering up the sides of the towers and the tendrils and vines that hung between them, and then up onto the tops of the towers. Overhead, the red moon was in retreat, rushing on past its twin, receding into the night; and all over the city the enemy were in retreat. She hurried up to the tower-tops. Everywhere she looked, the raiders were rising up into the air, first up to the heights of the city and then, with great leaps, into the sky, throwing themselves recklessly into the red light as it faded. Their arms were laden with their spoils: fistfuls of beads, bottles, torn-off wings, scraps of bloody gore, pathetic handfuls of fern or flower or food, frantically struggling infants, some stones, some plant matter. A few meaningless scraps.

Not all of them made it. Gravity overcame some of them before they were half a hundred feet above the tower-tops, and they fell back into the city, where they were quickly dispatched. Most of them kept going, up and up, so many of them that they were a dark cloud obscuring the moon.

An hour or two, perhaps three—it was hard to say how long it had lasted. The red moon was already perceptibly smaller; soon it would be smaller still. Soon it would be too late to cross.

She gave chase—opening her wings wide to sail on the light of the red moon. The retreating pirates were slowed by their spoils, and she caught up to them. As she swooped in on a straggler, she was already so far above the city that the buildings below looked like sandcastles, mushrooms, bright empty shells. She cut at the straggler's back, broke his wings, and as he fell she took an infant from his arms. It struggled and clutched at her.

The straggler's comrades kept going, most of them, ignoring his shrieks as he fell. A few of them stopped, turned: five—no, six—of them, out of thousands, torn between their eagerness to return to their departing world and their hunger for spoils, their hate. They circled her.

She was alone. She looked down to see that none of the city's defenders but her had given chase.

Distant blue specks watched her from the tower-tops below. She was alone in the sky, except for the raiders.

She saw the rules of the game now: the fighting ceased when the raiders fled. The city's defenders let them go. Poised between the rose moon and the red she saw, as if in a vision, the whole thousand-year cycle of their shared existence: the moons endlessly circling each other; the struggle becoming an observance as natural as the seasons.

The moons were drifting apart and the rage of the city's defenders (which had been quite as savage and wild as that of its enemies) was subsiding now. The pressure of the storm was draining from the air.

She had misunderstood yet again, committed an error. This might be her last.

The raiders circled her, wary, angry, waiting to see what she would do. There were two of them above her and two below—if she fell back to the ground, they would cut at her as she passed, and the infant was a terrible weight in her arms, and a strain on her wings, its fingers digging in a panic into her neck.

A sharp wing struck out at her. She parried, spun, and fell twice her own height, then moved sharply sideways as another wing struck at her, and a hand reached for her leg. She kicked and struck bone. She fell again, turned again. They circled her, shifting their places, some of them behind, some above, some below. One of them held two red fistfuls of ferns in his hands, and he had a deep bleeding slash above his mouth. It hardly seemed worth it.

They closed in. The infant's clutching fingers were a wordless scream. She couldn't think clearly. She turned and turned, not daring to let her guard down for a moment.

Then she glanced down and saw a bright blue mist rising from the city below. A scattering of blue and green petals on the wind; dabs of colour—a dozen, twenty, thirty, men and women of Angel on the wing. Among them—not the first, but rising up at the rear—she saw the explorer Orpheus. She recognised him by his wings.

They were there in seconds. Sharp wings cut down the raiders. Strong hands took the infant from her so that she could answer their questions. Yes, she was unharmed. Yes, the infant was unharmed, she thought, probably. No, she didn't know what she'd done, or why. Why not? She'd hardly known she was snatching an infant, she confessed, she might just as easily have taken a handful of beads or a scrap of clothing; only the chase had mattered. Yes, yes, she was the Earthwoman . . .

She looked around for Orpheus. She saw him circling, watching her. His face was impassive. His wings—those extraordinary, beautiful wings—suggested curiosity, perhaps even amusement. Then he turned and swooped down towards the city.

Far above them, the retreating pirates were a distant fading shadow. They dwindled, swallowed by the light of the red moon, and then they were gone from sight. The red moon was passing on its way. At some moment in the course of their flight they'd go from *rising up* to *falling down*. It made her dizzy just to imagine it. She was so tired she could hardly think, or speak; so tired it was all she could do to gently drift down like a falling leaf. She looked around for Orpheus, but he was gone.

Over the rest of the long lunar night, and through the following day, there were countless feasts, and celebrations, and speeches and debates, and rituals she was hard-pressed to understand, both solemn and wild. The city was drunk on red wine, on survival, on stories and boasting and honour, Martians danced, wrestled, argued, swarmed, laughed, made love openly in the skies overhead. Josephine was questioned, flattered, embraced, propositioned. She was drunk too; she couldn't stop herself talking. She told the story of how she'd given chase to the retreating pirates perhaps a hundred times. Her feat was considered daring, mad, hilarious, absurd. This unexpected motion—this deviation from the settled course—was rich in philosophical and artistic implications. It was either a stroke of genius or such a remarkable and prodigious idiocy that it was worth talking about anyway. There was a school of thought that what she'd done was cruel and depraved, a sign that the Blue Sphere was a place of uncivilised monsters. She was both feted and condemned. The Martians debated her act as if it held the key to a total understanding of the Blue Sphere and its inhabitants. They argued, as disputatious and quarrelsome as dons or priests or poets or spiritualists. Before the next night fell—a month of days and nights might have passed in London—half a dozen different schools of thought had emerged regarding the significance (spiritual, military, or artistic) of her feat. She was called on to speak, to write, to defend herself. Soon she found herself drawn into the quarrels and politics and life of the lunar city so thoroughly and so pleasantly that there were times when she could almost forget about London.

The red moon dwindled rapidly. The feasts came to an end. She went looking for Orpheus.

THE EIGHTH DEGREE

{ *Vast Countenance* }

Chapter Thirty-two

The sun rose. A sharp little disc of blue, unthinkably remote. The angle of its motion was peculiar, and somewhat vertiginous. There was something chemical about its faint light, as if the sun had been subjected to some hitherto unknown industrial process, burned out, and then discarded. Behind it, the sky was a dome of rust. Beneath it there was gloom. Vast dust-clouds massed on the horizon.

Now that there was sun, they had orientation, of a sort. The expedition left camp and set off north-by-north-west. A mountain range visible on the horizon rose higher and higher as the hours went by, and then became clouds, which became a mere haze in the air. The expedition pressed on through.

Atwood led the way. He'd started the march with a dip into his supply of cocaine and was full of energy. The men followed, labouring under packs that would have crushed them under the conditions of Earth. To the eye of any observer (and they both longed for and dreaded encountering any such observer) they might have resembled a procession of ants carrying leaves. Dimmick pulled one of the sleds. Vaz and Payne and Arthur took turns pulling the other. The things made an awful unearthly racket, the steel runners scraping over stony ground and striking sparks; and from time to time a sled got turned over or suddenly hit a rock and jerked to a halt, causing Vaz and Payne and Dimmick to swear, and tins of ox-tongue to go rolling all over the surface of Mars, or get punctured on sharp rocks. There were sharp rocks everywhere. Hard to spot them in the gloom; impossible not to think of them as wilfully malevolent.

The sun achieved its zenith. The cold persisted regardless. It had been twilight on Mars for ten thousand years, it seemed, and the sun was too distant to have much say in how Mars did things. Frank lit one of the lanterns, as much for comfort as for light. He tried to start a sing-along, something from his military days, but nobody had much heart for it. It was bloody hard work to make a noise that could travel in the thin cold air of Mars; and then there was the awful sense that nothing was listening, anywhere, in all that vast unfriendly sky—or, worse, that something might be.

Something in the atmosphere irritated the throat. It smelled faintly metallic. Sometimes there was a sound rather like the noise on a telephone line when no one was speaking. Occasional gusts of wind rushed past them, carrying odd whispering—or, not quite whispering, because it was soundless: a mere ghost of sound, a motion in the air . . .

They marched across stony ground, up and down occasional rills or ripples or dunes of dirt; they manhandled the sleds across cracks and ditches. They encountered no trace of life; not so much as a scattering of moss or lichen; not a trickle of water. Nothing to look at but that strange violet light, glimmering from behind dust-clouds as vast as oceans, slowly streaming and shifting. A haze hung in the air, obscuring vision. God knows what might come lumbering out of it. Impossible to judge distances, or to distinguish shadow from shape. No wonder poor Ashton had started to hallucinate.

Discipline. That was the thing. The same techniques that disciplined the mind for the rigours of Gracewell's Engine would work for the surface of Mars. It was the same problem, when you got down to basics. Things that the human mind was not meant to think. Things that the human eye was not meant to see.

Atwood marched blithely on ahead, and the rest of them followed.

Shortly after noon, one of the sleds turned over for the third time and bounced into a ditch. Payne cried out as the rope skinned his hands. Vaz stumbled and fell on his back. Then he rolled over and scrabbled after the sled on hands and knees, muttering excitedly. He reached down into the ditch and picked up a rock.

"Look." He got to his feet.

"Bloody thing turned the sled over," Payne said.

"Yes, yes—but look! See, Mr Shaw? Atwood! Lord Atwood! Come look!"

Arthur took the rock from Vaz's outstretched hands. It was pinkish, and roughly the size of a house brick.

"See, Shaw?"

"I don't—"

Atwood snatched it away. "Thank you," Atwood said. He was grinning like a madman. "Well done, Mr Vaz. A sharp eye. See, Mr Sun? Mr Shaw?"

Arthur and Sun both peered at the rock.

On one side it was smooth, almost glazed, with jagged flinty edges. It resembled pottery as much as it resembled earthly stone.

Atwood turned it over. On the other side there was a neat right-angled corner.

"A fortunate discovery," Sun said.

"Manufacture," Atwood said. "Clear evidence of manufacture."

"One can't be certain," Arthur said. "It might be a product of natural forces we don't understand."

"Admirable scepticism, Mr Shaw. But you lack vision. Can't you see it, can't you simply see it: the tremendous column of which this was once merely a corner of a plinth, rising steeply into the Martian sky, an ornament to a great Martian temple?"

"Where are they, then? Where are its makers? Where's the rest of the temple?"

"Gone. Dead. As if we walked among the sepulchres of the Valley of Kings. Perhaps even Mars has its Egypt."

Then Atwood handed the rock back to Vaz, and told him to put it on his sled.

Sun bandaged Payne's skinned hands. Payne cursed and grunted, while Sun remained silent. Later Payne grumbled to Arthur that it was like being treated by a veterinarian, as if one were a carthorse.

Arthur and Vaz got the sled righted and loaded again, then they each took a rope over their shoulder and began to pull. Their route took them uphill, and into a zone of sharp little pebbles. No further evidence of architecture appeared.

"Together again, Mr Shaw."

"We are indeed, Mr Vaz."

They went some way in silence. It was an effort to speak.

Arthur quickly began to see why the sled kept tipping over so easily. It was the weird weightlessness. The damn thing bounced and wobbled at the slightest disturbance. It was like a child's toy.

They moved on, bringing up the rear. Nothing behind them but the far horizon, the black clouds. Best not to look back at all.

"You know, Mr Vaz—I rather think you might have saved my life, that night in the fire. I always wanted to thank you."

"Think nothing of it, Mr Shaw. Besides—we are in worse danger now."

"Dimmick—might have—if you—if you hadn't . . . well."

Arthur's breath ran short. He thought back on the incident at Dr Thorold's house in Bloomsbury. Blood all over the doctor's study, blood on Dimmick's boots. Long ago now, a long-forgotten horror. He'd seen worse since. A certain wolf-like aspect to the black clouds streaming overhead. Getting faster now. He decided it was better not to tell that story. No doubt Mars had nightmares enough of its own; no need to trouble it with London's.

"Misunderstanding," Arthur said. "Won't happen again, I'm sure."

Vaz glanced at Dimmick's back. He did not look entirely convinced.

"Shaw. May I ask a question?"

Arthur nodded.

"Mr Gracewell's Work."

"Yes. We built another one, you know. Another Engine. Near Gravesend. Would have hired you on if I'd known."

"It was for this, the Work?"

Arthur thought about how to explain Gracewell's Engine. He couldn't find the strength. "Yes," he said.

The sled's runners shrieked over stone. Up ahead Payne was grumbling about his feet, and beyond that someone—Dimmick, Arthur thought—was rather improbably whistling a cheerful little tune. Atwood was so far ahead that he could be seen only as a distant shadow, flickering in the haze like a black candle flame. Sun walked along beside him. The two of them were talking. They appeared to be arguing.

"Fog," Arthur said. "Damn fog. That thing—Milton, isn't it?—*darkness visible.*"

Vaz shuddered.

Ahead of them rose a dune. Atwood struck a heroic figure atop it: a silhouette of black velvet, limned with cold violet light, field-glasses in hand. Then he was gone again, replaced by Sun, and shortly afterwards by Dimmick. They had a dreadful time getting the sled over the dune, but after that it was downhill, and easier going for a while.

"You are a Christian, I presume?"

"I am, Mr Vaz. A fairly bad one, I suppose. Given all of this, I mean. Atwood and his magic, that is."

"Why did you . . . ?"

"All this? A woman."

"A woman? I would like to see that woman. Does the Bible say anything about Mars? I don't recall. Do you think God watches Mars? I can't stop myself from thinking these things, Mr Shaw."

"God? I took you for a Hindu, Mr Vaz."

They'd never discussed religion back in Deptford, but here the subject seemed inescapable.

"A Roman Catholic. Not a very good one."

"Ah. Well, well. I wouldn't know, anyway. Perhaps he does. There's a red star in the book of Revelation, isn't there? I suppose that must be Mars. But other than that, I don't recall. We may be outside God's bailiwick, one fears."

"Yes. Yes." Vaz nodded. "That is what I fear."

They walked for a while longer.

"Listen, Mr Vaz. I want to ask you a favour."

"Ask."

"I told you when we worked in Mr Gracewell's Engine together that I was engaged to be married."

"Yes. I recall."

"She's—unwell. If we—if you should ever happen to meet her, but I am . . . well, if things haven't gone well for me here . . . Would you give her a message for me? Tell her that I've made arrangements. If . . . when she wakes."

"Of course."

He gave Vaz the name of a lawyer, and the address of his office in Gravesend.

"It's all my fault, you see. All my fault."

Vaz maintained a diplomatic silence.

Up ahead, a cloud formed on the horizon. It resembled the smoke of a great fire.

"Will you do me a favour in response, Mr Shaw?"

"Of course."

"Tell me truthfully: Does Lord Atwood know where he is leading us?"

"I don't know."

They walked for a while in silence.

Vaz grunted. "Which would be worse, I wonder? If he doesn't, or if he does?"

The march stopped at intervals of roughly an hour, so that Dimmick could take out an ice-pick and a hammer and carve a number into a suitable rock: *1, 2, 3,* and so forth. This was to ensure that they could retrace their steps, and also to be sure that they weren't going in circles. Roughly once an hour, whatever that meant on Mars. No doubt by the time they got to *9, 10, 11* they were far off from the true hour. They kept going. *12, 13.* It was as easy to keep walking as to stop, as easy to stand as to lie down. That must be what it was like to be a ghost, Arthur thought. *14* and then *15.* He began to think that they might walk for ever, leaving meaningless signs that would never be read, watched only by the black clouds overhead. *16 . . .*

Shortly after the sixteenth marking, Payne announced that he'd had enough, and was damn well going to sleep. He snatched a blanket from the back of Dimmick's sled, and sat on the ground with it wrapped around his shoulders, shivering.

At first Atwood looked annoyed. Then he smiled and said, "Quite right! A rest. I'll go one further, gentlemen. A feast. We shall have a feast on Mars. A celebration of our triumph."

Frank lit a second lantern. They set up the tents, then shared out cigarettes and cold soup.

"A wondrous thing," Atwood said. "Soup. Every sensation on Mars is to be treasured for what it can teach us."

Payne prayed, but without a great deal of enthusiasm, and nobody joined him. One never knew what might be listening, Vaz observed.

At last they all went to sleep—except Sun, whose energies appeared boundless, and who sat down cross-legged beside a lantern, apparently deep in thought.

Sleep on the surface of Mars was not terribly different from waking. In fact, Arthur passed from sleep to marching again without quite noticing it. Before he knew it, he was walking along beside Vaz, the sled rattling along behind him, and Dimmick was carving *2—4* into rocks as they went, and then *2—5*, and *2—6*, and so on.

It was shortly after *2—10*—the tenth hour of their second day on Mars—that they sighted the ruin.

At first, in the far distance, it resembled one of the bent tin cans they'd left behind, dented and leaking, hours and miles ago. A tiny black shape on the distant horizon, too oddly shaped to be a rock, butte, or mountain. It was not quite in the direction they were travelling, but close enough that when Atwood pretended that it was, no one argued.

A sign of civilization.

Frank started up another song, and this time everyone joined in, even Atwood—everyone but Sun, who continued to march in silence, hands folded behind his back, an odd smile on his face.

Arthur, remembering the Martian in Atwood's library, made sure that the rifles were loaded.

It was clearly a structure, the product of Martian architecture. Any doubt on that score quickly faded as they got closer. Within half an hour it was quite clear that it was a sort of tower. It rose up out of the flat dead plain, tall and slender, in splendid isolation. It had something of the look of a fortification, but there was nothing around worth fortifying for as far as the eye could see.

It was made of red stone, it was circular, and it was unornamented, save for a spiralling set of windows. Beneath each window jutted something a little like a drainpipe. Perches, perhaps, for winged visitors.

It had shattered long ago, like a lightning-blasted tree. It seemed to have broken roughly in half; the upper stories had toppled sideways, leaving a long snaky mound of rubble half-buried by dust. What was left upright was still tremendously tall—more so when seen from its foot, because its thinness played tricks with perspective, so that it seemed almost as if it hung from the sky.

"Bloody thing's got no doors," Frank said.

"See," Atwood said. "The Martians come and go by the windows."

"It's a ruin," Arthur said. "No one's come or gone from here in years—centuries."

"They fly. Remember the creature in my library? Winged. It was trying to fly."

"Not too well, as I recall."

"Why would they be endowed with wings if not to fly? Perhaps it was too heavy on Earth. Or perhaps it couldn't fly indoors—perhaps it needed wind and air and light. Imagine it. A race of flying men. Their feet might never touch the ground. Imagine what we might learn from such a people, Shaw. Their sciences, their arts, their magic; imagine how they must see the world! This must be a temple. A sacred place. They go down to the surface to pray."

He was practically standing on tiptoes, as if he hoped he might grow wings of his own, by sheer force of will.

Arthur felt a faint hope. Clearly the structure was empty, and abandoned; but if Josephine had been lost on Mars all this time, surely she would have sought out landmarks such as this, and possibly left some sign of her whereabouts.

No doors. The closest window was twelve feet off the ground, too far to jump even in the feeble Martian gravity. Payne had the bright idea of taking the ropes from the two sleds, tying them together, and throwing them up over the perch beneath the lowest window, so that if two men stood on the ground holding one end of the rope, another could climb up to the window.

Sun went first. Then Atwood, then Arthur.

Chapter Thirty-three

The windows of the tower were tall, but narrow, and they all had a devil of a time squeezing through, even Atwood. Inside it was dark.

Arthur called down to Vaz, who tied one of the lanterns to the end of the rope. He raised it hand-over-hand to the window, where he and Sun and Lord Atwood waited, wary of venturing farther into the dark interior.

The lantern revealed that they were standing on a narrow semicircular platform. Another step farther and Atwood would have fallen to the tower's floor—though he would have sustained no great injury, because the years had filled the tower, like an hourglass, with so much dust and dirt that the floor was now only a foot or two down from the window. Atwood smiled and hopped down. Hard-packed, the dirt held his weight.

The lantern's light flickered yellow and black on smooth glazed walls. The tower was made of the same odd ceramic substance as the fragment Vaz had discovered in the wasteland—not stone, precisely, nor brick. Overhead, a series of perches and struts and narrow beams spiralled up into the darkness. No cobwebs; no bats or owls or scurrying mice. Silence, and a smell of metal.

"Ancient," Arthur said. "It feels older than the hills, somehow."

Sun lowered himself gently to the floor, and looked up. "Isn't that always the way with ruins, Mr Shaw? The things of Man are measured in years; the things of God in millennia."

"True enough."

Arthur leaned out the window.

Outside, Payne and Frank held rifles at the ready. Vaz held an ice-axe in his hand. Dimmick seemed to have wandered off around the back of the tower.

"It's empty," Arthur called. "It's safe. For God's sake, stop waving those things about before somebody gets hurt."

"Empty?" Sun continued to stare upwards, hands folded behind his back. "Perhaps."

"Shaw," Atwood called. "Bring that lantern here."

Atwood knelt in the dirt, inspecting the wall on the far side of the tower.

"There, Shaw. Hold it up."

The lantern revealed scratches on the wall. A spider's-web tracery of shallow lines and curves.

"Markings," Atwood said.

"Hieroglyphics?"

"Perhaps—if you like."

"They look like scratches, to my eye—the wind and the rocks could have made them."

"Do they? Well. Look, though." Atwood scrabbled in the dirt. "Whatever they are, the greater part of them is buried—what a nuisance! Hidden by the years; swallowed by the sands of Mars themselves . . ."

"Well. We have shovels, don't we?"

"What a literal mind you have! Yes. I suppose we do. Then let's have Dimmick and Frank dig. Vaz and Payne should remain outside with the sleds. We may be here some time. Don't you agree, Sun?"

"I think I will defer to Your Lordship."

Atwood stood, rubbing his hands together. His palms were red—he'd cut them digging in the dirt. He put a hand on Arthur's shoulder. "Who knows what these markings may teach us, about Mars, about the heavens."

"Will they teach us how to find Josephine, or how to get home?"

"Be patient, Shaw. I said that we would find evidence of Martian civilization. And look: we have."

"Yes," said Sun, still staring up into the rafters.

Red dust drifted down and into their little circle of light.

Frank and Dimmick didn't share Atwood's enthusiasm for the tower; in fact, they found it positively eerie, and they kept their rifles close at hand as they dug.

After a while, Arthur stopped Frank and took a turn with the shovel.

Digging was something to do. Preferable to just standing around. Whatever Atwood saw in the scratches they were uncovering, it was all meaningless to Arthur. Certainly it resembled no language he was familiar with. How could it?

They piled up dirt under the window, and periodically heaved it out and over the side, creating a growing heap next to the sleds. Through some peculiarity of the arid Martian atmosphere, it was possible to work vigorously for hours without ever sweating. It was a strange sensation.

Frank took over again. Dimmick was indefatigable. Sun lowered himself down the rope from the window, and paced around the perimeter of the tower as if marking the boundaries—Arthur presumed there was some mystical purpose to this. Meanwhile, Atwood sat cross-legged on the stone platform, the lantern beside him, making sketches of the tower and its markings.

Every so often, someone's shovel slipped and made a fresh scratch on the wall. The first time that happened, Atwood flew into such a rage that it seemed he might have someone hanged. After a while, he became resigned to it, and merely sighed. Arthur began to wonder if perhaps *all* the markings had been made that way. Centuries of explorers, digging and scratching, the hourglass refilling after they were gone. Elizabethan mystics, medieval monks travelling to Mars in their visions, Romans and Greeks, Buddhists and Hindus and Aztecs too. Or Moon-men or Venusians, for that matter.

The setting sun found its way in through the windows and filled the tower with sharp angular shadows. Outside, it cast weird shadows across the dunes, which seemed almost to creep and ripple of their own accord. Or so Vaz reported, when Arthur and Frank and Dimmick came down from the tower, having decided, after long discussion, that they would rather sleep outside than in. When Arthur finally fell asleep, the lantern still glowed faintly from the window above. Atwood remained at work. Sun was still pacing the boundaries.

When Arthur woke, his bladder ached. First time since he'd set foot on Mars. The body's ordinary functions were slower here; or they were a mere illusion, a matter of habit. He ignored the urge, and it went away.

Eventually, reluctantly, he sat up. He ached all over. The aches didn't go away no matter how long he waited. He appeared to be developing an unpleasant rash on the back of his hands. Too much scrabbling in the dust and the dirt, perhaps.

Sunrise behind the tower. Cold and blue. He watched it for a while.

Vaz and Payne and Frank were still asleep. Atwood was presumably up in his tower. Since there were sounds of digging, Arthur supposed that Dimmick was in there too. Mr Sun sat on top of a nearby dune, watching the sunrise. Arthur went to join him.

"Shaw," Sun said, without turning around.

"Just think," Arthur said. "Somewhere that same light is shining on London."

"It isn't," Sun said.

"No?"

"It is not the same sun it once was. Nor are we the same men."

Arthur looked down at Sun. The back of the man's neck looked burned, as if he were starting to develop the same rash as Arthur.

"In a mystical sense, I suppose you mean. No man can step in the same river twice—that sort of thing? Well, fair enough. But I'm literal-minded, Sun. It's my refuge against madness."

"Then by all means believe what you will, Mr Shaw. I would not want to destroy your refuge against madness. Not now."

"Sporting of you."

The sun passed behind a dust-cloud. A shadow fell across the dunes. The whispering picked up slightly, as it often did in shadow.

"Atwood plans to keep us here for some time, I think."

Sun nodded.

"Studying the language. Does it make sense to you, Mr Sun? What he's finding—is it language?"

"Perhaps. I don't know. I have come to think that Lord Atwood knows more about this place than I had expected. Don't you think?"

"From the way he talks, you'd think we were all just things in his dream."

"Is it not a fine dream, though? Is it not beautiful?" Sun gestured out at the horizon. The sun now pierced through the black clouds with rays like needles of blue ice. He closed his eyes, and said no more.

"The men don't like this tower," Arthur said. "I don't either. When I said it was empty, you said *perhaps*—what did you mean?"

"I meant nothing, Mr Shaw. I know no more than you do. Do you think I travel to Mars often? Who knows what we may see tomorrow? Ask Lord Atwood. I meant what I said. *Perhaps*. Let me ask you a question. If Josephine is alive, she has been here for a long time, beneath this sun, this sky. Not dead, but changed; what do you imagine she has become?"

Arthur kicked at a rock, sending it skidding across the dust toward the tower. Damn the man! He didn't like Sun's insinuations; not about Josephine, nor for that matter about Atwood. If there was to be some rivalry between the two men, Arthur wanted no part of it. He had a job to do.

"You're right, Mr Sun."

"Am I?"

"Quite right. Just as you say. There might be anything in that tower. I should explore it for myself. Thank you, Mr Sun."

"Good luck, Mr Shaw."

He went back to the foot of the tower, where Payne and Frank and Vaz were waking, and proposed an expedition into the upper reaches of the tower.

"Go to hell," Frank said, speaking for himself and Payne. "We're not budging from these sleds, not for you or anyone else."

"I don't like the thought of climbing the tower," Vaz said. "But nor do I like the thought of spending all day with nothing to do but listen to the wind and these gloomy fellows moaning. I'll come with you. Besides, I am a first-rate climber, and good with ropes; that's why his Lordship brought me here."

The tower's builders hadn't needed stairs. There were nothing but the beams and ledges overhead, spiralling up into the dark and growing more remote every hour, as Dimmick's shovel steadily lowered the floor.

They had no ladder, but they had rope. They tied a kettle to the end of a rope, and after several failed efforts, one of which nearly concussed Dimmick, managed to lob the kettle over the lowest of the beams. Vaz, as the lighter and more athletic of the two, went up first, with Arthur and Dimmick supporting the rope's other end. Then Vaz secured the rope around the beam and Arthur followed him up. Balancing carefully, Vaz flung the rope again, over the next-lowest beam, and so on. They moved in this manner up through the tower's spiralling interior, pulling the rope up behind them as they went. It would have been quite impossible on Earth, but under the feeble Martian gravity, they made decent time. Within a quarter of an hour, the floor below was gone from sight. Atwood's lantern was a faint yellow glow. Soon even the sound of Dimmick's shovel faded.

There were windows every six feet or so, arranged haphazardly around the tower's circumference; a perch outside, and a narrow ledge inside. A view from the windows across endless plains. No furniture, or none that had survived. No decoration. No further markings. Perhaps the Martians roosted there to sleep, once upon a time. Dust heaped in the corners.

The top of the tower came closer. Faint daylight crept through the rafters overhead. They clambered up onto another ledge. There was another window, and another heap of dust—which, on closer inspection, appeared to contain bones.

They approached the bone-heap with trepidation, shoulder to shoulder, practically hand in hand.

"After you," Vaz said.

Arthur gave the heap a poke with his foot. A tangle of bones, held together by scraps of some ancient fabric—or, God forbid, skin—slid from the dust. The bones were plainly inhuman: long and tapering, light, paper-yellow. Whatever they were, there was no visible clue to the manner or cause of death. Vaz crossed himself.

They flung the kettle up over the next beam and pulled themselves up again.

After three more turns of the spiral—past three more windows, and more heaps of dust and bone, which they did not inspect too closely—Arthur stopped, overcome by a nagging sensation that there was something he'd overlooked. He put a hand on Vaz's shoulder and stopped him from throwing the kettle again.

"The windows," he said.

"The windows?"

"Yes—yes, Vaz. Or, rather, the view. Come, here, look."

At some point in their climb, the shape of the windows had changed.

Lower down, the windows were tall narrow slits, but farther up they were round, and hardly more than a foot in diameter—too small for anyone to enter; even, one would imagine, a Martian. The view through them had changed, too, some three or four revolutions ago, but Arthur hadn't fully noticed the change until now. He had to examine it closely to be sure he wasn't imagining it.

Though the window was empty, looking through it was somewhat like looking through a finely crafted lens. It commanded a view across vast plains and into the mountains; and yet it seemed somehow *focused* on one particular point in the distance, in the foothills of a mountain range, such that when one looked at that region—and only at that region—one could see it as if it were only a few yards away. The effect was tremendously disorientating. There was nothing to *see* in that distant region, nothing but rocks and hills and dust and shadow; and yet the fact that one could see it at all was extraordinary.

They lowered themselves back to the previous ledge. That window, naturally, faced in a different direction, and the point on which it was focused was different. It was almost equally nondescript, although this time, in addition to rocks and dunes, the zone of magnification contained a squat and empty-looking stone ruin.

"Lord Atwood will want to know about these," Vaz said. "Perhaps we can use them to plan our course."

"How do you suppose they work? Some sort of—some sort of ray, perhaps? Or something in the air, a gas or a . . . Yes. Atwood should know. Are there more? How do you suppose one controls them?"

They kept climbing. They passed by more bone-heaps without further curiosity. Next they found a window focused on a distant mountain, and then one that was focused on a region of cloudy sky. Perhaps, Vaz guessed, if they waited until nightfall it would illuminate a distant star, or one of the moons.

By the next window they had revolved half-way around the tower, and now they looked out west. The tower stood in a sort of shallow depression, they observed; the ground sloped up slowly into a great plain, under low-hanging clouds. In the far distance was an impossibly tall and tapering mountain. The window's zone of magnification lay at the mountain's foot. A storm was brewing there, great whirling winds rushing down off the mountain into valleys of dust and sweeping up enormous black clouds. Thrilling to watch, but terrifying; Arthur was very glad for the countless miles that lay between him and the storm.

After a while, Vaz scratched his head and asked if it was just his imagination, or wasn't the storm, miles wide, moving in their direction, and rather rapidly?

"Good Lord," Arthur said. "Good Lord. I believe you're right."

"I've seen enough, Mr Shaw. Let us return to Lord Atwood and make our report."

They went for the rope—both hurrying, unable to resist the sensation that the dreadful storm was somehow right at their backs. Arthur stumbled across a heap of bones and dust. There was a sudden agony in his leg, as if a snake had bitten his ankle, or as if he'd received an electric shock. There was a smell of burning in his nostrils, as if his moustache was on fire. Vaz cried out in pain. Arthur felt something clawing at him—clawing in his head, as if fingernails were scraping the inside of his skull. Vaz fell forward and toppled off the ledge into the darkness. Arthur recalled the training in magic that Thérèse Didot had given him—how he'd grumbled at the time!—and summoned into his mind a sigil of warding, of peace, of calm. The thing in his head shrieked wordlessly and battered at his defences. He fell to his knees. Before him, a tall shape—two tall shapes—rose up out of the heap of bones and dust. He looked up at long legs, narrow shoulders, long axe-thin faces, expressions of madness. They opened pale and ragged wings. They were creatures of the same species as the thing in Atwood's library—Martians. Not dead, these two, not like the others—not mere bones. They'd looked like bones because they were so terribly, excruciatingly thin. Not dead, but sleeping—for how long?—on a dead world. One of them reached for Arthur. He lunged forward between their legs and seized the kettle, which he swung up into the nearest face. That one crumpled. The other one spun, slashing its wing's ragged edge towards Arthur, and he stumbled back and slipped off the edge of the ledge. He landed on one of the beams, and slid off—bouncing off the next beam down, and falling again. He landed on a ledge, rolled off, and finally came to rest, panting and in agony, God knows how much farther down.

"Vaz!" he called. From somewhere in the darkness above, Vaz answered him. He couldn't see Vaz, but he could make out motion overhead, glimpses of those horrid pale wings, as the half-skeletal creatures were hopping down from ledge to ledge. From below, he heard Atwood calling up, demanding to know what was happening. Since there was clearly no way he could get up to Vaz at present, and since he didn't fancy wrestling with those monsters alone, Arthur began lowering himself—carefully, but not carefully enough; he slipped again, bounced again, and before he knew it, he was lying on his back on the sand, looking up at Dimmick's grinning face. In the next instant, Dimmick heard the buzz and click of the creatures' wings and the grin disappeared from his face, along with whatever joke he'd been about to make at Arthur's expense. He grabbed for his rifle as the creatures descended out of the rafters; shot one and it fell. The other kicked out at his head and knocked him sprawling. Arthur tried to get to his feet but seemed to have momentarily lost the use of his legs.

"Stay!" Atwood shouted. He seemed to be speaking more to the monster than to Arthur.

The monster stopped. It hung in the air, watching. Arthur craned his neck. He couldn't quite see Atwood, who stood behind him—he could see only Atwood's shadow on the wall, cast by the lantern behind him, as Atwood performed—Good Lord, what was he doing? It began with subtle and occult passes and worked up into jerking inhuman motions of hand and arm—he appeared liable to dislocate his shoulder or break his neck. The creature hovered—an extraordinary motion, not buzzing or beating its wings, but *rippling* them—and then it turned and fled for the nearest window, nearly knocking Sun over as he climbed into the tower.

Atwood stretched out a hand and helped Arthur to his feet. Sun looked out the window for a moment, then apparently decided that the creature was gone.

"Very well done, Lord Atwood," Sun said. "You must teach me that trick."

Arthur sat against the wall and caught his breath. No bones appeared to be broken, for which he supposed he had the feeble gravity of Mars to thank. He watched Sun and Atwood and Dimmick go up into the rafters, and he watched Vaz—whose condition was much the same as his—come clambering down.

When Atwood came back down, he was in a near-faint from exertion. Sun helped him to sit against the wall, and called for cocaine.

"Well?" Arthur said.

"A storm is coming," Sun said. "Perhaps they are common here. In any case, we cannot evade it on foot. And so we will remain here in this tower until it has passed. In the meantime, we will continue our study. Dimmick, please fetch Payne and Frank and bring in what we can of the supplies. And bury the rest."

Atwood waved. "Go. Good shooting."

"Sir," Dimmick said, and went.

"The remaining bones," Sun said, "are merely bones. As to the two creatures that attacked us, Lord Atwood and I have conferred, and our conclusion is that they were survivors of whatever catastrophe broke the tower, and laid waste to the countryside around. We suppose that Martians, like certain organisms of Earth, may enter in times of drought into a state of suspended animation. We believe they were the builders of this tower. The manner of their attack on you, Mr Shaw, suggests considerable telepathic gifts; the manner of their flight appears at least partially telekinetic. But no doubt they were quite mad, after centuries of hunger and thirst and uneasy dreams. If not for Mr Dimmick's quick shooting and Lord Atwood's peerless will, who knows what they might have done."

Dimmick stretched out the dead monster on the ground. It was nightmarishly thin, and paler by far than the specimen in Atwood's library, as if it had been bleached by the centuries. The bullet-wound was nearly bloodless. Sun and Atwood performed a somewhat undermanned version of the Rite of Jupiter, which they'd previously used in London for speaking to the dead. They didn't wait for any particular hour, on the theory that they had no way of knowing what the appropriate hour of Jupiter was on Mars, and so any hour was as good or as bad as the next. In any event, they got no answers out of the corpse. It remained stubbornly inert, as if it were relieved to at long last be dead.

The storm appeared at sunset. The darkness of evening became solid. The clouds descended from the heavens and swept towards them. The storm seemed to boil at its edges, and the faint light of the sun sparked across it like frozen fire. It was too dreadful to look at for long. The expedition retreated from the windows and hunkered down on the floor of the tower, where they crouched, wrapped up two to a blanket, and waited for the storm to pass.

Everything went dark.

It was soundless at first. Then, all of a sudden, there was a dreadful thundering that seemed to come from all directions at once, and to have always been there. The tower trembled. Dust roared in through the windows. Some of it roared out again; some of it heaped against the wall and began to weigh down on the blankets. Rather a lot of it went directly down Arthur's throat, it seemed to him, and he began to cough and splutter. The storm thrashed against the tower until the whole structure sounded like a drum being beaten. Several of the stone beams overhead cracked and fell—smashing, they learned later, a lantern, some tins of food, and some of Atwood's paints. The noise was like great beasts roaring and crashing against the walls.

It went on for an hour, perhaps two. Long enough for Arthur to become convinced, as he huddled in his blanket, pressed up against a shivering Vaz, that the screaming of the storm was a voice, that there were words in it, though none he could understand. Long enough to imagine that he heard Atwood's voice, answering it. Long enough to convince himself that he was imagining things, and then to change his mind again, and again.

When the storm passed, they crawled out of the tower. The rocks and dunes were much the same as ever. There was a weak light in the sky, and the air felt scraped clean.

The storm had shattered so many of the beams overhead that there was no way of climbing up to the windows again, certainly not by means of rope and tea-kettle.

Atwood announced that it was time to move on. He waved away questions about the markings in the tower as if they'd been merely a childish obsession, one he had long since outgrown. There was a new certainty in his manner as he told them that he had a destination in mind, where they might—if they were lucky—find what they needed to plan their return home.

"A library, of sorts," Atwood said. "A laboratory, one might say. More to our purpose, an observatory."

"Excellent news," Sun said. "And how did you learn of this place?"

"While you have been pacing, Mr Sun, I have been translating the markings of the Martian language. I think you can all see that the Martians are—or were—astronomers of great learning. Consider the windows upstairs. What are they if not telescopes? A marriage of science and magic. Wondrous. But sadly ruined by the passage of time, and useless to us. There are others, and better; and I can find them."

Arthur said, "Where?"

"Where? Where are we going? High ground, of course."

Arthur said, "How far?"

Atwood said nothing. He stood at the window and pointed into the distance; westwards, through the violet gloom, into the weird slanting half-light and shadow. On the far horizon, there was a mark that might have been the tapering mountain Arthur had seen through the telescopic window upstairs. It shifted in and out of visibility. First a mountain, then no mountain, then a mountain again.

"Good God, Atwood. You must be joking."

"You find our predicament funny, Mr Shaw? How odd."

"What if another storm crosses our path?"

"It won't. Rest assured."

"Atwood—"

"Shaw. Have you ever had a dream . . ." Atwood stared at the mountain and the sunrise and collected his thoughts. "Have you ever had a dream, Shaw, in which—for a moment, for a brief, tremendous moment—it appeared to you that you stood upon a high mountain-top, and that beneath you was laid out all the world, as God must see it, day and night at once? And the sky, Shaw, as if a great black veil had been pulled aside, so that you could see the stars—and hung between them the silver thread of your life, as you have lived it and now live it and will live it, the beginning swallowing the end?"

"I don't believe I have."

"I did once. In the Alps. I had a fever, the doctors said. I was no older than you are now."

"This is no dream, Atwood."

"Of course it's not."

Clouds obscured the mountain. The sun glowed faintly through them.

"Cheer up, Shaw." Atwood began to try to light a match. "We shall find her."

"Hmmph."

"Blasted thing!" Atwood threw the dead match on the ground.

Sun lit a match, cupped it, and handed it to Atwood, who thanked him and lit his cigarette.

"It's a pity," Sun said, "That you didn't climb higher, Mr Shaw."

"Excuse me?"

"Yesterday, Mr Shaw, in the tower. His Lordship and I went up after you and what's-his-name—the sailor. Had you climbed a little higher you would have seen a window that looked on Earth. A blue gem in a bed of velvet. It was a thing worth going a long way to see."

"It certainly was," Atwood said. "Now, Shaw, perhaps you should go and help Dimmick; I hear him tossing our supplies about, and we have little enough to spare as it is. If he breaks the bottle of champagne, I'll have to have someone shot."

It took an hour or two to gather up their supplies and dig out the sleds. Atwood smoked and stared into the distance. Payne was silent throughout the work, scratching grimly at his rash. After a while, he took one of the revolvers and wandered around the back of the tower. Nobody made any move to stop him. But for whatever reason, he decided not to shoot himself after all, and fell in with the rest of them as they headed west.

Chapter Thirty-four

Time flattened, as if the weight of the sky pressed it down. As the expedition moved westwards across the face of Mars, Dimmick marked the days and hours, his ice-axe ringing out through the gloom. Sometimes it seemed to Arthur that that was the purpose of their expedition: to mark their presence on the planet. To show that they had been there, should anyone else happen by, a thousand years from now.

The light was unnatural, the emptiness unbearable. Shapes swum in and out of the gloom. Sometimes it seemed that Atwood was suddenly very far in the distance, and at a weird angle, as if the expedition had somehow become scattered. That never failed to induce panic. When they camped—at irregular intervals, when full darkness and treacherous terrain made progress impossible—they huddled for warmth, like a picture Arthur had once seen: penguins on a frozen rock.

They were tormented by visions. Fragmentary, momentarily alarming horrors or absurdities. The wind carried telephone noises. A flicker of hell-fire dancing on the horizon. Rats underfoot, or the noises of London traffic. A column of ants crawling endlessly across the dunes. Mosquitos. Perhaps there really were mosquitos, or something like them. Certainly there was something in the air that buzzed and whined. Something that bit them. They watched the skies for more of those half-dead monsters they'd met in the tower. Did they see them? They weren't sure. Something seemed to move through the clouds, casting long shadows that slipped across the plains like hunting wolves. Once Frank reported that the sun had become a vast eye. He became convinced that the expedition had somehow shrunk to the size of germs, and that the vast eye of a scientist in London was studying them. He sat on the ground, saying that he refused to be anyone's experiment, and it took over an hour to talk him out of this delusion.

Everyone's hair grew wild. They ate sparingly, and rarely slept. Atwood and Sun maintained that they needed neither food nor water nor sleep, but even they seemed to struggle to believe it. They practiced exercises of discipline and self-denial. Even so, the expedition's supplies dwindled. Ropes frayed and snapped, as if something had been gnawing at them. Teeth yellowed and fell out. Hair thinned. They began to look like monsters, even to one another. The rash on Arthur's arms spread and thickened and climbed onto his shoulders. Everyone suffered from it, even Atwood. Arthur began to see patterns in it, shapes, of unclear significance—it drove him mad that he couldn't see what it was writing on his back, no matter how he craned his head! It began to resemble the shimmering skin of the Martians, their mottled wings. Perhaps that, too, was a hallucination.

They passed other ruins. The structures were days apart, and solitary, like the houses of desert hermits. No two were exactly the same. A stepped pyramid. A high crescent wall, half-enclosing a dome of empty stone. A cluster of towers growing out of each other like the stalks of a cactus. Minarets, monoliths. Structures that looked oddly familiar, like earthly houses or a Scottish castle or a London railway-station or a Bombay temple; other top-heavy structures that could make sense only to winged creatures, that could exist only in feeble gravity. They didn't explore them. Atwood would allow no detours from their path.

They pressed on. The mountain grew larger and larger.

Atwood marched up ahead, flickering through the haze and half-light, a black candle flame. Had Arthur thought that before? Well, he thought it again. He stared at Atwood for hours, paying particular attention to the pistol in Atwood's belt. He was developing deep suspicions regarding His Lordship's intentions.

Atwood rarely spoke. He muttered sometimes, as if talking to the wind. When he did speak, he no longer talked about exploration, or conquest, or the treasures of Mars, or the friendly natives. He had quite forgotten about Josephine, and he hardly even seemed to care about finding a way home any more. He spoke of Mars as a trial, an ordeal of the spirit, a refining fire for the magician's will: *per ignem ad lucem*. He spoke of the burning away of weakness, the purification through adversity of the inner eye, and so on and so on.

As a matter of fact, Arthur was developing deep suspicions of everyone, not just Atwood. The wind whispered unpleasant notions. Dimmick, for example: a thug, a common criminal, a killer. Dimmick might turn on them at any moment. Certainly he *would* turn on them, if Atwood commanded it. Hairy and filthy, he was starting to look positively bestial. Frank and Payne were little better. Soldiers turned mercenary—deserters, probably. God only knew where Atwood had found them, or for what purpose. Even Vaz seemed suspect—with his mysterious origins, his cleverness, his ratty little beard. Was it merely a coincidence that Vaz had been chosen for this expedition? Had Atwood chosen him to spy on Arthur? And if so, when? Had Vaz been spying on him even back in Gracewell's offices in Deptford? And what about Josephine, for that matter—how long had she been secretly working with Atwood? Was it really an accident that had sent her to Mars, or . . .

How did Atwood know where he was going? Why was he so certain that they would find what they were looking for on the mountain?

If they had to stop Atwood, who was strong enough? Not Arthur, not if it came to magic. He well remembered the thrashing Atwood had given him in his library all those months ago; he didn't relish the prospect of a rematch. Sun, perhaps; if any of them was a match for Atwood's tricks, it would be Sun. If only Arthur could talk to him, somewhere in private, without Dimmick snooping around! Sun was no fool. He shared Arthur's suspicions, that was plain. Why didn't he act? He was so patient—as if he were waiting to see what Atwood would do next; as if he were drifting along in a dream.

One night, Sun told a story.

"Once upon a time," he said. "Let us say, in India. Or perhaps in China. In any case, a very long way from London, gentlemen. One upon a time there lived many magicians, and they performed many wonders."

They were all huddled together for warmth in utter darkness. Sun's voice seemed to come from nowhere.

When they first started their long march, they'd told stories more often. Payne and Frank had talked about their campaigns, and Vaz had a good line in sea stories. But they'd all run out of stories a long time ago. This was the first time Sun had volunteered to speak.

"They lived on a great mountain, the greatest in their country. Of all the magicians in their country, they were the most learned, and the most powerful, and it seemed to them right that they should demand obedience from lesser magicians, and tribute. And I would say they were right, and I don't doubt that Lord Atwood would agree. I know all this because that is the way of great magicians. It is the way of great men everywhere."

"Enough," Atwood said.

"Enough? The tribute of one world would not be enough for them, I think. Mastery is greedy by its very nature. They would have looked to the heavens. They would have looked on their flesh as a burden. Suppose that one day they learned to shrug it off, like an old coat, and go walking— the way one might go walking and then forget where one left one's coat."

"That's enough."

"Well. Lord Atwood perhaps knows this story better than I. Let him tell the rest of it."

There was a long silence before Atwood spoke again, and when he did his tone was politely menacing.

"Would you like to take a walk with me, Sun?"

"No, thank you, Lord Atwood. I have more thinking to do."

Sun lay down. No one said anything further. Payne began to cough.

They moved on at dawn. Arthur tried to talk to Sun, but Dimmick was watching them both.

Five miles a day, they reckoned; perhaps ten on their best days. It was hard to tell. What was a mile on Mars, anyway? They marched through the night. Despite all their exercises of discipline, their supplies ran low. A mouthful of stale water a day. Soon there would be nothing at all. Then they'd march on will alone, Atwood said. The prospect excited him. His lips were cracked and bloody, his eyes unfocused. The mountain grew day by day until it dominated the horizon; a shadow that rose into the heavens, impossibly tall and thin, like the funnel of a whirlwind inverted.

There was a vision of wings overhead. Shadows pursued them across the dunes. Pale emaciated shapes fell from the sky shrieking and buzzing. At first Arthur thought it was another hallucination. He'd been half asleep as he marched, dragging the sled. Now something slashed through his vague dream: patterns and motion, flashes of pale blue and faded rose, screaming. Ahead of him, Payne cried out and fell to his knees, and suddenly there was something standing over him: a tall, desperately thin shape, long-legged, mottled wings outspread. A Martian. Was it the one that had escaped from the tower? Payne tried to crawl away, but it held his hair in its long, deathly blue fingers. Payne was screaming, and another shrill and inhuman scream came from all around—from nowhere—from inside Arthur's head. The Martian threw Payne onto his back on the ground, then swept up its wings as if it meant to strike with them. An ice-axe appeared with a *thump* in its back. A little splatter of thick pink blood, and it toppled forward onto Payne.

Dimmick had apparently thrown the axe. He now pushed past Arthur to snatch up one of the rifles from the sled.

Up ahead, Sun was wrestling with another of the creatures. How many were there? Arthur let go of the sled rope and looked around, trying to rouse himself from his dream.

Atwood drew his pistol, pointed it at Sun's assailant, then stopped. He seemed paralyzed by fear—or perhaps he, too, was struggling to tell dream from reality.

Shadows swept across the ground. Arthur looked up to see a half-dozen wings approaching through the air. They came in a hectic, clumsy rush, landed messily, like squabbling geese in a pond, some of them falling flat on their faces, then jumping up and running. An odd, high-stepping run, bird-like. Wings raised like weapons. Arthur threw himself to the ground behind a sled as a ragged wing slashed through the air where his head had been. A shot sounded, slow and muffled, and continued to echo for some time.

Arthur got up on his knees. Dimmick had taken the rifle, but there was another ice-axe on the sled, somewhere under the blankets. Arthur reached for it just as one of the Martians landed on the sled. He retreated, but the thing wasn't interested in him—it rummaged through the supplies, tossing aside tins of food and boxes of matches. It lifted up two small glass jars of coloured ink and leapt up into the sky, spreading its wings. It appeared to be trying to eat them.

Arthur reached under the blankets, took the axe, turned, and buried it in the back of the first Martian he saw. More blood. He acted without thinking, lifting the axe again. Well, there would be time to think later. He looked around for another target. He saw, without a great deal of surprise, that Sun lay dead on the ground. There were two deep slashes across Sun's chest and another that had almost taken off his head. He appeared to have lost a hand, as well. Two of the Martians were dead—Atwood appeared to have recovered his nerve, and was reloading his pistol. Dimmick was holding three of them off at once, jabbing at them with the end of a rifle. He didn't have a moment to reload. He jabbed one Martian in the eye with the rifle's muzzle, then clubbed another with the butt. Bleeding from a half-dozen cuts, he nevertheless advanced indefatigably on the third Martian. It fled—they all fled—snatching what they could from the back of the sleds as they went, then taking to the air. Payne fired wildly into the air at the retreating Martians, and Vaz roared in fury and hurled a tent-pole after them.

I blame myself," Atwood said. "In my haste to reach our destination, I allowed discipline to lapse. Did I think that this place would give up its secrets without a struggle?"

The Martians had made off with a few tins of ox-tail soup, some paint, some creosote, and a length of rope. Nothing very valuable. They appeared to have taken Sun's hand, too.

"He was a great magician," Atwood said. "And a brother to me."

There wasn't much they could do to bury him.

Frank spat at Sun's body, then swung a fist at Atwood's face, clipping his jaw and making him stumble.

"Discipline? Discipline? Atwood, you've ruined us, you bloody—"

Dimmick struck Frank in the back of the knee with a rifle-butt, knocking him to the ground. Then he beat Frank about the head and shoulders until he started to sob. Vaz, pale and sick, turned away. Arthur closed his eyes. Eventually Atwood said: *Enough.*

Chapter Thirty-five

T he Martians' flight was erratic. They were half-starved, half-
dead, half-mad. Some of them had been wounded in the
fight. Some were dead. The survivors—there were five of them—
were burdened by the things they'd seized from the interlopers.
Unfamiliar things, things they had no names for in any of the old languages of Mars. Food, they hoped.

They had no destination in mind. They didn't know where they were.
The skies were not the skies they remembered from before their long
sleep; the face of Mars below was so hideously blighted that they could
hardly bear to look down at it.

None of them remembered the world they'd gone to sleep in more
than dimly. They were of various nations and of various philosophies and
faiths. Once upon a time that would have mattered, but now their colours
were faded, their names forgotten. They were already half-dead, and they
expected to die soon.

They remembered the end of things: storm-clouds swallowing the
skies, driving them out of the air and onto the ground; nonsense words
screamed into the wind; shadows that crawled and laughed and pounced;
men and women struck down by madness; the rivers sucked dry by some
tremendous and bodiless hunger; the forests turned to ash. None of them
knew the cause. Sometimes it seemed to have happened in an instant
and sometimes it seemed to have been a thousand-year decline. They remembered rumours of its cause—nothing more. There was no point in
talking about it now. At the end they'd all come to the same place: alone,
separated from their dying nations, they'd found some corner of a ruin
somewhere to hide in; and there they'd dreamed, stiffening and wither-
ing and becoming like stone.

Something had prowled the edges of their dreams, screaming and murmuring, driving them mad. Now that they were moving again, it was only a matter of time before something found them, and ended them.

One of them remembered a little more than the rest. She was their leader, in so far as they had one. The first to awaken, she'd had more time to think. How long had she slept, in a remote corner of some meaningless ruin? She forgot what that ruin was, or who'd built it, or why. Perhaps she'd never known. She'd lain tangled with—who? A lover? A child? A parent? Some stranger who'd fallen there with her? She couldn't remember, no matter how hard she struggled. She'd been asleep for so long, and she'd had such terrible dreams, and she was so hungry.

Then someone had moved her—a mind had touched hers. In that moment she'd woken, screaming with fear and hunger. Whoever had slept at her side had woken too. The thing that had moved her was a sort of monster: huge, square, heavy-footed, wingless, an awful mixture of pink and white and brown. At first she took it for a new sort of nightmare. There'd been a struggle, in the course of which her sleep-mate died. Then one of the monsters had spoken to her in a language she half-remembered: the language of the Eye, a language of pride, and command, and power. Though she didn't fully understand what he was saying, she felt compelled to obey. At the monster's command, she fled.

When night fell, still following that command, she circled back and found the monster and its companions, and watched them from a distance.

She could hardly believe what she was seeing. These extraordinary, ungainly, heavy-footed creatures, trudging across the blasted face of her world; dragging behind them a nonsense of clutter, as if they meant it as some sort of offering—but for whom? They passed through hungry dust-clouds and weathered storms unharmed, as if the ghosts of Mars had for some incomprehensible reason decided to spare them, or had found them too strange and too foul to eat. Even their leader, the one who'd spoken, was hideous—yet there was something about him that compelled her to follow, to watch him. He might speak again. He might tell her what had happened.

She was afraid of him. He had power; his followers had strange and deadly weapons. She hung back, drifting high above them. They didn't seem to notice her.

From time to time they passed ruins, and in some of them she found others like her. She woke them from their sleep. Because she'd been awake longer, and her hunger had been sharpened to a finer point, she was able to subdue them and make them follow her.

At night she circled closer, confident that she was unseen. Some nights the creatures marched on by moonlight; some nights they gathered around a fire, and slept.

One night their leader got up from the fire, after all the others were asleep. He walked some way, until he was separated from the rest of them by a tall dune, and then he lit another, smaller fire—he had carried it with him somehow—and placed it at his feet. Then he looked up into the sky, as if he knew she were there watching him, and began to speak. The way he spoke was horrible—ugly and unsubtle, clumsy and lurching, colourless and crude, empty of everything but power and command. Like last time, it spoke to her on some deep level she couldn't quite understand; something drilled into her by centuries of fear and hiding responded, and she fled.

In the morning she returned. The others came with her. They attacked. She felt compelled to do so—as if the insult these creatures represented could no longer be tolerated.

It went badly. The creatures were slow and stupid-looking, but dangerous. Nevertheless, they killed one of them, a squat dark thing with a white fuzz on the top of its head and under its ugly mouth. After that, their fury vanished, replaced by fear. They fled, snatching up a few things they hoped might be food.

They found a high tower-top to perch on. They sliced the tins open and found that some of what was inside was vile but nourishing, while some of it was vile and poisonous. They gnawed on the rope and the creature's severed hand. She began to feel stronger. Faintly, she felt memory returning. More urgent than remembering her own name was remembering the name of her sleep-mate; but she couldn't. She began to feel shame at her own degraded state. She trembled and scraped at her own faded withered skin. A fight broke out over the creature's hand and she killed one of her fellow survivors. She never knew or asked his name. She snatched what she could and fled. One other came with her.

✳   ✳   ✳

Days and nights swirled beneath her. Then there were wings following her; she didn't notice until it was too late. Someone swooped down on her out of the clouds. They struck her in the back and grappled with her and bore her down to the ground. A half-dozen of them, more than she could fight, even if she still had strength to fight. She crouched, clutching at her spoils as if they were children to be protected.

They were people like her—winged people—but there the resemblance ended. They were strong, well-fed, and unafraid. Their colours were still bright. She couldn't understand how that was possible. She hated them terribly for their good fortune.

They paced, and circled overhead, threatening and babbling and asking questions that she couldn't understand. They spoke some dialect she didn't know—stiff and formal and grand.

One of them—it was a female—came rushing forward and snatched her trophies from her grasp. She was too weak to resist. The female held up the thing she'd snatched—a metal cylinder—as if it were the most astonishing thing she'd ever seen.

She summoned up the strength to rush at this impertinent stranger, this thief. She raised her wings to strike. Someone cut her down from behind.

Chapter Thirty-six

Josephine held the tin in her hands, turning it around and around. Cold metal; heavy; a squat, functional cylinder. A worn and ragged label, with stiff black markings that were at first strange to her eyes. A form of writing, but how could it mean anything without motion? There was a picture in the middle, familiar, but of wildly fanciful creatures: a lion and a unicorn holding up a shield. Above that were the words *BY APPOINTMENT*; and above those, *CROSSE & BLACKWELL, LTD.* At the bottom, an address, which was as fantastic and as familiar as the unicorn: *No 21, Soho Square.* And above *CROSSE & BLACKWELL* it said *OXTAIL SOUP.*

She had the strangest urge to cradle the thing as if it were a long-lost, much-loved doll.

~ *These poor wretches,* Orpheus said, indicating the dead Martians at her feet. *These are all that remain. They are better off dead. I wonder, though—what woke them?*

~ *My friends. My friends—or, if not them, then someone from the Blue Sphere. This—this is theirs.*

Not just men of Earth, but Londoners, or at least Englishmen. Atwood had come looking for her, or Arthur, or both of them. At last. Not the fragile psychic exploration that had left her stranded, but an expedition, with food. What other explanation could there be? But when had they arrived, and what had happened to them?

Orpheus reached out with some trepidation and touched the tin. His finger traced the words on the label.

~ *In all the times I have made the crossing, this is the strangest treasure I have ever found, and the strangest I ever expect to. What is it?*

She tried to explain. Meanwhile, the rest of Orpheus' party went to investigate the other dead Martian, who'd been killed in the struggle in the air and had fallen among the dunes a little way away.

After the night of the red moon, Josephine had spent a day and a night hunting for Orpheus; but his movements were unpredictable, and he had no fixed abode. If he didn't want to be found, everyone told her, no one could find him; and it seemed that was that.

She tried to petition for access to the Fates—the moon's council of matrons—but the bureaucracy of the lunar city proved as confusing and impenetrable as Chancery. She went looking for their courtroom, the little workshop she'd met them in before, and discovered that theirs was a mobile court. The place where she'd met them before was now just an ordinary workshop. They might be anywhere.

She pleaded, cajoled, begged anyone who'd listen: *please help me go down to the surface*. She boasted, in case boasting might help. She tried to trade, promising secrets of the Blue Sphere in return for passage. She began to wonder if she could survive the crossing alone.

She was on the verge of giving up when the Fates sent for her.

She was sitting in a window overlooking the city's rose-pink river, trying to remember what the Thames smelled like, when she saw a young woman standing by the water's edge, beckoning her down. She shrugged, opened her wings, and drifted lazily down to the stone embankment. The young woman was already fluttering away, south of the river and deep into narrow streets, stopping sometimes to beckon Josephine after her.

At last she was in the presence of the Fates again. Another workshop, a little crescent-shaped room cluttered with tables and tools and dust and noise. The one she'd called Clotho stepped forward, and touched her hand.

~ *You want to go down to the surface*, Clotho said.

~ *I do.*

~ *Why?*

~ *If I could search the ruins—*

~ *You will find death. Have we not been kind to you here, treated you as a guest?*

~ *Wouldn't you return to your home if you could?*

~ *We could all return, if we liked. But it would mean death. So we don't. Perhaps we should.*

Clotho moved from one side of the room to another, and sat at a new table, where she began methodically sorting beads, tossing out every tenth or twentieth specimen.

~ *Why did you bring me here, if the answer is no?*

Clotho stopped her work and spoke. ~ *Is that the answer? I didn't know. I thought I had brought you here to say* yes. *Though you will most likely meet your end down there, and we will be sorry; we could have learned so much more from you. But you are inflexible.*

~ *Why now?*

~ *Now, you suspect me? Why not? We are not heavy, solid, inflexible things like you people of the Blue Sphere. One day we say one thing, the next another.*

~ *I don't believe that.*

~ *No?*

For a while Clotho went back to working. Then at last she spoke again. ~ *We saw your coming. Did you know that? We haven't lost all of the science of Mars. We knew it when your people first came into our sphere and left you behind. We didn't know what you were, or where, or how, but we knew that something had changed. Our dreamers and sky-watchers tell me that you looked like a falling star. Two days ago they saw it again. Eight stars, falling onto the great face.*

Josephine's heart raced. She felt it in her wings, as if she were about to take flight.

~ *Eight? Not nine?*

~ *See—you do know something. Why are they here? Do you think they are looking for you?* Clotho looked up from her work and watched Josephine closely, waiting for her answer.

~ *I don't know. I hope so. It's been so long. They may be different people. There are so many people in the Blue Sphere—more than here.*

~ *I will tell you what I hope, and what I fear. What I hope is that they have come to take you back to your people, and if that's true, then*

*it would be wicked to keep you from them. Isn't that so? But I fear that
they have come for another reason. I fear these people who have learned
to venture from one sphere to another have come to plunder the ruins,
to steal secrets of the Eye that are better left where they are. I fear that
they have come to make war.*

~ *Then let me talk to them, and tell them to go home.*

~ *Good, child. I see we are in agreement.*

Orpheus was chosen as the leader of the expedition to the surface.
There were six members of his party, counting Josephine. They'd
been on the surface of Mars for seven days, which was already far too
long, far longer than any previous expedition had dared. Orpheus' second was a lanky woman whose name meant something like *One-who-
stays-in-their-proper-place-from-love;* Josephine dubbed her *Hestia.*
Hestia knew as much of the history of Mars-before-the-fall as any scholar
in the city—which was to say, not a great deal. *Xanthos* was an artist.
Poet and *Far-Traveller* rounded out their number; Poet was known for
his sharp vision, and Far-Traveller for her swift flight.

~ *If you die,* Orpheus said, *you die. They asked me to take you, and
I will. I don't know if this is right or wrong, wise or foolish. But I saw
that you are brave, and so I won't stand in your way.*

The moon circled Mars, approaching periapsis. The party ushered
Josephine blindfolded through the streets and into a certain tower
at the edge of the city. When they let her remove her blindfold, she saw
that the tower was windowless, and dark except for the faint red light in
Orpheus' hand. A steep staircase wound up into the dark, and the walls
around it were covered with carvings of a kind she'd never seen before on
the white moon. They were on the verge of reminding her of something,
but Orpheus said, ~ *Don't look.*

~ *What are they?*

~ *Not everything was forgotten,* Hestia said. Orpheus shushed
them both. They climbed the stairs in silence at first, and then Hestia
began to lead them in a solemn chant. The chanting was like a drug,
like Atwood's incense; Josephine felt that she was dreaming. After a
long time, the stairs fell away beneath them and they spread their

wings. Together they forced their way up into the dark shivering, in the terrible cold, struggling with all their wills against a terrible weight; until suddenly everything turned on its axis and they were hurtling down through blinding light and heat and thick streaming clouds of violet dust, their wings screaming in pain as the clouds parted to reveal Mars beneath them.

There'd been a seventh of their party when they set off from the city. His name was Born-into-Storm. When they came down through the clouds, he wasn't with them. That was to be expected. It was a dangerous journey, and sometimes people got lost on the way.

Mars rolled out endlessly beneath them. Orpheus led the way. The rest of them trailed behind in a V, like geese. They flew high. It was safer that way, Orpheus said. The surface was haunted.

You could see the things that haunted the surface sometimes, he said. They were clearest at noon. It took Josephine a long time to see what he was pointing to: not so much a *thing* as an absence, cloud-shadows on the land where no shadow should be. These, Orpheus said, were death to enter—he said no more. Whether they were a natural phenomenon or an unnatural one, they were everywhere, when the light was right and you knew where to look for them: like mould growing on the floor of an abandoned room.

Born-at-Midnight was as talkative as Orpheus was taciturn. She was a risk-taker, a scholar, restlessly curious. She told them stories about what was below them. A dust-filled crater was a sea, in Born-at-Midnight's telling; and not just any sea, but the Sea of Second Sky, which the Nation of the Long Arm had claimed as theirs, and into which the great heroine Bright-Blue-Wing had once fallen, convinced that the water was a world as rich in treasures as the sky. There had been a legend that one day she would return. There was nothing for her to return to now, Orpheus remarked.

A wave-like sweep of sharp little mountains marked the western edge of the migration of the Nation of the Tooth. A crescent ruin in the middle of a jumble of hills was once the library of the Nation of the Pinion—it was long since picked over. Something that looked a little like an amphitheatre sounded, from Born-at-Midnight's description, as if it had in fact been something roughly theatrical—it was hard to say. They'd lost the art of drama on the white moon, and Born-at-Midnight struggled for words. She was better at battles. This battle or that, acts of heroism, great feats of philosophical disputation, had taken place at one rock or ruin or ravine or another.

There were no borders. This was no one's country, no one's home. Thousands of years of history had moved through it. Everything that was now still and dead had once been in motion. Empty skies were once crowded. Desolate purple plains were once forests. What were now dry channels were once rivers, marking the route westwards. Dunes were once hunting-grounds. Born-at-Midnight told them about the animals of Mars: the lopers, the crawlers, the diggers, the stilt-walkers, the balloon-ists.

Josephine guessed that it was all about a quarter true. That was all right. Her narration was distracting, and calming. Whenever Born-at-Midnight stopped talking, a cold and nameless dread set in: the voice of Mars.

They headed north-west, towards the mountain of the Nation of the Eye. They didn't like it—those territories, those ruins, that mountain, were taboo to them. They all suspected that Clotho's fears were true.

One afternoon, to their great amazement, they saw wings in the distance and below. Life and motion on a dead and empty planet. Two ragged creatures, withered to the point of starvation, faded to a dreadful dead colour. Orpheus gave the signal to attack.

Born-at-Midnight and Exalted dragged the other dead wretch over and laid it out in the dust. *~ Poor thing*, Josephine thought.

~ Suppose a straight line of motion, said Orpheus, *from where this happened.*

~ He was holding this when we killed him, Born-at-Midnight said, holding up a grisly object. *What is it?*

~ I don't know, Josephine said.

~ Nor I, Orpheus said. *Nothing I've seen on Mars before. Suppose that they flew straight, all the way from where they met your people to where they crossed our flight. Then they met your people in the country of the Eye. Perhaps not far from the mountain.*

After a moment's further thought Josephine recognised the object as a human hand. She recognised the golden ring on its finger; it had belonged to Mr Sun. It had been severed at the wrist by the blow of some sharp blade.

Chapter Thirty-seven

The terrain climbed steeply, sweeping up and up into the great mountain. Better not to think how *far* up. Better not to look at the mountain at all, if you could help it. Even Payne and Frank, who boasted of their campaigns in the mountains of Afghanistan, said that they'd never seen anything like it, and confessed that it made them feel so small they practically vanished. Better to keep your eyes on your feet, anyway. There was sharp flint underfoot, treacherous scree. There were ravines, crevasses, sudden drops that you might not notice in the gloom and the dusty wind. One had the sense that the mountain had once risen quite violently from the plains, spinning up like a whirlwind, leaving the land all around ragged and cracked. They tied themselves together for safety, looping the rope around their hungry waists and clutching it in their bony fists.

They'd left one of the sleds behind. It would only slow them down, Atwood said. Their destination was at hand, and a few tins of soup wouldn't make much difference one way or the other. It was time, he said, to abandon the comforts of home; it was time to depend on their inner resources.

The second sled broke after half a day's upward struggle. After that, Arthur and Vaz carried what they could in their packs. A little food, a little water, some lanterns and matches, Atwood's most essential papers. Payne and Frank took the rifles, and watched the sky, in case the raiders returned.

They were being pursued again. There was no doubt in anyone's mind about that. Neither Frank nor Payne could ever quite see the wings of their pursuers, though from time to time one of them would yell and fire into the sky. The air was too gloomy; it grew darker and colder and harder to breathe as they climbed the mountain, and the shadows lengthened in a predatory way. They *knew* that they were being hunted, whether anyone could see their hunters or not.

Dimmick walked at the front of their procession. When night fell, he held a lamp. It was unnerving to walk in the dark, but at least, Vaz remarked, they didn't have to look at where they were going any more.

Atwood refused the rope. He went on ahead, setting the pace. Dimmick held the rest of them to it. When they slid, Dimmick pulled them along. At times they ascended at such a steep angle that on Earth they would have had to go on all fours.

Some time in the evening, Arthur found himself walking alongside Frank. He blinked. It seemed that Frank had for some time been hissing *Shaw! Shaw!* in his ear.

"Shaw? Are you with me? Please, Shaw." Frank whispered and whined. He sounded like a man pleading for his life, or his sanity.

"Shaw?"

"What, Frank? I was somewhere else entirely."

"Atwood, Shaw. Atwood. We have to kill him, Shaw. It's our only hope of ever waking from this terrible nightmare. Weren't you listening, Shaw? I've tried—by God, I've tried to wake up. It's Atwood's will that keeps us here. A bullet will settle this."

"You have the rifle, Frank."

"If not for that ape of his, I'd do it. He killed Sun, you know. He planned it; he planned it somehow. Sun knew—Sun knew what he was up to. I don't. Thank God I don't. I'm afraid, Shaw. I hear voices, whispering the most terrible things."

"That's enough, Frank."

"Of course. You don't want to wake, do you? You're in it with him. You're all as mad as each other."

"I think perhaps I should take the rifle for a while, Frank. What do you say? You could do with a rest."

Frank released the rifle without a struggle.

"I have a boy, you know. My son. In London. Studying to be a doctor, of all things. Atwood promised to pay for his education."

"Good man, Mr Frank. Good man."

Dimmick watched all of this, grinning nastily.

✳   ✳   ✳

That night Atwood permitted them to stop and sleep if they could. Arthur slept. When he woke—to Atwood's boot poking his shoulder—Dimmick and Frank were both gone. Atwood held up the lamp. Vaz was still asleep. Payne sat upright, staring fixedly at his boots.

What appeared to have happened was that Frank had murdered Dimmick in the night, killing him with his own ice-axe while he slept. Some bloodstains, snagged threads, and other clues suggested that Frank had then wrapped Dimmick's body in a blanket and rolled it over the rocks into a crevasse, before fleeing into the darkness, where probably he, too, had ended up in a crevasse. The motive was unclear. Mutiny of a sort, presumably. Madness. Revenge. Nobody had much interest in investigating further.

"I thought Dimmick might outlast us all," Arthur said.

"He had his strengths," Vaz said, judiciously.

"See here," Atwood said. He crouched down and held the lamp low. There were bloody bootprints on the rock next to where Atwood had been sleeping.

"He meant to kill me, too, as I slept. Gentlemen, did you know what he planned? Know this: if I die, you are at the mercy of this place."

"Don't threaten us, Atwood. We've come this far with you. We'll see it through. What other choice do we have?"

"I know, Shaw. I know. I'm sorry."

Suddenly, and to Arthur's surprise and disgust, it looked as if Atwood might be about to cry.

"You've been a good friend to me, Shaw."

"Well, Atwood. Well. If you say so."

"I shall miss Dimmick; he would have been very useful in what's to come. My trials are not done."

They were already on the march again when the sun rose. At their current dizzying elevation, the sunrise was a sudden explosion of blazing violet light. It revealed that a field of glittering flint lay before them, and in the middle distance, there was a ruin.

It was much larger than the tower they'd explored in the lowlands. Sweeping walls enclosed a dozen smaller structures: a strange too-steep dome and a scatter of broken towers. A bewildering profusion of sharply perpendicular objects—crenellations? fortifications? spires? obelisks?

ornaments?—somewhat recalled the Houses of Parliament. The outer wall's stone was laced with flint or mica or crystal, and with the full force of sunrise falling on it, it shone as if it were on fire. The whole structure stood on the edge of a wide impassable crevasse. A sheer cliff loomed behind it. Beyond that, the mountain continued to rise for mile after mile into streaming black clouds.

There was no time to study it. Atwood clapped his hands together and croaked, his voice suddenly choked with relief, or joy, or fear. *There! It exists*! At the same moment, Payne cried out and fired his rifle into the air. Arthur turned to see what he was shooting at.

A thousand miles of sunlit geography lay behind them. Terrain that had seemed flat and monotonous as they marched revealed itself, when seen from above, as an endless rolling sea of hills. Valleys they'd crossed revealed themselves as hundred-mile shadows, ancient gouges in the face of Mars, radiating outwards in every direction.

Payne lifted his rifle to the sky and fired again. There were wings overhead, blue and red and purple. Six, seven, eight Martians, maybe more, airborne, just a few hundred yards away. They'd been circling in the dark, waiting for dawn to reveal their prey. Now they descended. A strange sawing hum filled the air; Arthur recognised it now as the sound of Martians in flight.

Payne reloaded, fired again. His third shot caught one of the Martians square in the chest, and it fell from the sky.

"Not now," Atwood shouted. "Not now! Run, run all of you, run!"

He ran for the shelter of the ruin, and Arthur followed, scrabbling over the sharp stone. The sun was behind him and his shadow was long and sharp before him, legs and arms madly stretching and shrinking, shrinking and stretching. Long wing-shadows streamed closer. The castle ahead was almost too bright to look at, and the glare underfoot nearly blinded him. The wings were so close that the glitter in the stones underfoot reflected beads of blue.

Arthur ran in great bounding leaps, sliding and skidding on the stones. The pack on his back threatened to tip him head over heels or side to side. Wings whirred. Something swept with a rush of wind over his head. Then he stumbled, gasping, and one of them had seized his collar in its fist. For a moment he thought it might lift him into the air, like a hawk with a mouse; but it clearly hadn't reckoned with his weight. Starved as he was, he was still three times the spindly Martian's weight. He remained earthbound and the thing went heels-over-head. A blue face fell upside down past him, silver eyes wide with astonishment. It sprawled along the stones. He skidded on its splayed wings—an eerie, icy sort of surface.

He came to the ruin's outer wall. True to form, there was no door, only high windows, in one of which stood Atwood, his hand outstretched.

"*Jump*, Shaw!"

He jumped with all his strength, thanking God for Martian gravity. Atwood caught his hand and pulled him into darkness. A moment later Vaz fell on top of him, then Payne.

Chapter Thirty-eight

As the sun rose and its angle shifted, the field of stones grew dim again.

Orpheus, who'd severely underestimated the weight of an Earthman, was bruised and bloodied and somewhat humbled by his roll over the stones.

Hestia was dead.

Poet and Far-Traveller lifted her up by her arms, and together the whole party rose and hurried her away from the plain of stones. They flew sunwards. The ruin shrank beneath them.

~ *Dead,* Orpheus said.

~ *Yes,* Josephine said. *They have weapons . . .*

It was no easy matter to explain what a gun was. The Martians had few tools, made little use of fire, and regarded their own bodies and minds as quite adequate weapons. The concept of a machine for a killing was foreign to them.

~ *Like something the Eye might have made,* Orpheus said. He was appalled, terrified. ~ *You didn't tell us.*

She said nothing. It was true. It had never occurred to her that the humans might be armed.

~ *We should have acted sooner. We should have swooped on them in the dark.*

They'd caught sight of the expedition's lantern during the night. She had persuaded them to wait until morning to act, in the hope that by daylight they might be able to avoid violence.

~ *How far? How far can they kill?*

~ *I don't know. Not this far.*

~ *Those are your people?*

~ *I think so.*

Orpheus asked no more, and looked away from her.

They rose in silence, save for the sound of their wings.

She hadn't been able to see them clearly as they ran. The glare from the sunrise reflecting off the stones had made them into silhouettes. Ragged shadow-shapes, clumsy flailing arms and legs, bobbing heads; she could hardly tell one from another. She thought she might have seen Atwood, standing in the window of the ruined wall. Bearded, wild, sunburned, bruised; had it been Atwood? She couldn't be sure. Perhaps one of the others was Arthur. Perhaps not.

~ *They killed Hestia*, Orpheus said.

~ *Yes.*

~ *Why?*

~ *They were afraid of us*, she said. *We came on them too suddenly. They are lost in a strange place and they cannot tell us from the ones who attacked them.*

~ *Or they are mad already. They have crawled about on the surface too long and gone mad. We'll kill them if we must.*

~ *No!*

~ *No?*

~ *Let me talk to them. Isn't that why I'm here?*

~ *Talk if you can. They won't listen.*

They went up and up until the air thinned and the sky grew black and cold. The peak of the mountain-top was still far above them. Below them, the valleys were like a rough blue sea, and the ruin was a distant ship lost in a storm.

When they could go no higher, they dropped Hestia. She fell fast and was lost to sight almost at once.

It was a kind of honour, as Orpheus saw it; to end in motion, swallowed up by the face of Mars.

They circled over the ruin, descending slowly. Nobody fired on them. The walls described a half-moon, cut off by the crevasse at the rear. Towers stuck up at precarious angles. A strange, steeply swelling dome was cracked through, revealing a vault of dust below. Barbicans and watchtowers sat at the edges of the outer walls. The structure was divided in the middle by a wide open courtyard, which was choked with dust, dirt, rubble, the tops of half-buried obelisks, carved with worn illegible designs.

It was by far the largest structure Josephine had seen on Mars, and by Martian standards it was squat and ugly. It had a forbidding and warlike aspect, a little like a castle, or perhaps a battleship. A place fit for giants, or for the imprisonment of monsters.

What was it? Perhaps Hestia could have told them. All that they knew was that it had once belonged to the Nation of the Eye, who had claimed the mountain as their territory. It might have been a fortification, or a laboratory, or a temple, or any number of things. No telling what secrets it might hold. No telling what Atwood might be looking for down there.

They entered through the crack in the great bulging dome at the northern end of the complex, and were quickly lost in a maze of shadowy dust-choked corridors.

THE
NINTH
AND
FINAL
DEGREE

Chapter Thirty-nine

Bloody things are moving again," Payne said, lifting his rifle.

Vaz scrambled to his feet and joined Payne at the window.

"Where?"

They stood in what they'd dubbed the South Gallery, a long row of arched windows with a commanding view of the courtyard. Payne and Vaz had the rifles. Arthur had an ice-axe, which was good enough, in his opinion: if one of the bloody things got in through the window, he'd rather have an axe in his hand than a rifle.

He didn't see what Payne was pointing at. It was twilight, and the towers and crenellations and buttresses and arches and whatchamacallits around the courtyard were so numerous and so oddly shaped that they were easy to mistake for enemies on the move.

"There. Follow my bloody—there!"

Payne fired, swore, worked the lever, and fired again. Nothing moved.

Vaz lowered his rifle, and Arthur relaxed his grip on his axe.

They'd been in the castle for a day. Following a brief, chaotic midmorning skirmish, in the course of which Payne had put a bullet in a Martian's leg, the battle-lines had been clearly drawn. The Earthmen held the southern part of the complex, and the Martians the north. In between them was the gloomy, windswept courtyard.

"They're patient, by God," said Payne. "Cunning—not like the last lot.

This lot have a notion they can wait us out. And they've learned to fear rifles. Rightly so. I always say: God may abandon you in heathen country, but Mr Winchester never will!"

The prospect of something to shoot had rather raised Payne's spirits. Since they'd been in the castle he'd been dispensing military advice, barking orders, and playing look-out, eagerly expecting further sorties from the Martian lines. None had come since evening, but sometimes one or two of the Martians circled high overhead, out of rifle range. Otherwise, they kept themselves hidden.

The southern part of the complex was a honeycomb of dust-choked corridors, sloping chimneys, vaults open to the sky. Floors had apparently been considered a luxury on Ancient Mars; for the most part, if an Earthman wanted to get anywhere he had to tightrope-walk across uneven stone beams. If they chose to, the Martians might sneak in from any direction, from above or below. That they hadn't was something of a mystery. Payne's theory was that they were too superstitiously terrified of his Winchester rifle.

"Perhaps they're asleep," Vaz said. "God—I wish I were asleep."

Vaz leaned his rifle against the wall and sat back down on the floor. He poked glumly at his left boot. It had been much abused on the long march, and the race for the castle had been the final straw—now the sole flapped loose. He would be marching no farther on it. For a while he had pretended manfully to find this amusing.

"For all we know, they don't sleep," Arthur said. "We don't know a bloody thing about them. Least of all what they want with us."

"Makes no difference," Payne said. "There's them and there's us. That's all there is to know—except that we have guns and they do not."

A whir and a flash of wings crossed the window. Payne cursed and snatched up his rifle. Arthur felt the now-familiar sensation of telepathic assault—a wave of emotions so confusing that he nearly dropped to his knees—and he defended himself again, the way Atwood and Miss Didot had taught him. The sensation passed.

"Missed," Payne said. "Where'd it go? Do you see it?"

"Shaw!" Atwood called up from the depths below. His voice was a faint ghostly echo, muffled by countless tons of stone and dirt and by the thin Martian air. "Shaw! I need you. Come here."

✳   ✳   ✳

Atwood was holed up in an odd little windowless room on a recessed mezzanine floor beneath the South Gallery—to get to it Arthur had to clamber down a narrow slippery-sided chute. He suspected it had once been used for disposing of waste, or feeding something.

The room was roughly pentagonal in shape. Atwood had been working there for hours by the light of a hurricane lamp and the place reeked of soot and oil. Atwood's eyes were bloodshot and his fingers were ink-stained. His condition—both physical and mental—had degraded rapidly since entering the castle. He resembled a feverish monk in his cell, or a mad prisoner. All around him on the floor were his papers: sketches he'd made of the carvings on the castle's walls.

The castle was almost empty. Wind and dust had long since eroded most traces of ornament or furnishing or daily life, with the exception of a series of heavy ceramic tablets, which they'd found scattered haphazardly throughout the corridors. Almost a dozen of the things so far, and no doubt there were more. Some were mounted in recesses in the walls. Others were mounted on the sides of obelisks. Some were high out of reach; others were buried in drifts of dust. A few had shattered. Atwood's first instruction that morning, as soon as a comfortable stalemate with the enemy had been achieved, had been to collect half a dozen specimens and bring them to his cell. He'd spent the afternoon scraping dirt from them with a pen-knife to reveal the carvings beneath.

"I need your help," Atwood said. "Sit, sit."

Arthur cleared papers to make a space.

"No! Don't—it's a map, Shaw, it's a map! For God's sake, be careful. Sit there. Give me that and sit there."

Atwood's pistol occupied an empty spot on the floor. Arthur handed it to Atwood and sat down.

"That was our first encounter since sundown," Arthur said. "Payne thinks they fear the rifle. I don't know—they seem a little different from the last lot."

"Hmm? Oh—yes. Perhaps. There used to be many nations on Mars, Shaw. You see, their science is jumbled together with their history. I'm not sure that they made quite the same distinctions as we do."

"You've been reading their carvings, then."

"Yes. They were many nations, and not all were so wise or so civilised as the builders of this observatory—that's what it is, Shaw, or you might say a library or a tomb. The builders were plagued by barbarian tribes. Let's suppose that the creatures that have plagued us are descendants of those barbarians of Old Mars—devolved further, into a truly primitive state."

"If you like. What do these carvings say about how to get home?"

"Home?" Atwood said. "What about Josephine?"

Arthur blinked. For a moment, he was confused. He hadn't thought about Josephine in—how long? Not since Sun's death, at least. Since then he'd had no time to think of anything but the march, hunger and fear, the flight from the Martians.

"She's gone, isn't she, Atwood?"

"Gone? Pull yourself together, Shaw—now is no time for a nervous collapse."

"She's gone, Atwood. She's gone. It was madness to ever think otherwise. I let you trick me here—I did terrible things to help you—and she was always gone, wasn't she? I let you—I played a trick on myself, Atwood—as if I'd . . . like the sort of poor fool who lets some crooked medium play nasty tricks on him. I'm a fool. A fool."

"We have travelled across the void, and survived the surface of Mars. Now is no time for despair. But I need your help."

"If you mention her name again, Atwood, I shan't be responsible for what I might do."

"Hmm." Atwood edged a hand towards his revolver. Then he shrugged. "To business, then."

"That would be best, Atwood. What did you want?"

Atwood stood. His legs nearly went out from under him.

Arthur jumped up.

"Sorry, Shaw. Bit stiff. Thank you."

As Atwood stumbled past, Arthur noticed his rash—an awful purple mottling on his neck. He'd torn his nails bloody scraping at the carvings. The man was falling apart. Well, weren't they all?

"The trial that remains is one of the will, Shaw, not the body. There are ghosts here—did you know that? Echoes, one might say. Sometimes we speak of a writer putting his soul into his words, don't we? This was a great centre of learning and they were great magicians. More to learn here than in Athens and all of Egypt and every library in London. I wish I had a hundred years."

Arthur stepped over Atwood's papers and crouched to examine the tablets stacked in the corner. Scraped clean, the tablets displayed clear evidence of writing—far clearer than the faint scratches in the tower. Perhaps the eroding winds were less severe in the lee of the mountain. They were covered in swooping vectors, odd geometries, and inscrutable hieroglyphs that were somehow uncomfortably *dense*, in a way that suggested that they might move if you took your eyes off them; or that they were already slowly moving.

"They didn't quite see the stars the way we do," Atwood said. "Their language, their way of thinking, was very different from ours. A matter of translation, that's all. Mathematics. Should have brought Jupiter after all. Ah, well."

"The stars."

"Yes. Before—before the disaster that destroyed them, they were engaged in a study not so very different from ours. I told you, didn't I? They were attempting to explore the spheres. To move *up*."

"Up? You mean to Earth."

"Yes! Earth. The Blue Sphere. But it's hard to go *up*. Much easier to go *down*. This very room—this very room once contained a creature that they brought up from below—a thing from the Black Sphere, Shaw. Saturn. Can you imagine it?"

"No."

Arthur picked up a page of Atwood's sketches. The same hieroglyphs, over and over, with notes in Atwood's erratic handwriting.

"Listen. I've seen these before. In the *Liber Ad Astra*. On the floor of your library. When I first saw them I thought a madman or a drunk had painted them. Yet here they are on Mars."

"But that was down," Atwood said, as if he hadn't heard. "Into the dark. They never rose up—or else certainly history would have recorded it. They never solved the puzzle, Shaw."

"Then what good are they to us? We're stuck here—is that what you're saying?"

"No." Atwood snatched his papers back. "Leave that alone, Shaw. Listen. In this place they summoned up creatures from the lower heavens; and they peered into the higher heavens and prayed. They could not unlock the gates above them, but perhaps we can."

He sat down against the wall and pulled his journal from his pocket. "Our calculations. The stars from our sphere. What they didn't know. And so we can close the circle. We must think like them, Shaw—we must become them. And then become greater than them."

"Who were they? What were they?"

"Scholars. Magicians. The greatest of their kind. They left these carvings for us—they knew we would come. Someone would come. Do you think they knew it would be me?"

"What happened to them? This is a ruin—this is a wasteland."

"An excellent question. I don't know."

"But you knew about this all along. Even back in London, you meant to come here."

"Yes. I didn't remember it all, of course. Some of it I only remembered in the tower—thank you, Shaw, for finding those telescopes—and some of it I remembered only when I listened to the wind. But I have always known. Ever since . . ." He closed his eyes.

"I am the greatest magician who has ever lived. That's plain fact, not a boast—who else could have brought us here? What's *time* to a magician? Nothing but another circle, Shaw."

"What other secrets have you kept from us?"

"What right do you have to all my secrets? How have you earned them? Will you help me or not?"

"I should break your neck."

"Then what chance would Josephine have?"

"I told you not to say her name, Atwood."

"Only I could bring us here; only I can bring us back. By my will, Shaw." Atwood showed an unpleasant smile. Bloody gums, loose teeth.

Arthur looked around Atwood's cell again. It was defensible; that was why Atwood had chosen it, of course. Atwood was dug in. If the Martians overran them, this room would be the last to fall.

"Ghosts," Arthur said. "You say ghosts speak to you here. I don't hear them."

"Pray that you never do. You wouldn't be able to bear it."

From the gallery above them came the sound of Vaz shouting in alarm, a rifle-shot, then the whirring of wings.

Atwood called up the chute. "Report, please, Payne."

Payne shouted down to confirm it: they'd spotted a Martian, hovering just above their window. No one was hurt. They'd winged the thing but not killed it, and it had fled. Stalemate was preserved.

"Looked like a female," Payne opined.

Arthur called up. "How can you tell?"

"I don't know, Shaw. Maybe I'm going native."

"They're moving," Atwood said. "We have no time to waste."

All through the night Payne kept a look-out from the gallery, while Atwood beavered away in his cell, and Arthur and Vaz went clambering through the rafters and narrow corridors in search of carvings. Every corridor looked alike; they got lost. There were windows that had the odd telescopic power of the windows of the lowlands tower, but since their walls had collapsed they faced onto the ground, or towards other walls or windows, and they were exceedingly confusing to look through. If there had ever been any rhyme or reason that a human mind could comprehend in the locations of the carvings, it had long since been lost, as successive centuries of erosion and subsidence and collapse had rearranged the chambers. It rather reminded Arthur of Gracewell's Engine in Deptford, after the fire. He began to suspect that the castle had once been taller, and possibly beautiful; that it had collapsed in on itself to make this squat claustrophobic maze.

Sometimes the carvings could be prized out of the wall, with ice-axe or shovel, and carried back to Atwood's cell. Sometimes they were wedged too tight to move. Arthur spent half an hour balancing with one foot on a rafter, the other on a wall, a sheet of paper pressed with one hand against the ceiling while he sketched hieroglyphs in charcoal with the other. Later he squeezed into a crack in the wall, feeling entombed, to take notes. Once Vaz cried out for help, and Arthur came running, sliding down fallen pillars and climbing up broken walls, axe in hand. He found Vaz standing with a heap of spilled Martian bones at his feet, cursing colourfully.

"Rather a surprise," Vaz conceded. "I apologise. One would think we were far past the point of being frightened by skeletons."

"Far past all points, Vaz. Far past all. God! Is this what it's come to, after all Atwood's talk. This—this *tomb*? Looting the bloody thing?"

Vaz shrugged, as if to say that it came as no great surprise to him.

Together they dug a broken stele from beneath the bones and brought it back to Atwood, who had by that time covered the floor of his cell in papers and tablets, arranged in a sort of complex spiralling pattern of unclear significance.

Some time in the course of the night, bad weather blew in. The usual dry Martian weather—whirling dust-clouds that shrieked and scraped across the rooftops and blew in through the windows to sting the eyes and choke the throat. When morning came, the clouds obscured the sun.

Around what was probably mid-morning, Atwood emerged from his cell.

"Payne," he said. "Shaw. Vaz. Listen. It's not enough. That's why they're here, of course. I should have seen it. The Martians, I mean. They're here to stop me."

"Slow down, Atwood."

"From escaping, Mr Shaw. From returning home, with all that I've learned. I was wrong, you see. There is one more trial. And what else should I have expected? This is Mars, after all."

"You are not well," Vaz said. "Mr Shaw and I have been talking and we think—"

"Oh, have you? Have you? And what have you determined? No—listen. It's very simple. A very simple, practical problem, of the sort that you gentlemen are eminently suited to solve—that's why I brought you here! We have only half the carvings. And half are in the territory that the enemy occupies. What we need, gentlemen, is a plan of attack."

Chapter Forty

Josephine scouted out the southern half of the complex—the Earthmen's territory.

Arthur was with them. She first caught a glimpse of him early that morning, through a crack in one of the walls. A bony, and bearded, and sickly looking apparition, but unquestionably Arthur. He *had* come for her after all. She felt such a rush of relief and excitement, love and hope and fear, that her wings trembled. For a moment she thought she might fall.

How could she possibly explain her *wings* to him?

When she saw him, he was busy heaving a stone tablet down from the wall. That would be at Atwood's instructions, no doubt. She didn't know where Atwood was. She hadn't set eyes on him since he entered the castle. She supposed he was hidden somewhere safe, while Arthur and the strangers did all the work, faced all the danger. That would be just like Atwood. Just like Arthur, too. What were Atwood's plans, and what did Arthur know of them? Did he have any notion how much danger he might be in?

She tried to call out to him, but her throat and her tongue weren't suited to the task. *Arthur* came out as a croak and a shriek. She attempted to call to him telepathically, but his mind was locked tightly against intrusion—they were all wary of telepathic assault. She called out her love and her joy to him and he took it as an attack. It was intensely frustrating.

She scouted, and made reports to Orpheus. Names, numbers, movements. One or possibly two rifles. They didn't seem to be very good shots. Arthur and the two ragged strangers lay in wait overlooking the courtyard; Atwood was hidden.

In the evening she grew over-confident, flew too close, and one of the strangers shot her in her wing. A sudden stinging—more shock than pain. She fell to the ground, scrambled in the dust, ran across the courtyard and leapt for the safety of the northern complex, through a window and into the chamber where Orpheus, Exalted, Poet and Far-Traveller waited.

The room was empty. It was high-ceilinged and many-windowed. A pillar in the middle of the room had once held a carved tablet, but Orpheus and Exalted had tossed it from the window. The carvings unnerved them. Everything about the place unnerved them. They were far more afraid of the ghosts of the Eye than of the Earthmen or their rifles. They said that they were planning. She suspected that their courage had run out at last; they were afraid to leave the room.

~ *They hurt me*, she said. There was no word for *shot*.

Orpheus examined her wound. He poked its neat round edges with his finger.

~ *Harmless*, he signed. *Is there pain?*

~ *No worse than the Great Flight.* That was a popular idiom in the lunar city, which she'd picked up somewhere along the way. It meant *worse things happen at sea.*

~ *Look*, Orpheus said. *A perfect little circle. In and out. What a strange weapon. But I think perhaps you were lucky.*

~ *I need to talk to him.*

~ *You should be more careful. Not your life to throw away, like a gift you don't want.*

She bridled at that. ~ *Who are you to tell me where I should go! I was sent here to talk to them. I was sent here to save them.*

~ *It's too late to save them. It was too late when they came here. Do you think they came here for you? To this place?*

Wind howled across the rooftops. Dust swirled in the window. Orpheus went to the window and looked out.

~ *I hear a storm coming*, he said.

Far-Traveller sat awkwardly against the wall and stared at the bullet wound in her leg.

~ *This is the place*, she said. *Is it? Isn't it? Hestia would know. This is where they crossed. It is. It must be. I wish Hestia were here with us. I feel them, I feel them whispering, don't you? Their ghosts. When they crossed they left part of themselves behind. Their shadows—I feel them.*

~ *No*, Orpheus said. *I feel them too. But it's not the ones who crossed. It's the ones who made this place.*

Poet rushed to the window in a sudden frenzy, as if he meant to hurl himself from it.

~ *The men from the Blue Sphere are waking them*, Orpheus said.

~ *They don't know*, Josephine said. *They don't know what they're doing.*

Orpheus made his hands into fists. That meant, *enough*. He turned and began to talk with the others.

She couldn't follow what he was saying. He was talking the curt, crude language of tactics and war, and she'd never learned it.

Night fell. A dust-storm blew in and quickly surrounded the ruin in darkness. It howled and scraped and shook the walls. Little whirlwinds spun pillars of dust in the courtyard. The clouds made a roof overhead, hiding the mountain from sight. It wasn't safe to fly. They were trapped.

They talked war. They planned to charge—to assault the southern complex. They could not be dissuaded from their plan. Nor did they seem able to put it into effect. Poet stood by the window and Far-Traveller moaned on the floor and Orpheus paced around and around the room in endless circles, talking to himself, arguing with shadows.

She left them to it.

She went exploring. She drifted through narrow corridors and up and down deep circular shafts until they opened onto the vault below the great dome. Through the crack she could see storm-clouds, an indigo storm-light.

She leapt up and spread her wings. A slight ache, no more. A clean wound, just as Orpheus had said. Lucky. She was owed some luck. She rose up and settled on the rafters.

There were carvings set into the ceiling, all around the underside of the dome. She'd seen them before, when they entered the castle, but she hadn't had time to look closely at them. Now the memory of them nagged at her.

She counted a dozen carvings. Others had fallen from their settings and were no doubt buried in the dust below. They must once have covered all of the ceiling, like the frescoes of a cathedral—a map of the heavens, perhaps.

She ran her fingers along the carved symbols. Somehow it was easier to make them out by touch than by sight. To the eye, they appeared to move, to shift in an untrustworthy way. A terrible heaviness to them. They were in no earthly language, and no language known to the refugees of the white moon.

She'd seen them before, painted on the floor of Atwood's library.

Orpheus was right. This was what Atwood had come for—this knowledge. He'd lied to her, or told her half-truths at best. He'd known what waited on Mars, before he'd ever come.

Something on the surface of dead Mars had reached out to him across the void, before he'd ever left London, and had told him what lay here beneath the dust. Something—the ghosts that whispered here—had tempted him with knowledge, had taught him enough to make this voyage. What had Atwood offered them in return? What could these ghosts, trapped and starving on a dead world, want? What else could he have promised them but a way back to Earth?

An image of Atwood's smile came into her mind, and for the first time she truly hated him. He'd lied to her. He'd lied to her, and used her, and discarded her, and now he'd done the same to Arthur.

Beneath her the shadows of the vault seemed to shift and thicken.

She fled out through an archway and across the courtyard, wings tightly folded as the winds battered at her. If anyone shot at her, she didn't hear it over the storm.

Chapter Forty-one

Atwood's genius apparently did not extend to military matters, and Payne had always been an indifferent soldier at best. They didn't know where the enemy were located, their numbers, their goals, or their capabilities. After hours of planning they had come up with little more than variations on the theme of: *charge*. They had a bottle of whisky left: Payne proposed sharing it four ways, for courage.

"And if we beat them?" Vaz said. "What then?"

"If, Vaz?" Atwood scowled. "If? There's no *if*—we prevail or we perish here."

Arthur picked up his axe and a candle and walked away.

"Shaw—where do you think you're going?"

"The call of nature, Atwood."

He seemed to have lost the habit of urination. Instead he just paced through the corridors, wishing that there were still cigarettes. One could call it deserting, he supposed. So be it. Hadn't he given Atwood enough already?

At the end of the corridor, there was a flash of blue and a sound of scrabbling.

He hefted the ice-axe.

After a minute's thought, he decided to investigate.

The end of the corridor opened out into a honeycomb of passages. The shadows were thick. In the dust at his feet, someone appeared to have written the letter *A*.

A cryptic message. *A* might mean *Arthur* or *Atwood* or God knows what. Who could have left it? Vaz might once have enjoyed playing that sort of game, but his sense of humour had been notably diminished by his time on Mars. And so far as Arthur knew, no other human being had ever walked those corridors.

Hadn't Atwood said there were ghosts here? And hadn't he said that there were difficulties of translation, that their way of thinking was strange?

He waited and listened for further messages.

There was another flash of blue at an arched window overhead. He jumped up and clambered over a steep-angled stone beam to find that someone had drawn an arrow in the dust on the window-sill. It pointed across a small yard.

Clearly the sensible course of action would be to report back to the others; and yet his distrust of Atwood was now too deep. It seemed to him that Atwood knew far too much already. If this message was meant for Atwood, he did not want him to have it.

He ran out across the yard. Shadows gathered and whispered; they seemed to stick to him like threads as he passed. He ducked in through an archway on the other side.

At the end of a corridor he came to a tower. It was narrow, and conical; a little light came in through the upper windows.

There was rustling. Dust fell on him. He looked up to see blue light descending through the gloom: faint sunlight through wide, bright stained-glass wings, wings that filled the tower as the creature descended. It must have come in through one of the upper windows. Lean body, silver eyes. Angelic and dreadful. He lifted the axe over his head, but the creature was already on top of him. A sharp-edged wing flashed out and cut the axe in half, leaving a wooden stump in his fist. He stabbed out with the spiked handle, but the creature dodged. He swore. The creature was making a sound that he couldn't understand. Something like a wind lifted him and threw him against the wall. He slid in the dust and fell on his back.

Muscles moved on the creature's back and the panes of a bright glass-like wing creaked and shifted and complexly folded back until they were almost invisible. The creature stood over him. He closed his eyes and waited for the death-blow.

Nothing happened. He opened his eyes again.

The creature was long-legged, stiff, and regal in its bearing. A loose blue shift hung around its narrow waist, attached by a chain of blood-red beads and rather battered-looking flowers. Its face was a mask of obscure intensity.

He thought it might be a female.

It reached out a long-fingered hand and touched his face. Its touch was cool, tingling, almost tender. She was producing a noisy high-pitched thrumming, of increasing volume.

He scrabbled in the dust, picked up the stump of the axe again. He held it out in front of him like a dagger.

She crouched down, reached out a finger, and drew his name in the dust.

He lowered his weapon.

"You know my name, then. What do you want? Do you want to make peace?"

The look she gave him was sad.

She drew a *J* in the dust, and then an *O*. Then she pointed at herself. But even before she'd begun drawing the letters he'd known what she was about to say. He knew without question who she was.

Not dead then; alive. But transfigured.

He slid down against the wall to fall in the dust, and she moved to catch him. He observed that her wings appeared to make their own faint light.

He said, "How?"

Perhaps this was simply what happened when one died on Mars. Perhaps this was what happened when anyone died anywhere. Reborn as a Martian; no stranger than Heaven, really. He felt like laughing.

She remained silent. Well, of course! What sort of angel would speak in the tongues of Man, or to such an unsuitable prophet as Arthur Archibald Shaw?

"I'm sorry," he said. "I was too late. I came too late."

Ridiculous. As if he were blaming a late train.

"And it was all my fault in the first place. Better if I'd never walked into Borel's shop—better if the storm had blown me away. Oh, God, Josephine, but I tried."

She reached out again and put a hand on his head. She blinked her silver eyes and he saw a parade of visions behind them: spinning moons of fire and rose, cities of ivory, Mr Borel's stationery shop, a vault of sleeping blue bodies, the scarlet rivers of Mars when it was in full vibrant flower . . .

✻   ✻   ✻

She left the way she'd come. He sat against the wall, his mind and his heart racing, his skin still tingling from her touch. He could still hear the thrum of her wings echoing in the empty tower—a faint eerie music. He knew that it would be a long time before he could make sense of what she'd shown him, if he ever did. There'd been too much to communicate, and it was all too strange. He understood only a handful of things, but they were enough.

He understood that dead Mars was an aberration, a flaw in the universal scheme. Elsewhere the universe was alive and beautiful.

Elsewhere, somehow, she was alive.

He stood. He didn't know how much time had passed. It was still dark out. It felt as if their embrace had lasted for a year; he remembered a long season on the moon. It felt as if it had lasted for no more than an instant.

He took out his ice-axe and carved into the wall:

A A Shaw
Man of Earth
1895

After a little thought he added:

Here I Found Josephine Bradman

That felt inadequate, but it would have to do. There was no time. That was the other thing he'd understood.

She knew something about Atwood. She'd told him. He didn't quite comprehend it. He had an image of an eye, and a circle, and a black sphere, and princes with the wings of angels and the faces of devils.

He knew where the Engine had come from, and Atwood's magic, and the secrets of the *Liber Ad Astra*.

Ghosts lingered in this ruin. She'd tried to tell him what they were—that image of an *eye* again. He didn't understand. It didn't matter.

They meant ill. Whatever they planned to use Atwood for—or whatever Atwood planned to use them for—it had gone far enough.

I understand, he'd told her, before she went back to her people. He thought it unlikely that he would see her again.

* * *

He went back through the chambers and corridors until he was close enough to the gallery to hear faint echoes of Atwood's voice. He sat down on the ground against a wall and moved a heavy fallen stone to lean against his leg. Then he called out, "Vaz! Mr Vaz! I've bloody well fallen—Mr Vaz, come here, give me a hand!"

Chapter Forty-two

The flapping of his ruined boot came first, then Vaz's face, candle-lit, appeared from the shadows.

He looked sideways at Arthur's leg.

"Bloody clumsy of you, Mr Shaw."

"I'm glad you came, Mr Vaz."

Vaz crouched on the far side of the chamber, rather pointedly outside of Arthur's reach.

"I hope you don't plan to hit me over the head with that stone, Mr Shaw."

"Not at all."

"Or with the axe, for that matter, if you have that hidden somewhere about you."

"As a matter of fact, I lost it."

"Then if you do not mean to ambush me—and yet you're lying in wait, as if you distrust me—then it must be that you want to talk. You want to know if I will help you turn against Lord Atwood."

"Thank God, Mr Vaz. Thank God. That certainly saves time. Yes. Two against two is better than three against one."

"I did not say yes. The two of them have rifles, and we have nothing—not even an axe. Do you have a plan?"

"I don't suppose I do. Element of surprise; that's all."

"And then? Without Atwood, how will we get home?"

"We won't, Mr Vaz. We won't."

"I see." Vaz picked up his candle again, and held it up, studying the recesses of the room. Shadows moved from window to window.

"After a while," he said, "one ceases to hear the wind. Lord Atwood promised me a ship of my own, you know."

Arthur patted his pockets. "I can't even offer you a cigarette, I'm afraid."

"Let's think. There are four of us at present. Nine when we started; four now. Bad luck all round, old chap. I have counted six of the the natives. That is half again as many as four, and it would be twice three if Payne joins us, and three times two if he does not."

"They mean us no harm. It's Atwood they want to stop. But he's dug in—they can't get to him. They need our help. I think perhaps they'll help us, if it comes to it."

"There is also the small matter of right and wrong, Mr Shaw. What you are proposing is murder."

"He means to do something dreadful. We—all of us—we are only . . . Mr Vaz, I saw Josephine."

Vaz raised an eyebrow.

"She's alive. I swear to you. She spoke to me. She knows his plans, and she spoke to me."

"And what did she tell you, Mr Shaw?"

When they returned to the Gallery, Atwood and Payne were waiting by the windows. Payne marched briskly up to them.

"About bloody time. Where've you layabouts been hiding? It's now or bloody never, so pull yourselves together."

Payne shoved a rifle into Arthur's hands and seized Vaz roughly by his elbow, as if he were an errant schoolboy. Vaz slapped his arm away and Payne scowled and cuffed Vaz's ear. Arthur hit Payne under his chin with the butt of the rifle. He toppled backwards and his head struck the window-sill with an awful crack.

Atwood was already gone. At the first sign of violence he'd turned and fled, throwing himself on his belly down the tunnel that led to his cell.

Arthur crouched by the side of the chute, peering down to see lamplight at the bottom of it.

Atwood's voice called up from below.

"My last trial, then. In the form of you, Mr Shaw, and you, Mr Vaz."

"Stop talking like that, you bloody lunatic."

"Remember that I have a pistol down here, Shaw. If I see your head coming down that chimney, I will shoot it off."

Arthur crept over to the window, where Vaz was inspecting Payne's body.

"I think he is probably dead," Vaz whispered.

Arthur couldn't bring himself to care either way. He doubted anyone back on Earth had ever loved Payne very much.

"Atwood's right," he whispered. "He's dug in there, the bastard."

"I can hear you both quite clearly," Atwood said.

Arthur swore, picked up a chunk of stone, and threw it down the tunnel.

Atwood laughed. "Don't be ridiculous, Shaw. You're not thinking clearly, either of you. But listen. Listen."

Atwood's voice became friendly, ingratiating. "You're afraid, I know. You're tired. Good Lord, don't you think *I'm* tired? The human body, the mind, they're not made for this place. For the things we've seen. I know that you hear the voices of despair, the voices of madness. No wonder. But don't falter now. Shaw—don't falter now! Josephine depends on you. Josephine—"

"She's alive, Atwood. I spoke to her."

Arthur heard Atwood shifting about in his cell. He crept over to the side of the tunnel. Over by the window, Vaz readied Payne's rifle.

"He's mad, you know, Vaz," Atwood said. "Shaw has gone mad."

There was another long silence, except for footsteps and the scraping of stone below.

"I didn't know," Atwood said. "I didn't know that she was alive. I'm very pleased. I never intended what happened to her."

"Come out. Come out and we can talk this out."

"That was a nasty-looking blow you struck Payne, Shaw. I didn't know you had it in you. Is he dead?"

Arthur didn't answer.

"Yes," Vaz said.

"Come out, Atwood. Come out and talk. Tell us what you're planning to do. I think—I think perhaps you've become confused, Atwood."

There was a noise of scraping stone.

"One of us is mad," Atwood called up. "Not me. Perhaps I shouldn't have brought you here, Shaw. I thought you were strong enough. Now I see I made a mistake."

Arthur glanced at Vaz. His face was set, apparently unmoved by Atwood's words.

"Come out, Atwood."

"And if I do?"

"Then we'll let bygones be bygones. We can work together to get home."

"Home!" Atwood's laughter echoed up from the cell. "Home? We three, gentlemen—we have conquered Mars. We are the greatest magicians ever to have lived. And you want to go *home*."

"Conquered? Not without help, I think, Atwood. What did they promise you to bring you here?"

Atwood stopped laughing.

"Answers, Shaw. I was promised answers. If I closed the circle. And I nearly have, Shaw; I have nearly unlocked the puzzle. A little more time. That's all."

"Answers? And what did you promise them?"

There was another long silence.

"One world for another," Vaz said. "Is that right, Lord Atwood?"

Atwood called, "Is Josephine really alive, Shaw?"

"Come out, Atwood, and I'll take you to her."

There was no answer.

Vaz crept closer. The silence deepened. Lamplight reflected steadily on the tunnel's walls.

"Are you there? Atwood, damn you, are you there?"

It is a disgusting thing to do," Vaz said, "but these are desperate times."

He picked up Payne's body by the shoulders. For an awful moment Arthur thought he was suggesting cannibalism, as if they were shipwrecked sailors. Then he indicated by pointing that Arthur should take Payne's feet, and pointed a pistol at Payne's head, from which Arthur understood that he was proposing to throw Payne down the tunnel, in the hope that Atwood, if he was still there, would reveal himself by shooting the corpse.

They threw Payne head first. Nothing happened.

The experiment was inconclusive.

Arthur swore and threw himself down. He landed on Payne's body and scrabbled to his feet, expecting a bullet at any moment.

The cell was empty. The lantern, abandoned in the middle of the floor, illuminated a spiral of tablets etched with deeply shadowed carvings.

The rifle came clattering down. Vaz followed it.

At the far corner of the cell there was another tunnel, just large enough for a man to crawl into. They hadn't known it was there. Last time Arthur was in the cell, Atwood had leaned the tablets against the wall to hide it.

They got down on their hands and knees and gave chase.

A little way along its length the tunnel began to slope upwards, and soon it turned into a smooth vertical chimney. Faint light beckoned at the top of it. It was narrow enough to climb. It would be a death-trap if Atwood began shooting down into it. But they were committed now.

They had to leave the rifle. They shouldered their way up.

After what felt like hours they emerged onto a rooftop. The courtyard was to their left. They looked out across a square expanse of stone, made chaotic by dust-dunes and by collapse—a steeplechase of fallen obelisks and weirder ornamentation. In the distance, the rooftop swelled up into the cracked stone egg of the castle's dome. Beyond that the mountain, and tremendous black clouds. There was moonlight—the pale moon was rising behind the mountain.

Arthur saw Atwood in the distance, dodging fallen masonry. He had his pistol in one hand and held his papers precariously under his arm. Overhead, bright blue wings struggled through the storm towards him. There were two of them—no, three or more. Perhaps one of them was Josephine—Arthur couldn't tell. Atwood fired his pistol. The sound was a dull crack over the howl of the storm. One of the Martians jerked, wings spasming, and fell from the sky.

Arthur charged, sliding in the dust, leaping over great holes that opened up into utter darkness below, roaring nonsense.

Atwood turned and pointed the pistol at him. Arthur kept running. The pistol wavered in Atwood's hand, between Arthur and the Martians overhead. Atwood looked more frustrated than frightened, as if he were thoroughly annoyed with himself for the tactical blunder of fleeing the safety of the cell and exposing himself to the Martians. He fired at Arthur once and then turned and ran. He darted erratically across the uneven rooftop, clambering over obstacles and jumping over chasms. Wings swooped towards him; he ducked behind a pillar. Then he was off and running again. Arthur kept chasing him. Blue wings harried him back and forth. He saw Vaz running too, though they'd been separated by the wind and by various obstacles. Now Vaz was attempting to flank Atwood, as if they were playing a rough sort of sport. Atwood seemed to be searching for a window or bolt-hole by which he could return to the safety of the castle's interior.

Atwood came to the edge of the roof. The dome rose on the other side of a narrow chasm. Atwood stopped as if considering jumping. It was clearly impossible without dropping his papers. Instead he turned, pointing his pistol at Arthur across an empty and shelterless expanse of rooftop.

Josephine circled behind Atwood and swooped, meaning to kill. He stepped lightly aside, dancing along the edge of the rooftop, as if some sixth sense had warned him of her approach, or as if her shadow had betrayed her. She scrabbled in the dust and turned—faster than he was expecting—and struck the gun from his hand.

His eyes widened—not in alarm, but as if in recognition. He rubbed his bruised hand and smiled.

He opened his mouth. For a moment she thought he might be about to offer an apology, or an explanation. Instead, he lifted the papers in his hand, waved them, and shouted something that she couldn't hear over the wind. She lunged and struck the papers. The wind whirled them away, scattering some over the rooftops, swallowing others up into the shadows. Atwood looked around wildly. When he turned back to her, there was nothing in his expression but a cold inhuman hatred.

He raised his unbruised hand in a peculiarly unpleasant devil's-horn gesture—what was peculiar about it was that it seemed to involve too many fingers, or shadows of fingers. As she leapt towards him again, the wind picked up, seizing her with cold hands and sending her helplessly tumbling through the air, so that one moment she was staring up into the sky, the mountain above her like a whirlwind, and the next she was looking down at the castle, its mad turrets and arches and windows all askew. Somewhere off in the sky she saw Orpheus struggling in the same wind. Beneath her, Arthur and a ragged stranger approached Atwood across a chessboard of dense shadows.

✳ ✳ ✳

Vaz, seeing the Martian strike the pistol from Lord Atwood's hand, shouted with hoarse joy, jumped out from the stone he'd been sheltering behind, and ran, boot flapping, his head down and a hand up against the wind. Mr Shaw, he observed, was half a ship's length away and had fallen on all fours in a drift of dust—and no wonder, because it did seem that the whole castle had started to sway in the wind. If this was a dream, then this frantic chase was as good a way to end it as any. If he could just get his hands around Lord Atwood's throat, then perhaps he might wake with a jerk in London . . . Or he might not. One way or another it would be over.

He looked up at the Martians, thinking he might wave to them, to acknowledge comradeship—they were beautiful creatures, who belonged in a bluer sky! He could hardly make them out. A whirlwind overhead flung them to and fro among clouds of dust; as he watched one of them seemed to plummet, wings broken by the wind, to slam into a sharp-cornered obelisk. That was an outrage. Distracted, he nearly stepped out into a hole in the rooftop. He teetered on the edge.

A long stone beam led across the chasm. At the other end of it he saw Atwood standing on the roof's edge, arms raised; it was hard to say whether he was conducting the winds, or whether the winds were jerking him about like a puppet. Vaz inched out across the beam, tightrope-walking. "Your Lordship," he called. "Your Lordship—one moment, if you please."

The wind had picked up, and he felt unsteady on his feet. When he was three-quarters of the way along the beam Atwood turned to him and gestured with one hand. Vaz took another step forward and the sole of his boot finally tore off, as if it had caught on a nail (there were no nails—as if some invisible hand had snatched at it).

He threw himself forwards, in one of those great leaps that were possible only on Mars, and seized Atwood by his wrist. Atwood stumbled. It seemed to Vaz that the winds went still for a moment. Then Atwood pushed him backwards and his bare foot slid in the dust and he fell back through the hole in the roof.

He fell fifteen feet down into a drift of dust.

After catching his breath for a moment he stood, patted himself down, and looked around for a way back up. He was in a large, dark, dust-choked pentagonal room. When he lit one of his last remaining matches, he saw no obvious exits other than the hole far overhead. The far corners of the room were cloaked in shadow. There might be a door there; it was too early to panic.

Something moved in the darkness ahead and for an instant he saw them as they were now—the makers of this ruin. He saw them the way that sometimes one could quite clearly see a storm approaching on the horizon without quite knowing exactly what it was one had seen; perhaps nothing but a distant flickering, a certain bruised quality of the light. First they weren't there; then they were, whether one liked it or not, in their dozens, their hundreds, pressing together, their overlapping wings darker patches within the shadows of the room. They filled the whole castle, perhaps.

He closed his eyes and prayed and pushed through them. Cold; dry; fluttering; electrical. His prayer became a wordless moan. Slipping and sliding through the dust toward the wall he tried to recall the symbols of the Engine, Atwood's tricks of magical defense. He couldn't remember a bloody thing. Perhaps it was better that way. "Not a bloody thing! Ha! Not a thing."

As Arthur struggled to stand, he saw Vaz fall from fifty feet away. The wind seemed for a moment to have died down; Atwood was fleeing along the edge of the rooftop, holding his right arm as if Vaz had wrenched it. With a bull's roar Arthur ran at him, head down. Atwood turned and raised his hand again. Arthur stumbled, moaned. A hand of ice clutched his heart; fingers of ice reached into his skull. A hundred voices screamed and buzzed nonsense-words at him. He pressed forward.

He almost came close enough to grab Atwood's collar; he reached out a hand, but Atwood dodged, turning and leaping from the rooftop's edge across the narrow chasm and onto the dome.

Arthur jumped after him. He had a revolting sensation of pushing through thick shadows, like cobwebs.

Atwood was already on all fours, inching his way up the dome, calling out names and incantations and God knows what. Arthur reached for Atwood's ankle, and he kicked back and caught Arthur's chin with a glancing blow. Arthur grunted and started crawling up the dome. He had the advantage over Atwood, for once: he was taller and stronger and a faster climber, and besides, Atwood seemed distracted by whatever he was muttering. The vital thing—apart from not looking down—was not to relent, not to let up, not to let Atwood out of his sight for one moment, even though the dust and the shadows swirled so thickly around the top of the dome that he was almost blind. If the bastard got away into the castle's corridors, they'd never flush him out again. If there was a *they*. It seemed quite likely that Vaz might be dead. He saw no sign of Josephine. Perhaps she had vanished again, having given her message. Well, that was more than he had a right to expect. More than most people got, and worth the trip.

He reached out again, and this time he caught Atwood's ankle and dragged him back down. Atwood shrieked in outrage. For a moment, both men slid down side by side. Then Atwood scrabbled to his feet and Arthur stood too, both of them teetering at what would on Earth have been a quite impossible angle. Atwood's eyes were blank. With one hand Atwood gouged at Arthur's face, while he made that dreadful devil's-horn gesture again with the other. Arthur's lungs constricted, his heart skipped, his legs buckled. He lunged, wrapped his arms around Atwood's neck, and, with the last strength in his legs, threw himself backwards.

They rolled together down the dome. Atwood screamed and struggled and bit at Arthur's ear, but Arthur refused to let go. Faster and faster, over and over they bounced. Bones broke. Arthur hardly noticed the pain. He couldn't breathe. He thought he might be about to fall asleep. They rolled out over the edge of the dome and into empty air. There were glimpses, through dust and shadow, of the courtyard rushing upwards. At last Arthur let go, and closed his eyes.

He heard a whir of wings and felt himself lurching upwards. Beneath him he heard Atwood shouting gibberish, as if commending his soul to things best not named; then silence.

Vaz reached the wall unharmed, rather to his surprise; he bumped into it with an outstretched hand. Cold and hard and painful. He walked along the wall in the dark, feeling for a door. He didn't really expect to find one, but it seemed that he walked for a very long time without encountering any corners, which was odd.

The dust drifts mounted and became finer and finer, until with every step he was sinking up to his knees, then up to his waist.

He was thinking of striking his last match when he saw a faint light ahead of him in the darkness, as if from a distant lamp. "Mr Shaw?" he said; but then he saw that there were a dozen other lights, or perhaps a hundred. He took one more step forward and sank into the dust over his head. He kept sinking, as if the dust were black water through which he could see the glimmer of stars above, or the lights of a distant shore.

Josephine held Arthur's hand in both of hers and strained upwards. He was a tremendous, impossible weight. Winds buffeted her; she felt she might tear in two. She struggled for purchase on the harsh and gloomy air. She looked down for a place to land, but saw none. She was already high over the castle—higher than she'd realised—and its rooftops were wreathed in shadow. Atwood's body was lost to sight. Orpheus and the others were faint blue lights that guttered like candle-flames and went out. A moment later, nothing was visible of the castle but a few claw-like spires that narrowed to mere lines and then were gone, as if the whole structure had dissolved into dust and shadow and been swept away on the wind. She struggled up through the dark, not with her body but with her will. The black mountain above her spun like a whirlwind, swelled, and became the whole sky. Then, after what seemed like an aeon of struggle, it whipped away like a black veil, revealing the stars. She was so amazed that she hardly noticed that Arthur's weight was gone, and that she was alone.

Chapter Forty-three

It was the smell that first woke her, after God only knows how long a sleep. The smell of the river, and then the sound of traffic. She opened her eyes.

Oak rafters. A cobweb.

Sunlight. Blinding and golden. High summer warmth.

She tried to speak. Her fingers were stiff. Her arms were wrapped in something heavy, some kind of smothering restraint. She panicked, struggled, finally forced her hands free of it.

It was a blanket. An itchy woollen blanket.

She held up a hand. Pink. Stubby fingers. Long, unkempt nails.

A croak emerged from her throat.

She tried to sit up. Her body failed her; she could no more sit up than flap her arms and fly. The exertion made her heart pound.

She croaked again, then worked her stiff dry tongue and her cracked lips until she was able to form an obscenity. It was tremendously satisfying.

Already the memory of her long waking was starting to fade. Her flight through the dark, up through the unfolding geometries of the spheres. And before that, the castle, the lunar city—had that been real, or a dream?

She stared at the spider's web. Its solid and sane geometry comforted her.

She bent her will to the task of sitting up.

Pain shot through her. Everything ached. A man's hoarse voice called out in surprise.

She began to panic. Her hands shook. She fought for control.

They were in a long narrow room, under a slanting attic roof. There were two beds in the room: hers, and the man's. He sat upright in bed, beneath the window, staring madly about, as if her voice had suddenly woken him. He was jabbering something, not in English. Not Arthur. The sunlight from the window was almost blinding. He wore an unkempt beard, a white nightgown, and a long white hat, which he tore off to reveal a shaved head. He appeared to be Indian. She patted her head and found that she, too, had had her hair cut short. In the corner was a wardrobe and a closed door.

She croaked, "Arthur."

The stranger pulled himself to his feet. A little man; skin and bones. He opened the window—not without difficulty—and let in the smells of the river, of sizzling food-carts, of flowers and perfume and horse-sweat, of coal and asphalt and bonfires; and the noise of traffic and pigeons and a hundred beautiful human voices. Mid-day bells were ringing.

"London," he croaked. "We have gone and come back."

"Who?"

He turned as if surprised to find that she was real. He hobbled over to her and leaned on the edge of her bed for support.

"Miss—Bradley? Bradford? Bradman? Bradman. Josephine? By God. By God! It is you. He said—Mr Shaw said—my name is Vaz. Mr Shaw and I—by God! We went to Mars together!"

"Vaz? Mars?"

"Yes! Yes! He said that you were there; he said that he spoke to you. By God. Is it true?"

She clutched his stick-thin arm. "He fell, Mr Vaz; I saw him fall from the rooftop. He fell, and I caught him. And then I was carrying him, and then I wasn't, not any more . . . Where did he go?"

His bloodshot eyes widened. "I don't know, Miss Bradman."

"How long have we been asleep, Mr Vaz?"

He looked out the window and shrugged.

Vaz flung open the wardrobe and found ointments, medicines, bandages, and eventually, folded in the dust at the bottom of a drawer, a moth-eaten suit of clothes that he recognised as his. Just as he'd left them the night of the departure, back in Deptford, he said. That had been winter. It felt like high summer now, he suggested. The clothes hung from his bony frame. He found a mirror and some scissors and attacked his beard and hair and fingernails until he thought perhaps he was presentable, though he confessed he no longer recalled what a presentable human being looked like.

Josephine sat on the edge of the bed. She couldn't move any further. Her legs were feeble and her will appeared to have deserted her. She recalled, over and over, the fall from the dome—catching Arthur—Atwood falling silent—the castle's dissolution into shadow, and an eternity of struggle upwards through the dark. Had she lost Arthur? Had she let go? Had he really been there at all, or had she dreamed it? This stranger—Vaz—seemed to suggest that she had not.

He came limping over to her bed. He carried a long robe, scarcely more presentable than the nightgown she was wearing.

"Quick," he said. "We must go."

"Where are we, Mr Vaz? How did we get here?"

"To London? I don't know. I remember—I fell from the roof. And then there were shadows; and then it seemed that everything was shadows; and then it seemed that I was drowning; and I fought for the light. I fought with all my strength and all my cunning, and I did not think I would win . . . and then after a long time I heard voices, and bells . . . How did we come to be in this room? I don't know that either. I went to sleep in a warehouse by the river and now we are—I don't know. But listen: Mr Shaw had come to believe that our employers were very wicked people. I believe it too. We should flee, before they know we are awake."

"I cannot leave Mr Shaw."

"He is not here, Miss Bradman."

He hurried over to the door, and found it was locked.

She forced herself to stand, and then to walk. She joined him by the door.

"Perhaps the window," he said.

Exhausted, trembling from the exertion of walking, she leaned against the door. The smell of oak and varnish was so delightful it almost made her cry.

Mr Vaz limped over to the window and reported that it was hopeless. They were three stories up and the climb would have been impossible even for a strong man in good health.

She pressed her head against the door. Through the wood she felt the heavy iron of the key, sitting in the lock on the other side of the door. She felt a tingling in the air; the memory of her wings. She reached out with her will, took hold of the key, and turned it. The lock clicked.

"By God," said Mr Vaz.

When she opened the door it caused a bell to ring: twice, loudly. Then it was silent.

They stepped out arm in arm onto a landing at the top of a staircase that led down into what was plainly someone's house. It was somewhat sparsely furnished by London standards, but after Mars, the mere presence of an old rug on the floor and a lamp on the wall seemed quite dizzyingly luxurious.

A woman's voice called out, "Come down, please, Miss Bradman."

Mr Vaz shook his head. "No, Miss Bradman. We must go."

"I have to, Mr Vaz. I have to know what happened."

"Come down, please, Miss Bradman! Mr Vaz. I want to talk to you."

The woman who'd sometimes gone by Jupiter, and sometimes by Moina, sat in a chair in the corner of a small and spare office on the second floor of the house. A window overlooked the river. Tower Bridge, still half-finished, loomed in the middle distance. Though to someone accustomed to the cold of Mars it felt like high summer, crowds on the riverbank were dressed for winter. Someone had painted a variety of occult-looking sigils on the window-sill and on the floor.

Jupiter wore a heavy black dress, and she appeared to have quite a lot more grey hair than when Josephine had last seen her. Her eyes were red and sleepless, her face was pale. On her lap was a Bible, and she was making annotations in it.

She put down her pen and stared. "It's true, then. I had almost ceased to hope."

She stood, and put the Bible down on the window-sill. "Sit," she said, "sit." She took Josephine by her arm and steered her into the empty chair.

Mr Vaz waited anxiously in the doorway.

"I mean you no harm, Miss Bradman, Mr Vaz—no further harm. Please. Please sit, before you hurt yourselves. Perhaps you mistrust me— and why shouldn't you?—but you are safe here. God knows you will have enemies enough, but I am not one of them."

"Moina—please—where is Mr Shaw?"

"Please—please." Jupiter paced. She appeared quite distracted. "We may not have long. If you've awoken at last . . . It's been such a long time since you left, Mr Vaz, and it's been such hell since then. The rules of conduct have not lately been observed, Miss Bradman. They have *not* been observed! I could tell you news that would turn your hair white! But I knew that I had to keep you safe—I had to have answers, I had to know. Even after Atwood—even after that, I had to know if we had succeeded; and what it meant."

Josephine felt a rush of panic. She struggled to rise from the chair, but her legs betrayed her.

"If you've awoken, others may know soon."

Mr Vaz spoke softly. "When did Lord Atwood die, madam?"

"Oh—some months ago. It was still summer. In his sleep. It was terrible—terrible. I've had such nightmares ever since. You've done nothing but sleep, but I've hardly slept a wink. *They* sent these nightmares, you know; Podmore, or Archer. Or worse. Or worse! Tell me, please—what did you see?"

"Moina," Josephine said. "Please: Where is Arthur Shaw? What have you done with him?"

"How did you return? How did you return, when Atwood didn't? When Sun didn't? What did you see?"

"Horrors," said Vaz.

Jupiter rounded on him. "What horrors, Mr Vaz? Explain yourself. Did you see Mars?"

"Yes," Josephine said. It seemed to her that Jupiter required very careful handling. "We saw Mars. After you left me—after that night, I saw the moons of Mars. There was an ivory moon and a red moon, and men and women with wings; and we saw Mars, too."

Jupiter closed her eyes as if in prayer. Then she opened them again and stared intently at Josephine. "What happened to Lord Atwood?"

"He fell."

"I see. And then the two of you woke as one."

"We did; but it was a struggle to wake, Moina. And I'm afraid Mr Shaw was not strong enough. There was a—there was a struggle."

"Yes. Atwood went in summer; and you began to wake when he died; isn't that so? I've sat over you long enough—I've listened to the beating of your heart, the fluttering of your breath. I listened to Atwood whispering. Oh God, I listened! It was by his will that you remained. It was with the cessation of his will that you were released."

She clutched at her necklace as if she meant to tear it off and hurl it into a corner of the room. "It was delusion all along. Don't you see, Miss Bradman? The fact of your waking proves it. You saw nothing but Atwood's dream. It was all for nothing."

"Nothing? Less than nothing, if Arthur . . . What did you hope for, Moina?"

"Or perhaps I only prayed it was a delusion. What *horrors* did you see, Miss Bradman? Mr Vaz?"

"It was a dead world."

"And?"

"Please, Moina: Where is Mr Shaw?"

Jupiter went to her desk and began removing papers from a drawer. "I see. I see. I knew it. I knew, when the nightmares began. When I sat by Atwood's bedside. I should always have known. Addington was right, damn him. That horrible *eye*. Did you see them—the Masters of that place—are they real, then, after all?"

"Perhaps."

"Ah—Atwood has damned us all—I knew it! And now he's gone. What are their intentions, Josephine?"

"I don't know; how could I know? They do not mean us well. You should have seen that place."

Vaz sat by the door, stretching his leg. He glanced up. "You should be afraid, madam."

"You *deserve* to be afraid," Josephine said.

"I see." Jupiter's face went white. "I see. And is that all you can say? Well. Your faces say enough. If only Sun had come back. Ah! Look what we've come to."

She hurried to the door. Vaz stumbled out of her way. Josephine cried out and stretched a hand toward the door on the other side of the room; and she gathered up her will; and the door slammed shut in Jupiter's face.

Both women were equally amazed.

Josephine leaned forward in her chair, heart pounding. "Where—"

"Dead! Gone! Mr Shaw has been gone for months."

"When, Moina?"

"Months. A few days after Atwood died. I don't know."

"Then perhaps he still lives. Perhaps he was lost on the way, and perhaps his soul still lives, in the void, lost as I was."

"I don't know, Miss Bradman. I don't know! Yes, no; he might, he might not. What do I know of the condition of his soul? What do I know of the heavens? Nothing. Everything I thought I knew was lies. For God's sake, get out of London. Get out of England. I intend to."

Jupiter pulled the door open and rushed out into the hall. Her footsteps clattered down the stairs, and the front door opened and closed.

They hobbled down the stairs after her. When they stepped onto the street, passers-by—giving them odd looks—informed them that the woman in the black dress had run off *that* way, and pointed towards the spires of the bridge.

The bridge's towers had undergone construction since she'd seen them last. The spired peaks were taller; yet more scaffolding had sprouted, like the tendrilled flowers of the moon. A year had passed in one night.

Josephine sat down in the street.

Mr Vaz struck his forehead and said, "Mr Shaw!"

For a moment Josephine thought he'd seen him walking down the street.

"He made arrangements, madam—with a lawyer. Before he left. In Gravesend. I promised him I would remember the name of the fellow, in the event that you and I ever spoke, and he . . ."

"Arrangements?"

He shrugged. "I don't know. It was a Mr Harvey, or Harold, or some name of the sort. I expect if we walk up and down the High Street we will find him soon enough."

She shook. She was starting to feel the cold.

"We can hardly travel to Gravesend dressed as we are, Mr Vaz."

"Miss Bradman, it seems to me that there is nothing on Earth I cannot do, now that I have gone and come back. I can hardly keep my feet on the ground! Doesn't everything look frightfully thin and pale, madam? After—that place—doesn't London look very small?"

* * *

Arthur's arrangement turned out to be two thousand pounds, in cash. The solicitor, Mr Harvey, didn't know where Arthur had got two thousand pounds. Mr Vaz believed it to have been siphoned from the operations of the Company of the Spheres, and put aside for her care.

No letter. Two thousand pounds, but no letter. That was *entirely* like him.

She began to cry. It made Mr Harvey very uncomfortable.

Outside the office on the High Street, she gave half of the money to Mr Vaz.

"I have done nothing to earn this," he said.

"Nor have I, Mr Vaz. Nor has anyone. You'll need it to flee London."

He took her hand very solemnly, and for a moment she thought he might kiss it. Then she thought he might ask her what it had been like; what she'd seen on the white moon. Instead, he simply wished her good luck, and turned and walked away.

Mr Vaz remained in Gravesend a little while longer, asking around until he had obtained directions to an enterprise outside town that sounded very much like Mr Gracewell's Engine. It had closed at the end of summer, ejecting a mass of unsavoury young men and questionable young women: London riff-raff, who'd swiftly succumbed to the gravity of the metropolis, and drifted away overnight.

Whistling, he set off through the woods. Try as he might, Vaz couldn't quite rid himself of the sensation that his left shoe was coming off, causing him to limp the whole way. On the other hand, the sun and the breeze were blissful, and every speck of green in the bare winter woods was more beautiful to him than diamonds or gold. He wasn't cold. He thought that he might never be cold again, no matter where on Earth he went. Not a bad thing for a sailor.

In a clearing he found the Engine, little more now than a maze of empty rooms and broken windows. He gathered up every scrap of writing he could find, and made a bonfire.

After that, he left England at the first opportunity. He changed his name, and set about turning his thousand pounds into a much larger fortune. By the early years of the new century he had become a prominent

importer and exporter, with offices in Chennai and in London, and interests in more than one ship. His alias was emblazoned on packages and
crates on shelves on two continents, and on a large stone water fountain
in Hyde Park—though he never returned to London himself. He had six
sons, who inherited their father's cleverness with numbers but not his
minor gifts for fortune-telling and magic. They were strongly discouraged from taking an interest in astronomy, fanciful novels, or the games
of the English aristocracy.

The magical war that the Company had started continued for many
years. Both Josephine and Mr Vaz were afraid for a long time that
Atwood's enemies might track them down—or, for that matter, his friends;
it was hard to say which was worse. Fortunately, it seemed that the
magical war was keeping everyone busy. Hints of the conflict occasionally made the newspapers—odd events, strange lights, wolves in the city
streets, mysterious deaths of aristocratic eccentrics in Paris, Berlin,
London, and New York. By the early years of the new century, most of
those who'd been personally involved in the events of '94 and '95 were
dead, or mad, or had retired from magic and taken an interest in art, or
gardening, or religion. One Lord Podmore lost a fortune on some bad
investments in 1901, and in 1902 there was labour unrest among the
printers in his employ, and in 1903 he was reported (in a rival newspaper) to have been discovered drowned in a vat of ink. True or not, he
vanished. In 1909, in Panama City, Josephine saw Jupiter's photograph
in a six-month-old copy of *The Times*, in a story about campaigners for
Indian Home Rule in Calcutta. When Josephine inquired further with
the Embassy, she was told that the troublesome woman in question had
gone missing.

There were a few rumours about the occultist Martin Atwood's mysterious disappearance. He was widely suspected to have killed himself.

It seemed to Josephine that the new generation of occultists were
mostly frauds. And then, of course, the War—the *real* War—absorbed everyone's attention for a time, and kept a lot of brave and clever young
men busy killing and dying and writing poetry. After it was over, and the
smoke had cleared from the battlefields and the guns had begun to rust
and the poppies grew in the wasteland, and so on and so forth—after that

the whole business of magic felt absurdly old-fashioned and nineteenth-century.

The War rather passed her by. By the time hostilities broke out in Europe, she was living in South America, writing stories about Mars.

1937

She passed on in September 1937. She'd changed her name more than once by then, and had lived in most places on Earth; she travelled restlessly through the United States, and South America, and India, and parts of Africa—though she was never able to get into Tibet. She spent most of 1911 on a series of steamships, drifting from port to port. She said that the best place in all the world to see the stars was from the deck of a boat. She said that the important thing was to keep moving, that to be everywhere and nowhere at once and always moving was the essence of the modern condition. It was hard for her to be still. She had a very strange way of thinking, which people generally put down to her being artistic. She married an Australian financier whom she met on board a ship between somewhere and somewhere else. He said that she lived as if she were running from something, or to something, which was charming but also exhausting. They had no children. Her accent became unplaceable. She struck people as rather grand, but of uncertain background. The Australian financier died in 1919, of influenza. He left her money; but she'd already made a small fortune of her own in the early years of the century, writing stories of Martian heroism and adventure, of alien princesses and chivalry and savagery. *The Wings of Mars* was something of a best-seller in America in 1908, and *Captain Syme and the Queen of Mars* outsold it in 1909, and *The Vaults of Mars* was serialised in the *Strand* in London in 1910. She wrote most of her novels on ships or trains.

She was quite mercenary about it. She wrote under a pen-name, and many people thought she was a man. She never returned to London, though she was frequently invited there to speak or to meet with publishers. Once she confessed to an interviewer from *Life* magazine that her first husband died young, after an accident; subsequently, every interviewer tried to ferret out the facts of her tragic youth. She stopped granting interviews. Her books, beginning with 1915's *The Libraries of the Moon,* took an occult turn which was by that time rather unfashionable. 1917's *Tiphareth of Venus* was a commercial disaster. It didn't matter; she was already as rich as she needed to be. She spent 1918 learning to fly planes, then gave it up.

In 1921 she settled outside Flagstaff, Arizona. She had a house constructed in the middle of more land than she knew what to do with. Solitude made for good neighbours, she said. She became a local eccentric—not quite a recluse. She discouraged admirers of her books from visiting, but she was friendly with a couple of local lawyers who handled her affairs. She read the newspapers out of London and Berlin and New York and half a dozen other cities very closely. She kept up with the latest astronomical discoveries. She built a rather imposing library of exotic volumes in Greek and in Latin. She wrote poetry; she had no interest whatsoever in publishing it. She learned Hebrew, and Chinese. She studied mathematics. She could afford to bring the best tutors to Flagstaff. In 1924 she began a correspondence with a few occult figures in parts of Europe. She didn't give them her true name, but by certain signs and words she let them know that she was a woman of occult learning. She dropped Atwood's name, and Jupiter's; there were people who still remembered them. She was generous with her money, and that usually got their attention if all else failed.

In the spring of 1927 she was diagnosed with cancer. In the winter of that year she invited an eccentric crowd to Flagstaff, for a sort of party, as she called it. It more closely resembled a pagan jamboree. It made the local newspapers. There were reports of strange bonfires out on the low hill at the southern part of her land, and chanting and dancing and the taking of Indian drugs and a lot of un-Christian carrying-on. Nobody in town much liked it, but she was rich, and bloody-minded. She was still alive in 1928, so she did it again. The police were called, but no obvious law-breaking was discovered. She was small and frail and by now silver-haired, but she had a way of speaking that could make a Chief of Police go pale and stare at his feet.

She continued to sicken, but still didn't die. She liked to say that she knew a thing or two about death, and would not be going anywhere until she was *quite* sure that the destination was to her liking. Her winter jamborees were repeated in '29 through '33, regular as clockwork or Christmas, newspaper outrage and visit from the police and all.

She ended them in '33. Her young friend (and occasional lawyer) Mr Merriweather asked why, and she said, as if it were obvious, that she'd already learned all there was to learn that way. He didn't know quite what she meant, but that was all right. He rarely did. He was relieved, as her occasional lawyer, not to have to deal with the Chief of Police yelling at him anymore.

A round and pleasant and baby-faced fellow of twenty-seven, Merriweather had grown up reading *The Wings of Mars* and *The Vaults of Mars* and Captain Syme's other adventurers, and rather idolised their author. He said that in his opinion she was far superior to Edgar Rice Burroughs, who'd stolen all his best ideas from her anyhow, and he'd fight any man who said different if it came to it, which it never did. He considered her a kind of grand English dame. He was pretty sure she was English; she was certainly grand.

In '35 a Hollywood man came to town and Merriweather got to talking to him at the bar of his hotel. Merriweather was also a big admirer of the moving pictures.

"You know what," Merriweather said. "We got a famous author right here in town. What I wouldn't give to see Mars in the moving pictures, just the way she writes it—you should talk to her. I happen to know her as well as anyone."

The Hollywood man shook his head. "What do you think brings me to town? Your Madam Grand and Famous Author doesn't believe in telephones, I guess. Well, I don't mind sweet-talking the old lady a little. But she's crazy, you know that? She's crazy. Maybe she's sick, I don't know. She says she doesn't care for the money. Worse—I swear—she believes every word of it. They've had moving pictures on Mars for a thousand years, she says. Crazy. More trouble than it's worth."

"Listen, friend—there's no call for that sort of talk."

Merriweather had been thinking of buying the Hollywood man a drink and trying to talk business. Instead he picked up his hat and walked away.

✳   ✳   ✳

In '36 Merriweather was permitted to visit the author's study, to discuss her will. By that late date she'd become something of a hermit. He dressed up in honour of the solemn occasion. There were heaps and drifts of paper in the study, pages densely covered with the author's handwriting. At a single furtive glance it was clear that they concerned Mars, but not the Mars of Captain Syme, but a Mars of white moons and red, and flowers. The author informed Merriweather that they were written in a trance. He took that to be a figure of speech. When he tried to read more, the author rapped his knuckles—by God, she was still quicker than she looked—and advised him in a croak not to pry into secrets that did not concern him.

He reported to his wife that night that the author was at work on one last story. He waited anxiously for further news. The old woman was clearly on her last legs. Terrible to think she might die with her last work undone. He invented excuses to write and call, but the author had ceased to answer her mail, and rarely answered her telephone. She'd never liked telephones. She said they were too lonely.

He drove out past the author's house a few times but got no answer at the door. On one of the rare occasions when the author *did* answer the telephone, she apologised and said that she'd been travelling. Merriweather took that for a joke. She was too ill to go anywhere these days.

He asked after the progress of the book.

"Oh, that. I think I've written quite enough books, Mr Merriweather."

"Not in my opinion, ma'am."

"God bless you; but everything must end, and there comes a time when one must turn one's thoughts to what comes after."

"Oh, ma'am, I don't know about that."

"You remind me of him sometimes, Mr Merriweather."

He took her to be referring to her first husband, the lost love of her youth—the one who'd died in an accident, or of an illness, or whatever the sad story was. In another country, and before the War. She talked about him more often these days.

"But of course," she said, "we were very young then."

"He must have been quite a fellow," Merriweather said.

"He is," she said.

"Oh. I thought—that is, ah, I didn't know he was alive—I guess I don't know who we're talking about, ma'am."

"Oh, no." She smiled distantly. "Oh, no, no, Mr Merriweather." She didn't seem inclined to explain further. He supposed perhaps she was getting confused. Or perhaps the dead man seemed alive to her now; surely she expected to meet him again soon.

Merriweather was a Baptist, himself, and he guessed he believed in an afterlife. He didn't really know. One of those things folks couldn't see clearly in their own minds until they started to get old.

"The pearly gates," he said, to fill the silence. "Ah-ha. The angelic host with their wings and harps. Of course."

"Wings, Mr Merriweather? That would be something to look forward to, wouldn't it?"

"Hmm, hmm," he agreed.

"Have you ever thought of writing, Mr Merriweather?"

"Stories, you mean? Oh, no, ma'am. Don't have the head for it. Couldn't keep all the names straight. I write a mean will, though." Then he blushed, and stammered. "I mean, a lease, or something." But she hadn't taken offense, or even noticed.

"I could tell you a story or two, Mr Merriweather."

"I bet you could, ma'am. By God, I bet you could."

It seemed like the next thing Merriweather knew—business boomed and time flew and his wife and his law partner both thought he was spending altogether too much time on that old woman, who, after all, was just a crazy old recluse who'd once written some children's books—anyhow, the next thing he knew, he was getting a call from his friend the Chief of Police to say that the author was dead. A fire had destroyed most of her property overnight. There were clear signs of arson. In confidence, the Chief of Police informed Merriweather that it was quite probable that the author herself had set the blaze. Virtually everything was gone. A tragedy. She'd left $250,000 to Merriweather, along with a box of papers which she'd placed in the care of the post-office.

"By God," Merriweather said. He held out the telephone at arm's length and stared at it, as if it had appeared in his hand by magic.

The author herself had not perished in the blaze, but had been found lying out under the sky on the low hill at the southern corner of her land. She wore a simple white shift; beneath it she was skin and bone. Her arms were folded. There was frost in her hair—not remarkable, given the cold—and some weird pinkish flowers. The flowers blew away when the firefighters moved the body, and they couldn't say what they had been—roses maybe. She was dead of exposure. Who could blame her, said the Chief of Police; it beat waiting for the cancer.

When Merriweather visited the author in the morgue, on his way to pick up the papers from the post-office, there was a photographer there from New York. They both agreed that she had a remarkably beatific smile for a corpse, and the photographer had seen a lot of corpses in his line of work. That evening Merriweather drove out past the house, but there was nothing to see from the road but a ruin, which still seemed to give off a few ghostly wisps of smoke. Behind it, the sky was warm violet and the stars were coming out.